RACHEL VINCENT

SHIFT

MIRA

ISBN-13: 978-0-7783-2760-8

Recycling programs
for this product may
not exist in your area.

SHIFT

For questions and comments about the quality of this book please contact us at Customer_eCare@Harlequin.ca.

www.MIRABooks.com

Printed in U.S.A.

To #1,
who takes care of everything I forget and
makes it possible for me to do what I love. Thank you.

One

"You should leave. Now." My father's growl of warning resonated in some dark, primal part of me, and suddenly I craved torn flesh and fresh blood glistening in moonlight. Wave after wave of bloodlust crashed over me and I swayed beneath the onslaught, struggling to control it. We would have justice for Ethan. But this was not the time. Not the place.

Though my father's office practically sizzled with the rage that flowed through me and my fellow enforcers, Paul Blackwell, acting head of the Territorial Council, seemed completely unaffected. I watched him from my place near the closed office door, both arms—my right still in a cast—crossed over my chest.

Blackwell planted his old-fashioned wooden cane firmly on the Oriental rug and leaned on it with both hands. "Now, Greg, calm down… I'm only asking you to consider the greater good, which is exactly what you claim you'll honor, if you're reinstated as council chairman."

Unfortunately, that seemed less likely with each passing day. In the week since we'd buried my brother, Nick Davidson had announced his support of Calvin Malone as council chair, which meant that my father now needed the last remaining vote—from Jerold Pierce, my fellow enforcer Parker's dad—just to tie everything up.

And a tie wasn't good enough. We needed a clear victory.

My father sat in his wing chair at the end of the rug, and his refusal to rise was—on the surface—an uncharacteristic show of disrespect toward a fellow Alpha. But I knew him well enough to understand the truth: if he stood, he might lose his temper. "You're asking me to let my son's murder go unavenged." His voice was as low and dangerous as I'd ever heard it, and I swear I felt the rumble deep in my bones. It echoed the ache in my heart.

"I'm asking you not to start a war." Blackwell stood calm and steady, which must have taken substantial self-control, considering my father's comparative youth and bulk. And his obvious rage. Even in his late fifties, Greg Sanders, Alpha of the south-central Pride and my father, was a formidable force.

My dad growled again. "Calvin Malone started this, and you damn well know it."

Blackwell sighed and glanced around the room, and as his tired gaze skirted the three other Alphas grouped near the bar and the scattering of enforcers along the walls, I got the distinct impression that he would much rather have been alone with my father.

The other Alphas and two enforcers apiece had arrived

early that morning for one last strategy meeting before the south-central Pride and our allies launched the first full-scale werecat offensive the U.S. had seen in more than six decades. It was Saturday. We planned to attack in three days—just after sundown on Tuesday night. Anticipation hummed in the air around us, buzzing like electricity in my ears, pulsing like passion in my veins.

We could already feel the blows, every last one of us. We could taste the blood, and hear the screams that would soon pierce the still, cold February night. We were living on the promise of violence in answer to violence, and several of the toms around me teetered on the thin edge of bloodlust, riding adrenaline like the crest of a lethal wave.

Surely Blackwell had known his mission was a failure the moment he walked into the house.

Our allies were expected, but Paul Blackwell's arrival had been a total surprise. Just after lunch, he'd pulled into the driveway in a rental car driven by his grandson, a cane in the old man's hand, determination in his step. But that wouldn't be enough, and neither would the authority of the Territorial Council, which he wore like a badge of honor. Or more like a badge of shame, considering that nearly half of the council's members were present, and not one looked happy to see him.

Blackwell shuffled one foot on the carpet and closed his eyes, as if gathering his thoughts, then his heavy gaze landed on my father again. "Greg, no one is happy about what happened to Ethan, least of all me. Calvin has been formally reprimanded, and the enforcers involved—"

the surviving ones, presumably "—have been suspended from duty indefinitely, pending an investigation."

"Who's leading this investigation?" My uncle Rick asked from across the room, a half-full glass of brandy held near his chest. "And who will be allowed as witnesses? Do you honestly think the council is capable of justice, or even impartiality, in its current state?"

Blackwell twisted awkwardly toward my uncle— my mother's older brother. "Frankly, I think the current state of the council is nothing short of a disaster. But abandoning the very order that defines us is no way to repair the cracks that have developed in our foundation." Then he turned to face my dad again. "Fortunately, I believe you dealt with the actual guilty party yourself."

In fact, my father had torn out Ethan's murderer's throat before my brother had even breathed his last. The offending tom was disposed of in the industrial incinerator behind our barn, his ashes dumped unceremoniously on the ground several feet from the furnace, then stomped into the dirt by everyone who tread over them.

But that small act of revenge did little to ease the blazing wrath consuming all of us.

"Calvin Malone is ultimately responsible for Ethan's death, and he will pay that price." My father's words came out cold, as if he didn't feel a word he'd said. But on my right, Marc's hands clenched into fists at his sides, and Jace went stiff on my left. From the couch, Michael was nodding grimly. We were ready. Vengeance was overdue.

"The council has taken official action on this matter," Blackwell continued. "I know you're not satisfied by that action, and that's understandable, but if you strike at Malone after he's accepted censure, *you'll* be throwing the first punch."

"Are we children, playing this blame game?" My father finally rose from his chair, and Blackwell had to look up to meet his fury. "Are you so focused on who's at fault that you can't see the larger picture? Calvin Malone is out of control, and if the council can't rein him in, we *will*."

On the other side of the room, Uncle Rick, Umberto Di Carlo, and Ed Taylor nodded in solidarity. They'd thrown their support behind my father and pledged their manpower to fight alongside us.

"The larger picture is exactly what I'm looking at." Blackwell held his ground as my father stalked toward him. "You're talking about civil war. How does that benefit the greater good?" He glanced down at his cane, but when he looked up, resolve straightened the old man's thin, hunched spine. "My eyes may be old and weak, but I see this clearly, Greg. The U.S. Prides can*not* afford to go to war."

My father met his gaze steadily. "Neither can they afford to be led by Calvin Malone." He stepped around the older Alpha and took the glass his brother-in-law held out to him, sipping from it as Blackwell turned slowly, leaning on his cane while he scanned the room.

The council chair's gaze fell finally on my mother, who sat stiff and straight in a leather wing chair in one corner, half-hidden by the shadows. Long before I was born, she'd sat on the council, but I couldn't remember her ever taking active part in council business during my lifetime. Yet no one had objected when she'd filed into the room behind our unexpected guest, after showing him into the office.

"Karen…" Blackwell said, and the irony of his appeal to her irritated me like a backward stroke of my fur. The old man's record on gender equality was solidly *con,* yet he had the nerve to address my mother in her own home. "Would you really send your sons to die at war, if it could possibly be avoided?"

My mother's eyes flashed in anger, and my breath caught in my throat. She stood slowly, and every face in the room turned toward her. "In case you haven't noticed, Paul, I don't have to send my children to war to watch them die. Less than two weeks ago, Ethan was murdered on our own land, the result of an action *you* sanctioned." She stepped forward, arms crossed over her chest, and suddenly the resemblance between me and my mother was downright scary. "Yet you stand here, in my own house, asking me to speak against justice for his death? Asking my support for a council leader who stands for everything I hate? You're a bigger fool than Malone."

Blackwell stared, obviously at a loss for words, and the tingle of delight racing up my spine could barely be contained.

And my mother wasn't done. "Furthermore, if Calvin Malone takes over the council, the status quo will sink to an all-new low. What makes you think I want you, or him, or any other man to tell my daughter when and whom she should marry, and how many children she should bear? Yes, I want to see Faythe married—" my mother glanced at me briefly "—but that's because I see in her—sometimes *deep down* in her—the same fierce, protective streak I feel for my own children. And because I want to see her *happy.* That's a mother's right. But it is not *your* right. And you won't convince a single soul here that you bear the least bit of concern for her happiness."

"Karen…" Blackwell started, but my mom shook her head firmly.

I squirmed, in both embarrassment and pride, but my attention never wavered from my mother's porcelain mask of fury and indignation. "Listen closely—I won't say this again." She took another step forward, her index finger pointed at the council's senior member, and those spine-chills shot up my arms. "Do *not* mistake my even temper and my contribution to the next generation of our species as either docility or weakness. It is that very maternal instinct you're appealing to that fuels my need for vengeance on my son's behalf, and I assure you that need is every bit as great, as driving, as my husband's.

"Now," she continued, when Blackwell's wrinkled jaw actually went slack. "You are welcome here as a guest. But if you ever again insult me or any other member of my household, I will *personally* show you the exit."

With that, my mother tucked a chin-length strand of gray hair behind one ear and strode purposefully toward the door, leaving the rest of us to stare after her in astonishment. Except for my father. His expression shone with pride so fierce that if he hadn't still been mourning the loss of a son, I was sure he would have called for a toast.

Silence reigned in my father's office, but for the clicking of my mother's sensibly low heels on the hardwood. Without looking back, or making eye contact with anyone, she pulled open the door—and almost collided with a pint-size tabby cat.

"Kaci, what's wrong?" My mother took her by the shoulder and guided her away from the office, obviously assuming she'd been about to knock on the door. But I knew better. Kaci wasn't knocking; she was eavesdropping.

At least, she was *trying*. But I could have told her from personal experience that she wouldn't have much luck. The office door was solid oak and beneath the Sheetrock, the walls were cinder block and windowless. While those features didn't actually soundproof the room, they rendered individual words spoken inside nearly impossible to understand. Even with a werecat's enhanced hearing.

"I..." Kaci faltered, glancing at me for help. But I only smiled, enjoying seeing someone else in the hot seat for once. "You guys're talking about me, aren't you? If you are, I have a right to know."

My mom smiled. "Your name hasn't come up."

Yet. But now that Blackwell had been shot down on the uneasy-peace front, I had no doubt he'd start in about Kaci. Calvin Malone was desperate to place her with a Pride that supported his bid for control of the council. His own Pride, if he could possibly swing it. In fact, Ethan had died defending Kaci from an attempt to forcibly remove her from our east Texas ranch.

And Kaci knew that.

"What's going on, then? Is this about Ethan?" Her

chin quivered as she spoke, her gaze flitting from face to solemn face in search of answers, and my heart broke all over again.

Kaci had been closer to Ethan and Jace than to any of the other toms, and though she'd known him less than three months, she was taking my brother's death every bit as hard as the rest of us. Maybe worse. At thirteen, Kaci had already been tragically overexposed to death and underexposed to counseling. And in addition to the grief and anger the rest of us suffered, she felt guilty because Ethan had died defending her.

"Come on, Kaci, let's get you something to eat." My mother tried to herd her away from the office, but the tabby shrugged out from under her hand.

"I'm not hungry. And I'm tired of being left out. You keep me cooped up on the ranch, but won't tell me what's going on in my own home? How is that fair?"

I sighed and glanced around the office, loath to miss the rest of the discussion. But now that Ethan was gone, no one else could deal with Kaci as well as I could except Jace, and I wasn't going to ask him to leave. The impending war had as much to do with him as it did with me; Calvin Malone was his stepfather, and Ethan was his lifelong best friend.

"Come on, Kace, why don't we go kick the crap out of some hay bales in the barn?"

She looked at me like I'd just gone over to the dark side, but nodded reluctantly.

Marc took my hand, then let his fingers trail through mine as I stepped past him toward the door. Then I stopped and deliberately brushed a kiss on his rough cheek on the way, inhaling deeply to take in as much of his scent as possible, lingering for Blackwell's benefit, as well as my own. To reiterate for the old coot that I would choose my own relationships.

But on my way into the hall, my gaze caught on Jace's, and the tense line of his jaw betrayed his carefully blank expression. As did the flicker of heat in his eyes. We'd agreed not to talk about what happened between us the day Ethan died. There was really no other way to keep peace in the household, and keep everyone's energy and attention focused on avenging my brother. And I'd sworn to myself that Marc would be the first to know. That I would tell him myself. He deserved that much, as badly as I dreaded it.

And there had been no good time for that yet. Not even an acceptable time. Every time was a *rotten* time, in fact, and each time Jace looked at me like that—each time I felt myself respond to the connection I wanted to deny—my internal pressure dialed up another notch.

If I didn't break the tension soon, I was going to explode. Or do something we'd all regret.

I forced myself to walk past Jace with nothing more than a polite, sad nod—exactly what I would have given any of my other fellow enforcers—and closed the door as I stepped into the hall.

My mother was already standing there with my leather jacket and Kaci's down ski coat. Sometimes I forgot she could move just as fast as the rest of us, if she chose.

Sometimes I forgot she had a mouth on her, too. *Guess that's where I got mine...*

"Thanks." I took the jacket and shrugged into it. "Mom, that was...awesome." There was just no other way to describe it.

Her lips formed a straight, grim line. "It was the truth." She pulled Kaci's long chestnut waves from beneath her collar and forced a smile. "Come in and warm up in half an hour, and I'll have hot chocolate."

On the way down the hall, Kaci shoved her bare hands into her jeans pockets and glanced up at me, her frown almost as stern as the one my father typically wore. And in that instant, I wanted nothing more than to see her smile. To see her look—just for a moment—like any other thirteen-year-old. Like a teenager who knew nothing of violent death, and soul-shredding guilt, and spirit-crushing fear.

"What was awesome?" she asked, shoving the front door open.

I grinned, my mood momentarily brightened by the memory of my mother's bad-ass monologue. "My mom just handed Blackwell his shriveled old balls in front of everyone."

Kaci's eyebrows shot halfway up her forehead. "Seriously?" I nodded, and for a second, I caught a glimpse of what a happy Kaci could look like. "Cool."

We stepped onto the porch and I had actually gone two steps before I realized we weren't alone. Mercedes Carreño—Manx—sat in the wrought-iron love seat with my brother Owen. They both looked up as we approached, but their easy smiles said we hadn't interrupted anything. No conversation, anyway. They were simply sitting together, enjoying the winter silence. And somehow their easy comfort seemed more intimate than many kisses I'd seen.

"Hey," Kaci said, oblivious as I raised a curious brow at my brother. "Where's Des?"

Manx shrugged deeper into her wool coat. "He is sleeping."

My eyebrow went even higher, and Owen flushed, sliding his cowboy hat back and forth on his head. Manx never left Des. *Never.* The baby slept in her bed, and she sat with him when he napped. And she wouldn't even go to the bathroom until she'd found someone she trusted to watch him while she was gone.

Yet here she sat next to my cowboy-gentleman brother, doing nothing, her hands resting easily in her lap, butchered fingernails concealed by stretchy, crocheted gloves.

"Can I play with him when he wakes up?" Kaci asked.

Manx smiled. She'd already realized that playing with the baby—though that amounted to little more than letting the one-month-old grip her finger—set Kaci at ease as little else could. "Of course."

Kaci's shoulders relaxed, and I couldn't help wondering if two babies might mean twice the therapy, for Kaci and for us all. We hadn't had time to verify it yet, but Ethan's human girlfriend, Angela, was pregnant, and I had no reason not to believe that the baby was his.

My mother was cautiously optimistic over the news, with occasional, unpredictable bouts of unbridled delight in the moments when she let herself believe it was actually true. Nothing could fill the hole that Ethan's death had left in all of our hearts. But his son— my mother's first grandchild—could go a long way toward healing the wound. She couldn't wait to meet Angela, but we'd all agreed that for the new mother's safety, introductions would best be done after our troubles with the Territorial Council were over.

Kaci's gaze roamed the yard in the direction of the barn. Then her eyes narrowed and a frown tugged at the corners of her mouth. I knew what she was looking at without turning.

Ethan's grave.

We'd buried him beneath the apple tree, halfway between the front yard and the eastern field, and his headstone forever changed the familiar landscape. But that was the plan. We wanted to see him every day. To remember him without fail. To mourn for as long as we saw fit.

"I'm goin' on ahead," Kaci mumbled, then jogged down the steps without waiting for a response.

I hadn't intended to linger with Owen and Manx, hesitant to interrupt…whatever they had going on. But Kaci clearly wanted a moment alone with Ethan, and I had to respect that.

"How are the digits?" I asked, sinking into a wicker chair at the end of the porch.

"Pardon?" Manx frowned until I nodded at her hands, then she held her fingers up, as if to check on them. "Oh. Much better. They only hurt when—" she paused, searching for the right word in English "—bump things." She pushed her hands forward against nothing to demonstrate.

Nearly two weeks after being declawed, her hands had almost completely healed, but the scar tissue where her fingernails had been was still bright red and puffy. She hated the sight of them, and wore thin gloves whenever possible, only taking them off to care for the baby or herself.

I turned to glance at Kaci—halfway to the apple tree, and loping at her own pace—and idly noticed a pair of hawks circling overhead.

"How is your arm?" Manx asked, recapturing my attention.

I held up my cast, smiling at the doodles Kaci had drawn between the enforcers' perfunctory signatures. A flower with purple petals and X-shaped eyes in the center. A pink skull and crossbones. I'd sat still for several of her masterpieces. Anything to make her smile. Though, I'd threatened to paint over them with black nail polish if she plastered any more pink on my arm.

Still, I had to admit that thinking of Kaci when I looked at my cast was much better than thinking about how I'd broken it. About the bastards who'd stolen Marc and beaten him to get information out of me—when beating me hadn't worked.

"It's fine. Dr. Carver says I can try Shifting in a couple of weeks." Because broken bones take longer to heal than simple cuts and gashes. I was already itching for the transformation—and from the cast, which somehow made my arm sweat, even in the middle of February.

"She really misses him." Owen nodded at something over my shoulder, and I twisted to see Kaci on the ground beside Ethan's headstone, one knee brushing the freshly overturned earth.

"Yeah, she—"

"What the hell?" Owen demanded, and I peered over the porch railing. "Have you ever seen hawks that big? They must have spotted something to eat, from the way they're circling...."

I was on my feet in an instant, a sick feeling churning in my stomach. "Those aren't hawks...." They were too big, for one thing. And their wings were all wrong. Especially the tips. Even from a distance, the ends looked...weird. The birds must have been really high up before, because now that they'd flown lower, swooping in from over the woods behind the eastern field, they looked huge.

My heartbeat suddenly felt sluggish, as if it couldn't keep up with my body's natural rhythm. The birds were *too* huge. And too low. And too *fast*...

Oh, shit... "Kaci!" I screamed as the first bird dove toward her. She looked up and screeched, and I was already halfway across the yard.

Kaci leaped to her feet, then ducked as the first bird swooped, huge talons grasping perilously close to her head. She screamed again, and when the bird rose into the air, beating giant wings so hard I could hear the air whoosh from two hundred feet away, she stood and took off toward me.

Kaci raced across the dead grass, screaming at the top of her lungs.

I kept moving toward her, unwilling to waste energy on screams of my own. But in human form, neither of us was fast enough. I was a heartbreaking fifteen feet away when the second bird swooped, his powerful wings displacing so much air I was actually blown back a step. His talons opened wide, then closed around her upper arms.

For a moment, as he regained his balance with his new burden, I had a breathtaking view of the magnificent creature. Smooth, brown wings. Terrible, curved beak. Powerful, horrifying talons. And long, sharp wing-claws, protruding from beneath the feathers on the tips of his wings.

An instant later, the bird was aloft again, and I came to a stop with my fingertips grasping air three feet beneath Kaci's dangling sneaker.

My heart raced along with my feet as I followed them, knowing my chase was futile. I couldn't fly, and I couldn't run fast enough to keep up. Because Kaci hadn't been picked up by hawks. Our new tabby—my own beloved charge—had just been kidnapped by the first thunderbirds seen by werecats in nearly a quarter of a century.

Two

"Kaci!" I screamed as I ran, adrenaline scorching a path through my body so hot and fast I could feel nothing else. Not the biting February cold, not the ground beneath my feet, and not the bare branches slapping my face and neck when I broke into the woods behind the house.

Overhead, Kaci screamed and thrashed, skimming mere feet from the naked treetops. If it had been summer, I could never have seen her through the foliage.

The thunderbird dipped and wobbled wildly as Kaci threw her legs to one side, then he straightened and pushed off against the air with another powerful stroke of both wings. In seconds, he was ten feet higher up, and still Kaci fought him, shrieking in wordless terror.

"Hold still!" I shouted as loud as I could, hoping she could hear me over the wind and her own screams. If she fell from that height, she'd be seriously injured, even if the limbs broke her fall. And if they didn't, she'd be dead.

Beyond Kaci and her abductor, the second thunderbird flew in a wide arc, rounding toward us again. I had a moment of panic, assuming he'd dive-bomb me, until I realized he couldn't while I was shielded by the forest; there wasn't enough room between the trees to accommodate his impressive wingspan—twelve feet, easy. Maybe more.

Instead of diving, the second bird simply turned a broad circle around his cohort, playing lookout and probably backup.

If the thunderbirds hadn't been slowed by Kaci's weight, I would have lost them entirely. Even with their top speed dampened considerably, they flew much, much faster than I could dodge trees and stomp tangles of undergrowth on two human legs. Especially considering that my focus was on the sky, rather than on my earthbound obstacles.

Within minutes, they were a quarter mile ahead, at least, though they never rose more than about forty feet over the skeletal forest canopy.

How long can he carry her? I shoved aside a long, bare branch just in time to avoid a broken nose. But then I glanced up again and tripped over an exposed root, and tumbled forward like a felled tree.

My hands broke my fall, but the impact radiated up both arms, shooting agony through the still-broken one. I barely paused for a breath before shoving myself back to my feet, brushing my scraped and bleeding hands on my jeans. But before I'd made it back to full speed, my tender, broken arm now clutched to my chest, a black blur shot past on my right, leaping easily over a tangled evergreen shrub I would have had to circumvent.

Backup. Thank goodness someone had Shifted. If I'd taken the time, we'd have lost sight of Kaci.

The tom moved too fast for me to identify by sight, but a quick whiff as I dodged a reed-thin sapling and skirted a rotting stump gave me his identity. Owen. And surely more were on the way.

Not that there was anything any of us could do from the ground…

My brother sprinted ahead of me and out of sight, but I could still hear him huffing and lightly breaking twigs, since speed was more important than stealth at the moment. And I pressed on at my infuriatingly human pace, my throat stinging from the cold air, my hands burning with various cuts and scrapes.

After about a mile, I was blindly following both Owen and Kaci, and had completely lost track of what heading we were facing. I was pretty sure we'd changed directions at least once, and I could see no logic in the birds' flight path, other than trying to lose us. And staying over the trees, presumably so that cars couldn't follow.

So when the birds—and Kaci—suddenly dipped out of sight, I totally panicked. My heart tripped so fast I thought it would explode, yet I couldn't urge my feet into motion fast enough. I lunged ahead, slapping aside branches with both arms now, heedless of my cast, barreling through the woods in the direction I'd last seen Kaci. I could no longer hear Owen over the whoosh of my own pulse in my ears.

Until he roared, up ahead and to my right.

I put everything I had left into one more sprint, and seconds later, I burst through the tree line onto the side of a country road less than two miles from the ranch.

And froze, staring at the spectacle laid out before me.

Owen raced down the deserted street, already ten yards ahead, heading straight for a car parked on the shoulder a good three hundred feet in front of him. Over his head, both birds soared swiftly toward the car, descending as they came, Kaci still clutched—now struggling anew—in the talons of the nearest bird.

I ran after Owen as the driver's side door opened and a man stepped out of the car. Owen huffed with exertion. My quads burned. The man pulled open the car's rear door. The first thunderbird swooped gracefully toward the earth—and shock slammed into me so hard it almost knocked me off balance.

Three feet from the ground, the bird had feet. Bare, pale human feet, where there had been sharp, hooked talons a moment before. Then his head was human, but for the wicked, curved beak jutting in place of both his mouth and nose.

Surprised to the point of incomprehension, I slowed to a jog, my gaze glued to the most bizarre Shift I'd ever seen in my life. I could perform a very limited partial Shift. A hand, or my eyes, or even most of my face. But this was beyond anything I'd ever even considered. No cat could Shift so quickly, and what the thunderbird had just done was tantamount to a werecat Shifting in midleap!

This scary between-creature thumped gracefully to

the ground several feet from the car, naked legs half-formed, torso mostly feathered, wings still completely intact. An instant later, Owen pounced on him.

Powerful wings beat the air—and my brother. Long brown feathers folded around Owen, stealing him from sight for an instant before they spread wide again, and the fight began for real.

Claws slashed. A beak snapped closed. Blood flowed. Owen hissed. The bird squawked, a horrible, screeching sound encompassing both pain and fear, and other things I couldn't begin to understand. And a set of thin, gruesomely curved wing-claws arched high in the air, then raked across my brother's flank.

Owen howled, and his own unsheathed paws flew. The car's driver—a short, bulging man with a sharply hooked nose—stood carefully back from the melee, unwilling to intercede on either side in his current, defenseless state. Then his head shot up, and I followed his gaze to see the second bird swooping for a landing, twenty feet from the car, Kaci dangling from his talons.

I was running again in an instant.

The second bird dove lower and spread his huge wings to coast on a cushion of air. Then he opened his talons and unceremoniously dropped Kaci three feet from the ground.

The tabby landed hard on her left foot, then fell onto her hip with a dull thud. Her mouth snapped shut, cutting off a scream that had already gone hoarse. A heartbeat later, her captor simply stepped out of the air and onto the ground a yard away, on two human feet, his feathers already receding into his body, wings shrinking with eerie speed into long, pale arms.

He lunged for Kaci before his hands were even fully formed, but on the ground, she was faster. The tabby rolled out of reach, then shoved herself to her feet and raced across the road toward me. She had a slight limp in her left leg and her eyes were wide in terror, cheeks still dry. Though she'd been screaming for ten straight minutes, the tears hadn't come yet. They wouldn't until the shock faded.

The now fully human—and naked—thunderbird started after the tabby, but I was already there. Kaci collided with me so hard we almost went over sideways. Her forehead slammed into my collarbone, and her shoulder nearly caved in my sternum. I spun her around in my arms, putting my body between her and the would-be kidnapper. He'd have to go through me to get to her, and claws or not—hell, *cast* or not—I'd go down fighting.

At the car, Owen had the first bird pinned, muzzle clamped around his human-looking throat. At some unintelligible shout from the driver, the naked thunderbird glanced back, then turned and raced toward the car, having evidently given up on Kaci.

The driver slid into his seat and slammed the door, and the car's engine growled to life. The last thunderbird glanced at his wounded cohort, hesitated, then dove into the backseat through the open door. An instant later, the car lurched onto the gravel road, showering Owen with rocks, and the vehicle raced around a corner and out of sight.

As soon as it was gone, Kaci seemed to melt in my arms, and it took me a moment to realize she'd just eased the death grip she had around my ribs. I stepped back and lifted her chin until I could see her face, then spit out the only coherent thought I could form. "You okay?"

"I think so." Color was coming to her face, and her teeth started to chatter.

"What about your arms?" I held her coat while she carefully pulled one arm free. Then winced when she pushed up the baggy sleeve. Just below her shoulder were three thick welts, two on the front and one on the back, already darkening into ugly blue bruises. Her other arm no doubt held a matching set. "And your leg? You were limping."

"I was?" Kaci frowned and took a careful step forward, then winced. "I think I twisted it when I…landed."

"A quick Shift should fix that." Kaci nodded, and I led her back across the street slowly, already pulling my cell from my pocket.

"Faythe?"

"Hmm?" I glanced down to find the tabby staring up at me, the shocked glaze in her eyes finally fading.

"I think I'm afraid of heights."

I laughed. "I would be, too, after a ride like that." I autodialed Marc while we walked, and he answered on the first ring, as I stepped onto the shoulder a good ten feet from Owen, who still had the bird—now unconscious—pinned to the ground.

"Faythe?"

"We're on county road three, less than two miles from

the ranch," I said, and he exhaled heavily in relief. "I have Kaci and Owen has a prisoner, unconscious and bleeding. Owen's bleeding, too." From several obvious gashes on both flanks and across the left half of his torso.

"We're on the way. How's Whiskers?"

"Stunned, but okay. Her arms are bruised and she twisted one ankle, but it's nothing a Shift and some hot chocolate won't fix."

Another relieved sigh, echoed by a satisfied noise from Jace. They were together?

"We're on the way."

I hung up and slid my phone into my pocket, then extracted myself from Kaci so I could inspect the prisoner without dragging her any closer to potential danger. "Wow. Good work, Owen."

My brother huffed in response, and whined as I knelt and ran one hand gently over his flank, angling my body away from the bird, just in case he woke up. Owen's injuries weren't life-threatening, but they weren't comfortable, either. If the bird had gotten near his stomach, he'd have been disemboweled.

"Thunderbirds…" I whispered, standing to inspect the bizarre half-bird at my feet. What the hell did they want with Kaci?

Jace pulled up three minutes later, with Marc in his passenger seat—Marc's car had been left at his house in Mississippi—and they were both out of the vehicle before the engine even stopped rumbling.

"What the hell happened?" Marc demanded, running

his hands along my arms, as if I were the one hurt. Jace paused almost imperceptibly beside me, and his heavy gaze met mine. Then he stepped past us to kneel by Kaci, inspecting her shoulders, gently prodding her ankle, and generally fussing over her as if she were the only tabby on earth. In spite of her shock, pain, and lingering grief, she blushed beneath his innocent attention and held herself straighter than in the moments preceding his arrival.

I almost felt sorry for Owen, all by himself and bleeding, still standing with his front paws on the unconscious bird-monster.

"They just swooped out of nowhere and snatched her from the front yard." I gestured toward my brother, and Marc turned with me. "We need to get Owen back to the house."

Marc followed me to the downed bird, as my brother moved away to give us a better view. "Is that what I think it is?"

"If you think it's a thunderbird, then, yeah, I think so."

Marc prodded one feathered half-arm with the toe of his boot and whistled. "Look how big his wings are."

"They were longer than that in flight," I said. He started to kneel, but I pulled him up by one arm. "Trust me, if he wakes up, you don't want to be anywhere near those talons." I pointed at the curved two-inch claws, the points of which were finer and sharper than any knife I'd ever seen.

"Okay, let's tie him up and haul him in," he said as I knelt next to Owen, gently stroking the fur on his good side. He whined again and laid his head on my shoulder as Marc looked over my head. "Jace, get some rope." Because handcuffs designed for humans would never restrain those narrow bird wrists.

Of course, if the bastard woke up, he could slice right through rope, or even duct tape.

But on the edge of my vision, Jace stiffened and made no move to follow Marc's order.

Well, shit. That was new.

Technically, Marc hadn't been accepted back into the Pride or formally reinstated as an enforcer, in large part because we were busy with other things, and Marc's return to the fold felt normal without official proclamations. None of the other enforcers would have hesitated to follow an order from him. Except maybe me.

Yet there Jace stood, arms stiff at his sides, jaw clenched and bulging. And he wasn't looking at me. He was staring at the ground, as if trying to control his temper.

But Jace didn't have a temper. *Marc* had a temper.

I stood, shooting Jace a silent warning, but he wouldn't meet my gaze. Kaci stared up at him in confusion, and a moment later Marc noticed that his order had not been followed. He glanced from the bird that had thus far held his fascination and raised a brow at Jace. "What, you don't have rope?"

And finally, Jace looked up. He glanced briefly, boldly, at Marc, then turned toward his car without a word.

"What's with him?" Marc brushed a comforting hand over the top of Owen's head, where my brother stood ready to chew the bird's throat again, should he wake up.

I shrugged, hoping my casual gesture looked authentic. "He's probably freaked out by the giant bird attack. What is this, Hitchcock?"

Jace came back with a coil of nylon rope and a pocketknife, and in minutes we had the thunderbird's human feet bound, and his wing-claws awkwardly tied in front of his half-feathered stomach. Even with his wingspan shortened to less than nine feet in mid-Shift, I didn't think we'd ever get him wedged into the cargo space without further injuring him or waking him up, but Marc finally got his wings/arms bent toward his face and the hatchback closed. Barely.

Still, since we were far from sure the ropes would hold him if he woke up during the five-minute drive, Kaci rode up front with Jace, and Marc and I took the backseat, with Owen stretched over the floorboard at our feet.

Alphas and enforcers poured out of the house when we pulled into the driveway, and my father actually had to bellow for quiet to be heard. After that, my mother helped Owen into the house, and everyone else watched in silence as Marc and Jace carefully pulled the thunderbird from the back of the Pathfinder and lowered him to the dead grass in the arc of the half-circle drive.

Then the whispers began.

The Alphas made their way to the front of the crowd and my father stepped forward, pausing first to put a broad, gentle hand on Kaci's shoulder. "Are you okay?" he asked, and she nodded, her eyes huge. "Manx, can you take her inside and get her cleaned up?"

"Of course." Manx wrapped one arm around Kaci's

shoulders as she escorted the limping tabby toward the front door. For the first time since the allies had descended upon the ranch, Kaci wasn't the center of attention. And she seemed just fine with that.

Jace closed the hatchback and stepped aside to make room for his Alpha. My father knelt next to the bound, unconscious creature and began a slow, thorough visual examination, no doubt cataloging every detail in his head. If the council weren't fractured—possibly beyond repair—he would make a formal report of the incident as soon as possible. And though that would almost certainly not happen under the current circumstances, I had no doubt that he would record his observations.

Sightings of thunderbirds were rare enough to be historic, and I'd never heard of a werecat making actual physical contact with one. Much less being snatched and carried off like a giant worm for a nest of monstrous chicks. A kicking, screaming worm.

"What *is* that?" Ed Taylor, Alpha of the Midwest territory, eased forward slowly, as if his curiosity barely trumped his caution and blatant disgust.

My Alpha stood but didn't take his gaze from the spectacle. "I believe this is a thunderbird."

"Greg, it has feet," Blackwell pointed out evenly, leaning on his cane from several feet away.

"As do you," my dad said. Several toms chuckled then, and I couldn't disguise a smile. "He's obviously partially Shifted."

"And they're much better at it than I am. Than *we* are," I corrected, glancing around to see several of the toms who had already mastered the partial Shift. "They can Shift in the middle of a landing. Rapidly. That's why he has feet and wings at the same time. And they have these wicked wing-claws." I pointed to where his non-hands were tied, and several toms edged closer for a better look. "Owen could tell you all about those."

"What on earth do they want with Kaci?" Uncle Rick knelt at my father's side for a closer look. "They aren't known to attack people. If they were, we'd know more about them. As would humans."

But no one had an answer to that, so I shrugged as Marc's arm slid around my waist. "Maybe they didn't want her in particular. Maybe she was just the first one they saw." Because the rest of us had been under the porch roof. "Or maybe she's the only one light enough to carry."

My father gave me a vague nod. But the truth was that we had no idea.

Marc started to say something, but Jace beat him to the punch, stepping up to my other side. "What do you want us to do with him?"

Marc scowled, but looked to our Alpha for an answer, as did everyone else.

For a moment, we got only thoughtful silence, as my father stroked the slight, graying stubble on his chin. "For now, we'll put him in the cage, and when he wakes up, we'll question him. In the meantime, let's see what we can find out about thunderbirds."

It took some careful maneuvering, but finally Marc and Jace were able to carry the bird down the narrow concrete steps into the basement, then into the cage. They left him tied, because as easily as he Shifted, we had no doubt he could get out of his bonds as soon as he woke.

On my way to my room to shower after my race through the woods, I passed the room Owen had shared with Ethan. At first I couldn't make myself go inside. Ethan's death was still too fresh. His memory too immediate. His room still smelled like him, and entering it felt like walking through his ghost.

But then Kaci beckoned me with a wave, and I steeled my spine and stepped through the doorway, pausing to smile to Mateo Di Carlo, my fellow enforcer Vic's older brother. Teo hardly noticed me, and he didn't seem particularly interested in Owen, either. However, he watched Manx tend to her patient as if her every motion fueled a single beat of his own heart.

I sighed and turned to my brother. Owen lay on his bed in human form now, naked but for his green-striped boxers. The gashes across his ribs looked horrible, and the one bisecting his left thigh looked even worse.

"You okay?" I asked, as Manx knelt to gently blot his leg with a sterile cloth.

"I've had worse," he said, and forced his smile. That was the standard enforcer reply, but in his case, it wasn't true. Owen had seen less action than Ethan or our oldest brother, Michael, or even me. Not because he couldn't fight, but because he was just as happy tending the farm while the others patrolled and went on assignment. Only Ryan, the second born, had done less fighting, and we all considered that a very good thing; he was still officially on the run after having broken out of the cage two weeks earlier.

But I nodded. Owen had stepped up in Ethan's absence and likely saved Kaci's life. He'd earned his scars, and like the rest of us, he would wear them with pride.

When I bowed out of the room several minutes later, I found Jace waiting for me in the hall. Suddenly irritated, I glanced around to make sure no one was watching. Fortunately, most of the toms were in the kitchen devouring leftovers from my mother's Mexican lunch buffet, and Marc, Vic, and the Alphas had disappeared into the office, already looking for information on thunderbirds. So I grabbed Jace by the arm and hauled him into my room without a word.

"Wow, I haven't been in here in a while." He grinned the moment the door closed behind us. "But I feel at home already."

Anger flooded me, tingling in my nerves as if my whole body was losing circulation. "This isn't funny!" I hissed. "What the hell are you doing?"

Jace's flirtatious facade crumbled to reveal the weathered pain, anger, and grief that had fueled his every action since the day Ethan died. "I don't know." He pulled out my desk chair and sat backward in it, crossing his arms over the top. "I just…for a minute out there, I couldn't do it. I couldn't bend to him."

"It's not bending, Jace. It's working. Marc gives the orders in Dad's absence, and we follow them."

"I know," he said, and I breathed a silent sigh of relief that he hadn't called me on Marc's lack of an official position. I couldn't have handled that without losing my temper. "But it felt different this time, and I couldn't do it."

"Jace…" I sank onto the end of my bed wearily, brushing long black hair from my forehead. I didn't want to get into this so soon. I wasn't ready to talk about what had happened between us. Not so soon after Ethan's death. Not with everything else going on.

"It has nothing to do with you," he said before I could find a good finish to my hasty start. "I can't explain it. But I'm over it. I can play my part until you're ready to tell him."

But what the hell would I tell him? That I'd slept with Jace? That was true, but incredibly—miserably—that wasn't the worst of it. The worst of it was that I wasn't sure how I felt about it. I desperately didn't want to hurt Marc, and I couldn't stand it if I lost him. I wasn't sure I could actually force another breath out of my body if I thought I'd ever lost him for good. But I didn't want to lose Jace, either.

And I wasn't even sure what that meant.

I didn't *have* Jace. But we'd connected after Ethan's death, and it hadn't been a simple grief-stricken moment of comfort. Though, it was certainly that, too. But the truth was that grief had crumbled my resistance to a bond we'd formed earlier. One I'd been denying, because of what I had with Marc.

But I wasn't ready to understand what that meant. And I sure as hell wasn't ready to try to explain it to Marc. So Jace and I had agreed to stay…apart. Completely hands-off. But if he wasn't more careful than he'd been today, we'd soon be explaining ourselves to more than just Marc.

"You have to watch yourself," I whispered, glancing at my hands in my lap.

"I know." He stood, heading for the door, but I shot up and jogged ahead of him.

"Wait, let me check." I grabbed the knob, but before I could turn it, Jace was in front of me, so close I could feel the heat of his cheek on mine. But he wasn't touching me. He held his body so close, a sheet of paper would have wrinkled between us, but he didn't make contact.

"Jace…"

"I know," he whispered again, this time against my cheek. "It's not the time. But that time will come, Faythe. I'm not asking you to choose. You know that. But I am asking you to be honest with yourself. You owe us both that."

With that, while I stood breathing so hard my vision started to darken, he pulled the door open a crack—pushing me forward a step—and peered around me into the hall. When he was sure it was clear, he stepped out and closed the door.

Leaving me alone in my room, haunted by possibilities too dangerous to even contemplate.

Three

"What did I miss?" I sank onto the couch between Marc and my uncle Rick and glanced around the office full of Alphas. Ed Taylor and Bert Di Carlo sat across the rug from me, on opposite ends of the love seat. Blackwell was in the chair my mother had previously occupied, which someone had moved to the corner of the rug nearest the couch. And my dad sat in his wing chair at the end of the rug and the head of the room, where he could see everyone all at once.

"Very little, unfortunately." My father sighed and folded his hands over the arms of his chair. "It turns out that we know almost nothing about thunderbirds, other than what you and Owen just learned."

I shrugged and folded one leg beneath me on the center cushion. "How much is 'almost nothing'?"

Marc huffed. "They fly, and they're shy."

Umberto Di Carlo—Vic and Mateo's father—leaned forward on the love seat. "Other than today's incident, we've found no record of any thunderbird sighting since your dad saw one, had to be, what?" He glanced at my father. "Thirty years ago?"

My dad nodded, both hands templed beneath his chin. "At least."

Di Carlo turned back to me and continued. "We don't know where they live, how many of them there are, or even how their groups are organized. And we don't know anyone else who knows any of that."

"None of the other Alphas?"

"Who would you suggest we ask?" Marc turned to half grin at me.

Good point. All the Alphas who weren't with us at that moment were allied against us. Even if they knew something and were willing to help, how could we trust anything they told us?

"I'll make some calls," Blackwell began. "But I'm sure that if anyone else had had recent contact with thunderbirds, we'd all have heard about it."

Heads all around the room nodded. This was big news. Huge.

"Okay, so what are the facts?" My father glanced around his office like a teacher at the front of his classroom.

"They evidently Shift in motion." Ed Taylor ran one hand over dark, close-cropped hair. He looked like a retired marine, and maintained the best physical shape of any of the Alphas, most of whom were beyond the enforcing age.

Di Carlo nodded. "They know where we live."

"They can carry human passengers," Uncle Rick added.

"Yeah, but they can't fly very high or fast under the burden. Or very far." Based on the fact that they'd had a car and driver waiting. I pulled my other leg beneath me and sat yoga-style on the couch, barefoot. "In fact, I'm not sure they could carry anyone much heavier than Kaci. Not without doubling their efforts, anyway."

"Do you think they're gone?" Marc glanced around the room for opinions, but only Blackwell seemed to have one.

"I doubt it, considering we have one of theirs."

"And hopefully we'll know a lot more about this once he wakes." Something shuffled on the floor behind me, and my father glanced over my head. "Yes?"

I twisted to see Brian Taylor—Ed Taylor's youngest son and our newest enforcer—standing in the doorway, arms crossed over his chest. "Sorry to interrupt, but, Dad, have you seen Jake?"

Each of the visiting Alphas had brought a son and one other enforcer, as both bodyguards and requisite entourage, so the house was practically bursting with testosterone. Jake had come with his father; my uncle had brought my cousin Lucas, the largest tom I'd ever personally met; and Di Carlo had brought Mateo, his second born.

"Not lately. Why?" Taylor frowned at his son.

"He went out on patrol about an hour ago and didn't come back when the whole air raid went down. I kinda got a bad feeling...."

Taylor's frown deepened, and my father stood, instantly on alert. "Everyone in the office!"

Toms filed in from the kitchen, and my mother

stepped in after the last one, with Kaci peeking around her shoulder.

"You're going out in pairs," my father began, as the other Alphas stood. "Spread out, but stay with your partners."

"We're looking for Jake?" Jace asked. He hadn't looked at me since he'd entered the room, and that very fact told me he wanted to. If we hadn't *connected,* he wouldn't go to such obvious trouble to avoid me.

Better decide what to tell Marc soon... Because if Jace couldn't get it together, someone was going to notice him acting weird around me. And Marc.

"Yes. It doesn't make much sense to Shift, in case the birds are still in the area. You can't slash overhead without exposing your underbelly. And hopefully you'll see them coming from a way off."

Now that we knew to look for them...

"You'll hear them, too, once they get close," I added. "Those wings are strong, but not exactly stealthy."

My father nodded. "What can we scrounge up in the way of weapons?" Because in human form, even with that swing-overhead advantage, we were pretty defenseless against talons.

"Tools," Marc said. "Hammers, crowbars, tire irons, a couple of big wrenches." All of which had gotten plenty of use two weeks before, when we'd fought a huge mob of strays trying to kill Marc in front of us to send a message.

"Knives," my mother added softly. "I have three sets of butcher knives and several boning knives, all of which should work just as well on live birds as on dead ones."

The only person who looked more surprised than I felt was Paul Blackwell, who surely realized by then that his appeal to my mother as the "gentler sex" had fallen on not only deaf, but grief-hardened ears.

"And a meat mallet." Jace crossed thick arms over his chest, and that time he did smile at me, while most of the toms chuckled. Even those who hadn't been present had heard about me taking out a stray with a massive meat mallet in lieu of my claws, during my trial in Montana three months earlier. Apparently that one was going to stick with me.

"Good." Even my father cracked a small, brief smile. "Karen, will you arm the troops?" Anyone else would have gotten a simple order. My mother got a request.

She nodded solemnly, then ushered Kaci into the kitchen as Dad turned back to the rest of us. "Pair up, and report to my wife to be armed. Call your Alpha if you find anything. Dismissed."

Marc and I stood as the others filed out of the office and across the hall. He took my hand, and Jace watched us, forgetting to look away for a moment. To look uninterested. But then Brian stepped into his line of sight, just before Marc looked up, and surely would have noticed.

"You ready?" Brian had been paired with Jace since Ethan's death, and now that Marc was back, we'd been reunited in the field, even with his unofficial status. Owen and Parker were still partners, but since my brother was temporarily out of commission, Parker would head out with Vic, who was currently partnerless because of the uneven number of enforcers.

Jace nodded and followed Brian across the hall with one more glance at me.

"He'll be okay." Marc nodded toward Jace's back as he slid one arm around my waist. "Ethan's death hit us all pretty hard, but it *changed* him."

My heart nearly burst through my chest and I struggled to get my pulse under control. "What do you mean?"

He hung back to let me through the doorway first, so he didn't see my eyes close in silent, fervent hope that he hadn't seen *too* much difference in Jace. Or in me. "He's serious all the time now. Morose and angry. It's creepy."

"He's a better enforcer for it," I said, and Marc nodded without hesitation. I knew what he was thinking: too bad it took my brother's death to bring out Jace's true potential.

A line had formed in the kitchen, leading in through the hall and out through the dining room. Kaci and my mom stood behind the bar, handing out an assortment of makeshift weapons that would have made any action-movie bad-ass proud. Toms left in pairs, clutching knives or tools someone had gathered from the basement and from assorted car trunks.

Ed Taylor and my uncle Rick were at the head of the line, and right behind them stood my father and Bert Di Carlo. The Alphas selected weapons, then headed toward the door with the enforcers, and I blinked in surprise. Then nodded in growing respect. Most Alphas were past their physical prime—although a glance at Taylor would undermine that assumption—and while they still had to Shift and exercise to maintain good health, they didn't often patrol or hunt with their men.

The fact that they were all going to go out in search of our missing man filled me with more pride than I knew how to contain. They knew that every life was valuable, and unlike Calvin Malone, they were willing to put their own tails on the line to prove it.

Jace and Brian accepted their weapons in front of us and headed outside without a backward glance.

"Here." As I stepped up to the counter, Kaci reached to the side of the dwindling selection and picked up a large hammer with a black rubber grip. "I saved this one for you. Figured you'd need an advantage, working left-handed." She nodded toward my casted right arm.

My mother watched out of the corner of her eye, sliding a large wrench across the counter toward Marc while I arched one brow at Kaci. The tabby hated violence, which, on the surface, should have made her the ideal young tabby. But Kaci was raised as a human, by human parents who'd had no idea they'd each contributed the recessive gene necessary to transform their youngest daughter into a werecat at the onset of puberty.

Considering what she'd been through—accidentally killing her mother and sister during her first Shift, then wandering through the woods for weeks on her own, stuck in cat form—Kaci's die-hard pacifist stance was no surprise. But it wasn't enough to make her into what the opposing half of the council wanted. Because she was raised as a human, Kaci had human expectations from life, none of which included marrying the tom of her Alpha's choosing and siring the next generation of werecats—as many sons as it took to get a precious daughter.

And Kaci had a mouth, and she was not afraid to use it. Which made certain elements of the council even more determined to get her out from under my *questionable* influence.

"Thanks." I forced a smile, and met my mother's gaze over Kaci's head.

"Be careful," she said, and I nodded. Then Marc and I went out the front door after the others.

Several pairs of enforcers had gone into the woods, but Jace and Brian were headed for the west field, so Marc and I started out in the opposite direction, walking several feet apart, and breathing through our noses in spite of the February cold burning my nostrils. We didn't want to miss a scent.

It was eerily quiet in the field, other than the whisper-crunch of our boots crushing dead grass. Though the temperature had risen dramatically from the ice storm a couple of weeks earlier, it was still hovering in the mid-thirties, and my fingers had gone stiff with the cold. I tried to shove them in my jacket pockets, but my cast stopped my right hand at the first knuckles. My nose was running, and I sniffled as we turned at the edge of the field, eyeing the periwinkle-colored sky in distrust.

Danger had never literally come out of the blue before. Out of tree branches, yes. Overhead beams, second stories, and even porch roofs. But never from the sky, and suddenly I felt unbearably vulnerable standing in a wide-open field, where before, such surroundings had always made me feel free and eager to run.

And my paranoia was not helped by the fact that, though no one had said it out loud, we were obviously looking for a body on our own land.

On our third pass through the field, I dug a tissue from my left pocket and held it awkwardly to blow my nose—yet another simple activity rendered nearly impossible thanks to my cast. Then I froze with the folded tissue halfway to my pocket. My first unobstructed breath had brought with it a familiar scent, and an all-too-familiar jolt of fear.

Blood. Werecat blood.

"Marc," I said, veering from the path in search of the source of the scent. He followed me, sniffing dramatically, and his pace picked up as he found the scent. Cats can't hunt using only their noses. Unlike dogs, we just aren't equipped for that. But we could find the source of a strong scent if it stayed still.

And this scent was horribly, miserably, unmoving.

The scent grew stronger the farther north we went, and after race-walking for less than a minute, glancing around frantically for any sign of the missing tom, I froze in my boots when my gaze snagged on a smear of red on a stalk of grass, half hiding a pale hand lying limp on the ground, fingers half curled into a fist.

I made myself take that next step forward, in spite of the dread and fury pulsing inside me. And when the body came into full view, I gasped, horrified beyond words.

If the whole mess hadn't been nearly frozen, we would have smelled it sooner.

Jake Taylor lay on his back, so covered in blood that at first I couldn't make sense of the chaotic, violent images my eyes were sending my brain. There were too many gashes. Too much blood. Too little sense.

"Oh, *hell*," Marc said, and I flinched, though he'd spoken in little more than a whisper. He flipped open his phone and autodialed my father with the hand not holding the wrench while he squatted next to the body, careful not to step in the blood.

But I still stared.

I'd seen a good bit of carnage in my seven months as an enforcer, but nothing like this. Nothing so utterly destructive. So senselessly violent. Not even the scratch-fevered stray I'd seen perched in a tree, consuming a human victim. Even that had made a certain mad, gruesome sense compared to Jake's death. The stray had been hungry, and had only damaged his victim in the process of eating him.

But Jake was damaged beyond all reason. His face was a mass of shredded flesh, eyes ruined, his nostrils and lips almost torn from his face. His arms had fared no better; the sleeves of his jacket were ripped along with his skin, from wrist to elbow, probably in defense of his face.

But the worst was his stomach. Jake had been completely and thoroughly eviscerated from so many lacerations—any one of which would have been fatal—that it was impossible to identify individual wounds.

"East field, near the tree line." Marc glanced up to

see if anyone else was nearby, the phone still pressed to his ear. "But it's…gruesome. Don't let the Taylors over here. They shouldn't have to see this."

"Thanks. We'll be right there," my father said from the other end of the line.

Marc pocketed his phone, and I knelt before he could ask if I was okay. I was fine. An Alpha-in-training was always fine, right? There was no other choice.

"Damn, these bastards are brutal," Marc said, and I nodded, plucking a brown-and-black chevroned feather from the grass where its tip had landed in blood, like the devil's quill. It was easily twice the length of my hand.

"But this wasn't either of the birds who took Kaci. Couldn't have been. We'd have seen blood on them. Smelled it. We were only a few yards away when they landed."

"The driver, then?" Marc asked.

"That's my guess. I didn't get very close to him, and he was dressed. So it's certainly possible." I hesitated, unsure I really wanted the answer. Then I pressed on, because I needed to know. "Have you ever seen damage like this?"

"Never." And that was saying a lot, coming from my father's most experienced enforcer. "Cats don't do this. Not even the crazy ones."

Footsteps crunched toward us from behind, and we turned to see my father headed across the field, Bert Di Carlo on his heels, both frowning in grim certainty.

My dad came to a stop at my side and his jaw tightened when his gaze found Jake Taylor. Di Carlo's face went completely blank. Without a word, my father pulled his phone from the pocket of his one casual jacket and pressed and held a single button.

"Hello?" Jace said.

"Take Brian back to the office and pour him a drink."

For a moment, there was only silence. Then, "I'm on it."

My dad hung up, then scrolled through his contacts list as Di Carlo reached out for the feather I still held from the puffy, bloodless end. I gave it to him gladly, and he whistled, morbidly impressed with the size.

"Rick?" My father said into his phone when a muffled, scratchy voice answered.

"Yeah?" My uncle came in loud and clear that time.

"We found Jake, and we're taking him to the barn. Take Ed back to the house, please."

"Will do."

The last call my dad made, while Marc rubbed my upper arms to warm me, went to Vic. His order was simple. "Grab a roll of plastic and come to the east field, near the tree line. You'll see us." He hung up without a word from Vic.

"Well, Greg," Di Carlo said, as my father slid his phone into his pocket. "I don't know what they want, but it looks like they've got our number."

"Kaci…" I whispered, horrified by the possibility of what might have been. But then merciful logic interceded. "But if they'd wanted to hurt her, they could have. They wouldn't even have bothered with the car. Right?" I needed to hear that she hadn't come close to a horrible death. A horrible kidnapping was quite enough.

The Alphas nodded, and Marc took my good hand in his. "So why kill Jake, then?"

My father sighed and finally looked up from the dead tom. "My guess is that he saw them coming. Didn't you say they flew out in that direction?" He pointed toward the trees to the east.

"Yeah. So they killed him to keep him from warning us?" I glanced from face to face in disbelief, but the question was largely rhetorical. We all knew the answer. "Why didn't he call?"

"Reception's spotty in the woods, but it looks like he tried." My father gestured to something in the grass behind me and I turned to see a cell phone lying on the ground, smeared with blood, already flipped open and ready for use.

"They couldn't have gotten to him in the woods. Their wingspan has to be twelve feet or better. They'd have broken both arms trying to flap in there."

Marc's frown deepened. "They waited until he came into the open, then attacked."

"And they must've done it fast to keep us from hearing." Di Carlo shook his head. "This was planned. They want something."

"What could thunderbirds want with us?" I wondered aloud, as Vic and Parker appeared from around the barn, one carrying a large black bundle.

"We'll find out when Big Bird wakes up," Marc said.

My father shook his head. "We'll find out now. Wake him up and make him sing."

Four

Marc and I headed for the house while Vic and Parker took Jake to the barn. On the way to the basement, we passed the silent office, where Ed and Brian Taylor were seated on the couch with their backs to us. Jace met my gaze briefly from the love seat, and I shook my head, confirming what he'd already guessed. What the Taylors surely already knew. That we'd found a body, not an injured tom.

I felt guilty walking by them without a word, but it wasn't my place to tell an Alpha that his son was dead. Thank goodness.

The kitchen was empty, but I could hear Kaci talking with Manx and Owen in his room as I jogged down the concrete basement stairs after Marc, only pausing to flip the switch by the door.

Two dim bulbs inadequately lit a cinder-block room almost as large as the house overhead. The thick blue training mat was scattered with huge feathers the thunderbird had lost on his way down the stairs, and most of our outdated but well-used weight-lifting equipment had been shoved into the far corner near where the old, heavy punching bag hung. The door to the small half bath stood open, and a weak rectangle of light from within slanted over a folding table holding stacks of cassette tapes and an ancient stereo.

The room was damp, grimy, and one of few places in the house that my mother had attempted to neither clean nor decorate. It was strictly utilitarian, and well used.

It was also a prison.

The corner of the basement nearest the foot of the stairs was taken up by a cage formed by two of the room's cinder-block walls and two walls of steel bars. The cell held only a cot in one corner, with no sheets or pillows. Just outside the bars stood a water dispenser and a single plastic cup, narrow enough to fit through the bars, if held by the top or bottom. A coffee can—serving as a temporary toilet—sat next to the water dispenser.

They were miserable accommodations. And yes, I knew from personal experience. I once spent an entire month in the cage—most of that time in cat form— when I threatened to run away again, after having been hauled back the first time. What can I say? I was intemperate in my youth. And in much of my early adulthood.

And I have to admit that I prefer the view from outside of the bars.

"He's still out," Marc said, and I followed his gaze to the half-bird still unconscious on the concrete floor, just as we'd left him. He lay on his back, weird, elongated wing-arms stretched to either side so that the feathers on one brushed the bars. The end of his opposite arm lay hidden from sight—and likely folded—beneath the cot.

Even half-Shifted, the creature's arm span was at least ten feet.

"Suggestions?" I asked, my fury and fear muted a bit by sheer amazement as I stared at the bird up close, half-repelled by the thick, curved beak where his human mouth and nose should have been.

Marc never took his gaze from the cage. "Get the hose."

I pulled open the door beneath the staircase and rummaged in the dark for a minute before my hand found the smooth, textured hose coiled around what could only be a broken weight bar. I slid my good arm through the coil and carried it to the utility sink near the weight rack. When I had the hose hooked up to the huge faucet—moderately encumbered by my cast but determined to do it on my own—I uncoiled it loop by loop until it stretched across the room to Marc.

He raised both brows, finger poised over the trigger of the high-pressure nozzle. "This should be interesting...." Marc squeezed the trigger, and a long, straight, presumably cold stream of water shot between two bars of the cage, blasting the back concrete wall and lightly splattering the unconscious bird. Marc adjusted his aim, and the jet of water hit the bird squarely on his sparsely feathered chest.

The thunderbird sat up with a jolt, gasping in air—and a little water—through his malformed beak. His right wing-arm shot up an instant faster than his left, too quick to be anything other than instinct, protecting his face and torso, though his feathers were instantly drenched.

The bird made a horrible, pain-filled squawking sound and backed against the wall, where he slid to his knees and wrapped his long, feathered arms around his torso.

Marc released the trigger and the water stopped, but the bird remained huddled and dripping on the floor. In the sudden silence, he gasped for breath and I heard his heart racing with shock. But his pulse slowed quickly as he regained control of himself, and when he lowered his wings, the bird glared at us through small eyes as dark as my own fur, his expression as hard as the concrete blocks at his back.

"Stand up and Shift so you can speak," I said, desperately hoping he spoke either English or Spanish. Because he could be from Chile, for all we knew. Or Pluto, for that matter.

For a moment, he only stared at us, hostility gleaming in his shiny eyes. Or maybe that was water from his rude awakening. But when Marc re-aimed the hose, the bird stood slowly and spread his arms. His left one was reluctant, and he flinched as he forced it into place, flexing his wing-claws as if to show them off. Then he cocked his head to one side, like he was thinking, and closed both eyes. A very soft, eerie whispering sound seemed to skitter across my spine, and I watched in fascination as his feathers receded into his skin and his arms began to shorten.

It happened in seconds.

Marc and I stood in silent shock.

The fastest Shift I'd ever accomplished was just under a minute, and I was one of the fastest Shifters I'd ever met. Probably because I'm smaller than most toms—thus have less body to change—and more experienced than most teenagers, who have less to change than even I do.

But this bird—*every* bird, if the sample we'd seen was any indication—had me beat, paws down. Or talons down, as the case may be. And his Shift was weird. The fur that receded in my own was only an inch long, and not much thicker than human hair, but feathers had long, stiff quills. There was no way feathers twelve to fourteen inches long should have slid so quickly and easily into his skin.

Yet there the thunderbird stood, fully human and unabashedly naked, watching us in obvious, wary hatred. He was short—no more than five foot four—and thin, with a disproportionately powerful upper body and spindly legs. He would pass for human if he were clothed, but he would definitely stand out, though most people would be unable to explain exactly why.

While we stared, he ran his right hand over his thick chest and narrow waist, casually touching the gashes Owen had carved into him. His hand came away bright red. The water had washed away dried and crusted blood and had reopened the wounds. He held his left arm stiffly at his side, and when I looked closer, I could see that it was lumpy. Obviously broken, and certainly very painful. But he made no sound, nor any move to cradle his injury.

"What is this?" The thunderbird's voice was gravelly and screechy, as if he spoke in two tones at once. It was a strange sound, oddly fitting for his unusual build.

"I'm Marc Ramos. This is Faythe Sanders. We ask the questions." Marc knelt to set the nozzle at his feet, then stood and met my gaze, gesturing with one hand toward the prisoner. He wanted me to take the lead. Just like my father, he was always training me.

My dad had told us to start without him—he wanted to break the news to Ed Taylor personally—so I stepped forward, careful to stay out of reach of the bars. Waaaay out of reach, because of how long his arms could grow and how fast he Shifted. Even injured. "What's your name?" I crossed both arms over my chest and met the bird's dark glare.

He only blinked at me and repeated his own question. And when I didn't answer, he smiled—an expression utterly absent of joy—and cocked his head to the other side in a jerky, birdlike motion. "This is your nest, right? Your home? That ground-level hovel you cats burrow into, for what? Warmth? Safety? You huddle in dens because you cannot soar. I pity you."

My eyebrows shot up over the disgust dripping from his every syllable. "Maybe you should pity yourself. You're still bleeding, and it looks like you've broken a wing. You're in good company." I held up my own graffitied cast. "But mine's been fixed. If yours doesn't get set properly, you can't fly, can you? Ever."

His narrowed eyes and bulging jaw said I was right. That I'd found his weak spot.

"Our doctor is just a couple of hours away." Dr. Carver had already been called in to treat Owen. "But you won't get so much as a Band-Aid until you tell us what we want to know. Starting with your name."

The thunderbird cradled his crooked arm, but his gaze did not waver. "Then I will never fly again." He looked simultaneously distraught and resolute—I'd seldom seen a stronger will.

"Seriously?" I took a single step closer to the bars, judging my safety by distance. "You're going to cripple yourself for life over your *name?* What good will you be to your…flock, or whatever, if you're jacked up for the rest of your life?"

Doubt flickered across his expression, chased away almost instantly by an upsurge of stoicism. "The rest of my life? Meaning, the three seconds between the time I spill my guts and you rip them from my body? I'd say a broken arm is the least of my problems."

I rolled my eyes. "We're not going to kill you."

"Right. You're going to fix me up and toss me out the window with a Popsicle stick taped to one wing." He shrugged awkwardly with the shoulder of his good arm, leaning against the cinder-block wall for support. "I've seen this episode. This is the one where Sylvester eats Tweety."

"If memory serves, Sylvester never actually swallowed, and while I love a good poultry dinner, we can't kill you without proof you've killed one of ours. And you don't match this." I reached into my back pocket and pulled out the fourteen-inch feather I'd found next to Jake's body. I'd stored it shaft-first, to preserve the pattern of the vane.

The difference was subtle but undeniable. Our prisoner's feathers were dark brown, with three thick, horizontal black stripes. But the one in my hand had two thick stripes and one thin, in the middle.

Marc stepped up when the thunderbird's forehead furrowed as he stared at the feather. "We can't kill you, and you're entitled to water and two meals a day." At least, that's what the council said a werecat prisoner was entitled to. We didn't actually have any precedent for how to treat prisoners of another species. "But we don't have to tend your injuries or let you go, so you'll stand there in pain for as long as it takes you to start talking."

"Then I suppose I should make myself comfortable." The thunderbird's gaze openly challenged Marc, who had at least ten inches and thirty pounds on him, without a hint of fear.

Marc's inner Alpha roared to life; I saw it in the gold specks glittering madly in his eyes. I laid my casted arm across his stomach an instant before he would have rushed the bars. Which would only have convinced the prisoner he was right in refusing to talk.

I'd just realized something that might actually come in handy. The bird was clearly devastated by the thought of never flying again, in spite of his willingness to endure it. He hated our low-lying dwelling and the thought of "huddling" in it.

"Yes, make yourself comfortable." I extended my good arm to indicate the entire basement. "It stays pretty warm in here, thanks to the natural insulation of earth against cinder block...."

The bird's forehead furrowed and his legs twitched, as if he were fighting the impulse to stand. Or to try to flee. His dark gaze roamed the large, dim room and finally settled on one of the only two windows—short, narrow panes of glass near the ceiling, which came out at ground level outside.

"We're underground?" His odd, raspy voice was even rougher than usual.

"Yup. You're not only in our 'ground-level hovel,' you're *beneath* it. Trapped in the earth. Completely buried, if you will." He flinched at my word choice, but I continued. "You won't see the sky again until you answer our questions. And I can have those windows blacked out right now, if you want the full effect."

Panic shone in his eyes like unshed tears. I was right. Our prisoner—and likely most thunderbirds—suffered from a fascinating combination of claustrophobia and taphephobia, the fear of being buried alive. And I was more than willing to exploit that fear, if it made him talk without endangering either of us.

"Or, I can open them and let you see outside."

The bird's silent struggle was obvious as he fought to keep his expression blank. To hide the terror building inside him with each breath. But I knew that fear. I'd been locked up more than once, and while I wasn't afraid of being swallowed by the earth, I did fear the loss of my freedom just as keenly as he feared his current predicament.

But the bird was strong, obviously unaccustomed to giving in, to either his fear or his enemies. He'd need a little shove….

"Can you feel it?" I scooted just far enough forward to be sure the motion caught his attention. "Those bricks at your back? They're holding back *tons* of dirt and clay. Solid earth. There's nothing but eight inches of concrete standing between you and death by asphyxiation. Or maybe the weight would crush you first. Either way, live interment. Can't you almost *taste* the soil…?"

Marc was staring at me like I'd lost my mind. Or like I'd crossed some line he would never even have approached. But I'd seen him work. He'd readily pound the shit out of a prisoner to get the information he needed. How could my calm, psychological manipulation be any worse than that?

The bird had his eyes closed and was breathing slowly, deliberately, through his mouth, trying to calm himself.

"Honestly? I can't let you out. Even if I wanted to, I don't have the authority." I shrugged, lowering my tone to a soothing pitch. "But I can make this much easier for you. We can open those windows, and even the door." I pointed at the top of the staircase. "In the morning, you'll see sunlight from the kitchen. That'd be better, right? Might just make this bearable?"

"Open the door," he demanded, the dual tones of his voice almost united in both pitch and intensity. Feathers sprouted from his arms, and one fluttered to the floor. He flinched and his left arm jerked. Startled, I jumped back and smacked my bad elbow on Marc's arm. He steadied me with one hand, and I stepped forward again. The thunderbird hadn't noticed. His focus was riveted on the closed door, as if he were willing it to open on its own. "Open it," he repeated.

"Give me your name."

"Open the window." He forced his gaze from the door and met mine briefly, before his head jerked toward the closed windows and his hair disappeared beneath a crown of shorter, paler brown feathers.

"Your name."

He groaned, and his legs began to shake against the concrete floor, his knobby knees knocking together over and over. "Kai."

"Kai what?" I stepped closer to the bars, thrilled by my progress and *fascinated* by his reaction.

"We don't have last names. We aren't human." He spat the last word as if it were an insult, as if it burned his tongue, in spite of the sweat now dripping steadily from his head feathers.

"Get the window." I turned to Marc, but he was already halfway across the basement. He flipped the latch on the first pane and tilted the glass forward.

Cold, dry air swirled into the room, almost visible in the damp warmth of the basement. Kai exhaled deeply. His crown feathers receded into his skull and he opened his eyes. He wasn't all better. It would take more than a fresh breeze for that. But he could cope now.

"Good. Now, let's get acquainted." Metal scraped concrete at my back, and I sank into the folding metal chair Marc had set behind me. "Where do you live? Where is your flock?"

"It's a *Flight*," he spat. "And you couldn't get there if you wanted to. But you don't want to. Trust me."

"Why not?"

"Because they'd shred you in about two seconds."

"Like your friend shredded ours? In the field just past the tree line?"

Kai cocked his head again and raised one brow. "Something like that."

"Why can't I get to your home?"

"Because you can't fly."

"What does that mean?" Marc set a second chair beside mine. "You live in a tree? 'Cause we can climb."

But Kai only set his injured arm in his lap and pressed his lips firmly together. He was done talking about his home.

"Fine." I thought for a moment. "How 'bout a phone number? We need to talk to your Alpha. Or whatever you call him. Or her."

Kai shook his head and indulged a small smile. "No phone."

"Not even a land line?" Marc asked, settling into the second chair.

"Especially not a land line." The bird paused, and after a calming glance at the open window, he let contempt fill his gaze again, then aimed it at both of us like a weapon. "Your species has survived this long by sheer bumbling luck. By constantly mopping up your own messes. We've survived this long by staying away from humans and by not making messes in the first place. We don't have phones, or cable, or cars, or anything that might require regular human maintenance. Other than a few baubles like programs on disk to entertain our young, we have nothing beyond running water and electricity to keep the lights working and the heat going."

I grinned, surprised. "You need heat? Why don't you just migrate south for the winter?"

Kai scowled. "We *are* south for the winter. Our territorial rights don't extend any farther south than we live now."

I filed that little nugget of almost-information away for later. "Okay, so you live like the Amish. How can one get in touch with your…Flight?"

Kai almost smirked that time. "In person. But in your case, that would be suicide."

I couldn't stop my eyes from rolling. "So you've said. Why exactly is your flock of Tweetys ready to peck us to death on sight?"

The thunderbird's eyes narrowed, as if he wasn't sure he could trust my ignorance. "Because your people— your *Pride*—" again he said it like a dirty word "—killed one of our most promising young cocks."

I blinked for a moment over his phrasing and almost laughed out loud. Then his meaning sank in. Male thunderbirds were called cocks. Seriously. Like chickens.

And he thought we'd killed one of theirs?

"We will attack until our thirst for vengeance is sated, even if we have to pick you off one by one."

I glanced at Marc in confusion before turning back to the bird. "What the hell are you talking abou—" But my question was aborted for good at the first terrified shout from above.

I glanced up the stairs toward the commotion—deeply pitched cries for help and rapid, heavy footsteps—then back at Kai. The thunderbird was grinning eagerly. His anticipation made my stomach churn.

Then Kaci's panicked screeching joined the rest, and I raced up the concrete steps with Marc at my heels.

Five

I threw open the door and we burst into the kitchen in time to see my uncle Rick and Ed Taylor tear down the wide central hallway toward the back door, momentarily shocked out of fresh grief by whatever new horror had just ripped its way into our lives.

Marc passed me in the hall, and I was the last one out of the house—other than Owen, who looked frustrated and furious to be confined to his bed. By the time I made it onto the small, crowded back porch, the screaming had stopped, though I could still hear Kaci sobbing softly somewhere ahead. The only other sounds were the quiet murmurs of several Alphas trying to figure out what had happened and someone's agonized, half-coherent moans.

My heart thumped as I made my way down three steps and onto the pale winter grass, politely nudging and tapping shoulders to make a path for myself. Fifty feet from the porch, the Alphas stood huddled around a masculine form whose face I couldn't yet see. My mother knelt on the ground by the tom's head, but she seemed to be talking to him rather than administering first aid.

At the edge of the surrounding crowd, Manx stood with Des cradled in one arm, the other wrapped around Kaci's shoulders as tears streamed down the young tabby's face.

A shallow breath slipped from me in relief when I saw that she was okay, if terrified. Until I realized Jace wasn't with her.

No…

I edged toward the form on the ground, my pulse racing as I tried to remember whether or not he had a pair of brown hiking boots, which was all I could clearly see of the injured tom. But I didn't know Jace like I knew Marc. I didn't have his wardrobe memorized, nor could I predict what he would say or do in any given situation. Yet my relief was like aloe on a sunburn when Jace stepped up on my left, miraculously uninjured. His hand brushed mine, but he didn't take it, well aware that Marc was on my other side. And that we were surrounded by people.

"It's pretty bad," Jace whispered.

"Who is it?" I made no move for a closer look.

"Charlie." Charles Eames was my uncle's senior enforcer. His older brother was John Eames, the geneticist who'd discovered the truth about how strays were infected, and about Kaci's "double recessive" heritage. Their father had been an Alpha up north when I was little, but none of his sons married. When he retired, his territory went to his son-in-law, Wes Gardner. Who was now firmly allied with Calvin Malone.

That particular tangle of family ties was just one example of why civil war would devastate the U.S. Prides. There were only ten territories, and everyone I knew had friends and relatives in most of the other Prides. Drawing lines of allegiance was very delicate work, and keeping them in place would be nearly impossible.

Charlie groaned again, and I steeled my spine, then stepped forward for a closer look. Marc came with me, and we knelt opposite my mother beside the downed tom. It took most of my self-control to hold in my gasp of shock and horror at what I saw.

Charles Eames lay with his head turned toward my mother, staring at her as if she were a meditative focal point. Perhaps the only thing keeping him conscious. Both of his arms and one leg were crooked—obviously broken at multiple points—and the bone actually showed through the torn skin of his left arm, where someone had ripped his sleeve open to expose the injury. Blood pooled from his arm, still oozing from the open wound.

"Needed a cigarette," Charlie whispered to my mom. "Was only a few feet from the porch." His eyes closed and he flinched as he drew in a deep breath.

My mother frowned and began unbuttoning his shirt. Gently she pulled the material from the waistband of his jeans and laid his shirt open to expose his torso. The left side of his chest was already blue and purple; at the very least, he'd broken several ribs, on the same side as his broken leg and the arm with the open fracture. He'd landed on his left side.

"How many were there?" My father bent to help my mom pull the rest of the shirt loose, and Charlie started shivering.

"Two. From the roof." He flinched over another short inhalation, as every single head swung toward the house, to make sure we hadn't just walked into a trap. But the roof was clear now. The birds wouldn't take on so many of us at once. Hopefully.

I crossed my arms against the cold as Charlie continued, and my father shifted into his line of sight so the injured tom wouldn't have to strain to see him. "I heard this whoosh, and when I turned around, they were *on* me." He coughed, then swallowed, eyes squeezed shut against the pain. "Then I was in the air. One had my arm, one my ankle."

"I can't believe they could carry you," I said, thinking of how the first thunderbird had struggled with Kaci, as little as she weighed.

"Weren't trying to." Charlie closed his eyes again, and spoke without opening them. "They took me up about thirty feet, then let me go."

My own eyes closed in horror. They'd dropped him on purpose. And if he'd weighed any less, they might have dropped him from higher up. They weren't trying to take him. They were trying to kill him.

When I opened my eyes, I found my father watching me, and I saw the same bitter comprehension behind the bright green of his eyes. Thunderbirds were unlike any foe we'd ever faced. They swooped in out of nowhere, then flew off once they'd inflicted maximum damage. We couldn't defend ourselves from their talons, nor could we Shift fast enough to truly fight them. And we certainly couldn't chase them across the sky.

In the span of a single hour, they'd injured Owen, gravely injured Charlie Eames, and killed Jake Taylor. We were down three men, at the worst possible time.

The lump in my throat was too big to breathe around. How could we fight Malone if we didn't survive the thunderbirds?

"Greg…" Vic emerged from the crowd and my dad stood to take the phone he held out. "I got him on the line."

"Thank you." My Alpha turned to pace as he spoke into the phone, while my mother did what she could for Charlie. "Danny? How close are you?" He paused as Dr. Carver said something I couldn't quite make out over the static. "Can you get here any faster?"

I squeezed Marc's hand when it slid into my good one, and we followed my father away from the crowd to listen in on his call. If he hadn't wanted anyone to hear, he'd have gone inside.

"Depends. Do you want me in one piece?" Carver asked, and my father sighed.

"Just hurry. These damn birds dropped Charlie Eames from thirty feet up. At best guess, I'd say he's got six or seven broken bones, and he's not exactly breathing easy."

"Thirty feet?" I heard astonishment and horror in Carver's voice, and faintly I registered his blinker beeping, unacknowledged by the distracted driver. "It's a wonder he survived a fall like that."

"He wouldn't have, if he'd landed on his head. Or on anything other than the grass." Fortunately, last week's ice storm had melted and dampened the ground so that it squished beneath our feet, no doubt softening Charlie's landing somewhat. "I think he has a concussion and he's in a lot of pain. What should we do for him?"

Marc and I headed toward the gathering as my father nodded and "uh-huh'd" the doctor's directions on how best to get Charlie inside without damaging him further. Kaci caught my attention, still sobbing softly on the edge of the crowd. Manx had taken the baby inside—it was still cold out, and Owen was alone in the house— so Jace had moved in to comfort the poor tabby, but he could do little in that moment to truly calm her.

"You need your coat," I said, rubbing her arms when she started to shiver. But her problem was more than just the temperature.

"Is that what they were going to do to me?" Kaci stared straight into my eyes, refusing to be derailed by my concern for her health. "Were they going to drop me?" Her eyes filled with tears and her pitch rose into a near-hysterical squeal.

Jace frowned at me over her head, and I glanced to the left, where my mother and several of the enforcers were trying to follow Dr. Carver's instructions. "Let's go inside, where it's—" *safer* "—warmer," I said, thinking of Kai's prediction and his fellow thunderbirds perched on our roof.

"No!" Kaci scowled, and my heart ached to see a younger version of an expression I'd worn time and again. "You can't just tuck me away in some safe pocket and keep me in the dark." People were looking now, and my mother frowned at me, warning me silently not to let Kaci upset Charlie any more than his numerous broken bones already had. But the tabby wouldn't be quieted, and I recognized the determination in her expression—from my own mirror. "That was almost me, so I'm *entitled* to answers," she insisted. "What do they want?"

I sighed, well aware that nearly everyone was watching us now, including Charlie. "They want revenge."

My father's eyebrows shot up, then his forehead wrinkled in a deep frown. He pushed Vic's phone into my uncle's hand without a word and stalked toward me. "I think it's time I met this thunderbird."

My father stood just in front of the folding chairs, staring down at the prisoner, who'd made no move to stand, even after my dad introduced himself as an Alpha. "I understand your people—your *Flight*—" he glanced at me for confirmation, and I nodded "—thinks we're responsible for the death of one of your own? A young man?"

The thunderbird nodded but remained seated, his broken arm resting carefully in his lap, but not quite cradled, as if showing pain would be admitting weakness. Werecats had similar instincts. Weakness means vulnerability, and admitting such to an enemy could get your head ripped right off.

But his refusal to stand was an outright insult, and his bold eye contact said he damn well knew it.

"Your name is Kai?" my father continued; we'd filled him in upstairs. The thunderbird nodded again. "Do you have some kind of proof I can examine, Kai? Because to my knowledge, none of my men has ever even *seen* a thunderbird before today. And killing someone of another species is precisely the kind of thing I would hear about."

Though, there were always surprises. Toms like Kevin Mitchell, whose crimes went unnoticed until it was too late.

Kai sat straighter, though it must have hurt the still-oozing gashes across his stomach. "We accepted evidence in the form of sworn testimony from a respected member of your own community."

"Wait…" I crossed both arms over my chest and ventured closer to the bars, confident that the bird was now too weak and in too much pain to lunge for me. And that if I was wrong, I could defend myself from one caged bird with a broken wing. "Someone told you we killed your…cock?" I resisted the urge to grin. What was a crude joke to us was serious business to him, and making fun of our prisoner would not convince him to cooperate.

Still, that joke was begging to be told. Later, when we needed a tension breaker. Where Kai wouldn't hear.

"Who?" I demanded, frowning down at him.

"Even if I wanted to tell you—" and it was clear that he did not "—it's not my place to say."

"So you won't even tell us who's accusing us?"

"No." He turned slightly, probably looking for a more comfortable position on the floor, but flinched instead when the movement hurt.

"How is that…just?" I almost said *fair,* but bit my tongue before someone could remind me that life wasn't fair. Few enforcers knew that better than I did.

The bird heaved a one-shouldered shrug with his back pressed against the cinder blocks. "We gave our word that we would guard his identity in exchange for the information he offered. We swore on our honor." He looked so serious—so obviously committed to keeping his promise—that I couldn't bring myself to argue. Instead, I turned to my father, shuffling one boot against the gritty concrete floor.

"It's Malone." To me, it seemed obvious. Of course, in that moment I was just as likely to claim that Calvin Malone was the worldwide source of all evil. So maybe mine wasn't the most objective of opinions….

For a minute, I thought he'd argue. But then my Alpha nodded slowly, rubbing the stubble on his chin with one hand. "That's certainly a possibility…."

"It's more than that." I unfolded my arms to gesture with them, careful not to turn my back to the caged bird. "Who else would try to frame us for killing a thunderbird?"

Marc raised one brow in the deep shadows, silently asking if I were serious. "Milo Mitchell. Wes Gardner. Take your pick."

"If it was either one of them, he was acting on Malone's behalf. It's all the same."

My father waved me into silence and turned back to the

thunderbird. "If we don't know who's accusing us, how can we defend ourselves? Or investigate the accusation?"

Kai stared back steadily. "That is not our concern."

"It's in the interest of justice," I insisted. "If you guys value honor so highly, shouldn't you be interested in justice?"

"For Finn? Yes." The bird nodded without hesitation, his good hand hovering protectively over the open wounds on his torso. "That is our only motive. For you? Not in the least."

"But you're not getting justice for…Finn?" I raised my brows in question, and he nodded. "…if you're attacking the wrong Pride." Not that I was trying to pin the tail on another cat. I was just trying to get the name of our accuser. "Right?"

Kai actually seemed to consider that one. "I agree. But that's not my call."

"Whose call is it?" My father stepped up to my side. Marc was our backup, a constant, silent threat.

"The Flight's."

I frowned, uncomprehending. "So who decides for the Flight?"

Kai scowled at my ignorance. "We do."

"All of you?" I couldn't wrap my brain around it. Without a leader—someone to spearhead the decision-making process and keep the others in line—how could they function?

My father had gone still, and I couldn't interpret his silence, or his willingness to let me continue questioning the bird on my own. But I wasn't going to complain.

If I messed up, he'd step in. "What if you disagree? Isn't there some sort of…pecking order?"

The thunderbird nodded reluctantly. "It is only invoked in extreme cases."

"Like this one?" I spread both arms to indicate the bird's assault on our entire Pride.

That time Kai smiled, showing small, straight teeth he hadn't possessed in bird form. "We were unanimous about this."

I shook my head as if to clear it, and my hands curled into fists. "You unanimously decided to hold an innocent child responsible for an unfounded allegation of murder that has nothing to do with her? How is that honorable?"

The prisoner's expression twisted into a mask of contempt. "We would not have hurt the child, even if she is our natural enemy. Nor would we have hurt you, if it could be helped. Finn was killed by a male cat, and in exchange for that information, we also agreed to try to remove the female cats from your encampment before the true melee begins."

Melee?! Were these *ninja* birds? Green Berets with feathers?

My father went stiff on the edge of my vision, and Marc growled at my back. And for a moment, I was actually too surprised for words. But then indignation surfaced through my shock, singeing my nerve endings with infant flames of anger. "You agreed to *remove* us?" I turned to my father before the bird could answer. "I told you it was Malone." He'd initially tried to get his paws on Kaci through political maneuvering, and when that didn't work, he'd breached our boundaries to take her by force. My brother Ethan had died defending her, and Kaci's blossoming sense of security was shattered. As was her confidence in our ability to protect her.

"I think she's right, Greg." Marc stepped between us and I could see that he wanted to put an arm around me. But a public display of affection would be unprofessional in front of the prisoner. Even simply comforting me would make me look weak.

My father nodded, convinced. Then he turned toward the bars. "You have no phones? So how can we get in touch with your Flight?"

That cruel smile returned, though this time it seemed less confident. "You can't. They can only be reached in person, and even if I told you where to go, you couldn't get there on your own. And in this shape—" he lifted his broken arm, jaw clenched against the pain "—I can't take you."

"Then how did Malone do it?" I demanded, stepping close enough to touch the bars. I wanted to wrap my hands on them, shake them in anger. But I knew from experience that they were too strong to rattle, and that gripping them in my current state of desperation would make me look like the prisoner rather than the interrogator. Especially since he currently had the upper hand. And damn well knew it.

"If you mean our informant, he was never in our nest. Our search party found him with Finn's body."

"How did you make a deal with him, if you weren't

all there to agree?" Marc asked, and I was relieved to realize I wasn't the only one who didn't understand this hive mentality thing the birds evidently had going on.

Kai shrugged again. "We function as a unit. A promise from one of us will be honored by all."

"So, if we were to convince you of our innocence, you would promise to stop dive-bombing our toms, and the rest of you would honor that promise?" I could work with that. I was good at convincing....

But Kai shook his head, and his lips tightened beneath another grimace of pain. "I cannot offer my word in contradiction to a standing agreement. Even if I wanted to. It would dishonor my Flight."

Damn it!

My father turned away from the thunderbird without a word and headed for the stairs, which was our signal to follow. On the third step he paused and glanced at me over his shoulder. "Feed him, then close the door, but leave the window open." Which would make us look merciful for the moment, and ensure that we'd get maximum effect out of closing it later, if we had to.

I nodded, and as my father left the basement, I turned back to the caged bird. "Do you eat normal food? People food?"

He grinned nastily. "I don't suppose you have fresh carrion?" None that we were willing to let him eat. My stomach churned at the very thought.

But Marc only smiled coldly. "Personally, I feel more like poultry. Extra tasty crispy."

Six

"No one leaves the house in groups smaller than three," my father said, and I groaned on the inside, though I acknowledged the necessity. We'd had similar manpower restrictions in the Montana mountains during my trial, thanks to the psychotic band of strays trying to forcibly recruit Kaci. But at least then we'd been able to fight back.

Unfortunately, we had no idea how to fight the thunderbirds, and no way of knowing when or where they'd strike. And we could neither chase nor track them. We were out of our comfort zone and out of our league, unless we could find a better way to defend ourselves. Or a way to contact Kai's Flight.

"And if Kaci's with you, make that four," my father amended, as his gaze fell on the young tabby pressed so closely against me I felt like I'd grown an extra four limbs.

We'd assembled in the living room this time, because it was bigger than the office and because this was a mandatory briefing for every cat on the ranch. My dad had left the door open, to make it easier for those in our makeshift triage center to hear. They'd carefully lifted Charlie into Ethan's bed, after stabilizing his neck as the doctor had instructed. Ideally, he'd have been left where he landed until Dr. Carver could examine him, but it was too cold on the ground to leave him there, and none of us were safe outside at the moment. With all the questions still unanswered, that much was clear.

I sat on the couch, smooshed between Kaci and Marc. Jace sat on Kaci's other side. Around us, the room was full of toms and Alphas, though only Blackwell sat, in the white upholstered armchair. The old mule looked like he was about to collapse, and only sheer stubbornness kept his spine straight. Well, that and outrage over our latest crises.

Rage buzzed throughout the room, and the word *shock* didn't begin to describe our bewilderment over the sudden invasion from above.

"Although, Kaci…" my father continued, his voice stern but gentle, "I think it'd be better if you stay inside for a while."

Kaci nodded mutely. I could only imagine how she must have felt. A few months earlier, she'd been a normal thirteen-year-old, largely ignored by her older sister and crushing on human boys her own age. Now she was priceless, when she'd once been common. Coveted, when she had once been merely accepted. Fragile compared to those around her, in spite of her exponential gain in strength, when she'd once been considered strong and healthy for a girl her age.

Everything had changed for Kaci, and she had yet to find balance in her new life. Peace and acceptance of her past would be difficult to come by when someone was always trying to snatch her from her home.

Especially this most recent attempt.

"Here's what we know...." All gazes tracked my father as he began to pace across the center of the room. "The thunderbirds think we killed one of their young men." He held up one hand for silence when questions were called out from all over the room. "We'll get to the particulars of that in a moment. But first, the bird Owen captured is named Kai. No last name—they don't use them."

"How do they tell one another apart?" my uncle asked, leaning against the far wall next to a morose and silent Ed Taylor. Jake's family would not have time to truly mourn him until life returned to normal, and no one was willing to hazard a guess on how long that would take.

My dad shrugged. "My theory is that there are too few of them to necessitate repeating names."

"Or they have a bunch of names," I suggested. Dad started to frown at me, but I held up a hand to ask for patience. "I'm serious. They keep themselves completely set apart from human society. If we did that, even with our relatively large numbers, including the strays—" Blackwell scowled at that, but I ignored him "—would we need last names? We can tell at a single sniff what family a fellow cat is from, and if we didn't live and work within the human society, why would we need last names?"

To my surprise, though Blackwell still scowled, everyone else actually seemed to be considering my point. "All I'm saying," I continued, aiming my closing statement at Blackwell, "is that just because they only have one name apiece doesn't mean there aren't bunches of them. If their population was really that small, would they risk picking a fight with us?"

"Okay, that's a valid point," my father conceded. "We'll hold off any assumption about the size of their population until we have further information from Mr....Kai."

"Did he give you anything useful?" Blackwell tapped his cane softly on the carpet.

"In fact, Faythe and Marc did get two valuable bits of information from him. Without pulling out a single feather." I couldn't help but grin at that. My father would seize any opportunity to emphasize my worth to the other council members. Ditto for Marc. "First of all, thunderbirds have no Alpha."

Bert Di Carlo spoke up from behind me, and I twisted to see him frowning. "You mean they're currently without an Alpha, or they never had one?"

"Never had one," I answered. My father raised one brow but let me continue, so I bobbed my head at him briefly in thanks. "According to Kai, they make decisions as a group."

"Like a democracy?" Kaci's bright brown eyes shone with the first glimpse of curiosity I'd seen from her in more than a week—since I'd evaded her questions about my sex life. "So they, like, vote?"

"I don't think it's quite that simple. Or maybe it's

not quite that complicated." I shrugged and altered my focus to address the entire room. "I don't entirely understand, but the impression I get is that they make decisions as a single unit, but that it's nothing so formal as an actual vote. And their word is their law. Literally. Kai refuses to break a vow from his Flight, or even contradict it. Even if we convince him that we're innocent."

"So, they're honorable murderers?" Jace shifted on the couch to look at me around Kaci's head, but my father answered.

"They don't see it as murder. They're avenging the death of one of their own, and they've been told by one of *our* own that we're responsible for that death—a young thunderbird named Finn."

"Who told them that?" Ed Taylor demanded, pushing off against the wall to stand straight, his still-well-toned arms bulging against the material of a pale blue button-down shirt.

"Is it true?" Blackwell asked softly, before anyone could answer Taylor's question.

My father sighed and stopped pacing to face the elderly Alpha. "I don't think so, but we can't confirm that without more information, which Kai is unwilling to give us at the moment. But as soon as we're finished here, we'll begin contacting our Pride members for questioning one at a time. That will take a while, but I don't see any better course of action right now."

Blackwell nodded reluctantly, and my dad turned to Taylor.

"As for who's accusing us…" He glanced at me, then back to his fellow Alpha. "Logic and—frankly, gut instinct—would point to Calvin Malone."

I was watching Paul Blackwell as my father spoke, and as I'd expected, his face flushed in anger and his chest puffed out dramatically. If he'd had fur in that moment, it would have been standing on end. "You cannot go around accusing Calvin of everything that goes wrong, just because you don't like him. You have no proof he was involved in tagging those strays, and none to show for this, either!"

No, we had no proof that Malone was responsible for implanting tracking devices in several of the strays we'd fought when Marc was missing, but we *did* have proof implicating Milo Mitchell—Malone's strongest ally. Unfortunately, while tagging strays was immoral without a doubt, it wasn't illegal, technically speaking, and we currently lacked enough votes on the council to remedy that. So our case against Mitchell—and against Malone by extension—was on hold. Indefinitely. Another massive thorn in my already tender side.

My father remained much calmer than I felt, though I was proud of myself for biting my tongue. Literally. "We're not accusing him, Paul. We're suspecting him. Strongly."

"Because he's opposing your bid for council chair?"

"Because at their informant's request, the thunderbirds have agreed to try to remove the tabbies from the ranch before the height of their assault. Calvin Malone has publicly stated that he wants Kaci and Manx removed from the Lazy S, and that he'd rather see Faythe set back on the 'proper' path for a young woman. Who would *you* consider a more likely suspect?"

Blackwell faltered, and the flush faded from his cheeks as his gaze dropped to the curve of his cane. "He wouldn't do this. I know you and Calvin don't get along—I don't see eye to eye with him on everything, either—but he would never do this. Conspiring against a fellow Alpha with a hostile third party—one of another species! That's…treason."

"Yes." My father let the quiet gravity of his voice resonate throughout the room. "It is."

Blackwell stood unsteadily and stared at the ground before finally meeting my dad's expectant gaze. "You know I can't act without proof, and I only have a week left as council chair, anyway. But I will launch a formal investigation into this. Today."

"Why should we trust your investigators?" Bert Di Carlo looked almost as outraged as Blackwell looked suddenly exhausted. And every bit of his seventy-two years.

"Because you just volunteered for the job." The old man met Di Carlo's gaze gravely. "I'll pair you with Nick Davidson, to keep things even." Two days earlier Davidson had officially thrown his weight behind Malone. "If Calvin is responsible for this, you have one week to bring me proof. After that, the point is moot."

Di Carlo nodded and Blackwell turned back to my dad. "Where can I make some calls?"

"My office." My father waved one hand toward the

door, gesturing for the older Alpha to help himself. Blackwell made his way to the hall, and my dad turned to the rest of us. "My enforcers, start at the top of your call tree and work your way down. Pass me the phone if you find someone who's ever seen a thunderbird, or knows anything about them. Even if it's just a rumor, or an old Dam's tale. If they know anything more than that thunderbirds can fly, I want to talk to them."

We'd made out the call lists the week before, after Owen had spent hours calling on south-central Pride toms to help patrol the borders and search for Marc in the Mississippi woods. Now each of us had a roster, and—my idea—every tom in the Pride had a contact at the ranch. A go-to guy for problems or reports, in case my father was out. Or busy with any of one of the myriad disasters currently plaguing our Pride.

For the next hour, I sat at the long dining room table with my fellow enforcers, slowly crossing name after name off my list. The other Alphas had set their able-bodied men to similar tasks, searching for information among their own members. Because regardless of who killed this thunderbird, chances were slim that the murder happened on our land. We'd been patrolling pretty obsessively since Ethan died; the non-enforcer toms had been taking shifts at the borders ever since. We'd insisted, though two had lost their jobs due to excessive absences.

A lost job meant little compared to another lost tom.

I set the phone down after my last call and looked up to find Jace watching me from across the table. In the hall, Marc was in an animated discussion with one of the newly unemployed toms, who was not happy with his current assignment. All the others were still speaking into their own phones, so for a moment, I let Jace look. And I looked back, my heart aching with each labored beat.

After several bittersweet seconds, the rumble of a familiar engine outside pulled my gaze from Jace. *Dr. Carver.*

My father rushed toward the front door, cell phone pressed to one ear. "Pull as close as you can to the porch. We'll come out and get you." Because on his own, Dr. Carver would make just as appealing a target for any nearby thunderbirds as Charlie had. More so, if they knew who he was. "Marc? Vic?" my father called, out of sight now. But I beat the guys into the hall.

"No," my Alpha said as I reached for the doorknob. He held up my arm by the wrist of my cast. "If you don't give yourself a chance to heal, you won't do us any good when we go after Malone."

"Good point," I said, and he looked surprised as I reluctantly stepped aside so Vic could open the door. Marc brushed one finger down my cheek and shot me a sympathetic smile before following his Alpha and his former field partner outside.

I watched through the tall, narrow sidelight window while they rushed down the front steps just as Carver swung open his car door. Two birds circled ominously overhead, low enough that their size and wing-claws were obvious. As Carver twisted to grab his bag from the passenger seat, both birds swooped to a sudden, staggeringly graceful landing in the middle of the front yard, Shifting even as their newly formed feet touched the ground. For several long moments, they faced off against Marc and Vic, with nothing but Carver's car and fifty feet of earth between them.

My father stood firm on the bottom step, and the doc sat frozen in his seat, staring in awe at our unwelcome visitors. Suddenly feathers sprouted across the arms of one bird and he stepped up onto his bare toes, as if to launch himself at the car. Marc slapped his empty palm with the gigantic wrench he carried, growling menacingly. The bird stood down, apparently content to remain a silent threat while they were outnumbered, and a soft sigh of relief slipped from me.

My father waved his men forward and Carver stepped from the car and was ushered inside by both toms. Our Alpha remained on the porch, alone and undefended as a show of strength. In truth, any one of us could have been at his side in less than a second. But sometimes appearance is as important as reality.

"Kai is alive but in a lot of pain," he called in a strong, steady voice. "If you want him back, put me in touch with your Flight." With that, he turned his back on the birds—a show of confidence as well as an insult—and walked into the house.

He pulled the door closed, and I turned to find the hall packed with toms. "There's nothing to see," my father declared, and as the toms slowly dispersed, he turned to Carver. "Good to see you again, Danny. What's it been? A week?"

"Sounds about right." Carver hefted his overnight bag higher on one shoulder. "I have less than a week of vacation left. At this rate, I'll be looking for a new job soon, Greg."

My father sighed. "That makes two of us," he said, referring to his spot on the council, not his career as an architect.

Carver flinched and nodded. "Hey, Faythe," he said as Marc locked the front door and Vic took our latest guest's overnight bag. "How's the arm?"

"Ready to come out of the cast." I fell into step beside the doc and my dad, and Marc and Vic followed us.

Carver grinned. He was almost always in good spirits, no matter who he was sewing up—or cutting apart. In his day job, Dr. Danny Carver was a medical examiner for the state of Oklahoma. He spent more time with dead people than with live ones. "Give it a couple more weeks, then we'll cut it off and let you try Shifting."

"We don't have a couple of weeks, Doc." I stopped in the hall, and he had to stop with me to maintain eye contact. "We're going after Malone in three days." I whispered the last part, because I wasn't sure how much of our battle plans Blackwell had overheard. Or whether we could trust him, even with the investigation he was initiating against Malone.

Dr. Carver frowned and glanced at the heavily decorated cast I held up. "You may have to fight in a cast, then. It'll protect your arm better, anyway."

"But I can't Shift in a cast. I'll be stuck in human form."

Carver shrugged and tightened his grip on his

medical supply bag. "We could cut it off and let you Shift several times, but a broken bone isn't like a laceration, or even a torn rotator cuff." Both of which I'd suffered in the line of duty. "They take longer to heal, and if you don't heal properly, the damage could be permanent. And Shifting before broken bones have at least half healed hurts unlike anything you've ever felt. Just ask Marc."

I glanced at Marc, not surprised to see him nodding. He'd gotten several broken ribs at the same time I broke my arm. A chest couldn't be casted, so he'd been Shifting twice a day for the past week, and his ribs were only just returning to normal.

"So, what does that mean for Charlie?" I asked as we moved toward Owen's room.

"Let's see how bad it is...."

My dad and Vic followed the doc into our makeshift triage center, but I headed into the kitchen instead, and Marc followed me. "What's wrong?" he asked as I poured the last of the coffee into my favorite mug. I raised both brows, and his head bobbed in concession. "Okay, everything's wrong. But specifically?"

"This." I set my mug on the counter and held up my casted arm. "We're days away from going full scale against Malone, and in the meantime, we're under fire from above. And I'm about as useful as a three-legged dog."

"You're much more useful than any kind of dog, *mi vida.*" Marc purred and pressed me into the counter, his hands on my hips. I couldn't resist a smile. I was a real sucker for Spanish.

Except when he was yelling it at me.

I kissed him, and my arms went around his waist, my good hand splaying against his back. Feeling the restrained power, and loving it.

"Better?" he asked when we came up for air.

"A little." I sighed. "I just want to fight."

He grinned. "I love that in a woman."

"Stupid cast." I tried to twist and grab my mug, but he held me tight.

"I kind of like it. You broke your arm saving my life."

I had to smile at that. "And I'd do it again tomorrow. I just wish it wasn't going to hold me back the next time."

"I'm sorry."

I shrugged and grabbed my mug, then followed him into the hall. Marc hung back to keep from crowding Owen's room, but I pressed my way through the throng and stood against one wall with Kaci. My mother sat in a chair by Ethan's bed, holding Charlie's hand because she could do little else for him. Manx sat on the floor beside Owen's bed, one mangled hand on his arm.

Carver headed straight for Charlie, whose clothes had been cut off but left under him, because lifting him again would have hurt him worse. The doc shook his head when my mother started to give up her chair, then he knelt to dig in his medical bag. Seconds later he pulled out a plastic-wrapped disposable syringe and a small vial of something clear. Carver drew some of the liquid into the syringe, then carefully felt for a vein in Charlie's arm.

"Let's give this a chance to help with the pain, then we'll see what we can do for you," he said softly as he slid the needle into Charlie's skin. Charlie didn't even flinch. What was a shot, compared to being dropped from thirty feet in the air?

My mother took the used syringe, and Dr. Carver crossed the room to Owen, then sank into the desk chair to examine my brother's stomach. "These stitches look good, Karen." She murmured her thanks, and the doc turned to Owen's leg, which my mother hadn't been confident she could stitch up properly. "These are deeper. They're going to hurt for a while, but if you Shift a few times tomorrow, you should be good to go in a couple of days. Let's get you stitched up."

The doctor talked while he worked, to set his patient at ease, and it helped. I could attest to that personally. "This isn't so bad," he said when Owen flinched. "Faythe had similar injuries a couple of months ago, but Brett Malone had it much worse than either of you...."

But I missed the rest of what he said, because that name echoed in my head. Brett Malone. Jace's brother, whose life I'd saved with a meat mallet. Brett had insisted he owed me, even after he'd given us the heads-up about my father's impeachment. I'd tried to brush off his IOU—I was just doing my job—but he was insistent.

And now I knew exactly how he could repay his debt.

I ran one hand over Kaci's hair and whispered that I'd be right back. "Where are you going?" my father asked as I passed him, and when I gestured, he followed me into the hall, where Jace now stood with Marc and Vic.

"I'm getting evidence for Blackwell." Before he could press for details, I turned to Jace. "I need your phone."

Jace dug it from his pocket with neither hesitation nor questions, and I smiled at him gratefully. No one else would have done that. Even Marc would have asked why I wanted it.

I took Jace's phone and headed toward my room, calling over my shoulder as I ran. "I'll fill you in after I consult my source."

Seven

"Hello?" Brett sounded cautious and suspicious—and he didn't even know who was calling yet. Jace had his half brother on speed dial, as I'd known he would. Other than his mother, Brett was the only family member in his contacts—which I'd also guessed.

"Hey, Brett, it's me."

"Faythe?" he whispered, then something scratched against the receiver as he covered it. A few seconds later, he was back, and the background chatter was gone, leaving only the wind—a hollow-sounding echo in my ear. "My dad will kill me if he finds out I'm talking to you!"

"Yeah, well, welcome to the game. He tried to kill me in November." I was too nervous and upset to sit, so I walked the carpet at the foot of my bed, occasionally running the fingers of my casted hand over the scarred posts.

"It's not a good time, Faythe. What do you want?"

I took a deep breath and tried to keep in mind how

difficult this whole thing must have been for Brett. He knew his father was a lying, ambitious, hypocritical, sexist, bigoted bastard, and there was nothing he could do about that. Unlike Jace, he was Malone's actual son and couldn't just walk away from his Pride. Not without leaving his mother and the rest of his family. And not without permission, which Malone would never give.

But the time for easy choices had passed.

I sighed and let a hint of true fear and frustration leak into my tone. "There's never going to be a good time, Brett. I need a favor. Information."

For a moment, I heard only the whistling wind and the heavy rustle of evergreen boughs. He was in the woods behind his house, hopefully out of hearing range of the rest of his Pride, because if anyone overheard what I was about to ask for, he could be locked up for the rest of his life. Or worse.

Finally Brett spoke, and each word sounded like it hurt coming out. "I'm all out of favors, Faythe. Things are bad around here. They're going to notice I'm gone."

My heart ached for Brett. I knew what it was like to stand in conflict with the rest of my family. The rest of my Pride. But lives weren't at stake when I argued with my parents. My Alpha wasn't psychotically ambitious.

However, as strongly as I sympathized with his position, I had to think of my Pride first. Of Kaci and Manx. Of my father's precarious position on the council. If he lost it, he'd lose the ability to protect us all. So I steeled my spine and forged ahead.

"Are you enjoying life, Brett? Truly treasuring each

breath? Because if it weren't for me, you'd be rotting in the ground right now."

"I know, but—"

"You owe me. You said, 'Let me owe you, Faythe.' So I'm going to let you."

His sigh seemed to carry the weight of the world. "I already repaid you."

"Yeah, well, that bit of information didn't come in very handy." When he woke from the attack that nearly killed him, Brett had warned me that his father would try to take the council chair. "Your dad jumped the gun and challenged mine before I even had a chance to warn him."

"I had nothing to do with that."

"I know." I sank into my desk chair and picked up a novelty pen with a fuzzy purple feather sticking up from one end. "Okay, forget the favor. I'm asking you as a friend. We need this, Brett. You know what's going on with the thunderbirds, don't you?"

"Thunderbirds? What are you…?"

"Save it." I dropped the pen on my desk. "Don't insult me with lies. You're better than that. You're better than Calvin."

Brett's next exhalation was ragged, and twigs crunched beneath his boots. He was walking. Hopefully moving farther from the house. "I only have a minute. What do you want?"

"The truth. Is your dad doing this? Did he sic the birds on us?"

"Faythe, I can't… He'll kill me."

"Jake Taylor's dead, Brett. And Charlie Eames may

never walk again, if he survives." I shouldn't have disclosed our damages to the enemy; that was on page one of the don't-screw-your-own-Pride handbook. But you don't make gains without taking risks, and I believed in Brett.

Of course, I'd believed in Dan Painter, too, but then his double agent act had nearly gotten me killed. But Brett would come through for us. He *had* to....

"I'm sorry. I—"

"Apologies aren't good enough, Brett. They almost got Kaci. You know what your father will do if he gets his paws on her."

"He would never hurt her."

"No, he'd just whore her out to one of your brothers the day she turns eighteen. Earlier, if he can pass it off as in the best interest of the species. Are you going to let him do that? Are you going to let him sell her in marriage just so he can get his sticky hands on our territory? Or the Di Carlos'?" Because Umberto Di Carlo had no heir, thanks to his daughter's murder, and once he retired—or was *forced* into retirement— someone would have to take over his territory.

And in our world, he who has the tabbies has the power.

"Is that what you want for Kaci?" I asked when Brett didn't answer. "Hell, is that what you want for *Mel?*" Melody Malone was only fourteen, and already being courted by several toms handpicked by her father. By all accounts she'd bought into his propaganda and believed that her decision had the power to make or break her Pride. She took the responsibility very seriously and would have done anything to please her father.

Poor, warped kid.

"Of course not," Brett said at last, and his next pause was long. "But if I do this, I can't stay here." If his father found out he'd betrayed his Pride, Malone would take his claws and his canines and throw him in their cage so fast he'd still be reeling from the first blow. And he'd never get out. I had no doubt of that.

My toes curled in the thick carpet, as if they alone anchored me to the floor. Was he saying what I thought he was saying? "What can I do?"

"I need sanctuary. If your dad gives his word, I swear I'll tell you everything I know."

I exhaled in relief and actually felt the beginnings of a smile coming on. This was what Blackwell needed. With proof, he would have to revoke his allegiance to Malone and begin prosecuting him instead. The pendulum of power would shift back to my father. Or at least away from Malone.

"Let me see what I can do."

"Hurry…"

I threw open my bedroom door and tapped and shoved my way through the crowd to Owen's room, the tile cold against my bare feet. Dr. Carver sat in the chair by Charlie Eames's bed, drawing more clear liquid into a syringe from a small, inverted glass bottle.

I glanced briefly at Charlie and noticed that his skin was paler than I'd ever seen it. And that his stomach looked…puffy. But then my gaze caught my father's, and I waved for him to follow me. Dr. Carver only looked up briefly, but both Marc and Jace followed us into the hall.

Once we'd escaped the crowd, I held up Jace's phone, blocking the sound, already heading toward the living room since Blackwell still occupied the office. If Brett came through like I hoped he would, we could let him speak directly to the old man who would then have no choice but to believe Malone's involvement. "I have Brett Malone on the line, and he's willing to tell us what he knows, in exchange for sanctuary."

Marc's brows rose; he was obviously impressed. Jace beamed. "I wish I'd thought of that." But even if he had, half brother or not, Brett might not have talked to Jace. Not like he would talk to me. I'd saved his life. Plus, I was a girl, and like it or not, most toms weren't threatened by me. At least, not until I'd had reason to prove they should be.

My father frowned and sank wearily into an armchair angled in front of the picture window. "What makes you think we should trust him?"

I perched on the arm of the overstuffed couch, facing him. "He told us his dad was going to challenge you. For what little good that did us."

"Exactly." He templed his hands beneath his chin, a sure sign that he was considering my proposal, even if he sounded skeptical. "That made him look loyal and grateful, but the information came too late to be of any use. It sounds to me like he's been studying his father's playbook."

"He didn't know Cal was going to move so quickly," Jace insisted, sitting on the edge of another chair pulled near the window.

My father thought, and I bit my lip to keep from rushing him. "What does he know?"

I could only shrug, still holding the phone up with my hand covering the mouthpiece. "He's waiting for your word that you'll take him in."

"Then how do you know he knows anything?"

Jace frowned. "If Calvin's involved, Brett knows."

Marc nodded solemnly. "And he's probably risking a lot, just talking to Faythe."

"He is. And he doesn't have a lot of time." Too nervous to sit, I stood, watching my father anxiously. My heartbeat ticked off each endless second of silence. Then, finally, he opened his eyes and held one hand out.

"Give me the phone."

I handed Jace's cell over and my father held it up to his ear, then stood to walk as he spoke. "Brett? My daughter tells me you have information about your father's involvement with a Flight of thunderbirds? Are you willing to volunteer that information?"

"I am—in exchange for sanctuary." Brett's voice actually shook, and I took Marc's hand where he still stood, squeezing it to offer him the comfort I couldn't offer Brett. "I can't go back after this, Councilman Sanders."

"I'll go one better than that. If you can bring us proof of your Alpha's involvement, you'll have a job here as an enforcer."

Brett exhaled, and I could hear his simultaneous

relief and unease, all in that one breath. "Are you serious? Sir?"

"Completely." My father smiled, amused by the young tom's nervous doubt. "Anyone willing to stand against his own father in the name of justice belongs here with us."

"Thank you, sir. I accept."

My grin was so big it threatened to split my face.

"I'm in the middle of something, so I'm going to let you give Faythe the details. Then I want you to get your proof and come straight here. And be careful. That's an order."

"Yes, sir."

My father was almost truly smiling when he handed me the phone, but his worried frown was back by the time he made it to the hallway. He was concerned about Charlie. And probably about the rest of us. "Take notes," he instructed, then disappeared down the hall.

I leaned back on the couch, already digging in the nearest end-table drawer for a notepad and pen. Fortunately, my mother stashed them everywhere. "Thank you, Faythe," Brett whispered into my ear, and I had to blink back tears in order to speak clearly.

"You can thank my dad when you get here. For now, just tell us what you know."

Marc settled onto the cushion next to me, and Jace leaned forward in his chair, listening carefully as his brother began to speak. "Two days ago, one of our guys took down a deer, then went to ring the proverbial dinner bell. Before he was fifty feet away, this huge bird swooped down on his meal. Our man killed the thunderbird in a dispute over the kill. When we reported it, my dad went nuts. Said the last thing we needed was to piss off the thunderbirds. It took him a day or so to get there...."

I glanced at Marc to see if he'd caught that, and he nodded. How far out had they been, if it took their Alpha a full day to get to them? Of course, if they were expecting our attack, broad patrols made sense, but the Appalachian territory wasn't *that* big.

"...and by the time he did, he was almost...excited." And anything that excited Malone would be bad news for us. "He didn't want to bury the body. He said they'd come looking for their lost bird, so we had to sit still and wait."

"How did he know they'd come for it?" Marc asked.

Brett started to answer, but Jace beat him to it. "When I was little, there was a flock that migrated through our territory every year. Cal claimed he'd actually talked to one once, but I never believed him. Guess he was telling the truth for once."

"Yeah," Brett said over the line. "So we waited. Six hours later they showed up. Three of them. I have no idea how they found us. They can't smell for shit with those beaks."

"But they can see for miles from the air." Marc ran one hand slowly up and down my back. "At least, natural birds can."

"I always hated that phrase," Jace said. "It makes Shifters sound *un*natural."

"Anyway..." Brett ignored them both. "They landed, and it was totally bizarre. They Shifted in midmotion, with their feet first, so fast it looked like movie special effects."

I nodded, though he couldn't see me. "I know. We've seen the show."

"Oh. Yeah." Brett cleared his throat and continued. "Anyway, they landed and saw their boy dead, surrounded by, like, five of us. Three of us in cat form. They started to go feral. But before they could lunge, my dad said he knew who'd killed their man and wanted to make a deal."

"Then he set us up," I guessed, my eyes closed in frustration.

"Yeah. He told them that one of your cats had to have done it, because yours was the closest territory."

Marc growled. "Where the hell *were* you?"

Brett exhaled heavily. "Four miles from your western border in the free zone. I'm sure you know why."

Yeah. Sounds like they were just as ready to invade us as we were to invade them. So much for Malone's promise to Blackwell that he wouldn't start the war.

But then something even more infuriating occurred to me. They'd put five toms on our western border—the opposite direction we'd expect them to come from, because Malone was headquartered east of us, in Kentucky. But five wasn't enough for a large-scale offense. Which obviously wasn't what they were planning.

They were counting on *us* to start the war. Expecting us to take most of our men northeast, into Appalachian territory, leaving Manx, Kaci and my mother largely undefended. At which point those five or so toms would sneak in the back way and plunder our most valuable resources. Our most treasured, vulnerable members.

Fury crept up my spine in a white-hot blaze, but I

forced it down. Their plans had obviously changed, and I needed to focus.

"So, the thunderbirds promised your dad they'd get the tabbies out, then they'd rip us to shreds, one by one?"

"That's the gist of it, yeah." Brett sounded miserable.

"And you have proof?" Marc prodded.

"My testimony, and the dead bird's feathers, stained with his killer's blood. Dad told us to clean up the mess, and I kept a couple of the feathers. I had a feeling this would go downhill. But I'm not sure how much good they'll do. These birds can't distinguish one cat's scent from another's."

"At least it'll help with the council," Jace said, voicing my exact thought. "But we'll have to come up with some other way to prove it to the birds."

"If we can even find them." I frowned, suddenly overwhelmed by the new burden, when we could least afford it. Kai was going to have to talk—that's all there was to it.

"I have to go. They've probably already noticed me missing," Brett said, and twigs snapped as he made his way back toward the house from the woods.

"Wait, Paul Blackwell is here. You have to tell him what you told us."

"I don't have time now, but I'll speak to him when I get there. But there's one more thing. Our tom? The one who killed the thunderbird?"

"Yeah?" I stood, eager to report to my father.

"It was Lance Pierce."

Parker's brother.

Well, shit.

Eight

"Son of a bitch!" Jace pounded the arm of the couch and I jumped, his phone bouncing in my open palm. "To clear our name, we have to sell out Parker's little brother. How's that for a rock and a hard place?"

"We can't just turn him over…" I started, but my words faded into silence as soft sobs and footsteps sounded down the hall. I made it to the doorway just as Kaci flung herself into my arms. "What's wrong?" Though, really, the sheer number of ways she could have answered that question was staggering.

"He died. Charlie's dead."

"Oh, no…" I wrapped both arms around her as my father stepped out of the somber crowd of toms still gathered around Owen's room, now staring at their feet as if they were afraid that eye contact might trigger tears.

Kaci was crying freely. She'd only met Charlie Eames that morning, but at her age, with all the tragedy she'd already witnessed, any death would have been traumatic. Murder, even more so.

My father's gaze was heavy as Dr. Carver followed him into the hall, both of them headed our way. "What happened?" I asked, pulling Kaci into the room with me so they could come in.

"Internal bleeding." Dr. Carver laid a hand on Kaci's shoulder briefly, then sank wearily onto the couch next to Marc.

"Did we make it worse by moving him?" I had to ask. Not that the answer would change anything.

"Probably." Carver twisted on his cushion to face me. "But we had no other choice, and the truth is that with such major, full-body trauma, his chances were never very good in the first place."

Kaci whimpered in my arms, and I squeezed her tighter. Physical contact was the only comfort I had to offer.

My father sat stiffly near the front window, where crimson, late afternoon sunlight slanted across his white dress shirt like translucent streaks of blood. He leaned forward with his elbows propped on his knees, staring at his shiny shoes. He'd shed his suit jacket—the house was warm from all the extra bodies running on accelerated Shifter metabolism—but his shirt was still buttoned to his neck, his gray striped tie still neatly knotted.

I glanced at the hallway, where toms were now gravitating toward the kitchen, then at Kaci in indecision. Then I sighed and closed the door, gesturing for her to take a seat next to Jace. Keeping her in the dark wouldn't comfort or calm her, but being with those she trusted most just might.

She curled up on Jace's lap, resting her head on his shoulder as he wrapped both arms around her, cocooning her as if she were his little sister. Though, he and Kaci were already closer than he and Melody had ever been.

The living room wasn't soundproof, and anyone who really wanted to hear what was said would have little trouble. But in a house full of werecats, a closed door was a formal request for privacy, and our present company could be counted on to honor it. Including Blackwell, should he emerge from the office before we finished. He and my father might not agree on everything, but Blackwell would never intentionally do something he considered dishonorable.

My dad looked up when I closed the door. "That's two murdered toms, one attempted kidnapping, and one mauling, all in under three hours." The Alpha's voice was grave, with a strong undercurrent of anger and bitter frustration. And his expression was tense beneath the strain of what he wasn't saying: that we could ill afford the deaths of two allied toms less than two weeks after we'd lost Ethan. Not that there was ever a convenient time for so much death.

"Yes, but they both went out alone, right?" Dr. Carver glanced around for confirmation. "We know to avoid that now."

My father's eyes flashed in fury. "We shouldn't have to! This is our territory. *My* property. We will not cower in our own home while vigilantes pick us off one by one."

"We can't fight them," Marc said as I sank onto the couch between him and the doctor. "Not on their terms."

"I know." My father looked my way, obviously hoping for some good news. "What did Brett say?"

"He has blood-soaked feathers proving we didn't kill Finn. Unfortunately, while birds have great eyesight, they have little sense of smell, and we're pretty sure they can't differentiate between two cats' scents. The feathers will hopefully convince the council that Malone is pulling the birds' strings, but they won't do us much good with the thunderbirds themselves. Even if we do find a way to contact their…nest."

"Wonderful." My father's scowl deepened.

"It gets worse," Marc began, but Jace interrupted, gently stroking Kaci's long brown hair down her back, petting her like a kitten.

"The blood on the feathers belongs to Lance Pierce. He killed Finn in a squabble over a fresh kill."

Marc glowered at Jace, and my frown echoed his. But with more urgency. Was he trying to show Marc up? In front of our Alpha?

Fortunately, my dad was too distracted by the new information to spare the toms more than a brief glance. "Well, that's just wonderful." He stood and started across the floor, then stopped and glanced around as if surprised to find himself in the living room rather than the office. "That puts Jerold Pierce in a nice bind, doesn't it? Not to mention us."

"Why?" Kaci lifted her head from Jace's shoulder.

"Because now Councilman Pierce will have to choose between two of his sons," Marc explained.

Lance Pierce had been with Malone almost as long

as Parker had been with us, and their father was the only
North American Alpha who had yet to officially pick a
side in the council chair debate.

Kaci still looked confused, so I elaborated. "We
know Malone set the thunderbirds on us to weaken us
before we could attack him, but Parker's dad is just as
likely to see Malone as a hero for saving Lance's life."
I shrugged miserably. "And if *we* give Lance up to get
the birds off our backs, his father won't be very happy
with us." Understatement of the century. "Or very likely
to support Dad as the council chair."

My father needed Jerold Pierce on his side just to
bring him even with Malone. Then, if Blackwell
withdrew his support from Malone in response to Brett's
evidence, we'd be one up on Malone in the vote.

I was relatively confident that Blackwell would do
the right thing once he'd spoken to Brett Malone. Unfortunately, I was also pretty sure that if we turned
Lance over to the thunderbirds—even in name only—
we could kiss Pierce's support goodbye. Even with
Parker still in my father's employ. Assuming he wanted
to stay there after this.

"Poor Parker." Kaci glanced from one to the other of
us with huge hazel eyes. "None of this is his fault, and
he's going to be caught in the middle."

I nodded, impressed all over again by her perceptive-
ness.

"Does he know?" My father leaned with one hand on
the wall-length entertainment center.

"Not unless he's listening at the door," Marc said.

And he wasn't. Parker would never eavesdrop without the typical open-door invitation to do so.

"Faythe, bring him in here." I stood, and my dad turned to Kaci. "And why don't you go see if Manx needs any help with the baby? She and Karen have their hands pretty full right now." Because my mother was cooking for twenty people. No, make that eighteen, since we were down two men. And Manx was tending Owen very closely.

Kaci looked disappointed, but she climbed down from Jace's lap. She'd been permitted in a closed meeting and knew better than to push her luck. Most of the time.

She trudged off toward Manx's room and I crossed the hall into the kitchen, where four toms sat around the breakfast table with a deck of cards, a huge bowl of salsa, and several open bags of corn chips. Another group sat in the dining room with hot wings and no cards, but the atmosphere in both rooms was identical.

The toms had come to the ranch ready to fight, but had been benched instead. They'd been confined to the main house, yet exiled from the office and the living room. They were restless, irritable, and on edge from their Alphas' tension. The prevailing ambiance was somber, and quietly angry. Like hot water about to break into a boil.

"Hey, Parker, can you come here for a minute?"

Parker glanced up and ran one hand through prematurely graying hair, then laid his cards down and followed me. My mother raised both brows as we passed, but she never stopped stirring a huge pot full of ground beef, beans, and crushed tomatoes—the beginnings of the world's best chili.

I tossed my head toward the living room, and she nodded, then called Vic over to stir in her absence. But before we made it out of the kitchen, Paul Blackwell emerged from the office and marched into the living room, leaving us to follow.

"Thank you for the use of your office," the old Alpha said as I took up a post against one wall near the door. Parker stood nearby and my mother sat in one of the armchairs, but no one else had moved. Blackwell leaned on his cane several feet in front of me, facing the rest of the room. "I've spoken to the other Alphas, and no one admits to having any contact with thunderbirds in the past decade. In fact, they all sounded rather astonished. Including Calvin Malone."

"Do you believe him?" I asked, and at first I didn't think he would respond. But when my dad made no objection to my question, Blackwell turned unsteadily to half face me, utilizing his cane more than he had before. Maybe he'd gotten stiff from sitting in my dad's desk chair. Or maybe the stress was affecting the poor old man physically.

"I intend to refrain from judging until I've heard all the facts and seen all the available evidence." His voice was steady but doubt showed in every line on his face. And there were plenty to choose from.

"Well, we might be able to help you out there." I glanced at my father for permission to continue, but he shook his head and stood.

"Let's take this to the office."

We filed out of the living room and into the office, then took seats in our usual formations, centered on my father in his high-backed chair. When everyone was settled and Dr. Carver had pushed the door closed, my father's gaze found me. "Faythe, go ahead."

That's right: my source, my idea, my party. I couldn't help a little thrill of adrenaline at the knowledge that I'd made a vital contribution to the effort.

I sat straighter on the couch—between Marc and Jace, to my extreme discomfort—and faced Blackwell in the chair he'd claimed opposite my Alpha. "I just spoke to Brett Malone, who says he has proof that his father framed the south-central Pride for the murder of the thunderbird. Finn."

Blackwell took a moment to process the information, and to his credit, I had no idea what he was thinking or feeling. He'd had more than seven decades to work on his poker face.

Finally the elderly Alpha gripped the curve of his cane and trained a steady, surprisingly intense gaze on me. "Proof in what form?"

"His own testimony, and the dead bird's feathers, stained with his killer's blood."

"And who is this killer?"

I desperately wanted my father's guidance before answering that question, but couldn't get it without making an obvious glance in the opposite direction. So I went with as conservative an answer as I could. "One of the Appalachian territory's enforcers."

Blackwell frowned at being stonewalled but did not press the issue. "Did the Malone boy volunteer this information?"

"No." I fidgeted in my seat and had to remind myself that I'd done nothing wrong; I wasn't usually under such scrutiny from an Alpha other than my father unless I was in serious trouble. "I called him looking for evidence. For your investigation."

"And what did he ask for in return?" Blackwell may have been old, but he was no fool.

"Sanctuary." I felt no obligation to reveal my father's job offer because technically Brett hadn't asked for that, thus it fell outside the scope of the question.

Blackwell went silent again, and I risked a glance at my father. He gave me a tiny nod, and I exhaled silently, then returned my attention to the elderly Alpha as he began to speak. "When will you have this evidence?"

"Brett should have already left. So...tomorrow, hopefully." I wasn't sure whether he'd fly to save time, or drive to retain possession of his car.

Blackwell stood, leaning heavily on his cane. "Unfortunately, I can't wait that long. Present your evidence to Councilman Di Carlo, when it arrives. I'll be waiting for his report."

My father stood. "You're leaving now?"

"I think that's best. I'll be ready in half an hour." The elderly tom nodded to his grandson, who came to his side like a trained puppy.

"I'll send an escort with you to the airport."

Blackwell hesitated. Normally such precautions

wouldn't have been necessary. But if the sitting council chair were injured while leaving our territory, some of the other Alphas might consider that a reflection of our security. Or lack thereof.

Finally the visiting councilman nodded, and my father walked him to the office door. "Let me know when you're ready to go."

My mother checked on her chili, then rejoined us in the office and closed the door. My dad sighed and turned to Parker. "I hate to be the bearer of more bad news, Parker, but according to Brett Malone, it was Lance who killed the thunderbird."

For an instant, relief was plain on Parker's face. No one was dead. No one related to him, anyway. Then the ramifications sank in, and relief melted slowly from his features. He blinked, and I could almost hear the gears turning in his head. "So Malone was protecting him by blaming us?"

My father nodded, and Jace leaned forward with his elbows on his knees, anger flaming behind his bright blue eyes. "Yes, but I can guarantee that your brother's safety was *not* foremost on Calvin's mind. He was saving his own tail, and framing ours."

"We have a choice now, and I'd like to get your input before I make a decision," my dad said. "Once we get in contact with them, we can tell Kai's Flight the truth and try to clear our name, but in doing that, we'd be implicating your brother. Or we can keep quiet about it, in which case we have to find a way to either fight these thunderbirds or convince them to stop fighting us."

Parker stared at the floor, straight strands of salt-and-pepper hair hanging over his face. "You want me to decide whether or not to turn my brother over to the thunderbirds?"

"No." My father shook his head firmly. "That's my call. But I am interested in your opinion."

Parker sat up then, his face lined in pain and bitter conflict. "Okay, if we turn him over, they'll kill him. Right?" he asked, and the rest of us nodded. Even my mother, who sat with her ankles crossed primly beneath her chair, her expression just as guarded as my dad's. "But if we don't, they'll keep killing *us*."

"Yes. But it's a bit more complicated than that," my father said.

"Because of my dad?"

Again our Alpha nodded. "I'm assuming that if we turn your brother in, our chances of gaining your father's support drop dramatically."

"You might say that." Parker raked one hand through his hair, and in that moment he looked much older than his thirty-two years.

"Maybe there are choices we're not seeing…" I ventured, and both of them turned to me expectantly. "Maybe we could offer Lance sanctuary, too, in exchange for his testimony to the birds." My father started to object, but I rushed on before he could. "Via video, or something. I don't know. I don't have the details worked out yet, but there has to be some way to fix this without handing him over to be slaughtered."

But before anyone could argue—or agree—an electronic version of an old-fashioned telephone ring cut into the air, and I glanced down to see that I still had Jace's cell phone in my lap. I picked it up and glanced at the display, hoping to see Brett's name.

Patricia Malone. I reached across the rug to hand Jace his phone. "It's your mother."

Jace raised one brow at our Alpha, asking permission to take the call. My father nodded, and a sick feeling unfurled deep inside my stomach. Jace flipped open the phone. "Hello?"

"Jace?" His mother's voice was only vaguely familiar, and I realized I couldn't remember the last time I'd seen Patricia Malone. "I just thought you'd want to know that Brett's dead."

Nine

"What?" Jace went pale. His forehead crinkled and his blue-eyed gaze met mine as my heart threatened to collapse beneath the mounting pressure of guilt. "That's not possible. I just talked to him." He stood, and probably would have left the room if his brother's fate weren't of crucial consequence to our entire Pride.

"Don't tell me what's possible—I saw the body," his mother snapped, true anguish fueling her anger. But then her tone softened. "You spoke to Brett today?"

Jace sank back onto the love seat, almost seeming to deflate in front of us. "Well, Faythe did. But I was here." He glanced at me, and I could only stare back at him as I clutched Marc's hand with my good one. It was my fault. I'd pressured Brett into helping us, and now he was dead.

And we had no evidence.

"What did he say?" His mother's voice dropped even lower. Like she didn't want to be overheard.

"Nothing. They were just talking." Jace bent with

his forehead cradled in one palm. "What...? How did it happen?"

Mrs. Malone sighed, and her anger seemed to bleed away with that one soft exhalation. "It was an accident. He and Alex were sparring in the woods. Just training. Brett lost his balance and fell out of a tree."

"He fell out of a *tree?*" Jace glanced first at me, then at our Alpha, to see if either of us was buying the coincidence. My father's steadily darkening scowl said he was not, and my own expression hopefully mirrored his. We'd told the few humans in his life that Ethan had died when he'd fallen out of a tree, but it was no more plausible a story for Brett than it had been for my brother.

The tree bullshit was a message to us, from Malone. He'd found out what Brett was doing and had killed his own son as much to hurt us as to keep his own dealings from going public. And it sounded like Alex, Malone's second-born son, had done the honors.

The knots in Jace's family tree made mine look straight and strong in comparison.

"You can't be serious." Jace leaned back on the love seat and stared at the ceiling.

"Hon..."

"Mom, you don't really think Brett fell out of a tree. Today, of all days?" She started to interrupt again, but Jace spoke over her. "You can pretend you don't hear things, but you know what's going on. I *know* you do, so you can't seriously believe Brett was out goofing off in the woods—today—and fell out of a tree. What did they tell you? That he broke his neck?" His eyes watered, and his voice halted as he choked up. "How closely did you look?"

"Honey…"

Jace shot to his feet and stomped toward the bar but made no move to pour a drink. "Did you *see* his *neck, Mom?*" he demanded.

Patricia Malone sobbed over the phone, one great, heaving, hiccuping cry of despair that left me hollow inside, my guilt and regret a mere echo of her pain. Then she sniffled twice, and after a brief silence seemed to have herself under control. "I need you to come home," she said, in little more than a whisper.

"Mom…"

"Melody's in bad shape, Jace. She's not taking it well, and we need to be there for her."

Jace turned to face the rest of us, and my heart broke for him. He couldn't go back; if they'd kill Brett, they'd sure as hell kill Jace. We all knew that. Surely his mother knew it, too, whether or not she was willing to admit it, even to herself.

"You belong here with us," she insisted.

The last bit of self-control crumbled from Jace's expression, revealing raw pain and anger for an instant before he whirled to face the wall. "That hasn't been true since you married Calvin."

I stared at my cast in my lap, fiddling aimlessly with a puff of padding sticking out from the end. He should have been alone; we were all intruding on what should have been a very private agony. I glanced at my father and tossed my head toward the door, raising one brow in question. He nodded, then stood and motioned for us all to follow him into the hall. Whatever Jace said next would be personal, and of no value to our Pride. Marc took my good arm as we headed for the door, but if Jace noticed us leaving, he showed no sign.

"Don't do this, Jace," his mother begged as I rounded the couch. But her voice carried a sharp edge of warning.

"I'm not doing it." I'd never heard Jace sound so strong. So angry, and unmovable. "Calvin's doing it. He set the thunderbirds after us, and he killed his own son because Brett was defecting with evidence. If you can't see the truth when it's staring you in the face, we have nothing else to talk about."

I was halfway to the door with Marc at my side when a plastic *crunch* echoed through the room. I turned to see Jace holding the pulverized remains of his cell in one hand, small bits of plastic and electronics spilling between his fingers to clatter on the hardwood.

"Will you accept Marc Ramos as an escort?" my father asked from the hall, making no effort to lower his voice. Marc's hand tightened around mine beneath the table. At the peninsula, my mother froze in the act of ladling chili into bowls, and her gaze strayed to the doorway. Along with mine.

"Greg…" Blackwell hedged, but my father's footsteps never paused, and Blackwell had to either keep up or be left behind. Both men stopped in front of the dining room—no doubt strategic positioning on my dad's part.

"Marc is my best enforcer, Paul." My Alpha turned with his back toward the kitchen, putting me and Marc in Blackwell's direct line of sight, over his shoulder. "I can't in good conscience send you off with anything less than my best."

I glanced at Marc and found him watching in silence, his every muscle tense, his breath apparently frozen in his lungs.

Blackwell looked our way and sighed, then his focus shifted to my dad. "Of course. I'm sorry for the trouble, but I do thank you for the escort."

I might have been the only one who saw the almost imperceptible ease of tension in my father's shoulders. But then again, my mother probably saw it, too.

Marc stood when our Alpha motioned for him and Vic. They would drive Blackwell and his two toms to the airport in their rental car, then ride back with my oldest brother, Michael, who would be landing in a couple of hours, back from a business trip.

Michael had been out of town for the past three days, and he knew nothing about the thunderbirds or the damage they'd done, because he was out of touch while his plane was in the air. So my father had left him a voice mail telling him where to meet Vic and Marc, and that they'd explain on the way home.

Several minutes later, I watched through the front window as the four younger toms hastily escorted the elderly Alpha down the steps and into the rental car, where he squeezed into the roomy backseat between his own men. Vic drove down the quarter-mile driveway and out of sight, and though the thunderbirds launched dramatic—and frankly, scary—dives toward the car, they made no physical contact. Probably because the car would have emerged the clear victor over feather and bone in any kamikaze mission.

Moments after the rumble of the car's engine faded, the birds came swooping back into sight, then over the house, where they no doubt perched on the roofline, waiting for some foolish cat to come out alone.

But—as badly as we hated being prisoners in our own home—that wasn't going to happen.

Dinner was miserable, even with my mother's chili and homemade corn bread muffins. Jace sat across the table from me, staring into his bowl, aimlessly stirring its contents. I wanted to say something to him. To apologize for getting Brett involved, or lend him a tear-proof shoulder. After all, I'd just lost my own brother. But memories of the last time we'd grieved together stood out in my mind like a big, flashing "danger" sign, so I settled for meaningful looks of sympathy every time our gazes met, wishing I knew what to say.

I forced down two bowls of chili to encourage Kaci to eat, though neither of us had any appetite. In spite of a house full of guests, there were several empty chairs, and my gaze was drawn to them over and over as I ate. Marc and Vic wouldn't be back for several hours. Manx was still tending Owen in his room, and Jake and Charlie were gone for good.

After supper, Kaci went to help with the baby and some of the guys invited me to share a bottle of whiskey and a game of spades. But I was restless and out of patience, so I excused myself and headed to the basement. I couldn't take any more communal mourning. And the current of rage running beneath our common grief? Riding that was like sitting on a drum of gasoline, holding a lit sparkler. Eventually one of those tiny flames would fall in the right place, and my whole world would explode.

Part of me felt like that had already happened.

"You're distressed," Kai said as my left fist slammed into the big punching bag.

"No, I'm pissed off." I threw another punch, concentrating more on power than on form, and my shoulder ached in protest. I bounced on the balls of my feet, as I'd been taught, both fists held ready, though my broken right arm would not see active duty.

"Does that help?"

"Yes." But that was a lie. Usually, hitting something put me in an instant good mood, but punching one-handed only made me feel awkward and infuriatingly powerless.

Hopefully our unwelcome guest was suffering similar frustrations. The thunderbird stood with his own broken arm cradled to his bare and still-bloody chest. His good hand—fully human for the moment—clutched a steel bar at the front of the cage, through which he watched me vent my grief, anger, and frustration on the equipment in our homemade gym.

Upstairs, I could hardly breathe without wanting to kill someone, just from inhaling all the tension. But like the office, the basement was practically soundproof, by virtue of being underground. The small, high windows and the door at the top of the stairs were the only weaknesses in the sonic armor, and you'd have to be very close to them to overhear anything clearly. So my solitude would have been nearly complete, if not for the human-form bird studying me as if I were the circus oddity.

"What happened to your arm?" Kai asked as I threw another punch. I'd skipped the gloves, but what were skinned knuckles compared to torn flesh, bruised hearts, and everything else my fellow cats were suffering upstairs?

I swiped my good arm across my sweaty forehead without looking at him. "I broke it." And that reminder sucked up what little joy remained in my useless punching, so I shifted my weight onto my left foot and let my right leg fly. I hit the heavy bag hard enough to make it swing sluggishly, and the blow radiated into my knee and beyond. A tiny spark of triumph shot through me. Kicking was better. There was nothing wrong with my legs.

"How did you break it?" Kai asked, obviously un-bothered by my pointedly short answers.

I steadied the bag with my good hand and faced him, hoping I looked fierce in spite of the scribbled-on cast. "I broke it dispatching of the bastards who tried to kill several of my Pride mates."

I expected Kai to flinch, or laugh, or show obvious skepticism. Instead, he only nodded solemnly. Almost re-spectfully. "So you understand our need for vengeance."

"No." I whirled again and grunted as my left leg hit the bag. "We deal in justice."

"Justice and vengeance are the same."

"Now you're just lying to yourself to validate blood thirst." I kicked again, and the bag swung harder. "Justice is for the victim." Kick. "Vengeance is for the survivor." Kick. I stopped to steady the bag again and glanced at the bird now watching me in fascination. "You're not doing this for Finn." I threw a left jab and had to stop myself from following it with a right out of habit. "You're doing it for yourselves, and that's anything but honorable." Contempt dripped from my voice, and blood smeared the bag when my knuckles split open with the next punch.

"We punish the guilty as a warning to future aggressors," Kai insisted, and I turned to see him scowling, small dark eyes flashing in the dim light from the dusty fixture overhead.

"There was no aggression!" I threw my hands into the air. "Your boy tried to take a werecat's kill. That's fucking *suicide*. Don't you harpies have any instinct? Or common sense?"

Kai drew himself straighter, taller, though the movement must have stung in every untreated gash spanning his chiseled stomach. "We are birds of prey, but carrion will suffice in a pinch. The kill was abandoned in our hunting grounds. Finn had every right to a share."

"It wasn't *abandoned*. The hunter—" I was careful not to give out Lance's name "—just went to tell the group he'd brought down dinner. And for the record, a werecat is only obligated to share his meal with higher-ranking toms and his own wife and children, should he have them. Our custom says nothing about donating to any vulture who swoops out of the sky."

"He wasn't in werecat territory."

Okay, technically Kai had a point, but that was only by chance. In many cases, territories of different species often overlap, mostly because what few other species have outlasted werewolves exist in such small numbers as to be inconsequential to us.

Or so we'd thought.

"You know what? None of that matters." Frowning, I kicked a boxing glove across the floor and crossed my arms over my chest, annoyed that they didn't fit there, thanks to the cast. "The cat who killed Finn wasn't one of ours. If he had been, your bird would have died in our territory. But you just said he didn't."

Kai's scowl deepened, and his good hand tightened around the bar until his knuckles went white, the muscles of his thick hands straining against his skin. "If your people are innocent, where is your proof?"

Incensed now, I stomped across the gritty concrete into the weak light from the fixture overhead, careful to stay well back from the bars. "Our proof was murdered this afternoon. By your *honorable* informant."

The bird only stared at me, probably trying to judge the truth by my eyes. But I couldn't read his expression. Couldn't tell whether he believed me, or even cared one way or the other. "You need new proof."

"No shit, Tweety." I turned my back on him and stalked across the floor, then over the thick blue sparring mat to the half bath on the back wall. "Do you even care that while you guys are out here slaughtering innocent toms, the man you're after is hundreds of miles away, laughing his ass off?"

Okay, Lance probably wasn't laughing, but he had to be at least a little relieved that *he* wasn't the one being dropped from thirty feet in the air by a vengeful, over-grown bird.

I squatted and dug beneath the small, dingy sink until I found a bottle of rubbing alcohol and a gallon-size bag of gauze squares and medical tape. We had hydrogen peroxide, but frankly, I wanted the walking eight-piece dinner to sting in every single cut.

"Here." Back on the mat, I tossed the alcohol underhanded. It landed a little harder than I'd intended, then slid until it hit the bars, evidently undamaged. "I can't do anything for your arm, but maybe this'll prevent gangrene. Or whatever." While Kai stared at the bottle, obviously confused by my compassion, I tossed the bag of bandages, which smacked the bars then fell to the ground.

Kai bent awkwardly—and hopefully painfully—to pull the bottle through two bars. His gaze shifted from me to the alcohol, then back again, and his head tilted sharply to the side—a decidedly avian motion, which implied a very detached curiosity. "Why do you care?"

"For the same reason I don't go around killing innocent toms. Because my human half understands that sometimes compassion is the greater part of honor."

Ten

Sweaty from my workout, I headed for my shower, but I knew something was wrong the moment I closed my bedroom door. The door to my bathroom stood open and an amorphous shadow lay across my carpet, cast by the brighter light from within.

I held my breath but couldn't stop my heart from pounding. My first thought, as ridiculous as it would seem in hindsight, was that Malone had somehow breached not only our territorial boundary, but our home. I *hated* feeling unsafe in my own house.

Furious, I grabbed a hardbound book from my dresser—the only potential weapon within reach—but before I took the first step, a familiar voice called softly from the bathroom. "Relax. It's me."

"Jace?" I wasn't sure that was much better. My pulse slowed, but only a little, and a tingly feeling began deep in my stomach—half dread, half anticipation. "You shouldn't…"

"I know. Sorry." His shadow stood from the side of the tub and he stepped into the doorway. "This was the most private place I could find." And that's when I realized he'd been crying.

Sympathy rang through me, softening the sharp edge of my irritation and melting my willpower like chocolate in the sun. "Oh. Yeah, I guess it is." Because no one else—other than Marc and Kaci—would venture into my room without permission.

After Charlie died, the Alphas had banned trips to the guesthouse, even in groups, until we figured out how best to fight the thunderbirds. So we were packed into the main house tighter than clowns in a Volkswagen.

"Are you okay?"

He shrugged and wiped moisture from his cheeks with both bare hands, but his eyes were still red and swollen. "It just kind of hit me all at once. About Brett."

"And your mom?" I stood near the bed, afraid to move too close to him. Being near him made my heart beat too hard and my throat feel too thick. I was acutely aware of every tingling nerve ending, even under such grave circumstances.

Jace looked surprised for a moment, then he shoved his hands into his jeans pockets and nodded. "She knows what Cal's doing. She has to know. But I think it'd be easier if I could believe she doesn't."

"I'm sorry." I didn't know how to comfort him. I wanted to hug him. To hold him, like I would if it were any of the other guys in pain. Werecats tend to relax in big piles and to relate to each other through touch. But

Jace wasn't just one of the other enforcers anymore, and the last time we'd tried to comfort each other, things had gotten out of hand. Waaay out of hand.

Brett's face flashed through my mind, and I had to concentrate to keep from imagining his last moments, wondering if they had looked anything like Ethan's. My eyes watered and I sank to the carpet, leaning against my footboard. "It's my fault. I got Brett involved, and now he's dead. I'm so sorry."

"No." Jace strode forward and dropped smoothly onto his knees, inches from me. His cobalt eyes shone with unshed tears and flashed with resolve. "Brett was already involved. He kept those feathers for a reason. And if he wasn't willing to take the risk, he would have hung up on you the moment he heard your voice."

"But…"

"This is Calvin's fault, Faythe. Not yours, and not mine. Cal's going to pay for this. I'll make sure of that."

I nodded. Staring into his eyes, I believed him. I believed we could make Calvin pay, because Jace couldn't live with the alternative. And he wasn't the only one.

But killing Malone wouldn't make everything okay again. No amount of justice—or vengeance—would bring back Ethan or Brett, or make us miss them any less. Nothing could erase Kaci's trauma, or give me back the time I'd lost with Marc.

"We're gonna be fine, Faythe," Jace insisted, but that time I didn't believe him because his voice shook. He didn't truly believe himself. "You're strong, and so determined. Nothing ever knocks you down. People try, but you just get up swinging." He braved a grin in spite of obvious grief. "You're going to take over for your dad when he retires, and you're going to be an amazing Alpha."

"What about you?" I asked, and the room seemed to fade around us then, as if nothing else existed in that moment.

A pained shadow passed over his eyes, like clouds in front of the sun. He scooted closer and leaned against the footboard next to me. "I'll be happy if I'm still a part of your life."

I didn't want to ask, but I couldn't help it. "What part?" My voice cracked on the last word, and I blinked back more tears. Why was I crying? Why did my heart *ache,* like it was going to collapse in on itself?

"This part…" Jace whispered. Then he kissed me.

I tried to fight it. I tried to think about Marc, and how much I loved him. But Jace was everywhere in that moment. He was everything. Our pulses raced in unison, and the hollow ache in his heart echoed in my own. His lips were warm, but his hand on the side of my neck, his thumb brushing the back of my jaw— they were hot.

I couldn't pull away. And the truth was that I didn't want to.

That kiss went deeper than I'd been prepared for. Longer. It lit tiny fires within my veins, dripping little bits of flame that trailed to burn low in my body. When our kiss had finally run its course, Jace leaned back a few inches and my eyes watered as my tortured gaze met his. "Why is this so hard?" I whispered.

His pulse leaped crazily at my admission. "Everything worth fighting for is hard."

My hand trailed down his arm. "When did you get so smart?"

That shadow passed over his eyes again. "When I realized that nothing else matters. There's only my job, and you, Faythe. All the other stupid, petty shit is gone. There's killing Calvin and earning a place in your life. That's it. That's my whole world now."

No. It's too much. My head shook slowly. It was hard enough being the almost-constant focus of Marc's attention. I couldn't be fully half of Jace's world, too. That was too much attention. Too much pressure. Too much…trouble.

"Jace, this can't happen." I closed my eyes, thinking it would be easier to say without him looking back at me. But it wasn't. "This isn't just about us. I can't leave Marc." I opened my eyes again, hoping he'd believe me if he saw the truth in them. "I *love* Marc."

"I'm not asking…"

"I know." I let my hands uncurl uselessly in my lap. "You're not asking me to leave him. But he won't share. And I can't ask him to."

"Do you *want* him to?" Jace tried to don his blank face, but it didn't work. Maybe I was too close to him now, and could see past it. Or maybe he could no longer defend against me. Either way, I saw what it cost him to ask me that, and it broke my heart.

"I don't know." Frustrated, I let my head fall back

against my footboard. "I don't *know* what I want, but I can't lose Marc, and I will if you…if we…"

"Fine." He frowned, and his suddenly hard gaze searched mine. "Tell me you want me to go, and I'll walk away. I swear."

"Jace…" But I couldn't say it. And he knew it.

"You can't, because you *don't* want me to go." I tried to argue, but he cut me off. "You feel something for me, and it's not brotherly, and it's not sympathy. It's not even curiosity. Not anymore." The suggestive spark in his eye sent flashbacks racing through me.

Me and Jace, on the floor of the guesthouse.

Intertwined in mutual pain and need.

Easing fresh grief the only way we knew how.

"Jace, this isn't right. It'll mess everything up." It would tear the entire Pride apart.

He shook his head and held my good hand when I tried to pull away. "It's not wrong just because it isn't easy, Faythe. The only thing we've done wrong is keep it from Marc. We should tell him."

I nodded. That was only fair. "But not yet. It's not a good time." *And I have no idea what I'm going to say…*

Someone knocked on my door, and we both jumped, then flushed. "Faythe?"

Dr. Carver.

My door opened before I could respond and he slipped inside, then closed the door at his back. We both leaped to our feet and the doc took us in with a sad, cautious look. But he didn't seem surprised in the least. "Your dad's looking for you. Both of you."

I felt the blood drain from my face. Carver had caught me and Jace in the guesthouse the day Ethan died, and he'd promised to keep our secret, on the condition that I figure out what I was doing. Unfortunately, I hadn't made much progress in that regard.

"Does he…?" I couldn't finish my question.

"No. I told him I'd get you, but I didn't know Jace was in here until I got to the door and heard you both."

Good thing we were whispering…

"Thank—" I started, but he cut me off with a look that was part anger—probably over being put in such a position—and part aching sympathy.

Carver strode closer, and his voice dropped almost beyond my range of hearing. "If you're not ready to tell people about this yet, then you better learn to stay the hell away from each other, because if anyone else had passed by this door with an ear to listen, you'd be having an entirely different conversation right now. And that doesn't seem fair to either Marc or your father, considering everything else that's going on."

Jace bristled under the verbal censure, and I felt him go stiff at my side. I laid a warning hand on his arm and heard his pulse slow as he made himself relax.

Surprise flickered behind the doctor's eyes as he took in both the gesture and the response, but I spoke before he could ask questions or make assumptions. "It just happened. But it won't happen again. Right?" I glanced up at Jace, and he nodded stiffly. "Go out with the doc, please." Because the two of them seen leaving my room together would raise much less suspicion than Jace leaving alone. "I'll be **there in** just a minute." After I washed my face and brushed my teeth, to keep Marc from smelling my indiscretion. At least until I was ready to tell him.

Jace blinked at me, pain shining in his eyes like tears. He wanted to touch me, or say something private, but wouldn't in front of Carver. I could almost taste his frustration; it mirrored my own. Then he turned abruptly and followed the doctor out of my room.

Hot water poured over my head and down my back, washing away Jace's scent and my sweat, and blending with the tears I could no longer hold back. I cried quietly, hoping the running water would hide the evidence of my weakness from the house full of cats, most of whom needed to see me as Jace had described me. Strong. Determined. Someone who knew how to harness pain, and anger, and heartache, and use them to her advantage. To hone her leadership skills, sharpen her wits and senses, and fuel her drive for justice.

But I didn't feel much like that person at the moment. I felt…fractured. Fragmented. Like I was under fire from all sides, and each impact left a tiny crack in me. Soon, those cracks would spread and touch, and I would just fall apart.

Because I wasn't good enough.

I wasn't good enough to save Brett. To avenge Ethan. To raise Kaci. To protect Manx. To be…whatever Jace needed. To keep Marc.

To lead the Pride someday.

They needed better than me. They *deserved* better than me.

My shoulders shook and I threw my head back into the spray, shoving wet hair from my face with my right hand, grateful for the clear plastic cast protector.

"Faythe?"

I jumped and nearly slipped on the wet tiles.

"Whoaaa." Marc pulled open the shower door and steadied me, careful to grab my arm above the cast. "What's wrong?"

I blubbered something even I couldn't understand and threw my arms around him, heedless of his clothes. He stroked wet hair down my back and ignored the water soaking into his shirt and jeans. I didn't have to be strong with Marc. With him, I could just be me. I could say whatever I was thinking, do whatever felt right, cry if I was upset, and he thought no worse of me.

He picked me up.

I wasn't good enough for Marc.

When the worst of my sobs had eased, he gently peeled me away, then stripped while I stood beneath the spray. Then he stepped into the shower with me and closed the door.

"What happened?"

But I hardly knew where to start. "Ethan's dead. Jake's dead. Charlie's dead. Brett's dead. We have no evidence, and those damned birds aren't going to stop coming. There are more of them now." Ten, at my last count. And until we learned how to fight them, our only options were to hide in our own home or to flee it.

Neither was acceptable.

I sniffled and wiped my face with my good hand. "I thought I could fix it. I thought I could get the proof, and protect Brett from his dad, and prove to the council that Malone's behind this. But I can't. I can't do anything right. I can barely even wash my own hair." I sobbed again, gesturing to my shampoo bottle with my broken arm.

Marc leaned forward to kiss my wet forehead. "Then let me do it." He turned me around by my shoulders and gently tugged my head back by my hair to rewet it. Then he nudged me forward and squirted shampoo on top of my head.

He used too much and started at the top, rather than at the ends, but I barely noticed, because he was washing my hair. Massaging my scalp with strong, confident fingers as he fulfilled my need, in the most literal sense. Once again, he was there for me when I needed him, and I was...

Not good enough for him.

"You deserve better than me," I whispered, and the selfish part of me hoped he wouldn't hear.

He heard.

Marc spun me around so fast I would have slipped again if he weren't holding me up. We were so close drops of water from his chin fell onto my chest, and I had to crane my neck to see him. "You are perfect for me, Faythe, just like you are, because you're *not* perfect. You're headstrong, and impulsive, and outspoken, and I'm possessive, and overprotective, and too easy to piss off. We're both wrong for a lot of things, but we're right for each other. Do you understand?"

I nodded. I didn't know what else to do.

"There's nothing you could have done for Ethan or for any of the others, but we all know that you would have given anything to save them. Hell, look what you went through for me." He held up my broken arm and brushed the fingers of his free hand over the fading bruises on my ribs and stomach.

It was just pain. I deserved pain, if only for what I'd done to Marc.

"You're too good for me." I shook my head, digging deep for the courage to tell him the truth. It was the very least he deserved, though he didn't deserve the fallout. "You don't understand…."

Marc's mouth crushed against mine, and he kissed me so hard, so thoroughly, that I couldn't breathe. And didn't give a damn.

I kissed him back, tasting him, breathing him, hating the plastic encasing my arm because it kept me from properly feeling him. His chest was slick. The muscles shifted beneath my good hand as he moved. I let my lips trail over the harsh stubble on his chin, and he tilted his head back, giving me full access to his throat—the most vulnerable part of his body.

I could kill him in half a second, if I wanted to. Marc presenting me with his throat said he trusted me with his life. It was the biggest compliment one cat could give another.

But the scary part was that he trusted me with his heart.

I forced that thought away and stood on my toes to reach his jaw. His hands roamed up from my waist, brushing the lower curves of my breasts. My tongue traced the line of his neck, following it to his collarbone. I lapped at the water pooled there, then my tongue ventured back up, searching out his mouth.

I pulled his head down for another kiss, and Marc groaned. His tongue found mine, and he walked us one step backward. My back hit the cold tile wall, and he pulled away to lift me beneath both arms, his stance wide for stability. I wrapped my legs around his hips and clung to him, my skin slick against his.

My breasts pressed into his chest. My good arm went around his neck. He lifted me higher, and I half sat on the soap shelf to help support my weight as his fingers slid down my side, leaving trails of fire in their wake. His hand slipped between us, testing, guiding. Then he lowered me slowly.

I held my breath until he was all the way in, and my next inhalation was so ragged it almost hurt. I rocked forward, and he moaned. His eyes closed, and he rocked with me. I draped both arms around his neck, closed my eyes and rode him. I let him set the pace—slow at first, but gaining speed as friction built.

He drove into me, pinning me to the wall, drawing small sounds from me with each stroke. He rocked me back and forth with a grip on both my hips. I clung to the top of the stall with my left hand and lightly clutched the showerhead with the fingers protruding from my cast. Each breath came faster, each thrust harder. My legs tightened around him as I sought more contact. Greater friction. More heat.

Finally, when I was sure I couldn't hold back another second, Marc groaned and his strokes became frantic. I let go, and sensation washed over me, scalding compared to the now lukewarm water.

Spent, Marc leaned into me, and his head found my shoulder. His heart raced inches from mine, and I could hear each whoosh of his pulse.

After at least a minute like that, he lowered us until we sat on one corner of the shower floor, water spraying my back. I straddled him and leaned back so I could see his face. He stared at me, but he wasn't smiling. He looked…scared. Determined.

I started to ask what was wrong, but he spoke before I could.

"Marry me, Faythe."

I nearly choked on surprise. How many times was that request going to catch me off guard?

"This is the last time I'll ask. I mean it. Marry me so that when all this is over, we can get a house of our own. A little land. A lot of privacy."

"Marc…" But I had no idea how to finish that thought.

"We can do it however you want. We can have a ceremony, or stop by the courthouse on our way to Venice. You can wear a white dress, or a red dress, or jeans, or nothing at all. We can get married in the nude. I don't care. We'll do whatever you want. Just tell me you'll marry me, so we can get something good out of all this." His wide-spread arms took in every disaster the past few months had thrown at us, but his gaze never left mine. "Marry me, Faythe. Please."

His face broke my heart. His eyes seared my soul.

I wasn't good enough for him.

"Marc, we have to talk about…something." I swallowed thickly, and put my good hand over his mouth when he started to protest. "I'm not saying no," I insisted, and he relaxed visibly, as the spray of water across my back continued to cool. "But I can't…I can't do this now. There's too much going on, and we need to talk first."

He sat straighter, and I slid a few inches down his legs. "Whatever it is, it doesn't matter. If it's kids, or becoming Alpha, or whatever, it doesn't matter. We'll work it out."

He looked so hopeful, I wanted to smile, but didn't let myself. He hadn't heard what I had to say yet. "I—"

And that's when the power went out.

Eleven

"Someone give me a flashlight." My father's voice rumbled from the other end of the hall. A bobbing shaft of light accompanied heavy footsteps toward him, and a Vic-shaped shadow handed over his flashlight.

Marc tucked his towel tighter around his waist, and the thin beam from his own penlight showed off drops of water still clinging to his chest and dripping from his hair. Having anticipated neither the full-scale air raid nor my wet embrace, he hadn't brought a change of clothes.

In the deep shadows, the four parallel scars running across his chest looked terrible. Fresh. No doubt they were fresh in his mind, but he'd had them since he was fourteen, when the stray who'd raped and killed his mother had gored him, too, bringing him into my life.

For better or worse.

Three other beams crisscrossed the packed hallway as my father held an informal roll call, but a single steady pole of light caught my eye. Jace stood across from my room and several feet down, his face harshly lit by the beam from the small flashlight my mom kept beneath the kitchen sink. But even poorly illuminated, his expression was unmistakable. His focus jumped from me in my robe to Marc in his towel, and his jaw bulged furiously.

A tangle of emotions churned through me, threatening to wash me away in a tide of confusion, guilt, fear, and regret. And for a moment, I thought Jace was going to expose them all.

But when his gaze met mine, his anger softened into carefully controlled envy. Then he exhaled and dragged his focus to the end of the hall when my father cleared his throat to capture everyone's attention.

Marc's hand wound around mine. He hadn't seen Jace watching us; he was focused on the problem at hand. Like a good enforcer.

"Vic, you and Parker go downstairs and flip the circuit breaker," my dad said from his position near the front door. "And stay away from the cage. That thunderbird has an incredible wingspan, and he can Shift instantly."

Vic nodded, already headed into the kitchen with a flashlight. Parker followed, his steps heavy, his grim frown exaggerated by the dark shadows stretched across his face. To my knowledge, he hadn't spoken since he'd heard what Lance had done.

I knew how he felt—at least better than anyone else could. Lance had let Malone frame us for murder, putting all our lives at risk, including Parker's. My brother Ryan had sold me out to a serial rapist jungle stray who'd planned to sell me as a broodmare in the Amazon. Betrayal sucks, but I had more faith in my pound-the-shit-out-of-something therapy than Parker's drink-till-you-go-numb method of dealing.

"Karen, can you pass out candles and matches, just in case?" my dad said, drawing my attention back on track. My mother raised a handful of tapers she'd already collected, then ducked into the kitchen, probably to dig for matches. All of the enforcers kept two flashlights in their cars as part of the standard trunk emergency kit. Except for me; I didn't have a car.

Unfortunately, venturing outside to raid half a dozen trunks carried more risk at that moment than stumbling around in the dark inside. Especially considering that several of us could partially Shift our eyes, if necessary.

My father's stern focus skipped from face to shadowed face. "Everyone else, grab a candle and find something quiet to do while you wait. The lights should be back on any minute." Then, as the toms shuffled toward the kitchen, my father mumbled beneath his breath. "So help me, if one of you sets my house on fire, I will replace the rug in my office with your hide."

I snorted. An Alpha's sense of humor was a rare beast indeed.

But my smile died on my lips when Vic and Parker clomped up the basement stairs, yet the house remained dark.

Kai cried out from below, in a screeching, dual-tone

voice loud enough to echo in the crowded hall. "They've cut your power to draw you out. That means there are enough of us now to take you on in groups!"

"So, what do they expect us to do?" Jace demanded, while my father scowled from the center of a huddle with the other Alphas. "Walk out and surrender?"

"No." I drew my robe tighter and held my broken arm at my stomach. "They expect us to die."

My dad's scowl deepened, and he led the other Alphas into his office with the flashlight they shared.

"This makes no sense," Mateo Di Carlo said to the house in general, once the office door had closed. He stood as close as he could get to Manx without actually touching her while she nursed Des back to sleep. "Why would they believe Malone's bullshit story, but not our truth?"

"They'd believe us if we had proof." I waved Kaci forward when she peeked out of Owen's room. My injured brother lay inside, listening and watching by candlelight from his bed. Michael sat in a chair beside him, taking it all in. "And that would be enough of a reason for them to break their word to Malone," I continued. "To nullify the deal they made. But without evidence, they consider themselves honor-bound to uphold their word. And to avenge their dead."

"They're trying to kill us?" Kaci whispered.

I wrapped my casted arm around her. "Not you. They could have killed you earlier, but they didn't. They're trying to protect you and me and Manx."

She looked less than reassured.

"This is crazy." Brian Taylor stepped from the kitchen with a candle in one hand, its flame flickering over his freckles and the pale brown fuzz on his chin, emphasizing his youth. "How are we supposed to stop them? Shoot them out of the sky?"

"Yeah, that'd be great, if we had guns." Since our ranch had no livestock to protect, they weren't necessary for typical farm practicality and werecats hunted with their claws and canines. Carrying a firearm was like cheating, thus considered dishonorable in most Prides.

In fact, the only cat I'd ever even seen with a gun was...

"Here." I stepped away from Marc and nudged Kaci closer to him, for comfort. "I'll be right back." I could feel everyone watching me as I marched down the hall, and Jace's gaze in particular seemed to burn.

"What are you doing?" he whispered, falling into step with me.

"I have an idea." I stopped at the office door and gave three sharp knocks to announce my entrance; I wouldn't have been able to hear permission, anyway.

The door was unlocked, so I pushed it open to find all four Alphas watching me. "Sorry to interrupt, but I have an idea, and I need something from your desk. If that's okay."

My father raised a brow at my formality, and one corner of his mouth twitched as if he wanted to smile. He knew I was about to ask for something crazy; why else would I grease the wheels with manners?

He waved one thick hand toward his desk in a be-my-guest motion, and I marched across the room. Jace stopped in the doorway, and an intimately familiar breathing pattern told me Marc had joined him.

Eager now, I upended the marble jar on one corner of the desk. Pens and mechanical pencils tumbled onto the spotless blotter like pick-up sticks, and I pawed through them until I found a small, thin key ring, holding two identical shiny keys.

My father stood when I dropped into a squat behind his desk. "Faythe…" he warned, but I already had the bottom drawer open. And there it was: a blocky black pistol. Handheld death. According to the box of bullets next to it, the gun was a 9 mm, which was more than I'd known about it a second before.

I held it flat in my palm, getting a feel for the weight. It was heavier than I'd expected.

Across the room, Jace flinched, and I caught the motion in my peripheral vision. Manx had accidentally shot him with that gun five months earlier, and his recovery had been less than pleasant. And more than memorable. "Faythe…" he began, and I was surprised to realize that his tone almost exactly matched my father's.

My dad cleared his throat, and I looked up to see that all the Alphas were standing now. My uncle watched me in equal parts caution and curiosity. Taylor looked like he thought I'd lost my mind. And if I wasn't mistaken, Bert Di Carlo looked…almost impressed. "You don't know how to use that," my father said.

"They don't know that."

Jace flinched again when I flipped the gun over,

looking for the safety. Most cats I knew had an innate fear of guns, which went hand in hand with our fear of hunters. Thanks to our fantastic hearing and reflexes, there really wasn't much danger of us getting shot, but the chances of dying from a bullet wound were greater than the chances of dying from the average mauling. To which our scar-riddled bodies could attest.

Thus, no one looked particularly comfortable with me waving a gun around the room.

"What are you doing?" Marc started across the floor toward me—brave tom—but my father reached me first.

"I'm checking for bullets. To see how many are in there."

"What are you going to do, stand on the porch and hold a turkey shoot?" Taylor asked, running one hand over his close-cropped hair.

"I'm hoping it won't come to that." I frowned and turned the pistol over again. "How do you open this thing?"

My father calmly plucked the gun from my hand, then pulled back a lever at the top of the grip with his thumb. Something clicked, and the clip slid into his waiting palm. He held it up for me to see, then slid it back into the grip of the gun until it clicked again. "One in the chamber, fifteen in the clip. Safety's on."

He gave me back the pistol, and I gaped at my Alpha like I'd never met him. "How did you…?"

My dad lifted both graying brows. "When are you going to stop being surprised by what I know?"

"Where did you learn about guns?"

He sighed but looked pleased by my interest. "Facing your fears is the best way to overcome them. But that's a story for another day. And Ed's right. You can't just walk out there and start shooting."

"I know." Even if I wanted to kill one of the thunderbirds—and I wasn't willing to kill in anything other than immediate self- or friend-defense—if our gunman shot and missed, they'd know we were bluffing. "I was hoping to scare them off long enough for us to…come up with a better plan. Learn how to fight them, or work on finding more proof. Or at least get the power back on."

Without it, we couldn't access the Internet, charge our phones, or even cook. Much less heat the house. Heat wasn't an immediate concern, with all the bodies keeping things warm, but we would get cold eventually. And we would definitely run out of food. We'd stocked up the day before, but two dozen full-grown werecats go through food very, very quickly. We'd eaten fifteen pounds of beef in the chili alone.

"Okay, that's a solid, attainable goal." Uncle Rick nodded sagely.

Taylor frowned. "No, it's spinning our wheels. Even if we get the power back on without any trouble—and for the record, this smells like a setup to me—they'll just knock it out again. We need a permanent solution."

"We're not going to get rid of them without killing them," Marc said. "And that'll just bring more of them on the fly. Pun intended."

No one laughed.

"They'll lay off if we can come up with proof that

we're not involved," I repeated. That was our only hope for a peaceful resolution.

"Yeah, and they'd disappear into a wormhole, if we knew how to open one," Michael said from the doorway, adjusting his glasses on the bridge of his nose. "Why are you holding a gun?"

"I think we should try threatening them. Maybe clip a couple of wings in the process. We have to show them we're willing to fight back."

"Even if it brings more birds down on us?" My father eyed me with an odd intensity, as if he were looking for something in particular from my answer.

"Yes." I nodded definitively to punctuate. "We can't just cower here, waiting to be picked off one by one. They're birds of prey, and we're acting like a bunch of mice trembling in a field. We all need to remember that in the natural order of things, cats hunt birds, not the other way around."

"Agreed…" my Alpha began. But he looked less than convinced by my proposition, so I sucked in a deep breath and tried again.

"Look, even if they leave long enough to bring reinforcements, that'll give us time to arm ourselves and get the power back on."

"Arm ourselves?" Ed Taylor asked, and I turned to see him holding a fresh bottle of Scotch. I'd never seen Taylor drink, but with his eyes still red from crying over Jake, I could hardly blame him. "With guns?"

"Yes."

Taylor set his glass on the bar and poured an inch from the bottle. "We've never resorted to such crude measures before, and frankly, I'm afraid to think where a step like that might lead."

I met his gaze steadily, trying to strike a balance between confidence and criticism. "We've never been held prisoner in our own home before, either. And *I'm* afraid to think where *that* might lead."

"A valid point," Di Carlo declared, and I could have hugged Vic's dad.

My uncle Rick reached for the bottle of Scotch. "So, does anyone know how to fire that thing?" He looked pointedly at his brother-in-law.

My father rubbed his forehead. "I was a decent shot in college, but I haven't fired a gun in nearly a quarter of a century."

I shrugged. "Has anyone else ever shot a gun?"

No one spoke, so I held the pistol out to my dad. He sighed but took it and turned to his fellow Alphas. "Are we in agreement over this course of action? Should I call for a vote?"

"I don't think that's necessary," Uncle Rick said, and Bert Di Carlo nodded in agreement. Then, to my surprise, Ed Taylor nodded, too.

"We can't just sit here and take it," he said, and a swell of pride blossomed in my chest. They were actually listening to me! Not just my father, but the other Alphas, too. I couldn't resist a grin, but my smile faltered slightly when I saw it returned by both Marc and Jace. Neither noticed the other beaming at me.

"So, what's the plan?" Di Carlo sank onto the arm of the couch with the short glass my uncle handed him.

Uncle Rick screwed the lid back on the bottle. "I suggest an ultimatum. Call one of them out for a parlay and explain that if they don't flock on back home, we're gonna hold a turkey shoot." He winked at me, and I couldn't resist a grin.

"Then wound one of them," Taylor suggested, and I glanced at him in surprise—I hadn't thought they'd agree with that part of my plan. "As a warning. We have to prove we're serious, and it's best to do that without risking injury to one of our own."

My father nodded. "Better sooner than later." He glanced around like he was looking for something, but I got the impression that he was seeing something other than his office. "We'll have to do it from the steps—they won't be able to see us under the porch roof. And we'll need light. I'm assuming they don't see very well in the dark, because most birds are diurnal."

Heads around the room were nodding now, and we'd picked up several more observers in the hall, where toms had gathered to listen.

"I want two enforcers at my back." He looked up, and both Marc and Jace stepped forward immediately, and my cousin Lucas pushed his way in from the hall.

"Good." Our Alpha nodded. "Marc, get the tranquilizer gun from the basement, and grab both darts. If one veers too close, shoot it."

Marc took off immediately toward the kitchen.

"Lucas, get whatever you're most confident wielding." Because Lucas was the more physically powerful of the pair, and would be more effective with brute strength. In fact, he was the biggest tom I'd ever personally met. More than six and a half feet tall, and three hundred pounds—I wouldn't want to run into him in a dark alley.

Jace looked disappointed but didn't argue. He might have been chafing under Marc's authority, but he still held our Alpha in total respect.

Ten minutes later, we gathered in the front hall, my father facing the door with Marc a step behind on his left, my cousin mirroring him on the other side, each holding both a weapon and a candle in a jar. My uncle and I peered out the tall window to the left of the door. Taylor and Di Carlo watched from the opposite side.

In the living room, several toms had gathered to witness the action from the front window. My mother, Kaci, and Manx watched from the dining room across the hall, flanked by more enforcers, just in case.

My father took a deep breath, then opened the front door and stepped onto the porch, the gun in his right hand. Marc and Lucas followed him, then fanned out on the porch and set their candles down carefully out of the walkway. They took the steps together, the enforcers one tread behind my dad.

"Send someone to represent your Flight," my father ordered, in a strong, clear voice. "I demand a word."

There was a moment of near silence, then the whoosh of huge wings beating the air. An instant later, a single thunderbird swooped from our own roofline and landed ten feet in front of the porch on human legs. Its head and most of its torso were human, too, which is how I knew, to my complete surprise, that this thunderbird was a girl.

Or, more appropriately, a naked, winged woman.

"I will speak for the Flight," she announced, in a voice that almost hurt to hear. Her dual tones were both high and screechy, as if her throat hadn't fully Shifted. Which was a distinct possibility.

"What is your name?"

"Neve," she announced, and offered no further title or rank.

"I am Greg Sanders, Alpha of the south-central Pride." My father cleared his throat and made his formal pronouncement. "Hear this and consider yourselves warned. We did not kill your Flight member, nor do we bear any responsibility for his death, and we will not pay the price for a crime we did not commit. The next thunderbird who shows him or herself on this property will be shot on sight."

He raised the gun, and even from inside the house I heard Neve gasp.

A thrill of satisfaction raced through me. She hadn't seen *that* coming!

"You have to the count of three to leave, or I *will* make an example of you."

I glanced at Jace in surprise. I'd wondered, when the female bird had appeared, if my father would actually shoot her. Most toms would rather die than hurt a woman of any species. Protectiveness was ingrained in them from birth.

"One." My father aimed the pistol in a two-handed grip and flipped off the safety.

Neve made no move, so Marc raised the tranquilizer gun.

"Two."

She still stood frozen, so Lucas slapped his crowbar into his opposite palm.

"Three."

My dad fired the gun.

Neve tried to lift off. The bullet slammed into her left wing. She screeched and staggered backward. A powerful roar thundered from above. The next instant was a blur of wings, talons, and pale flesh against the dark night.

A tom screamed.

Lucas was gone.

Twelve

Kaci screamed and pounded on the window from the dining room, to my right. On the front steps, Marc spun to his left, tranquilizer gun raised and ready. But he had no clear shot. My father kept his pistol trained on Neve. His back and shoulders were so tense I was afraid his muscles would snap like stressed ropes.

Uncle Rick ran through the open front door onto the porch steps and I went after him, peering into the night for his son. My heart raced, demanding action. Instead, I sucked in a deep breath and forced myself to think.

A crescent moon shone through the cloud cover, too weak to illuminate much and the candles' light only penetrated a few feet into the dark. Lucas's enraged shouts echoed from somewhere to our left, and not too high up, giving us his general direction. But we couldn't help him if we couldn't see him.

I stepped to the back of the covered porch, out of immediate danger, and closed my eyes, already working on a partial Shift. Just my eyes. The bird was obviously having trouble with Lucas—no surprise, considering my cousin had to be nearly double his weight. If I could find them before they got too far away—or too high for Lucas to survive a fall—we could still save him.

I both heard and felt my fellow enforcers file onto the porch, and I smelled Jace at my side. But I blocked it all out as the first bolt of pain speared my eyes.

"Bring him back, now, or I'll shoot her other wing," my father warned, and distantly I realized Neve couldn't fly away with a hole in her arm. She was almost literally a sitting duck.

Fresh agony licked at the backs of my eyelids, and my eyes felt like they would explode. I gritted my teeth and rode the pain, focusing on what I could hear in the absence of sight.

Another set of wings beat the air in the distance, but it wasn't Lucas's captor. I could still hear my cousin shouting—slowly drifting farther away—from my left.

"Stay back, or we'll hobble you, too!" Marc shouted at whoever now approached, and I wondered if the birds could even hear him over the din of their own flight.

The pain began to ease behind my eyes, and I spared a moment of thankfulness that they were one of the fastest parts of the body to Shift—no bones, no large muscles, and no sprouting fur. Then I opened my cat eyes. My newly vertical pupils dilated instantly, letting in every bit of the little available light. And suddenly I could see in the dark.

In the arch of grass defined by our half-circle drive,

a naked, fully human woman sat on the frigid ground, shivering miserably. Neve held her left arm close to her chest, folded like a wing and dripping blood. She eyed my father in abject hatred, her jaw clenched.

At her back, another bird coasted straight for the confrontation, moonlight glinting off dark, glossy feathers. Neve glanced back and up, and relief washed over her. He was coming to get her, but not at top speed—not with the continued threat of gunfire.

My father watched the new bird's slow approach, tense with controlled fury. Marc stared after Lucas, tranq gun aimed in his general direction, judging by my cousin's screams. I wound my way around half a dozen enforcers and peered over the left railing. Lucas and his captor were almost to the apple tree, flying very low. The bird pitched and dipped as Lucas fought him, swinging his crowbar and kicking furiously.

When his feet skimmed the top branches, my cousin stopped fighting. He bellowed an impressive roar and rammed the end of the crowbar up through the bird's torso. The thunderbird screeched, and his next flap faltered. Lucas shoved the crowbar deeper. The bird screamed, sounding almost human. His talons opened. Lucas fell into the bare limbs of the apple tree.

Yes! Marc and my uncle peered over the rail with me, but they couldn't see far in the dark. Not with human eyes. "Lucas impaled the bird," I whispered urgently. "He fell in the apple tree, alive, but probably hurt. The bird fell somewhere past the tree."

"Come on," Uncle Rick whispered to Marc. Then he

jumped the porch rail in one smooth, lithe motion. Marc landed beside him, still carrying the tranquilizer gun, and they ran off into the night.

I scanned the darkness, looking for other birds, or any sign that this was a setup, but I saw nothing. With any luck, my father was right—their eyes were no better in the dark than a human's.

"Stay back!" my Alpha roared, and I turned to see that the approaching bird had almost reached Neve.

I jogged down the steps to my dad's side. "He can't hear you over the wind he's stirring up. Fire a warning shot."

My dad's mouth formed a thin, angry line. "I can't see him well enough."

"Then shoot her again." The girl bird sat in a pool of light from two different enforcers' flashlights. "Disable her other wing, so he gets the picture."

My father considered for less than a second. Then he fired again.

The bullet grazed the she-bird's right arm. Neve screamed. Blood ran from the new wound, fragrant in the night air. At my back, toms shuffled their feet as the scent fueled their rage, threatening to turn it to blood-lust. On a very large scale.

But the second shot accomplished its goal.

"Neve!" The bird in flight thumped to the ground in the darkness a good hundred feet behind her, now fully human but for his wings.

"I'm okay, Beck!" she yelled, without taking her glittering, black-eyed gaze from my Alpha.

"I don't want to kill her," my father shouted to Beck.

"But if you come any closer, I'll have…" His voice faded into an uneasy silence as the background whisper of wings beating the air grew to a thundering crescendo. I looked up. My cat gaze narrowed. My breath caught in my throat.

"What's that they say about birds of a feather?" Jace murmured from close behind me.

"They flock together.…" I eyed the sky, trying not to panic over the sheer number.

"How many?" My dad didn't bother to whisper; they couldn't hear us over the sound of their own wings.

I glanced down the line of huge bird-creatures, doing a quick estimate. "Fifteen, not counting Neve, Beck, or the one who took Lucas."

"That's too many," Bert Di Carlo said, having assumed a backup stance in Marc's stead.

"Without more guns?" My dad nodded firmly. "Yes, it is."

We stared in silence, and I grasped mentally for a plan, sure my father and the other Alphas were doing the same thing. Seconds later, the entire flock landed behind Beck in one eerie, graceful touchdown after another. They stood a good fifteen feet apart, on human legs. Most also had human heads and torsos, but they'd all kept their wings intact, for a quick takeoff.

At least five were women, long, dark hair trailing behind heavily toned, nude torsos. They looked like harpies, flexing wickedly sharp wing-claws, snapping strong, curved beaks.

Beck stalked forward slowly on thin human legs,

disproportionate to his massively muscled upper body. He knelt behind Neve without taking his gaze from us, then stood and pulled her up with him, cradling her with obvious familiarity and affection.

"If you are any wiser than the base creatures you lead, I advise you to surrender now." Beck's voice was only marginally lower and more tolerable than his girl-friend's. Or wife's. Or whatever. "Your men will die quickly—you have my word."

Was that supposed to be a mercy?

My father bristled, and fury emanated from him in waves I could almost feel. He shifted his aim to the new threat. "Leave now, or I will start shooting."

"So be it." Beck let go of Neve and Shifted so fast my eyes couldn't make sense of what I saw. My father raised the gun slightly, ready to defend us. But Beck only flapped his powerful wings twice, rising several feet into the air with each stroke, and clasped Neve's shoulders in his newly formed claws.

She screamed when he lifted her, and more blood poured from the wounds on her arms. Then the birds lifted off as one and flew into the night.

But instead of fading gradually into silence, the thunder of their exit ended almost all at once. They hadn't flown off. They'd landed, likely in the front field, just out of range of my cat eyes.

Grass crunched to my left, and I turned to see Marc and my uncle Rick headed our way, each half support-ing Lucas, who favored his right leg. We stood back to let them pass, and Marc gave me a bleak grin. "Your cousin's good with a crowbar." Then he saluted me with the bloody steel and continued into the house with the injured cat.

The rest of us followed them, and my father bolted the front door. He hadn't locked up the house since the night Luiz roamed free on our property. And even then, he'd only locked up the women—leaving me to protect Manx and my mother—while the rest of the enforcers went out to hunt him down.

But this was different. This was cowering. It felt wrong.

"What are we going to do next, nail plywood over the windows?" I whispered, following my father down the long main hallway to the back door. "Do you really think they'll try to come inside?"

"No." The dead bolt scraped wood, then slid into place. "With a twelve-foot wingspan, they'd be too confined in here to take advantage of their assets. And they couldn't fly away, which would practically cripple them. But I'm not taking any chances."

"In that case, maybe we should *invite* them in!" I trailed him into the kitchen, where my mother smiled wearily and slid the side door lock home.

Dad nodded to thank her, then glanced at Kaci—she sat at the peninsula in front of a vanilla scented votive, staring at a brownie—before heading into his office.

I wanted to follow him. I wanted to be a part of whatever critical decisions he and the other Alphas would make in the next few minutes. But Kaci needed me more than I needed to have my say.

"Hey." I pulled out a stool and sat, smiling in thanks

when my mother set a glass of milk in front of me. "How you holdin' up?"

"Fine." Kaci broke the brownie in half but made no move to eat either piece. "You?"

"Honestly?" I shrugged. "I'm kind of scared. And pretty sad. And really pissed."

Kaci stared at me for several seconds, then nodded solemnly. "Yeah, me, too."

"So, what do you think we should do?"

"About the thunderbirds?"

I sipped from my glass, then set it on the countertop watching deep shadows sputter on the front of the fridge. "Yeah."

She blinked in surprise, then seemed to consider, and I realized no one had ever asked her that before. At least, not about anything more important than what she wanted for dinner. "I think we should talk to them," she said at last. "I don't want anyone else to get hurt."

"Even one of them?"

She nodded slowly, then more confidently. "It's all a misunderstanding, right? They think we did something we didn't do, and they're trying to punish us for hurting someone. Like we're going to do for Ethan." Her eyes watered as she said his name, and I fought back tears of my own. "Right?"

"Yeah, I guess it's like a misunderstanding." A huge, gory case of mistaken identity. "And I agree with you. I'd rather talk this whole thing out." We'd dealt and been dealt more than enough death over the past few months, and yet more was on the horizon. "But that's hard to do, considering that they don't have a leader and we can't get in touch with the majority of their Flight."

Kaci started to say something, but stopped when Michael's voice reached us from the hallway.

"No. Holly, do *not* drive out here." He paused, but I couldn't hear how she replied over the raised voices now coming from the office. "Yes, another family emergency. I'm sorry, but I have to stay overnight. Owen…fell off the back of the tractor." Another pause. "Yes, he'll be fine, but there's nothing you can do for him."

Michael crossed in front of the wide doorway, carrying a red taper in a crystal holder, then reappeared almost instantly. He put his thumb over the receiver of his cell and met my gaze while Holly listed her objections in his ear. "Faythe, can I use your room? I need a little privacy."

Before I could answer, my mother spoke up. "Manx is using Faythe's shower. Take the master suite."

My brother shot her a grateful look, then disappeared down the hall.

"Poor Michael." Kaci frowned after him. "I don't know how he keeps her from figuring stuff out."

Michael was the only werecat I knew who'd married a human. Since there weren't enough tabbies to go around, most toms settled for endlessly playing the field with human women. But my oldest brother wanted something more—someone to love for more than a few months at a time—and Holly had seemed the perfect choice. She loved Michael, and thanks to her job—she was an actual runway model—she spent almost as much time on the road as she did at home. Which was good, because when Michael wasn't practicing law, he was at the ranch.

But when she was home, Holly wanted to be with her husband, and he'd been largely unavailable for most of the past few months, helping us deal with one disaster after another.

"Beats me. But she's more likely to think he's cheating on her than that he turns into a giant black cat in his spare time." I took another sip from my glass, and as my parents' door closed, my father's voice carried to me from the open office door across the hall.

"What we've done is show both them and ourselves that we can fight them—if only by nontraditional means."

"Yeah, that'd be great—" Taylor started, and in his pause, I heard the distinctive clink of glass on glass "—if we had more than half a box of ammunition and one gun."

At least they're taking us seriously now, I thought, then turned my attention back to Kaci.

"…think she's going to die?" she was saying when I brought her back into focus. "That girl bird?"

"No." I shook my head decisively as she bit into her brownie. "I bet the bullets went in one side and out the other. And considering how fast thunderbirds Shift, she probably heals even more quickly than we can."

Which was a problem I hadn't considered before. It would suck to come face-to-face with a healthy and once-again flying and newly pissed off Neve in a few hours.

"…couldn't carry Lucas very far, or very high…" Di Carlo said from across the hall.

"Yeah, but Luke weighs nearly three hundred

pounds," my uncle replied. "That's a good fifty pounds over the largest man here, and closer to seventy more than most of us."

Yeah, and if they hadn't been distracted by the gun, the birds would have double-teamed him, like they did with Charlie...

"...did he get the gun, anyway?" Kaci asked, and I was getting dizzy from trying to keep up with two conversations at once. "I thought Shifters don't use guns."

"It's the one Manx shot Jace with." But I didn't truly realize what I'd said until my mother scowled at me from across the counter, frozen in the act of wiping down the countertop.

Kaci's hazel eyes widened in horror. "Manx *shot* Jace?"

I cursed myself silently for not giving her my full attention. That was probably one of those things a thirteen-year-old didn't need to hear. At least, not without the full story. "It was an accident. She was aiming at...the bad guy behind me, but Jace thought she was aiming at me. So he jumped in front of me and got shot."

Though it hardly seemed possible, her eyes went even wider and glazed over with what could only have been total adoration. "Jace took a bullet for you?"

"Um, yeah." Actually, he'd taken a bullet for Luiz, but I wasn't going to downplay his heroics—he'd been *willing* to take the bullet for me. And he still was. Jace would have done anything for me, and everyone in the house knew it.

But so would Marc.

I'd been staring at her brownie when I got lost in my

own thoughts, and Kaci mistook my emotional turmoil for hunger. "Here." She pushed the saucer and half her snack toward me. "It's the last one. Take it."

I forced a grin. "Thanks." But as I chewed, Marc's voice floated my way from the office.

"…she's not going to go for that."

"It's not up to her," my father replied, and I dropped the remainder of the brownie on the little plate.

"Just a minute…" I mumbled, then slid off my stool and raced across the dark hall and into the candlelit office. *They're talking about Manx or Kaci*, I thought as I stepped past Jace and into the room. But that wasn't true. I could tell from the way they all stared at me, their eyes identically shadowed in the gloom.

"What's not up to me?" I demanded, in as respectful a tone as I could manage.

My father sighed and stood from his armchair. "We can fight them, but it isn't going to be pretty. So I want you to take Kaci, Manx, and Des somewhere safe until this is over."

No! But shouting at my Alpha—especially in front of his peers—would only make things worse. So I sucked in a deep breath and regrouped as everyone watched me, waiting for the fireworks. "I'd really rather stay and fight. Can't someone else take them?"

"Teo's volunteered to go with you," Di Carlo said. "But we're going to need everyone else here to fight."

I glanced at Mateo, but he was ostensibly absorbed in cleaning beneath his fingernails. I'd never known Mateo Di Carlo to back down from a fight; Vic and his brother were very much alike in that respect. But he might never have another chance to spend so much time almost-alone with Manx. He was willing to miss the action for a chance to convince her that she'd be better off with him than with Owen.

Most toms never got a chance to learn to be subtle in their affections.

"Dad…" I began, but stopped when his eyes pleaded with me silently.

"Faythe, in all honesty, you can't fight with a broken arm, and we want to send someone the tabbies trust with them. That's you. We're not trying to get rid of you, or even protect you. We're depending on you to protect *them*."

That was the truth; I could see that much. But it was only half the truth. He *was* trying to protect me.

"They won't be in any danger," I insisted. "The birds are supposed to get us out of the way, anyway, so they'll probably let us drive right off the ranch, completely unmolested."

My father nodded slowly. "That's what we're hoping. But just in case, we feel that you and Teo are best prepared to defend them."

Okay, he had a point there. Mateo was in love with Manx—at least, he thought he was—and I'd give my own life to keep Kaci safe. "I'm not going to talk you out of this, am I?"

"I wish you wouldn't try," my father said evenly. So I nodded once. Decisively.

"Fine. I'll go." I swear every eyebrow in the room shot up and a couple of jaws dropped. They didn't have to look so surprised. I wasn't *such* a shrew, was I? "Where are we going?"

"If it wasn't such a long drive—and through the free zone—we'd send you to Bert's place." Umberto Di Carlo ran his territory from a suburb north of Atlanta. But since Manx wasn't a legal citizen, and had no ID, we couldn't fly. "For now, head north to Henderson and get a room. We'll be in touch with more concrete plans soon." Fortunately, we all kept fully charged backup batteries for our cell phones, just in case. A lesson we'd learned the hard way.

"Okay," I said, and my father sighed in relief. I turned toward the hall to see Kaci standing in the doorway, clutching her votive. "Get packed, Whiskers. We're going on a road trip."

Thirteen

Manx was getting out of the shower when I got to my room, so I filled her in while she stood in the middle of my floor, her hair dripping on her robe as ever-leaping shadows moved over her face. She listened with her dark brows drawn low, her mouth a grim, straight line. The spark of irritation in her eyes said she'd rather stay and fight, but the twitch in her arm—as if she wished she were holding her baby—said she knew she could no longer protect her son on her own.

I couldn't stand to see her so…powerless. Dependent. And I knew well how close I'd come to sharing her fate. Or worse.

Manx cleared her throat, and I made myself face her silent suffering. "Twenty minutes. I will pack." Then she was gone.

I shoved the essentials into my bag, then grabbed my candle and headed for our former guest room to check on Kaci. On the way, I stopped in the doorway to the guest bathroom, where Lucas sat on a bar stool brought in from the kitchen. My mother was wrapping the ankle he had propped on the closed toilet seat by the light of several candles, while Brian Taylor applied a clear, goopy ointment to my cousin's shoulders.

Which looked like they'd almost been ripped from his body.

Three deep punctures pierced his skin below each collarbone where the talons had gripped him, and a fourth had apparently been driven *through* both his shoulder blades, completing the bird's grip in the back.

"Shit, Lucas!" I set my bag down in the hall and stepped into the bathroom for a closer look. My mother frowned over my profanity, but didn't look up from her work.

"Yeah." Lucas glanced at his reflection, then down at me. Even seated on the stool, he was a good six inches taller than I was. "Looks nasty, huh?" He flinched as Brian worked on his left shoulder.

"They carried Kaci a lot higher and farther than they did you. How come she doesn't look like this?" Brian asked, dabbing more ointment on the torn skin with a cotton ball.

"Because Kaci weighs about a third what Lucas weighs." My mother finished the wrap and secured it with a metal butterfly-shaped clip. "So she had a lot less weight pulling against their talons."

"That, and they had her by the arms, instead of the shoulders," I added. "And they were trying not to hurt her, whereas their plans for Lucas likely included a forty-foot drop."

My mom stood and carefully lowered his foot to the floor. "You'll have to Shift a couple of times before you…head outside." Her face went white at the thought of the fight to come, but her expression remained resolved. Strong. "But clear that with the doc, first. Those shoulders may not want to support your weight for a while."

I shot my cousin a sympathetic look, then continued down the hall.

But I only made it ten feet before Mateo's voice caught my attention and I stopped outside Manx's bedroom. I shouldn't have listened. The closed door said they wanted privacy, and the anxious whispers only underlined that fact. But across the hall, Owen was sleeping off his latest dose of pain pills, and while Manx and Teo weren't my business, they *were* my brother's business. So I told myself I was listening for him.

"…not safe here anymore, and our door is always open to you. You have choices, Mercedes. You don't have to stay here just because this is where you landed, or because you feel obligated to them."

A dresser drawer slid shut. "I like it here," Manx said, in her firm, lilted speech.

"I know. I just want you to know that we'd be happy to have you. *I'd* be happy to have you. I can take care of you, Manx. You *and* Des."

Her footsteps paused, and I pictured her staring at the ground, clothes in hand as she weighed what was best for her son against what was best for her heart. "Yes," she said finally. "I believe that you can."

That was all I could take.

Yes, Manx had choices, but sometimes choosing for yourself is just as hard as accepting someone else's choice for you.

Twenty-four minutes later, we stood by the back door, the women at center stage. Kaci wore a stuffed backpack and cradled a sleeping Des, who was blissfully unaware of the danger we were about to carry him into. I had my old college book bag, and just behind us, Mateo Di Carlo carried Manx's duffel over one shoulder, and his own smaller bag over the other.

My heart ached as I hugged my mother. We weren't sure whether or not she fell under Malone's orders to spare the women, since she was beyond childbearing age and long-since married. My father had tried to talk her into going with us, just in case, but she'd stubbornly refused.

"Are you sure you won't come?" I whispered as I clung to her. "You know how impulsive and bullheaded I am. I could use someone to keep me in line."

My mother laughed and pulled back so she could see my face. "You'll grow out of the impulsiveness, and you get the bullheadedness from me. No matter what your father says." She shot an affectionate glance at him over my shoulder. "But I need to stay here."

The way she eyed me intently, meaningfully—and the way she spoke her next sentence—sent a violent assault of chills up my spine. "Now, go say goodbye to your father."

I nodded, still staring into her eyes. Trying not to understand the message she was sending. But it was all too clear.

The man with the gun would be the first and most obvious target. My mother was staying because there was a good chance that this might be my father's last fight.

I blinked back tears, then turned to hug my father, acutely aware that this was unlike any other preassignment goodbye we'd ever shared. "Be careful," I whispered, breathing in his scent—the leather, coffee, and aftershave I'd always associated with absolute safety and authority, even if I sometimes chafed under the yoke of them both.

"I was going to say the same thing to you."

"If you guys make enough noise, we'll be fine." I sounded confident, though I was far from sure.

"Oh, we'll make noise," Jace promised, and I turned to hug him, too, holding him just a second longer than I should have. Then I went on to hug Michael, Vic, Parker, and Brian. I'd already said goodbye to Owen in his room, where frustration had gleamed like tears in his eyes. He hated missing the fight almost as much as I did. But he'd already struck his blow and given us our prisoner. And without Kai, we wouldn't know enough to even *think* about fighting his Flight members.

So I'd kissed the cowboy goodbye and called him my hero. Then ordered him to stay in bed and recuperate.

"Faythe…" Marc began when I faced him, the last of my farewells. But he didn't have to say any more. We'd said goodbye entirely too often in the past few months, and leaving him again was the last thing I wanted to do.

"Watch yourself." I went up on my toes to kiss him

and let the contact linger a bit longer than I normally would have in front of an audience. "And watch my dad."

"You know I will."

And I did know. Marc's role in the upcoming melee was to protect his Alpha: the man with the gun. And in truth, that would probably be easier without me there for them both to worry about. No matter how far I progressed in my training, no matter how well I fought in either form, there was always someone trying to defend me. Thus putting himself and others in unnecessary danger.

"I'll see you soon." I squeezed him harder.

He smiled. "I'd bet my life on it."

My father cleared his throat. "Everybody ready?"

"Where's Manx?" I scanned the small crowd and saw her stepping out of Owen's room. She flushed when she saw us watching, then her stride quickened and grew more confident.

"We are ready?" She took Des when Kaci held him out to her, obviously aware of all the eyes focused on her. Including Mateo's.

"We are." As ready as we were going to get, anyway.

My father stepped forward, holding the pistol, and gestured toward his left. The guys—all except Mateo—headed for the front door. My dad turned to me one last time. "Carey Dodd's already in place waiting for you. You have his number, right?"

"Yeah." I'd programmed it into my phone, just in case.

"Good. Even if they catch on, I don't think the birds will follow you into the woods, but keep your ears open, just in case."

"We will," Kaci said, clutching her small flashlight, and my dad spared a moment to smile at her.

"Call me as soon as you make it to the car," he said, and I nodded, one hand on the back doorknob. "Wait for your mother's signal," he warned, then jogged down the dark hall to join the rest of the men.

"Okay, let's go." My dad opened the front door.

My pulse raced, and I wondered if birds could hear well enough to know that.

My Alpha stepped onto the porch, the gun held ready. Marc and Vic fanned out to either side of him, Jace and Parker beyond them. Each enforcer carried a rudimentary weapon, and because we were all enamored of Lucas's impale-them-in-midflight approach, all the weapons had at least one sharp end.

The plan was simple: the guys would make a bit of a fuss, demanding the birds restore our power. There wasn't a chance in hell that would happen, but hopefully they'd cause enough of a distraction to let us slip out the back door and into the woods without the birds noticing.

It was a hell of a risk—but we were out of options.

"Beck!" my father shouted from the front porch, and through the windows, I caught the glare of someone's flashlight beam, streaking toward the sky like a spotlight. "We need to talk!"

For a moment, there was only silence, but for the racing pulses of those of us waiting, and I was sure our little ruse would fail. Manx, Des, and Kaci would be stuck here with the rest of us, in danger once the real fighting began.

But then that too-familiar thunder of wings roared from the front of the property, and I exhaled softly in relief. They were coming.

The noise of their approach would cover the sounds of us leaving, but we couldn't afford to break for the woods until they'd all landed, because their eyesight—while not as good in the dark as ours—was much better than their hearing, and they might easily catch a glimpse of movement in the backyard from the air.

So we waited, and I watched in the dark with my cat eyes as my mother peered anxiously through the front window. When the wind-beating racket finally faded and the last of the bird-bodies thumped to the ground, my father began his spiel. And my mother waved frantically behind her back with one hand.

That was our signal.

Kaci's pulse spiked. I put a supportive hand on her shoulder and gestured for her to kill her light. She turned off the flashlight, then shoved it into the water-bottle pouch on one side of her backpack as I slowly, carefully pulled open the back door.

No creaks; so far, so good.

The screen door was next, and I froze when it squealed, only halfway open. My mom went stiff, then bent to stare out the window again, to see if anyone had noticed. I'm sure the cats all heard, but if the birds had, she saw no sign. She waved us out again, and I opened the door the rest of the way, relieved when it stayed silent.

Mateo went first, with Manx and the baby on his heels. They snuck down the concrete steps on their toes, then took off across the dead grass toward the woods. Kaci was only a second behind Manx, and I went right behind her after handing the open screen door over to my mother to close after we'd made it to the trees, so that the closing squeal wouldn't give us away before we reached relative safety.

My pulse roared in my ears as I ran, careful to stay just steps behind Kaci.

Teo hit the tree line first, then stopped to wave Manx ahead of him. Des was fussing by then, but was too surprised by the bumpy ride to wail in earnest, thank goodness. And the moment she stepped into the woods, Manx was ready with his pacifier, to keep him quiet.

When Kaci made it to the trees, I stopped and turned to make sure no one had spotted us. I could still hear my father yelling, and caught the occasional screech of a bird's response, but there was no one in sight. We'd made it, at least this far.

I waved to my mother, and she nodded, then closed the screen door. I stepped into the woods as it squealed shut, and allowed myself one quick sigh of relief. Then I turned and jogged to catch up with the others.

"Who's Carey Dodd?" Kaci whispered as I fell into step beside her. Des sucked peacefully in front of us, where Manx and Teo hiked side by side.

"One of the Pride members," I answered, careful to keep my voice soft. We weren't out of the woods yet. Literally. "He's the closest nonenforcer tom we have." My dad had arranged for him to pick us up two miles from the ranch, on a road that cut through the woods behind our property, hopefully far enough away that the birds wouldn't see the car or hear the engine. Dodd would take us to Henderson and stay as added protection for Manx and Kaci. We weren't taking any chances.

Because we were in human form—and only I could Shift my eyes—our hike took nearly an hour, and the first half was the roughest by far. Kaci and Manx tripped often, and Teo and I scrambled to catch them until finally Manx handed off the sleeping baby to the tom, who was much more used to tramping through the woods in the dark.

When we were far enough from the house, I decided it was safe enough to risk a little light, and the walk was a bit easier with two flashlight beams lighting the way.

When the trees began to thin, I called Dodd's cell phone and had him start his engine. We used the rumble to guide us the last eighth of a mile or so, and were relieved to step out of the forest less than twenty feet from the waiting vehicle.

Dodd jumped from the driver's seat of his SUV and rushed to open the back door for Manx and Kaci. Kaci crawled in first, then took the baby while Manx got settled in the middle of the bench seat. Until we could stop for a car seat, she'd have to hold the baby on her lap.

Teo scooted in next to Manx and pulled the door shut, and I sat up front with Dodd. "Thanks for the ride," I said, pulling the seat belt tight across my lap.

"No problem." He shifted into gear, then pulled the car smoothly onto the road. "We're just lucky I'm not out patrolling tonight."

That we were. Otherwise, our walk would have been much, much longer.

Half a mile later, I Shifted my eyes back, then autodialed my father. "Hey," I said when he answered. "We're free and clear."

"Good. Call when you get to Henderson. We're scrounging up weapons, and plan to make the first offensive in about an hour."

For once, I had no idea what to say. Everything I could think of—be careful, watch out for Mom— seemed a bit obvious. Nothing an Alpha would need to hear. So I swallowed the grapefruit-size lump in my throat and told him the truth. "I love you, Daddy."

"I love you, too, Kitten. Watch out for them."

"I will. Will you tell Marc I love him?"

He laughed, a sound of genuine amusement, when I really needed to hear exactly that. "He already knows."

We said goodbye again, and I slid my phone into my pocket, then twisted to accept the tire iron Manx handed me. Kaci sat in the middle row, holding a hammer. "Hey, be careful...."

"Oh, shit!" Dodd stomped on the brakes. The van started to skid. Teo threw out one hand to protect Manx and Des. Kaci slammed into the back of the driver's seat. I flew forward, then my seat belt snapped tight against my hip.

Stunned, I dropped into my seat—and screamed. Fifty feet ahead, and closing with every second, the largest thunderbird I'd ever seen soared right for us, lit from beneath by our headlights. His talons clutched something big, and dark, and obviously heavy.

Before Dodd could safely change course, the bird opened his talons, directly over us. Whatever he was carrying slammed into the hood of the van.

We all screamed. The van swerved. I rocked violently from side to side as Dodd tried to control the vehicle. And I could only stare at the huge boulder deeply embedded in the hood, pinning the thick canvas it had been carried in.

The van swerved left. Dodd overcompensated. We swerved right, and I braced my good arm against the dashboard. Dodd swerved again. The van careened off the road and smashed head-on into a trunk at the edge of the tree line.

For a moment, there was an eerie, shocked silence. Then Des started screaming.

I took a second to assess my injuries—a single, rapidly forming lump on the side of my head—then twisted to check on everyone else. "Are you guys okay?"

Manx nodded, dazed, one hand patting the screaming infant. Kaci peeked up from behind the backpack in her lap, and after a moment of consideration, she nodded, too. "I think so—"

That's when Teo's door was ripped completely off the car.

Fourteen

Kaci shrieked as a vicious half-bird head appeared where the door had been an instant earlier. Human hands attached to long, muscle-bound arms hauled Teo out of the car and tossed him to the ground. Manx screamed and beat the bird with her right fist, while her left clutched the screaming baby.

The thunderbird made strange, aggressive screeching sounds deep in his human-looking throat, pulling on Manx's arm. But she was still buckled, and he couldn't reach the latch.

I jabbed the button on my own seat belt, then leaned over my seat to punch the intruder with my good hand. Dodd reached for Manx but was too far away in the driver's seat. I only realized he'd gotten out of the car when his door slammed shut.

A second later, Teo roared, and the thunderbird was hauled backward, out of my reach. Dodd wielded a crowbar and bared human teeth at the bird, who half

Shifted rapidly in Teo's grip. All three fell to the cold grass in a violent, snarling, snapping tangle.

I groped for my door handle with my bruised left hand, staring over the back of my seat at Manx. "Are you okay?"

Manx didn't answer. She was hunched over the baby, protecting her infant with her own life. Her back heaved. I heard sobs and saw tears, but I smelled no blood— none of Manx's, anyway. So I looked past her to Kaci— just in time to see the young tabby throw open her car door. I could practically smell her panic.

"Kaci, no!" I shoved my own door open, but she didn't listen. I wasn't even sure she could hear me over Manx's crying, Des's screaming, and the odd snarls and screeches coming from Teo and the bird-man. But it probably wouldn't have mattered even if she had heard me. Kaci was terrified of being snatched again, and she was not strong enough to defend herself.

That was my job.

"Stay here and stay buckled," I shouted to Manx, then I dodged the full-out brawl at my feet and took off after Kaci, putting everything I had into my sprint.

Unfortunately, I couldn't concentrate well enough to Shift my eyes while I was running, so once we'd gone beyond the dim red glow of the van's taillights, the young tabby's dark hair and jeans faded into the night. If not for her bright white ski jacket, the slap of her shoes on concrete, and the terrified sobs floating back to me in the wind, I would have thought I'd lost her completely.

Go into the woods! I thought desperately as Kaci frantically threw one foot in front of the other. Thunderbirds couldn't follow us there. At least, not in full bird form. But I couldn't afford to waste my energy shouting something that might not sink in, anyway. If she'd been thinking clearly, she would have headed for the trees in the first place, rather than racing along the shoulder of the road, fair game to anything that swooped out of the sky.

Then, as if my own thought had called it into being, a powerful *thwup, thwup* echoed at my back.

Oh, shit. Either Mateo and Dodd had lost their fight, or more than one bird had come after us. Probably both.

I dug deep and threw every spark of energy I had left into my sprint. My focus stayed glued to Kaci's back, an inverse shadow in the nightscape. I surged ahead, and she was only twenty feet ahead now.

The wind-beating sound grew steadily closer. The accompanying rush of air blew my hair out in front of me. Ahead, Kaci tripped and screamed. She went down only yards from the tree line.

She stood unsteadily, but I was closing on her. *Eighteen feet.* My lungs burned. She started running again, but more slowly, and with a limp.

Fifteen feet. My side cramped, but any minute, I'd have her.

Twelve feet. I was already reaching out, moments away.

Then the whoosh that had been a warning was suddenly a horrifying roar. I couldn't hear myself breathe; I heard only menacing wind. I couldn't feel my pounding heart or rushing pulse; I felt only the surge of air now pushing me backward, away from Kaci.

I squinted against the dust that terrible wind blew at me. A huge, dark shadow swooped low, only feet in front of me. Kaci screamed. Her white jacket shot off the ground and into the air, bobbing higher with each powerful flap of wings. She kicked, the stripes on her shoes reflecting the little available moonlight.

"Hold still!" I shouted, stumbling to a stop beneath her, terrified that her tossing and turning would make the bird drop her. But she couldn't hear me. I stared up at Kaci in horror, and the fresh ache in my chest threatened to swallow me whole. I'd lost her.

I was supposed to protect Kaci, and I'd lost her. I'd failed, and now she would pay the price.

What little I could see of the night blurred with the moisture standing in my eyes as I forced my legs into motion again. I couldn't catch her without wings of my own; I knew that. But I had to try.

I stumbled along, wiping tears on the sleeve of my jacket, hoping I wouldn't trip and further injure my arm. And that Teo and Dodd had won their fight. And that they could get Manx and the baby to safety. I couldn't see if any of that had happened without losing sight of Kaci. And I couldn't hear anything—not even Des scream-ing—over the roar of wings beating overhead and behind me.

Wait, beating *behind* me?

I spun, my heart trying to claw its way out of my throat. He dove the instant I saw him, a great hulking shadow blocking out the silver crescent moon. In that moment, the bird was everywhere. He was all I could see, and everything I feared. Talons. Hooked beak. And a possible forty-foot fall.

I couldn't outrun him, so I dropped to my knees, then onto my good elbow, half-convinced he would land on me and crush me. Or drop another big rock on me. But his huge, curved talons were empty.

I tucked my head between my knees and screamed, but could barely hear my own voice. An instant later something gripped my upper arms, then jerked viciously. My shoulders screamed in pain. The world tilted wildly around me. And suddenly the ground was gone.

Just…gone.

Squeezing my eyes shut, I forced myself to hang limp, afraid that thrashing would get me dropped. And so far, the only thing I was sure I'd hate more than flying was falling.

I'd had only seconds to adjust to being aloft when another grating screech ripped through the air behind me. Something grabbed my right ankle in midair. The world swerved around me again, and I squeezed my eyes shut even tighter, still screaming. Then I was horizontal, my stomach to the earth, my left leg and forearms dangling awkwardly.

After several deep breaths, which only calmed me enough to bring my terror into sharper focus, I forced my eyes open. Then immediately slammed them closed again.

Below me, the van was a two-tone spot of light on the ground: white from the headlights, and red from the taillights. I was already too high to make out the occupants—if they were even still there.

The woods stretched out for miles to the right of the van, and we flew over them. From my horrifying new perspective, the skeletal deciduous branches were as thin and tangled as steel wool in the moonlight, the evergreens dense spots of darkness. And in that moment I hated my abductor for turning my beloved forest—my refuge from all things human and artificial—into a place of nightmares.

And still I screamed. I screamed until I lost my voice. My arms and one leg went numb from being gripped so tightly. They felt like they'd be ripped from my sockets at any second. I chattered uncontrollably. If it was cold on the ground, it was literally freezing in the air, and my toes tingled painfully. I couldn't feel my hands. Couldn't move my fingers.

After several minutes, I lost it. What little composure I'd had could not survive two hundred feet in the air, with nothing to catch me. Nothing but the ground to break my fall. No way to save myself. I could see calmness in the back of my mind, but it cowered in the corner like a little bitch, leaving panic to rule the roost.

My free leg flailed uncontrollably. My arms tried to twist themselves from the bird-bastard's grip, though part of me knew that would only lead to my death. My mouth opened and I screamed again, though no sound came out.

I wouldn't survive this. No one could survive such torture. Cats don't fly without airplanes. We can't survive it—not physically, not psychologically. And if dangling two hundred feet in the air was enough to fracture my sanity, what must it be doing to Kaci?

Kaci. Fresh panic flooded me, oddly warm in my numb extremities. I lifted my head and forced my eyes open again, this time resisting the silent scream my abused throat wanted to indulge. I couldn't see her; it was too dark, and the wind too harsh. I couldn't hear her; the *thump thump* of giant wings was too loud. Then, just as my eyes started to close, a cloud shifted, gifting me with a weak beam of moonlight.

I twisted carefully to the left for a better view. Kaci's white jacket and reflective shoes were the last things I saw before a giant wing slammed into the side of my head.

"Faythe, wake up!" Kaci whispered, and something shook my left arm fiercely. "Faythe!"

"What?" I groaned and rolled over on the lumpy bed. My sore left arm flopped off the side, but I kept my eyes closed.

Wait, lumpy bed? I had a good mattress, and it was big enough that my arm shouldn't hang off. Alarm spiked my pulse. My eyes flew open as a barrage of unfamiliar scents flooded my nose. Raw meat, not all of it fresh. Wool and steel. People. And poultry. Lots of poultry.

Shit!

I sat up and glanced around the small, dingy room, taking everything in at once. Bare, wood-plank walls. Scarred hardwood floor. A single twin bed with a rough wool blanket and no pillow. One window made of a single pane of glass, flooding the room with daylight too weak to be anything but late afternoon.

And Kaci, who sat curled up next to my feet on the other end of the bed.

"Where are we?" I whispered, as sounds from the building around us began to filter in. Squawking, screeching, and human speech. Heavy footsteps, and light, sharp scratches against wood. And a television. Somewhere, someone was watching Looney Tunes. The one where Bugs Bunny directs the opera. My favorite episode.

"I don't know." Kaci's hazel eyes were wide with fear. She sat cross-legged on the twisted wool blanket, her hands clenched in her lap.

"How long have we been here?" I slid my legs off the side of the bed and onto the floor, then stood carefully, hoping neither the mattress nor the floor would creak and reveal that we were awake.

"I just woke up," she whispered. Kaci started to stand with me, but an old-fashioned metal spring groaned softly beneath her, and I waved one hand, silently telling her to stop. Then I dug in my front pocket for my cell. But, of course, it was gone.

"Do you have your phone?"

She shook her head. "It was in my backpack." Which she'd left in the van when she ran.

Great. "Are you okay?" I kept my voice as low as I could; I knew she would hear me, but wasn't sure about the thunderbirds.

Kaci leaned against the wall and pushed one sleeve up to expose her upper arm, which was ringed with a single deep bruise, thicker on the front than the back. "Just bruises." Talon marks. I pushed my own left sleeve up as I inched slowly toward the window, trying to avoid creaks in the obviously aged wooden floor.

My left arm was similarly marked, and I knew from the tenderness in my right arm that it would match. As would my right ankle. "Anything else?"

"I'm cold and hungry."

"Me, too." I made it to the window without a creak from the floor and noticed two things immediately. First, it wouldn't open. It was a single pane of glass built into place along with the house. Or whatever kind of building we were in.

Second, we couldn't have snuck out even if we could break the window without attracting attention. We were a couple hundred feet off the ground, jutting out over a cliff. And there was no balcony.

"Damn it!" That one came out louder than I'd intended, though it was still a whisper. I let my forehead fall against the glass and immediately regretted it. After my most recent flight, I wasn't eager to see the earth from on high ever again.

"What?" Kaci whispered, and the bed creaked again as she leaned forward.

"We're in their nest. And it's not exactly built in the treetops." The window was directly opposite the only door, so I edged my way along the wall to the corner, then made the turn, still hugging the wooden planks. The floor was much more likely to creak in the middle than along the edges.

"What do they want?"

"Oddly enough, I think they were trying to protect us." From the violence *they* brought forth.

Kaci glanced from the window back to my face. "I don't feel very safe."

"Me, neither." When I reached the door, I bent to study the knob. It was a plain, old-fashioned brass sphere with a small round hole in the center. Which meant the other side held a simple push lock. I twisted it slowly and the knob resisted. It was locked.

I could have forced the lock with one quick twist, but the *pop* might be heard, and I didn't want our captors to know we were awake until we knew a little more about our surroundings.

"How the hell did they get us here?" I wondered aloud, barely breathing the sound. "There's no way they could have flown us all the way here." I didn't know exactly where "here" was, but I couldn't think of a single cliff of any size within several hundred miles of the ranch.

"They didn't," Kaci said, and I turned to see her twisting the edge of the coarse navy blanket in one fist. "I must have passed out when they were carrying us, but I woke up later, in the back of a car. Something like Jace's, with a big area in the back for luggage and stuff. We were all tied up, and you were still out cold."

"They tied us with ropes?"

Kaci nodded. "Thin yellow ones."

Nylon. I glanced at my left wrist, but found no marks. A glance at my ankles revealed none there, either, which meant they hadn't tied us very tightly. If they had, the ropes would have left marks even through our clothes.

And we'd woken up unbound, barely locked into a room. Together.

Those were all good signs. They hadn't killed us because they'd made a promise to Calvin Malone, and they obviously didn't want to hurt us. At least, not until or unless we hurt one of them. Or pissed them off.

So, what now? Did they plan to finish slaughtering our Pride, then simply let us go? Had they *already* slaughtered our Pride?

My pulse raced, and I couldn't stop it. Sweat broke out on my forehead, in spite of the chilly room.

"Faythe? What's wrong?" Kaci scooted to the edge of the bed, and the old mattress let out a long, grating squeal. She froze, but the damage was done. Her eyes went wide and panicked, and her lip began to tremble.

"It's okay...." I crossed the room toward her, heedless of my own footsteps now; the nest itself was evidently holding up far better than the old furnishings. "We need to talk to them, anyway. We're not doing any good just sitting here."

Kaci bit her lip and blinked back tears. "You sure?"

"Totally." Not that we could do anything about it if I weren't.

From the hall came light, but obviously human, footsteps. Kaci's hand gripped my good one, and every muscle in her body tensed. "Should we Shift?"

"I think it's a little late for that. Besides, they might see it as an act of aggression." The footsteps stopped outside our door, and the knob turned. "Don't say anything unless I ask you something or give you a signal, okay?"

Kaci nodded as the door swung open.

The woman in the doorway was short, thick with muscle from the ribs up, and downright skinny from the waist down. She had a long, thin nose, almost nonexistent lips, and long, smooth dark hair—clearly her best feature. She was also completely nude.

Kaci flushed and looked away—she was raised among humans—and the bird-woman tossed a curious, head-tilted glance her way before focusing on me. "I am Brynn. Follow me." That was it. No *please,* no smile, and not even a glance over her shoulder to make sure we obeyed.

But there was nothing else to do. We weren't getting out through the window, and while our chances probably wouldn't be much better in front of a room full of thunderbirds, they certainly couldn't get any worse.

Our room was the last in a long second-story hall bordered on the left with nothing but a wooden rail, worn smooth by what could only have been generations of hands trailing over it. Beyond the rail, the floor ended, revealing the drop to a huge first-floor room where thunderbirds of all sizes and both genders mingled and lounged, in various stages of Shift. There must have been fifty of them. And I could hear even more moving around behind the many closed doors.

Our hallway wrapped around three sides of the building, and the two floors above were the same; we could see identical third- and fourth-floor railings across the large opening. The front of the building was a series of small glass panes built into the wall, forming a huge grid of windows. The effect was a stunning, patchwork view of a wooded mountainside. And at the bottom, near the center, stood a single door—the only entrance or exit we'd seen.

Kaci gasped, and I glanced down, then followed her gaze up. Way up.

Then I gasped, too.

The building was cavernous and could easily have fit at least three more floors, although none existed beyond the fourth. Instead, the empty space was crisscrossed with exposed beams, and ledges, and nooks, most occupied by one or more thunderbirds. Those on the beams were mostly in avian form, perched like blackbirds on a wire, while those resting on small nests of pillows and blankets on the many ledges looked more human. Some even held old, worn copies of books whose titles I couldn't quite make out.

It was like nothing I'd ever seen. This wasn't just a nest. It was a true aviary.

Brynn made an impatient noise at the back of her throat, and I forced my attention from the spectacle overhead and nudged Kaci. Then we followed her down an open flight of stairs to the huge room below.

Like the levels above, the first floor was surrounded on three sides by a series of doors, though they were farther apart on the ground floor. I was guessing the first-story rooms were the Flight's common areas, like the kitchen, dining room, and maybe more living areas.

As we crossed through the center of the open area, I glanced through several of the open doors. Most were sparse bedrooms, a bit larger than the one we'd woken in. But the doorway to one corner room revealed a large, bright space full of old-fashioned toys—most of the handmade doll and wooden block variety—and the distinctive flickering light of a television.

We'd found the source of the Looney Tunes. And based on the scratchy, low-quality sound, I was guessing they had only worn VCR tapes, rather than DVDs.

My steps slowed as my curiosity grew, and as I walked, I saw more of the room. And its occupants. At a glance, I counted half a dozen small children, none yet old enough to attend school.

But age wasn't the only thing keeping these kids out of the human educational system.

As I watched, a naked boy of maybe four years—the biggest in the room—shoved one chubby fist through a tower of brightly painted wooden blocks. The small girl who'd been stacking them—also nude, but for a cloth diaper—scowled so menacingly I half expected her to burst into flames.

Instead, she burst into feathers.

In a single, smooth motion almost too fast for me to understand, her arms lengthened and sprouted feathers. Her short hair receded into her head, and her naked scalp began to toughen, flush, and wrinkle, like the head of a vulture. Her thin legs withered until her calves were little more than sturdy sticks ending in tiny, sharp talons.

And her hands curled into petite but obviously lethal wing-claws.

The whole thing took no more than two seconds and appeared completely spontaneous. I couldn't stop staring.

The bird-girl tackled the larger boy, snapping her new beak at him and swiping with her claws, and when they fell, I got a look at the smaller children behind them. All four were quite a bit smaller. Toddlers, judging by their size. And they were all constantly Shifting.

Several arms were feathered, two with hands, one with claws. Two heads were bare and wrinkled, one had tangled dark hair, and the fourth was somewhere in between, patches of blond peach fuzz standing out on an almost bald avian skull. The children were continually in flux, and they obviously couldn't control their small bodies.

No wonder thunderbirds removed themselves from human society so completely.

I stared, transfixed, until Brynn made another angry noise in her throat, and I jogged to catch up with her and Kaci, though the strange images remained painted on the backs of my eyelids.

But when Brynn came to a stop, I looked up, and all thoughts of odd, ever-Shifting children flew from my mind. There must have been thirty different thunderbirds seated or standing in the back half of the large room. And they were all staring at us.

Fifteen

Kaci's cold hand slid into mine. Her lips were pressed into a thin, tight line and her jaw bulged, not with anger, but to keep her teeth from chattering, as they sometimes did when she got nervous. Her terrified, wide-eyed gaze flitted anxiously from bird to bird, as if she were looking for a friendly face.

But she wasn't going to find one, other than mine. We were in this together—whatever "this" was.

"What is your name?"

My head whipped up and I glanced around, waiting for someone to step forward, or otherwise claim his or her question. But no one did, even when I stood silent for almost a full minute. In fact, the only reason I knew the speaker was addressing me was that no one was looking at Kaci.

When I didn't answer, another voice called from above and I glanced up, but again failed to pinpoint the speaker. "Are you Mercedes Carreño or Faythe Sanders?"

Aah. They knew I was one of the adults, but not which one.

"I'm Faythe. Who's speaking, please? I'm getting a little dizzy trying to pinpoint you." And frankly, I wasn't sure where I should look. I didn't want to accidently insult someone by misdirecting my attention.

"You are speaking with our Flight."

Of course. I'd almost forgotten about the mob—I mean *Flight*—mentality. Fortunately, I actually saw the speaker that time, though she hadn't asked either of the previous questions.

Another voice spoke from my far left. "You and the kitten will be delivered to Calvin Malone tomorrow...."

"What?! No!" I shouted, and Kaci clung to me, terrified. "You can't do that. You have no idea what he wants with us!"

"We promised to remove you from danger and deliver you to him, and we will not go back on our word. We're only letting you live because we've been assured that you and the kitten were not involved in the death of our cock."

I turned and pinpointed an older male thunderbird with strong features and the typical top-heavy build. And nearly laughed aloud on the heels of his last word.

It's not funny! some horrified part of me insisted, from deep within my head.

But it *was* funny, in that scandalous way that inappropriate jokes are always irresistible at the most inopportune moments. Their Flight member was dead, they'd kidnapped us and were trying to kill the remaining members of our Pride, and this asshole sounded like a testimonial for Viagra!

For a moment, I couldn't speak for fear of bursting into laughter, and it took all my self-control to kill the irreverent smile that my lips wanted to form. But then Kaci squeezed my hand again, and the look of pure terror on her face sobered me instantly.

I cleared my throat. "That's right. We had nothing to do with it. But neither did anyone else in our Pride. Malone only told you that…"

"We're not interested in discussing Finn's death with you.…"

"Well, you should be!" I shouted—and immediately regretted it when a series of soft whoosh sounds and heavy thumps told me more birds had landed behind me from the overhead perches.

My pulse raced fast enough to make my head spin, and I barely resisted the urge to turn and face the new combatants. I was surrounded by the enemy, and my fight-or-flight instinct demanded that I make a choice. But neither of those options led to survival—I was sure of that.

"Look, I'm sorry. But this is the truth, and it's important. Calvin Malone lied to you, for his own gain. My Pride isn't responsible for your…Finn's death. One of Malone's men is."

I'd expected to be interrupted, but I could tell by the universal, uneasy shift in posture that I'd caught their collective attention with the word *lied*.

"Why would Calvin Malone compromise his honor

with a lie?" The speaker still looked skeptical, but was obviously willing to listen.

My mood brightened instantly. They were going to let me talk.

"First of all, he has no honor. But he has plenty of greed and he is hungry for power." Lots of confused expressions and eerily tilted heads met my declaration, but I rushed on before anyone could interrupt, my left arm around Kaci. "And second of all, I just gave you the reason—for his own personal gain."

There was an odd silence as the birds glanced back and forth at one another in quick, sharp movements, clearly conferring silently through expressions I couldn't interpret. I glanced down at Kaci to see her watching our captors in both fascination and fear, and I was relieved to see the latter winning out.

A tabby with enough curiosity to override her fear— aka: common sense—would turn out like me, and mine was not a life I wanted for Kaci. At least not until she'd matured enough to balance her mouth with a bit of wisdom. Or at least experience. I'd learned my lessons the hard way, and I would spare her that, if I could.

Finally, I looked up to see the birds all watching me, and the next voice came from behind me, so I turned again. "We will hear you speak on this matter. But we have no tolerance for ruses. If you transform, we will be forced to incapacitate you."

"No problem." I'd never put myself at their mercy long enough to "transform," anyway. My fastest full Shift ever took nearly a minute, and even if I could do it again, that was plenty of time for them to rip me from limb to limb, considering how incredibly fast *they* changed form.

Oh. And that's when I understood. They thought werecats could Shift the same way they could. Instantaneously. Miraculously.

I briefly considered explaining the truth, to make myself look less threatening and set them at ease. But in the end, I decided they were more likely to respect me if they felt just a little threatened by me. Right? That approach usually worked with toms, anyway....

"Speak," an elder female bird commanded, from near the windows on my left. So I spoke, fully aware that the safety of my entire Pride rested on me in that moment. Assuming I wasn't already too late to help them. And I had no reason to believe the birds would have told me if I were.

"Malone is running against my father for a position of leadership within our Territorial Council. But Malone doesn't fight fair." I glanced around, trying to make sure everyone was listening, but though the faces were different—and in various stages of mid-Shift—their expressions were all the same. They looked frustrated, angry, and impatient. "Anyway, according to a source of mine—a werecat in Malone's Pride—last week one of Malone's enforcers killed one of your...cocks in a dispute over a kill and feeding rights."

Several of the expressions hardened, and I spoke faster as my pulse raced; I was desperate to finish before someone cut me off. "I'm not saying your bird was necessarily the one at fault. Our two species have different laws, and I'm not qualified to sort that particular issue out. But what I am sure of is that Finn's killer does not, nor has he ever, belonged to my Pride."

"What does Calvin Malone stand to gain from misleading us?" another male bird asked from behind me, and that time I didn't turn. It didn't seem to matter which one of them I faced; I was speaking to them all, as unnerving as that concept was.

It's like the tribunal, I told myself, grasping for something familiar. *Everyone gets an equal vote.* Unfortunately, that made the whole thing feel a little too familiar—the majority of the tribunal had wanted me dead.

"He's gaining three things," I said, fighting to project confidence and authority. "First of all—me and Kaci. He's convinced you to remove us and turn us over to him, because in our world, he who controls the tabbies controls the toms. There are only a few female werecats of childbearing age in the entire country, and Malone wants us both married off to his sons, so he can keep all the power in his family. Thus under his thumbs. He tried to force me into a marriage I didn't want a couple of months ago, through political means, and when that didn't work, he resorted to brute force with Kaci."

"How so?" some nameless, faceless bird called out from behind us, and Kaci cringed against my side as all eyes turned her way for the first time.

"He snuck onto our property and tried to kidnap her."

A couple of the birds—mostly the women—looked upset, if I was reading half-avian expressions correctly.

But most of them just looked confused. They didn't know enough about our culture to understand why Malone would resort to violence over a potential daughter-in-law. So I moved on to point number two.

"Second of all, he now has you fighting his battle for him. You're weakening our offensive capabilities while we're on the verge of a very well-justified fight against Malone."

"How is your fight justified?" an exceptionally scratchy, gender-neutral voice asked from behind me and to my right. I gritted my teeth to keep from groaning in frustration as I resisted the urge to turn and search for the speaker yet again.

"One of his cats killed my brother almost two weeks ago, when they came after Kaci. Malone knows an attack is imminent. But this way, we bring fewer, weaker forces to the fight. Thanks to you guys."

To my horror, several of the birds were nodding, not merely in understanding, but in admiration! They approved of Malone's underhanded strategy! The bastards!

But even I had to agree that it was effective, if unconscionable.

"And in the third place, he's deflected both the blame and the consequence for Finn's death away from him. Which means his forces remain safe from your rage, thus intact. And you're not getting the justice Finn deserves, because while you're fighting us, the real killer is literally getting away with murder. In Malone's Pride."

Now they were frowning....

A throat cleared to my far right, and my head swiveled so fast and hard I heard one of my own vertebrae pop. My focus snagged on a single dark beak as it Shifted almost instantly into the creased lips and chin of the oldest thunderbird I'd seen yet. She had thick white hair halfway down her back, and her hands were even more wrinkled than her face, but her eyes shone with shrewd intelligence.

"You insist that Calvin Malone is willing to compromise his honor for success in war. What evidence can you give us that you are not, in fact, doing that very thing?"

Why did they always use his full name? Did they think that was how all humans addressed one another? By both names? Or did they run the whole thing together in their minds, as if it were all one word? Like their own names…

"You're asking why you should believe me instead of him?" My heart thudded in my ears when she nodded. I'd never delivered a more important argument than the one I was about to launch. Never before had so many lives depended on what I said next.

No pressure, Faythe…

"You should believe me because I stand to gain nothing from this except what we had before Malone interfered— the peace to assemble our troops in private and avenge my brother's murder. I'm not asking you to attack my Pride's enemies for us. Or to kidnap and deliver any members of his Pride to give us a political edge. Or to give up justice for your own dead by launching an attack against the wrong people. But Malone asked for all of that. He used you. Hell, he's probably laughing at you right now."

Okay, he was probably too busy plotting our destruction to literally laugh about the wool he'd pulled over the Flight's eyes, but my point stood. They'd been played.

And finally, they looked mad.

"If you're telling the truth, Calvin Malone must pay for his deception," a disembodied voice called from overhead.

My brows rose, but I didn't bother glancing up. "*If* I'm telling the truth?"

"We can no longer trust the unsubstantiated word of a werecat." This statement came from my left, from a young female bird, whose dark-browed scowl was genuinely scary. "You will bring us proof."

Proof. Shit. If I had that, all our problems would be over! "You didn't ask Malone for proof…."

"We are disinclined to repeat our mistake."

Another scratchy voice spoke up, but I whirled too late to catch the speaker. "You will bring us evidence in two days."

Two days! I glanced desperately from one impassive face to the next. "My whole Pride could be dead by then!" Though hopefully they'd take the thunderbird contingent with them. "You have to call a ceasefire."

"No." Short, simple, and spoken by the bird who'd begun this whole weird interrogation. "We will not stop the attack without proof that your people are innocent."

A growl began deep in my throat, and it took me a long moment to contain it. "If you don't call a ceasefire, I have no reason to go looking for your proof. What would I have to go home to?"

For a moment, there was more silence, as the birds conferred, cocking their heads at one another, and glancing from face to face. And finally they seemed to reach a mute consensus. "We will halt the attack against your Pride until you return with your proof. In two days."

Relief surged through me, cool compared to the flames of fear and anger licking at my heart. I'd bought time for the rest of my Pride—assuming they hadn't already launched their offensive. But my relief was short-lived.

"What kind of proof? And how the hell am I supposed to get it? I don't suppose you have a car I could borrow?" Otherwise, it could take me two days to climb down their damned mountain and find the nearest form of public transportation.

"No. How you get this proof is not our concern, and we don't care what form it takes, so long as it is irrefutable."

Great. And staggeringly vague. "Well, then, I guess we should get going. We're burning time."

"The child stays," said a firm, deep voice from behind me, and that time not only did I turn, but I turned Kaci with me.

"No. She goes with me, or I won't go."

A new voice joined the argument, from overhead again. "You will go alone, and be back in two days, or we will kill the child."

Sixteen

Kaci whimpered and clung to my arm.

Fresh rage and terror shot through me, singeing what was left of my nerves. Obliterating my patience. "No!" I shouted, and every muscle in my body went so suddenly, completely taut I couldn't move. "Kaci has nothing to do with this. Where's the honor in slaughtering an innocent teenager?"

"The honor lies in protecting our interests and avenging our dead," some faceless voice announced. I'd given up looking for the speakers. "The girl is merely your motivation."

"But she's just a kid!" And for once, Kaci was too terrified to insist that she was nearly grown.

"She is not *our* child."

My blood ran cold, chilling me from the inside out. Were they serious? Did they care about nothing but their own people? What about right and wrong? Good and bad? And I'd thought *Malone's* moral compass veered left of true north! Evidently thunderbirds had no concept of morality!

But I knew from Kai that they observed their own code of honor obsessively, even if it didn't fall into line with mine. Or anyone else's. Once they'd made a promise, they'd stick to it. And they'd vowed to try to protect the south-central Pride's tabbies....

"You can't kill her," I insisted, speaking lower now, as a deceptive calm settled through me. I recognized my father's influence in my bearing and voice, and that surprised me as much as the determination now steeling my spine, fortifying my nerve. Kaci was depending on me. The whole Pride was, though they didn't know it yet. I would *not* let them down. "You swore to Malone that you'd try to keep our tabbies safe. I'm thinking killing Kaci would be a pretty heinous violation of that promise."

There was another long pause while the thunderbirds conferred wordlessly. Wings flapped and feathers ruffled at my back as more birds dropped from their overhead perches. And finally, Kaci and I had to turn again to meet the gaze of the latest speaker.

"Your statement and Calvin Malone's statement are mutually exclusive—both cannot be true. Therefore, we conclude that a werecat's word cannot be accepted without proof. Calvin Malone provided no proof, thus our vow to him is null. You and the child are at our mercy."

Well, that certainly backfired.

Chill bumps popped up all over my body, and Kaci shuffled even closer to me. I opened my mouth to argue with the latest avian proclamation, but before I could, another bird spoke up.

"We would kill neither of you without cause. If you return in two days with proof, as instructed, we will give the child to you, unharmed. If you do not return on time, or return without acceptable evidence, the child will die, and our fight for vengeance against your people will resume."

I sucked in a deep, silent breath, trying to absorb the latest twist in thunderbird logic with decorum, though my temper raged inside me.

"Go now, Faythe Sanders. You are wasting time—yours, ours, and hers." The old woman-bird's gaze flicked to Kaci, who shook visibly in my arms.

They wouldn't hurt her if I kept up my end of the bargain. She'd be fine. Unless something went wrong.

What if I got hurt and couldn't make it back? What if I couldn't find proof, now that Brett was dead? What if I got caught sneaking around Malone's territory? Kaci would be dead before anyone else had an opportunity to negotiate for her life. If that was even a possibility.

And even if I made it back on time, with irrefutable proof, what would Kaci suffer while she waited? She wasn't in any physical danger—the birds would stand by their word, unless I gave them reason not to—but she was already emotionally fragile. Two days as the prisoner of a hostile foreign species—whose members were practically counting the hours until her execution—would do nothing for her mental health. She'd seen what they'd done to Charlie and Owen, and she had a great imagination. She knew what would happen to her if I didn't make it.

"No." My mind was made up.

"What's that?" a voice asked from my left, but my gaze stayed glued to the old woman.

"I'm not leaving her. Turn us over to Malone." At least he wouldn't kill us, and we stood a better chance of getting away from him than from the birds, if only because Malone lived on the *ground*.

"That is no longer an option. We want true vengeance for Finn, and you are our best hope of finding it. We believe you will do whatever is necessary to keep the child alive. You may stay or go, as you like, but if we have no proof in two days, the child will die."

Shit, shit, shit!

Wait a minute… "What about a trade? Kai for Kaci. Did you know he was captured?"

Several half-bird faces looked surprised, and several Shifted into human form, apparently just for that ability. But no one looked particularly upset. "The child is not a hostage. Her release is not negotiable."

"Why not?" I glanced from face to face, truly baffled. "Is his life worth less than Finn's?"

"Of course not," said a young man with fully formed wings, then a man whose feathers had begun to gray with age took over.

"But Kai volunteered to fight, and he knew the risks. To die in war is to die with honor. Finn was murdered. His death must be avenged."

For a moment, I could only stare, clutching Kaci to my side. They were serious. They were *not* going to let Kaci leave without proof of Malone's guilt.

As if to underline that fact, a bustle of movement drew my gaze to four of the largest thunderbirds as they moved to block the front door, the only exit I'd yet seen. None of the birds was over five foot two, but they were all powerfully built from the waist up, even without talons and wing-claws.

Kaci was dead, if I couldn't come through. Or at least come back with reinforcements.

I stood straighter. "How soon can you call a ceasefire?"

"We will dispatch a messenger immediately."

"In person?" They could *not* be serious. "Where's my cell? Somebody give me back my phone." One arm around Kaci, I glanced around the room until movement drew my attention to a mostly human woman— the only fully dressed person in the room, other than me and Kaci. She was pregnant, and evidently about to pop.

Please let her have a baby in there, and not a giant egg....

The woman slid her hand into the pocket of her maternity pants and pulled out my phone, then stepped forward to hand it to me.

"Anybody know how this works?" I held the phone up in my left hand, while my casted arm slid back around Kaci. A few of the younger birds nodded—likely those who conducted the Flight's few interactions with human society.

"Good. I'm going to call my dad—he's our Alpha, the one in charge—and fill him in. Then he's going to toss his phone to one of your birds, and I'm going to give mine to one of you guys. You call a ceasefire, then give me back my phone." I wasn't willing to negotiate on that part. Without some way to communicate with my Pride, I'd never get to the Appalachian territory in two days, much less find the necessary evidence and make it back to…wherever the Flight lived.

"Then I'll be on my way."

"No!" Kaci's head popped up on the edge of my vision, her cheek brushing my arm. I patted her back and squeezed her arm, telling her silently to stay quiet. I'd explain everything to her when we had a little privacy. Assuming we got that chance.

"Make your call," a voice at my back ordered.

I autodialed, and my father answered on the first ring.

"Faythe?"

I almost cried at the sound of his voice, relieved to find him still alive. No matter who we'd lost in the offensive, it wasn't my father.

"Yeah, it's me. Kaci's with me, and we're both fine," I added, before he could ask. "For now."

My father's barely there pause was the only indication that he understood the gravity of our situation, if not the details. "Where are you?"

"I don't know. We're in the Flight's nest, but they haven't been very forthcoming with an address." I closed my eyes briefly, as loath as I was to take them off our captors. "Is everyone…okay?"

My father knew exactly what I meant. "No new casualties, on either side."

My exhalation of relief was so ragged it was more like a sob. "Manx and Des?"

"They made it to a—"

"Time waits for no cat, Faythe Sanders," an intrusive, scratchy voice warned, and a deep, low growl trickled from my father's throat. "Your clock is already ticking."

"Who is that?"

"Um…we're kind of surrounded by thunderbirds. Literally."

"What do they want?" Leather creaked over the line, then floorboards groaned as my father paced, a sure sign that he was planning something.

"I'll explain in more detail when I get a chance, but the short version goes like this—they're giving me two days to find proof that Malone's Pride is responsible for Finn's death, and when I get back with the evidence, they'll let Kaci go."

Another half second of silence, but for steady, heavy footsteps. "And if you don't make it back on time?"

I couldn't say it, but my father easily interpreted my tortured silence. "No…" he whispered, and the footsteps stopped. Something scraped the phone, as if he'd covered the receiver, then he was back and fully composed. "Are they willing to negotiate?"

"Not about this." The circle of stony expressions said that fact hadn't changed.

"Have you exhausted all the other options?" Meaning, fight or flee.

"There *are* no other options." Not that wouldn't end with both me and Kaci dead.

My dad sighed. "What do you need?"

"I don't know yet, but I'll call you when I'm on the way. For now, though, I need you to call Beck back into the front yard. Then toss him your phone. I've negotiated a ceasefire for the next two days."

"Good work." I heard a hint of real pride shining through the fear and anger in my father's voice.

Something scratched against the phone again, and I was almost certain none of the birds heard my father's whispered order. "Get the gun and stand by the front door. We're going out." Then he was back on the line, and his heavy footsteps changed when he stepped from the hardwood in his office onto the tile in the hall. Other footsteps joined his, and I recognized my mother's distinctive clacking as well as Michael's tread, identical to my father's in tempo, but lighter, thanks to his rubber-soled loafers.

But if Marc was there, he wasn't walking; I would have recognized his footsteps, too.

I forced aside the deep pang of fear Marc's absence rang in me and made myself listen as my father gave instructions for whoever was backing him up in Marc's absence.

Then the front door creaked softly, and my father stepped onto the concrete porch. "Beck!" he shouted. Even over the phone I heard the rustle and wind-stirring flaps as at least half a dozen birds landed somewhere on my front lawn, who knew how many miles away. "Beck, your Flight wants to talk to you.

"Okay, Faythe, I'm going to toss him the phone."

I nodded, though he couldn't see me. "I'm handing mine over, too." I eyed one of the young birds who'd claimed he could use a phone—one of only two who currently wielded human hands—and feinted once, to make sure he got the picture, then tossed the phone for real.

My breath stuck in my throat when he caught it, then fumbled before tightening his grip and bringing the phone to his ear. "Beck?" he asked, and I had a moment of panic, suddenly sure Beck wouldn't know which end to talk into.

But then a vaguely familiar, scratchy voice answered from the other end of the line. "Ike?"

"Yes." The young bird glanced around and received small nods from his peers, then took a deep breath and continued. "We're calling a forty-eight-hour ceasefire, for Faythe Sanders to seek evidence of her Pride's innocence in Finn's murder. If you haven't heard from us two days from now…"

I cleared my throat to interrupt, and glanced at my watch. "By…5:23 p.m. on Tuesday."

"…by 5:23 p.m. on Tuesday," Ike repeated, after another round of nods, "resume the attack."

"I understand" was Beck's only reply. Ike tossed the phone back to me, and my father's familiar sigh of relief—or maybe disbelief—whispered over the line. Seconds after that, the front door closed on another series of footsteps, and the wind died in my ear.

And with that there was peace. At least temporarily.

"Okay, Dad, I gotta go. But I'll call you from the

road." For more updates, and advice on how the hell I
was supposed to get to Malone's territory on my own,
with no car, in time to get back with evidence I didn't
even have yet.

"Don't dawdle" was all he said, but it sounded very
much like "I love you" to me.

I hung up and slid my phone into my front pocket
before one of the birds could demand it back, then tightened my grip on Kaci and faced the old woman. "I don't
suppose you guys have another television, or some
video games or anything?"

I got dozens of confused looks, and at least five
shaking heads.

"Yeah, I figured. Books, then. You have books?" I'd
seen several birds reading in their perches overhead, so
I knew they had at least a few.

"We have hundreds of books," said a male voice I
decided not to track down.

"Good." The classics? That would explain their
stilted cultural awareness, and maybe their formal
speech patterns. "Would you please bring a good selection to Kaci's room? She's going to need something to
keep her mind occupied while I'm gone." I was willing
to fight for that one. If they gave her nothing to distract
her from the possibility of her own impending death,
Kaci would dwell on that, and on the fact that I'd left
her. And that would be torture. Literally, in my opinion.

To my surprise, my request met with several more nods.

We followed Brynn back to the second-floor room
and I studied the nest as we went, in search of anything

that might prove useful. Another exit. A potential weapon. Hell, even a bargaining chip they actually valued. But short of snatching one of their little ones and promising its release in exchange for Kaci's, I came up empty. And I could never hurt a kid, and if I bluffed them, I'd lose all credibility, which was the only asset I had in their eyes.

Besides, they'd probably cut me down long before I made it into the nursery. Assuming the kid I grabbed didn't do it herself. I'd seen how fiercely even the little ones fought.

In the room, Kaci and I waited through the departure of both Brynn and the young cock who'd brought an armload of worn paperbacks. Then I closed the door and sat across from her on the bed. But before I could say anything, she burst into tears, her chest heaving as if she'd been holding back sobs for the better part of an hour.

"Kace…" I started, leaning forward for a hug, but she shook her head and wiped tears from her cheeks roughly with the pads of both hands.

"I'm sorry." She hiccupped and her breath hitched, but though her eyes still watered, no more tears fell. "I know you have to go, and I understand why. And I know you'll be back for me. I just… I don't want to be here alone."

I could almost hear the sound of my own heart breaking. "If there was any way I could take you with me, I would. I'd fight them, if that wouldn't get both of us killed. But it would."

She nodded, wiping unshed tears from her eyes with the tail of her shirt.

"Two days," I swore. "I'll be back in two days, with either the proof they want, or enough cats to turn this place into a great big bird slaughter. I swear on my life." She looked skeptical at that, so I amended. "Okay, on Marc's life."

She didn't smile, but she gave me a single, solemn nod.

"It won't be that bad. Just stay in here and read, and try to forget about everything else. I'm sure they'll feed you here, so you only have to come out to go to the bathroom."

"Just like last time."

That took me a moment, then I realized she'd been under a similar house arrest when we'd met. "Yeah. Just like last time. Only without the whole run-for-your-life-in-the-woods finale." Hopefully.

"Yeah." She blinked and wiped away more tears.

"Okay, what else…?" I closed my eyes, running through all the potential tips and warnings I could arm her with. "Um…don't Shift. They'll see that as a sign of aggression. And if you have to leave this room, don't go near their kids. If they're anything like us, they're fanatically overprotective. Other than that, just keep to yourself and try to relax."

But the tension in my jaw and the sharp bolts of pain shooting through my temples said I needed to take a bit of my own advice.

"I trust you, Faythe." She blinked up at me, her vulnerability almost as obvious as her blind faith.

Another chunk of my heart fell away, and that one actually hurt. "Thank you, Kaci."

As I left her room and closed the door at my back, I sent up a fervent prayer that her trust in me wasn't sorely misplaced. Because like everyone else in my life, Kaci deserved better than I could give.

Seventeen

"Okay, so how does this work?" My voice came out clear and strong—a minor miracle, considering it was hiding anger, fear, and near panic as I stared down at the world from the front porch of the Flight's nest.

Beyond the edge of the porch was a two-hundred-foot drop, ending in a broken, boulder-strewn gravel road below, rendered scarlet in the light from the setting sun.

That's right; the porch ended in nothing but air. It was a sheer vertical drop guaranteed to stop my heart before I even hit the ground. That thought terrified me so badly I couldn't make myself let go of the support post I gripped with my good hand, my knuckles bone-white against the unvarnished, weather-aged wood.

"You go down the same way you came up," Brynn said from my left, and if I weren't skeptical that a thunderbird could have a sense of humor, I'd have said she was almost grinning.

"Yeah, well, I kind of slept through that part. Wanna

spell it out for me?" Another glance over the edge made my stomach pitch. "There's an elevator, right? Or a tunnel with a zillion steps carved into the middle of the mountain. Maybe under a trapdoor in the kitchen?" I'd take a long, dark, insect-ridden tunnel over another thunderbird-powered flight any day.

That time I was sure I saw Brynn stifle a smile. She was laughing at me on the inside. I knew it.

"No elevator. No tunnel. There is only Cade and Coyt." Brynn slapped a hand on one monstrous triceps of each of the huge cocks who'd stepped up on either side of her.

I almost choked holding back laughter at that thought.

"So, you're Cade, and you're Coyt?" I glanced from one impassive, craggy male face to the other, and when neither answered, I shrugged. "Doesn't matter, I guess." Then I shot a grin at Brynn. "Those are some big…birds you have there."

She frowned. So much for that sense of humor. But before Brynn could reply—or I could form a sincere-sounding apology—light, scratchy footsteps echoed from inside, and a small figure raced through the open doorway on mostly avian legs.

It was the little diaper-clad girl from the nursery, long brown hair now falling down her back. "Mama, catch me!" she shouted gleefully, and her arms Shifted rapidly into a diminutive pair of wings. She flapped furiously, and managed to put nearly a foot between her tiny feet and the ground before she started to sink. Brynn's eyes widened in alarm. Her arms shot out and she snatched the child from the air before she got near the edge of the porch, then settled her on one hip, unfazed when the small wings reformed into human arms.

Brynn was a mother! And suddenly I saw her in a completely different light.

"Listen…" I let go of the post—risking my fear that either Cade or Coyt would shove me off the porch—and turned to fully face Brynn. "I know you have no reason to trust me, but I am going to get your proof and help you avenge Finn. And I *will* be back for Kaci. But I need to know she's safe here until I get back. You can understand that, right?" I smiled pointedly at the girl on her hip and resisted the urge to touch the smooth skin of her now human—and chubby—cheek. Even human mothers were testy about stuff like that.

"You're the kitten's mother?" Brynn asked, obviously surprised.

"No." Damn, how old did she think I was? "Her mother's…dead. I'm all she has right now. Is she safe here? With you?"

Brynn hesitated, then nodded, rocking her daughter gently on one hip. The child's beak became a mouth and she stuck one thumb into it. "Of course. We wish the girl no harm. But if you fail, we will stand by our word."

I nodded uncertainly; that was probably the best I was going to get. "Thank you." After a deep breath and a moment to collect myself, I glanced up at Cade. Or maybe it was Coyt. "I'm ready, boys." Though truly, I was anything but.

Without even a glance at each other, the male thunderbirds Shifted almost simultaneously and rose into the air at the exact same time. Fortunately, the porch roof was very high, no doubt to accommodate just such a takeoff.

The upside to having no luggage is that there's nothing to accidentally drop when a giant bird swoops and grabs you by both arms, then dangles you over the earth from a height no cat was ever intended to experience.

From two hundred feet up, would I land on all four feet?

"Oh, shiiiiit!" I shouted, no more able to close my mouth than my eyes. The ground raced toward me, then the second bird grabbed my ankles in midair, halting our plummet. The birds flapped in unison, and we bobbed for a second—jarring my entire body—before soaring down again at a terrifyingly sharp angle. Three flaps later, they let go of my arms. I fell the last yard or so to land hard on my feet.

I squatted to absorb some of the impact in my knees, and to avoid falling over face-first; I couldn't afford to catch myself with my bad arm and risk hurting it worse.

I straightened just as the flyboys landed in tandem in front of me, and though they both watched me with evident disinterest—maybe even outright disgust— neither said a word.

"Jeez, could you two hold it down? I'm getting a headache from all the witty banter."

They only blinked.

We stood in a narrow valley between two small mountains—foothills, if I had my guess. When I turned, I saw that the nest was at one end of the valley, built on an outcropping jutting from the juncture of two hills.

YOUR PARTICIPATION IS REQUESTED!

Dear Reader,

Since you are a lover of fiction – we would like to get to know you!

Inside you will find a short Reader's Survey. Sharing your answers with us will help our editorial staff understand who you are and what activities you enjoy.

To thank you for your participation, we would like to send you 2 books and 2 gifts – **ABSOLUTELY FREE!**

Enjoy your gifts with our appreciation,

Pam Powers

SEE INSIDE FOR READER'S SURVEY

YOUR READER'S SURVEY
"THANK YOU" FREE GIFTS INCLUDE:
▶ 2 Suspense books
▶ 2 lovely surprise gifts

PLEASE FILL IN THE CIRCLES COMPLETELY TO RESPOND

1) What type of fiction books do you enjoy reading? (Check all that apply)
○ Suspense/Thrillers   ○ Action/Adventure   ○ Modern-day Romances
○ Historical Romance   ○ Humour   ○ Science fiction

2) What attracted you most to the last fiction book you purchased on impulse?
○ The Title   ○ The Cover   ○ The Author   ○ The Story

3) What is usually the greatest influencer when you <u>plan</u> to buy a book?
○ Advertising   ○ Referral   ○ Book Review

4) How often do you access the internet?
○ Daily ○ Weekly ○ Monthly ○ Rarely or never.

5) How many NEW paperback fiction novels have you purchased in the
past 3 months?
○ 0 - 2   ○ 3 - 6   ○ 7 or more
E4FP   E4FZ   E4GD

YES! I have completed the Reader's Survey. Please send me
the 2 FREE books and 2 FREE gifts (gifts are worth about $10) for
which I qualify. I understand that I am under no obligation to
purchase any books, as explained on the back of this card.

192/392 MDL

FIRST NAME	LAST NAME

ADDRESS

APT.#	CITY

STATE/PROV.	ZIP/POSTAL CODE

(SUR-SUS-10)   © 2009 HARLEQUIN ENTERPRISES LIMITED
® and ™ are trademarks owned and used by the trademark owner and/or its licensee. Printed in the U.S.A.

The Reader Service — Here's How It Works:

Behind Cade and Coyt, far beneath the nest, the gravel road ended in a huge pile of rocks, obviously fallen from the hills. Probably knocked down on purpose, to make the path to the nest inaccessible to humans. Which made choosing a direction a real no-brainer.

"So…where does this road go?" I gestured to the gravel trail leading away from the nest, and finally one of the flyboys spoke.

"North."

"Wow. Thanks." I squinted at them, shielding my eyes from the setting sun, and noticed that I was virtually eye to eye with both thunderbirds—they were the tallest I'd seen yet. "Could you at least tell me where we are? How am I supposed to get to Appalachia if I don't even know which way to walk?"

"We're in New Mexico," said the bird on the left. His partner hadn't even bothered to Shift his beak. "East of Alamogordo."

Now *that,* I could use. "Thank you."

"Two days," the vocal bird warned. Then they both took off, their powerful wings blowing hair back from my face.

I turned to watch, again shielding my eyes from the sun, until they landed smoothly on the front porch. They didn't look back, and no one came out to watch me leave. I was truly on my own, for the first time in my entire life.

Wait, is that right? While I was in college, my father always had someone watching me. Even when I'd been kidnapped by Miguel, I'd had my cousin Abby for company, and my brother Ryan to manipulate and spy on.

Now I had nothing. No company, no plan, and no transportation.

Fortunately, I had my cell, and already knew there was reception on the side of the mountain. *What are the chances I can get a signal in the valley, as well?*

Two bars. It could have been worse.

I walked as I autodialed, and again my father answered on the first ring. "Faythe?"

"Yeah." My boots crunched on gravel, and the rumble from my stomach reminded me that I hadn't eaten in…it had to be nearly fifteen hours. "I'm on some tiny gravel road in front of the nest, somewhere east of Alamogordo, New Mexico. Any idea how far it is to the nearest town with a car rental place? Also, I need a plane ticket to Kentucky. As near as you can get me to Malone's property."

"Whoa, slow down.…" Leather creaked as my dad sank into the armchair in his office. I wanted to be there with him. I wanted to be planning things behind the scenes, instead of hiking my happy ass across New Mexico alone in search of the nearest Hertz. Not to mention a restaurant. Fortunately, I'd visited the birds' bathroom before I left.

"I don't have a lot of time here, Dad." Twigs snapped beneath my feet when I stomped over fallen branches, gone brittle with age.

"Faythe, you cannot go looking for proof of Malone's guilt in his own territory."

I kicked a broken stick out of my way and stepped over a rain-filled dip in the road. "They're going to kill Kaci in less than forty-eight hours if I don't."

"You really think they'll go through with it?"

"There's not a doubt in my mind." I shoved hair from my face, where it had come loose from my ponytail. "They're not like us, Dad. They're fanatically loyal to their Flight members, but won't put themselves out on anyone else's behalf unless it will directly benefit them. They don't care if Kaci lives or dies, but they know we do. And they know they're only as good as their word. They'll go through with it."

His pause was heavy with thoughts I could only begin to imagine. He had to think about all of us. About what would be best for the Pride. Kaci was just one member, but she was *ours*, and she was defenseless. "Okay then, we have to get her out. If they won't negotiate, we'll have to go in by force."

I shook my head again, though I knew he couldn't see it. "Won't work. There're too many of them. And if we invade their home—where their children are—they'll fight even more fiercely. Unfortunately, they're not limited by space in their own home, like they would be in ours. Their nest is cavernous, with plenty of room to swoop and dive. And, anyway, we can't get up the side of the mountain in human form, and in cat form, we can't carry weapons."

Glass clinked over the line. *Scotch.* I could certainly have used a drink right about then. My father sighed. "I didn't say it would be easy. But it's better than taking Malone on."

"I'm not talking about fighting him, Dad. Not yet. This is a total covert op. I'll be in and out before they even know I'm there." *As soon as I figure out what I'm looking for…*

"No. You're too vulnerable on your own."

"So send me backup." I stepped over a rotting log lying across the gravel road and silently cursed the fading daylight. I wouldn't be able to travel very well or very quickly in human form, but if I Shifted, I couldn't carry my clothes or my phone. And it was cold in the foothills in February, yet I had nothing but my jacket to keep me warm. "Put a couple of the guys on a plane. I'll wait for them." *If I ever find an airport...*

"Marc and Jace are already on the way."

My initial massive surge of relief was eclipsed almost immediately by confusion. "How did you know where to send them?"

"We didn't know where they took you and Kaci, but we figured it'd be out West. So as soon as I got the call from Mateo, I sent them north through Dallas, then west on I20. They're waiting just this side of the territorial boundary."

"I already gave them their new heading." Michael spoke up from somewhere—probably from behind our father's desk. "They'll be there in about three hours, but we'll need you to narrow down your location a bit by then, so you can give them better directions."

"No problem." Surely I could find a landmark, or road sign, or something by then. If I ever got off the gravel road and onto something a little better traveled. "What about Teo and Manx? And Des? They're okay?"

Please, please, please let them be okay....

"They're shaken up pretty badly, and Carey Dodd and Mateo have some deep scratches, but there's no permanent damage. Teo says they only sent four thunderbirds after you. One took Kaci, and a second and third took you when you went after her. He and Dodd beat the fourth with a crowbar. Manx was upset that she didn't get a piece of the action."

"I bet." I'd never seen Manx fight, because she'd been pregnant when we…found her. But I understood her frustration over missing the fight. Unfortunately, without a weapon, or claws, even if she'd had time to Shift and someone to watch the baby, she could do little to defend herself beyond biting anything in her path.

"They killed the bird who stayed behind." My father sounded both proud and amused. "Teo called to tell us what happened, and Dodd called a tow truck to pick them up, and once he got Teo and Manx to safety, I sent him back to pick up Marc and Jace."

"Where are Manx and Teo now?"

"Dodd drove them to Henderson and helped Teo get cleaned up and bandaged in the hotel. They're fine for the moment."

Thank goodness. I'm not sure I could have handled it if anything had happened to Des. Or to Manx, for that matter.

"Speaking of hotels…" my father continued. "I don't suppose you're anywhere near one?"

I huffed and squinted in the dim light. "Not unless the Wicked Witch is renting out rooms in the ginger-bread cottage. I'm on a gravel road in the middle of the woods, in the foothills of some small mountain range."

Concern and anger thickened my father's voice, like

he needed to clear his throat. "Okay, what's your status? Did they give you any supplies?"

I rolled my eyes. "They didn't even give me a hearty farewell. I have my black leather jacket, my hiking boots, my cell, and my wallet. Which means I have ID and about thirty bucks in cash, if memory serves."

"No water? Food?"

"Nothing but the memory of my last meal." My mother's chili, the night before.

"I'll tell the guys to stop for supplies," Michael said in the background.

"Are you dehydrated? Injured?" My dad's words were clipped short in anger now, but his fury wasn't directed at me. It was for the thunderbirds who'd dropped me into the middle of nowhere without a thought for my well-being. And likely for Malone, who was responsible for this whole clusterfuck in the first place.

"I'm thirsty, but intact." The only marks on me—other than my broken arm—were deep bruises from the thunderbirds' talons. "I can manage a bit of a hike, so long as I know someone's coming for me."

That knowledge kept my anger and frustration from blossoming into despair and panic. Even if the idea of Marc and Jace cooped up together in a car did make my stomach churn with dread. "So, we're going after proof?"

My father's exhalation was too heavy to be called a sigh, and I pictured him rubbing his forehead. "Yes. But I need you all focused on the job. No petty squabbling."

I closed my eyes as a pang of dread rang through me.

Had he noticed tension between Marc and Jace? Had *Marc* noticed?

"Hopefully I don't have to tell you how bad things will be if you get caught."

"Of course not." My heart pounded painfully at the mere thought. After Brett's death, there was no doubt that if Malone found us on his property, he'd execute both Marc and Jace—and probably make me watch—then lock me up until he figured out how to make me cooperate. Which would never happen. He'd have to kill me first.

"Good. The rest of us will continue training for the real fight, and if you get caught, we'll just move up our plans and come after you."

But we both knew that by the time the cavalry arrived, should we need them, I might be the only one left to save. "I should probably go." I glanced at my phone, then held it back up to my ear. "I've got less than half power, and I need to be able to get in touch with the guys."

My father hesitated, and in that silence, I heard everything he wanted to say to me, and everything I wanted to say to him. "Faythe, be careful."

"I will. Love you."

"I love you, too."

By the time I hung up, the sun had set, and its crimson glow had almost completely faded from the sky. I slid my phone into my pocket and Shifted my eyes into cat form. Then I zipped my jacket to my neck and shoved my hands in my pockets, where I was surprised and relieved to find my gloves. If the temperature dropped much more they might mean the difference between frostbite and simple numbness.

I stayed on the road, but had to pick my way over more large obstacles along the way, including two long-ago-stalled rusted vehicles. If the thunderbirds hadn't damaged the road themselves, they'd certainly done no maintenance to keep it passable.

The next two and a half hours passed slowly and miserably. At first I moved at a good pace, determined to find a highway, or an intersecting road with a street sign, or even a cell tower. Anything I could direct the guys toward when they called. But it was eight long miles—by my best estimate—before I saw anything other than that stupid gravel road and trees to either side.

By the time I saw the water tower peeking over the trees to my east, bathed by floodlights, I was shivering uncontrollably, my teeth were chattering, and my toes, nose and the tips of my fingers had all gone numb. My pace had slowed to a crawl, and I was minutes from stopping to rub two sticks together on the chance that I turned out to be a naturally gifted wilderness survivor.

But the water tower fueled my resolve and I pressed on, desperate to read the letters wrapping around the sides of the tower. I forced my legs to move faster, bribing myself with promises of hot chocolate and homemade stew, though I was more likely to get protein bars and Coke, assuming the guys ever found me. I actually jumped when my cell rang and my fingers were so numb I could barely feel the phone as I pulled it from my pocket.

"Hello?"

"Faythe?" Marc said, and relief spread through me like sunshine, warming me from the inside out. "Are you okay?"

"Better now," I breathed, trying not to chatter in his ear.

"We should be getting close. Any specifics on where you are?"

"Um, yeah. Just a minute." I clenched the phone tight to make sure my numb fingers wouldn't drop it, then jogged forward with my gaze glued to the water tower until the bottom half of the letters rose above the tree-tops. "To the north, I see a water tower that says... Cloud...something."

"Cloudcroft," Jace said in the background, and I heard the rustle of paper closer to the phone as Marc unfolded a map. "Look, it's right there," Jace continued, and there was an electronic beep from his GPS unit. "We're only a couple of miles away."

Marc huffed, and more paper crackled as he folded his map. "Head toward the tower. We'll go south from there and find you."

"Hurry..." I said, but the end of the word was swallowed by chattering.

"Hang on. We're almost there."

Eighteen

Jace's Pathfinder pulled to a stop in the middle of the gravel road, and Marc was out before Jace could shut the engine down. He squeezed me so tight I couldn't breathe, and the talon bruises on my arms ached, but I was happy to exchange my breath for his warmth. Not to mention his company.

Jace stood with one hand on the driver's side door, watching us with a mixture of relief and frustration. I gave him a bittersweet smile with numb lips, then lost his gaze when Marc set me down and pulled his leather jacket off to layer it over my own.

"Come on, let's get you warmed up." Marc led me toward the Pathfinder by one hand and pulled the back door open for me.

"It's warmer up here," Jace said before I could climb in. I shot him a censorious glance, but he ignored me in favor of Marc. "All the vents are in the front."

"Good call." Marc pulled open the front door, and I

found myself seated next to Jace, bundled in Marc's jacket, before I even really processed what had happened. Jace restarted the engine and cranked up the heat, then turned all the vents toward me.

Marc got in and leaned forward as Jace pulled onto the side of the narrow road to turn the car around. "So, the nest is back there?" He tapped his window, facing the direction I'd come from, and I nodded. "How far?"

"Not sure. Maybe eight miles?" My words were choppy, spoken around my chattering teeth, but they both seemed to understand me.

Jace frowned and shifted the car back into Drive. "According to the GPS, the road's a dead end."

I pulled off my gloves and dropped them in my lap, then held my hands in front of the vents. "Yeah. But it dead-ends right in front of the thunderbirds' nest."

Jace hesitated with one hand on the gearshift. "Kaci's only a few miles away. We can't leave her there."

"You got a better idea?" Marc didn't sound hostile, exactly, but he was definitely impatient, and I was glad I'd missed the first half of the road trip, even considering the bitter cold and the airplaneless flying.

Jace shrugged. "She must be terrified on her own."

"She is." I used the toes of one foot to pry off my opposite shoe, then stretched my frozen toes toward the floorboard vent. "But we can't get her back without either evidence or a fight, and the three of us don't stand a chance against several dozen thunderbirds. Especially since they have the home field advantage."

Jace's jaw tensed and his hand tightened around

the wheel, but his foot stayed firmly on the brake pedal.

"Let's go," Marc insisted. "There's nothing we can do for Kaci without proof that Malone's guilty, and if we miss our flight, she's as good as dead."

"Please," I said when Marc's order had no impact on him, a fact which made me vaguely sick to my stomach. "You know if there was anything else we could do, I'd be the first one to suggest it."

Jace's hand twitched around the steering wheel, then he nodded once, briskly, and hit the gas so hard gravel spewed behind us. I'd have flown forward if I hadn't been buckled in. Marc hit his forehead on the back of my headrest and let out a string of Spanish profanities too fast for me to understand.

"Watch it, asshole," he finished at last, glaring at Jace in the rearview mirror. "We're no good to her if you plant us in a ditch."

Jace scowled, but slowed to a speed less likely to sling us into the next dimension. "You getting warm yet?" He glanced at me briefly and turned right onto the first paved road I'd seen, running perpendicular to the thunderbirds' long private drive.

"Yeah." But my teeth were still chattering. "How far to the nearest gas station? I'm starving."

"We gotcha covered. Marc, grab the…"

But Marc was already lifting a bulging white plastic bag over the front seat into my lap. "It's probably cold by now, but it's better than candy bars and soda. And there're a couple of bottles of Gatorade by your feet."

"Thanks, guys." For the next twenty minutes, I devoured convenience store chicken strips, potato wedges, fried mozzarella sticks, and corn dogs. I felt like I hadn't eaten in weeks. A Shifter's metabolism runs much faster than a human's, and if I'd had to Shift, I probably would have passed out from hunger.

When the bag was empty, I wadded it up and dropped it at my feet, then started on a bottle of purple Gatorade. "So, where are we going?"

"Roswell." Marc twisted in his seat, and his face came into focus in my side-view mirror. "We should be there in a couple of hours. Our flight leaves at nine-fifteen."

"You're serious? Roswell has an airport?"

"Nope." Jace grinned. "We're booked on the first available flying saucer. Hope you don't get space-sick."

I couldn't suppress a grin of my own; it felt good to finally be smiling again, after so much fear and pain. Even if the jokes were stupid, and the smiles were only temporary, and neither could truly hide the seething anger and growing bloodlust consuming us all on the inside. "You only think that's funny because you weren't on my last flight. Whatever we take off in better have jet engines. Or at least a couple of propellers."

Movement in the rearview mirror caught my attention, and I glanced up to see Marc scowling at Jace. I twisted to face him. "What's wrong?" My question seemed somehow too trite, yet too complicated to have any real answer.

"How safe do you think Kaci is with them? With the birds?"

"Having second thoughts about leaving her?" Jace's smile was gone.

"No," Marc growled. "We had no choice. I just want to know how bad off she'll be when we get there. Does she have anyone to talk to? Anything to do? Do they even know what to feed her?"

"Assuming we make the deadline, she'll be fine." I had little doubt about that, after seeing Brynn with her daughter. "They'll stand by their word, unless I break mine. I made sure she has plenty to read, but there's nothing I can do about the company. Fortunately, they seem inclined to leave her alone. They don't like outsiders, and as weird as it sounds, they think of us as practically human."

"Meaning what?" Jace asked.

"They look down on us, and they don't trust us. Including Kaci. But they don't want to hurt her, either. She'll be fine, so long as we make it back with the smoking gun in two days."

"What about food?"

"She's a teenager, not a baby." Jace swerved to pass the first car we'd seen since leaving the gravel road. "She eats the same things everyone else does."

But I knew what Marc meant; Kai had asked for carrion. "I told them to make sure her food was fresh and well cooked." In animal form, our stomachs can handle raw meat, but even a cat won't eat rotting flesh. And in human form, Kaci couldn't eat either one.

Marc nodded, apparently mollified, and scooted onto the driver's side of the backseat, so he could see me better. He leaned against the window, and when he blinked, his eyes stayed closed a little too long. He looked exhausted, and I realized then that he and Jace probably hadn't slept at all since Kaci and I had flown the coop. My father had sent them west immediately, hoping they'd be close enough to help by the time he heard from us.

"How did you guys get out?" I asked.

"Huh?" Jace frowned at me, and Marc blinked slowly in incomprehension. They really needed sleep.

"From the ranch. How did you get out? That was before the ceasefire."

"Oh." Marc rubbed both hands over his face, then blinked again. "Your dad went out the front door again, gun a-blazin'. While the birds were all flocking around him, we snuck out the back door and into the woods in cat form, each hauling a backpack."

"Why the hell would they fall for that again? They'd just caught us sneaking out!"

"They didn't fall for it." Jace gave me a lopsided grin. "It was a hell of a race, but they didn't follow us into the woods. I think they're totally helpless when they're earthbound."

"Well, at least now someone can go out for food and supplies. So, how did you get your car?" I ran the fingers protruding from my cast over the door handle, then stopped and glanced at Jace again. "Wait, this isn't yours." Now that I'd warmed up and eaten, I realized that the upholstery was dark gray, when it should have been black.

Jace grinned again, impressed. "Nope. Dodd took us to a rental place, then took Teo, Manx, and Des to Henderson in his company car."

No fair. Dodd had two cars, and I didn't even have one. But then again, Carey Dodd had a good job, and—like most toms—no family to support. Whereas I wasn't even drawing a salary, thanks to the tribunal, which had found me guilty of infecting my ex-boyfriend a few months earlier. Officially, working as an enforcer for free was considered my "community service." If it wasn't work I enjoyed, I'd have called it indentured servitude.

"Why don't you take a nap?" I suggested, reaching back to squeeze Marc's hand as he yawned again. "We'll wake you up when we get to the airport."

Marc started to refuse; I could see the frown building. But then he gave up and sighed. "Can you make sure smart-ass keeps us on the road, somewhere below light speed?"

I nodded and smiled, refraining from telling Marc that Jace was actually the better driver. Behind the wheel, Marc made *The Fast and the Furious* look like *Driving Miss Daisy*.

He looked unconvinced, but ten minutes later, he started snoring and I looked back to find him passed out against the window, using an empty backpack for a pillow.

"So, how come you're not falling asleep at the wheel?" I whispered, to keep from waking Marc. Normally he was a very sound sleeper, but I had no doubt that if he was ever going to wake without warning, it would be during a private conversation between me and Jace.

"He drove most of the way here." Jace's gaze flicked to the rearview mirror.

"And you could sleep through that?"

Jace shrugged. "I figure if he's planning to kill me, he'll wait until he has enough justification to avoid the death penalty." He was still smiling, but his eyes showed no humor. "So…how long do you think that'll be?"

My hands went cold in spite of the heater blowing full blast, and I twisted to look at Marc again, to reassure myself that he really was sleeping. "Jace, I can't do this right now." My words came out so soft I could barely hear them, yet they left a bitter taste on my tongue.

"Just give me a date," he whispered, sounding oddly…intense. "And I won't mention it again until then."

"You want to know when I'm going to tell him? You're seriously asking me this *now?*" No amount of cautious whispering could soften my irritation. Marc was in the backseat!

"There will never be a good time to talk about this, Faythe," Jace returned calmly, staring at the road. "We're about to sneak into enemy territory, and as mad as it makes me that Calvin Malone owns everything that was once my father's—" his wife, as well as the land "—it pisses Cal off worse to know my dad had it all first. He hates me for that, and if he finds us, he'll kill me. And this may be petty of me, but I'd kind of like to know where we stand before I die, if that's what's in the cards."

I sucked in a deep breath and held it, and when that

wasn't enough, I let it go slowly and pulled in one more. Jace wasn't looking at me. He couldn't. Or maybe he wouldn't. I wasn't being fair to either of them, and I damn well knew it. What I *didn't* know was how to remedy that without hurting someone. Or—more likely—all of us.

In that moment, with Marc snoring softly behind us, and Jace staring at the road like nothing else existed while he waited for my reply, I wished I'd never let him kiss me. That I'd never kissed him back. I wished we'd been strong enough to deal with Ethan's death without falling into each other physically. Without connecting on such a primal, emotional level.

If I'd never known what I was missing, surely this wouldn't be so hard.

But that was a futile wish, worth less than every penny I'd wasted on fountains as a child. And even if I could undo what I'd done, I wasn't convinced it would make any difference.

I didn't feel something for Jace simply because I slept with him. The truth was that I slept with him because I felt something for him. Even if we'd had the willpower to resist physical comfort in such emotionally fragile states, I would *still* feel something for Jace. And eventually something else would happen to weaken our willpower, and the result would be the same.

Only it would be infinitely worse if it had happened after I'd married Marc.

"Faythe?" Jace practically breathed my name, and I heard the filament-thin edge of panic in his voice. He couldn't interpret my silence and had assumed the worst-case scenario. "What are you thinking?"

I sighed, a fragile sound that was little more than the slide of air between my lips. "I'm thinking that I have no idea what I'm doing."

"That makes two of us."

I glanced at him in surprise, and he shot me a grin that was almost…shy. "What, you think I planned this?" I shrugged helplessly, and he turned back to the road. "Okay, maybe while you guys were broken up, I thought about it occasionally. Or more like constantly. But now? I like my teeth in my mouth and my face intact, thank you. I know what this means for me, and I know what it means for Marc. And I know what it means for the Pride."

"Jace…" I started, but he shook his head.

"Let me finish."

After a second of silence, I nodded hesitantly.

"If I love you more than you love me, I'm as good as dead. Yet I can't make myself take it back. I can't just walk away from you, because every time you pass by me without smiling, without touching my hand, or at least making eye contact, it feels like I'm dying inside. And I'm pretty sure that hurts worse than whatever Marc would do to me. Whatever your dad would do.

"Hell, Faythe, I'm pretty sure that never touching you again would hurt worse than the nastiest death Calvin could think up for me."

Nineteen

We arrived at the Roswell airport with an hour to spare, and since we had no luggage to check, we made a quick trip into a gift shop for an extra T-shirt and toiletry essentials for me—the guys had what little they needed in their backpacks—then picked up a new cell phone for Jace at a kiosk near our gate. Our plane left on time, and after a short layover in Dallas, we settled in for a longer flight to Lexington.

The plane had a row of three seats on one side of the aisle, and two on the other. Jace and I had adjoining seats on the two-seat side, with Marc right in front of us. But when we boarded the plane, Marc took Jace's window seat, and tossed an offhand gesture toward the one he'd passed over.

Jace scowled but took the seat in front of him without comment. For which I was endlessly grateful.

"So, what's the plan from here on out?" Marc asked once we were in the air, as a pair of flight attendants began the beverage service at the front of the plane. "What kind of proof are we looking for?"

I'd thought it over during my long walk from the thunderbirds' nest, but had yet to hit upon a stroke of brilliance. Or even sufficiency. "Um…I was thinking we could find the feathers Brett was going to bring."

"Why would Malone keep them?"

"I'm kind of hoping he never found them. Brett said he had them hidden, and right now Kaci's life is riding on the hope that Brett died before he could retrieve them."

As Marc thought, his expression cycled through doubt, skepticism and raw fear. For Kaci, most likely. I'd never seen him afraid for himself, because Marc was truly, completely selfless. Except where our relationship was concerned.

Finally he faced me, leaning with his temple against the back of his seat. "Do you have any idea where he hid them?"

"I was hoping Jace might have a little insight to share with us."

"How 'bout it, Hammond?" Marc kicked the back of Jace's chair. Jace dropped his seat back as far as it would go, wedging it against Marc's knees. "Damn it!" Marc shoved Jace's headrest, but Jace only grinned at me through the now-wide crack between his seat and the vacant one next to him.

"I don't know. Under his mattress? That's where he used to hide stuff he didn't want Mom to find. If you want anything more creative than that, I'll have to think about it. After my nap." With that, he winked at me and leaned against the window, out of sight, without raising his seat.

"What the hell is his problem?" Marc shoved Jace's chair one more time, then twisted to face me more fully, obviously uncomfortable in his newly tight quarters. "I swear, if he wasn't a damn good fighter, I'd send him home and ask for Vic instead."

Several minutes later, after the flight attendant had made another round, I leaned in to Marc.

"You think Jace fights better than Vic?" I hesitated to ask, because Jace wasn't sleeping yet. I could tell by the rhythm of his breathing. But my curiosity got the better of me.

Marc shrugged. "He put up a pretty good effort yesterday."

"You *fought* Jace yesterday?" Why had neither of them told me?

"We were just sparring. We had to do something while we waited to hear from you and Kaci, and we both had energy to burn. It was either spar or fight over the motel television's remote."

I hesitated, glancing through the crack between the seats again at what little I could see of Jace. He'd gone completely still. Listening. "And he was good?"

Marc nodded. "Put me flat on the ground twice. He's different since Ethan died. He takes everything more seriously. He's out for Malone's blood, and I'd bet my canines he'll get it."

I nodded thoughtfully, and Jace relaxed. No doubt Marc was right on all counts—he was attributing the obvious changes to Ethan's death and Malone's power play. So far, he was only missing one piece of the puzzle that Jace had become: me.

"So, why did my dad send Jace instead of Vic?" Vic and Marc had been partners for years, and even if Marc didn't know the details, he knew that Jace's feelings for me went beyond friendship.

"Because Kaci responds best to him. I think she has a crush on him."

"Yeah." I smiled a little at that, and couldn't help missing—just for a moment—the days when a girl's innocent crush was as complicated as my own personal life ever got. "But she's not really thinking along those lines right now. Because of Ethan." And because of everything else that had gone wrong.

By then, Jace's breathing had evened out, and his hand had gone slack on his own thigh. Finally I could relax with Marc, confident we weren't being overheard. Not by Jace, anyway.

I leaned on Marc's shoulder, and he curled his fingers around mine where they stuck out from my cast. He stared at my left hand, and I knew he was picturing his ring there. But I'd never actually worn it on my finger. It was on a silver chain in an envelope in the top drawer of my dresser.

"I was half-afraid they'd taken you both straight to Malone," Marc whispered, leaning his head against mine. "I thought we'd have to execute a full-scale rescue."

"You think it'd be that easy?"

Marc thought as the flight attendants pushed the cart closer. The metallic rattle and the hiss of soda being opened almost drowned out his words. "I think taking you would be the biggest mistake he's ever made. Possibly his first real tactical error."

I pulled away and twisted to meet his heated gaze. "Why is that?"

"Because nothing could make us fight harder than getting you and Kaci away from him. Me. Your dad. Hell, even Jace. Taking you would have been the last mistake Malone ever made."

The instant the plane landed, we became guilty of trespassing. In the south-central Pride, such an offense was punishable by immediate capture and expulsion, for a first offense. Unfortunately, since trespassing is not a capital crime, the exact consequences were left up to each individual Alpha. And something told me Malone wouldn't be quite as forgiving as my father.

In fact, I had no doubt he'd kill Jace and Marc on sight and trump up a charge later—unless either his wife or daughter was there to object. And something told me Malone wouldn't mind if it took a bit of *subduing* to get me under control, so long as no permanent damage was done. Because he had plans for me— or at least for my ring finger and my uterus.

Which made me the member of our team with the least to lose, since I had no intention of actually serving my sentence.

Since he hadn't yet been officially rehired, Marc didn't have his business credit card, so Jace put the rental car in his name. He looked a little too eager for the privilege—until we got to the parking lot and Marc held the back door open for me. Jace grumbled about being treated like a chauffeur, so I made Marc sit up front with him, so I could stretch out in the back.

A nap would have been awesome, but I had a feeling we'd need every minute of the two-hour drive ahead to plan our next moves.

The Appalachian Pride was headquartered in the southern end of Clay County, Kentucky, about a hundred and ten miles southeast of Lexington. It was nearly two in the morning by the time we left the airport. We'd spent almost nine of our allotted forty-eight hours and the return trip would take at least that long, which left us roughly thirty hours to find the evidence and get the hell out of the Appalachian territory in time to save Kaci. And that would be cutting it close.

Kaci was thirty-nine hours from death. I was thirty-nine hours and one minute from a total breakdown.

We stopped for burgers at the first all-night fast food place we found, using the drive-through to keep from leaving our scents on the door handles and seats, or even lingering in the air. The last thing we needed was for one of Malone's toms to tip him off before we even got to his property. The chances of any of his men actually living in middle-of-nowhere Kentucky were slim to none, but considering the stakes at hand, Murphy's Law seemed more like a guarantee.

"So, you grew up running around the Appalachian foothills?" Marc said a few miles later, folding the wrapper back from his burger.

Jace nodded and swallowed his own bite, one hand holding the top of the steering wheel lightly. "Technically, this is the Cumberland Plateau."

"Whatever." I loosened my seat belt and leaned forward to be sure I wouldn't miss anything. Like Marc, Jace hardly ever spoke about his past. They both knew everything about my childhood, but I knew nothing about Marc's and only that Jace's father had died when he was a toddler, and still an only child. "Did you run with your brothers?" Surely half brothers were better than no brothers.... "Did Malone let Melody run with you guys?"

"Sometimes, and almost never." He frowned, and I thought he'd clam up when he took another big bite of his burger. But then he swallowed, and in the rearview mirror, I could see that his eyes were focused more on the past than on the road. "Cal didn't let Melody do much of anything. But then, she was only seven when I left. Not old enough to Shift, or do much more than get on your nerves."

"Wow, you must have been a *great* big brother." I smacked him on the head.

Jace shot me a mock glare in the rearview mirror. "She's *Calvin's daughter.* You've seen *The Omen*, right?"

"She can't be that bad," Marc said, around his last fry. "She's your mother's, too."

Jace frowned. "I wish she were a little more like my mom. Hell, I wish my *mom* was more like my mom right now."

My heart ached for him during the uncomfortable silence that followed, and Marc stared out his own window, lost in his own thoughts. He never spoke about his mother or her murder, and I never knew how to tactfully broach the subject.

"What about your brothers?" I asked finally, when Jace wadded his burger wrapper and tossed it into the front floorboard at Marc's feet. Marc growled and made no effort to put it in the empty paper bag. "I know Alex is no gem, but Brett's…"

Oops. But it was too late to take back the mention of his murdered brother, so I finished with the only thing that seemed both true and appropriate. "I was starting to like Brett."

"Yeah. Me, too." Jace sipped from his soda, then set his cup in the drink holder and flicked on his brights as we pulled ahead of the only other vehicle on the dark road. "I was almost four when Brett was born, so I was closer to him than to the rest of Cal's kids."

His phrasing stuck in my head; he didn't consider himself one of them. I'd always known that, but hearing him say it wrung sympathy from my heart.

"Brett and I hung out a lot when we were little. But the others were a lot younger than me. They spent more time with Cal, and by the time most of them could speak, they talked to me just like he did. That bastard taught them to talk about my dad—" Jace broke off and stared out the windshield in silence, and the speedometer crept toward eight-five.

Then he spoke again, so suddenly I actually jumped in the backseat. "Those hills are the only reason I survived long enough for Ethan to get me out of there. For your dad to hire me." Jace exhaled, and Marc turned from his window to watch Jace in what could only be sympathy. "I practically grew up on the side of the mountain. Every time Cal would start in on me and I couldn't take another word from him without throwing a punch, I'd just Shift and run to the hills. I'd climb until I was too tired to move. Those hills saved my life."

Or, knowing what I now knew about Jace's fighting skills, maybe they'd saved Cal's life.

"So, you still know the area?" Marc asked, ever focused on the goal at hand.

"As well as anyone who still lives there. Better than most." Jace wasn't bragging; he was simply stating a fact.

I sent a silent thank-you to my father for sending him. Marc and I would probably have bumbled our way into some serious trouble without him.

"What about Brett?" I leaned forward with an elbow on each of the front seats. "Did you think of anywhere he might have stuck those feathers? Other than beneath his mattress?"

Jace hesitated, but I recognized an idea in the artful dart of his gaze from mine in the mirror. He wasn't sure. In fact, he was so unsure he didn't even want to mention it. But however small it was in his mind, his idea was the only one we had.

"Jace?" I prodded, and he looked at me reluctantly as our speed dropped back toward eighty.

"It's not going to be there. We'll waste hours hiking through the woods in the dark, uphill the whole way, freezing our asses off, and it won't be there."

"Where?" Marc asked, half a second before I would have said the same thing.

Jace sighed, still staring at the road. "There's this old deer stand. It's really just a platform and three wobbly rails for walls. If it's even still standing. We weren't supposed to go past the property line—the other side is public hunting ground—but that old deer stand was too much to pass up. Brett and I would raid the castle tower and storm the fort all weekend, by the time he was five or so."

"Your mom let a five-year-old and a nine-year-old wander the woods alone?"

Jace shrugged. "She didn't know. She was busy with the younger ones, and so long as we showed up again for dinner, she'd assume we were playing near the tree line. It seems stupid and dangerous now, but then…"

"Sounds like fun," Marc said, and I smiled, pleased that the two of them could be civil when it really mattered.

"Yeah. It was." Jace smiled distantly, as if he'd just then realized the truth in his statement. "There was an old wooden chest up there. We used it as an armory. Brett had a couple of toy pistols—you remember those pop guns?—and I had this plastic retractable knife…." Jace's voice faded again, and I spoke up to prompt him.

"And you think he might have hidden the feathers in there?"

"No." Jace shook his head firmly. "I doubt the old stand is there anymore, and even if it is, Brett probably hasn't thought about it in a decade." The present tense did not escape my notice, and judging by the look Marc shot me, it hadn't escaped his, either. "I know I haven't. But it's the only place I can think of." He shook his head again. "It's a total waste of time. It won't be there."

"It's worth a try," I insisted, and Marc nodded, though he seemed less convinced. "Especially considering it's our only idea so far. And if the feathers are there, we won't have to go anywhere near Malone or his men."

"That's a long shot, Faythe," Jace said softly.

I shrugged. "This whole damn thing's a long shot."

Marc frowned and turned from me to Jace. "Can you find it?"

"If it's still there, I can find it."

An hour and a half later, I stood beside the Pathfinder, staring up at the tree-covered hill in front of me. It wasn't as high or as sharp an incline as the Montana mountain where the Territorial Council had held my trial, but it would certainly be a workout compared to the relatively flat woodlands behind our ranch.

There was no sign of the sun at three-thirty in the morning, but dawn would come fast—I had no doubt of that—and we needed to be long gone before then.

"You ready?" Jace shut the driver's side door behind me, and I nodded as Marc tossed his backpack over one shoulder. We'd stopped about an hour away from Malone's property for bottled water and snack bars, and had no choice but to risk leaving our scents in the all-night gas station, hoping none of the local cats would stumble in at that hour.

"I still think you should Shift," I said, frowning at Marc. "I won't be much good like this if we run into a fight." I held up my casted arm, still pissed that I couldn't Shift. Heading up the side of a mountain in cat form sounded practically sporty. Half exercise, half game. But hiking up on two legs sounded like a huge pain in the ass.

"I'd rather keep you company." Marc stepped closer, and the heat from his body felt wonderful in contrast to the bitter February chill, even more pronounced at the higher elevation. His head dipped and his lips found my neck just below the right side of my jaw.

I shivered from pleasure, rather than the early morning cold, and my arms wound around his back as his mouth trailed lower.

Then Jace's footsteps crunched loudly on the loose gravel, and I sighed, pulling away from Marc reluctantly as he stiffened in irritation. "Besides," he said, as Jace's shirt hit the ground at his back. "You might need help. You can't afford to fall on this." He ran his fingers down the top of my cast, and for the millionth time, I wished I could feel his touch there.

Damn Kevin Mitchell for breaking my arm! But Kevin was already damned. Or dead, at least. Marc had made sure of that.

"Maybe I should just stay here. You guys could get there faster in cat form. I'll just slow you down."

"You can't stay by yourself…." Marc began, and when I frowned, Jace interrupted.

"You won't slow us down." He grinned and dropped his pants. And he wasn't wearing underwear. "And I think we'd *both* enjoy your company."

My face flamed, in both anger and embarrassment. What the hell was he *doing?*

Marc turned on Jace, already pissed over the innuendo. His hands bunched into fists, and his jaw worked as if he was either going to yell or break every one of his own teeth. But he didn't make a sound. And I understood in that moment that there was very little he could say without directing more attention toward Jace, which was the last thing he wanted to do.

Technically, Jace had done nothing wrong. He had to undress to Shift, and on the surface, he'd paid me a compliment on both of their behalf. But Marc wasn't stupid. He may not know how far things had gone between me and Jace, but he knew Jace was openly flirting and inviting me to look. And that bold of an invitation could not be blamed on any of our recent tragedies.

"Watch it...." Marc growled at last. Jace only grinned harder and tossed his clothes onto the backseat, heedless of my silent, wide-eyed pleading over Marc's shoulder.

Pissed now, I slammed the door, and Jace had to jerk his hand away to keep from getting it caught. I tugged Marc toward the trees as he resettled his backpack on his shoulder. "We're heading south, right?" I asked Jace as he scowled after us. He nodded and dropped to his knees. I led the way into the woods with Marc at my side, the sounds of Jace's Shift almost inaudible over my own footsteps. "Catch up with us when you've Shifted."

Twenty

Jace caught up with us eight minutes later, and his posture said "anger" just as clearly as his claws and canines said "approach at your own risk."

"What the hell is his problem?" Marc grumbled as Jace sprinted past, leaving us to follow the sounds of his progress.

"Just ignore him." I considered explaining that Jace's post-Ethan transformation went beyond a die-hard determination to see Malone pay. But that skirted too close to the truth, and I wasn't willing to flat out lie to Marc. I was only lying by omission because I had yet to find an appropriate moment to tell him what I'd done. A moment when Jace was several hundred miles away—to keep Marc from killing him—and when no one else's life depended on our ability to focus on the job at hand.

Such moments were rare lately. And hiding the truth made me feel like I'd swallowed a slow-working poison that was gradually rotting away my insides. Beginning with my heart.

Jace let us catch up with him a quarter mile later, and after that, the hike was blissfully uneventful, if tedious. Even though Marc and I had both Shifted our eyes, it was rough going. I tripped several times—my human body is much less graceful and coordinated than my cat form—and each time Marc caught me before I could even throw out an arm to catch myself. And I was too tired, cold, and worried about further injuring my arm to be anything other than grateful for his help.

To his credit, Jace never looked unsure of where he was going, though he hadn't been back to his birthplace once in the seven years since my dad had hired him. To me, that said the deer stand was a much more important part of his childhood than he'd let on, and if the same was true for Brett…we might just get lucky.

My pulse spiked at the thought of serving justice to Malone using evidence his own son had given us. The son he'd murdered. Malone's downfall was imminent. I could feel it.

After an hour and a half of hiking through the woods, Jace stopped and swished his tail to catch our attention. His bearing held no tension and no warning; he was simply telling us we had arrived.

A minute later, the forest gave way to a small clearing with irregular, undefined edges, as if someone had chopped down a few trees to gain just a bit of work-space. And there was the deer stand.

It was built into the branches of a large, sturdy tree on the opposite side of the clearing, maybe twenty-five feet off the ground. The wood was weathered and rough, and looked grayed even in the muted colors of my cat vision. A homemade ladder led from the ground to the edge of the platform overhead, its plank steps made from mismatched lengths of two-by-fours, several of which swung loose on one end.

"Well, at least it's still standing." Marc's voice sounded odd after an hour of hearing nothing but twigs snapping beneath our feet and the occasional rustle of some small creature through the winter-crisp under-brush. "But there's no telling if it'll hold our weight."

"I'll go. I'm the lightest."

"No." Marc grabbed my arm when I started forward, but let go when I winced from the pain in my talon-shaped bruises and turned on him with an angry scowl. "What if it collapses?"

I shrugged. "You'll catch me."

"And if I miss, you'll break your other arm, or a leg, and you won't be able to fight when we go in for real."

"Marc, in all the times I've fallen, you've never failed to catch me." I tugged my arm from his grip gently and stood on my toes to kiss him, acutely, uncomfortably aware that Jace was watching. Then I turned my back on them both and faced the deer stand.

I tested the first step with one foot before putting my full weight on it. When it held, I started up. The fourth step was hanging from one nail, and the fifth was missing completely, and with the grip of my right hand compromised by my cast, I was afraid to depend too heavily on it. I glanced back at Marc. "Can I get a hand?"

He was behind me before I'd even seen him move, and suddenly I was sitting in his cupped hands. He lifted me easily past the fifth and sixth planks, and I stepped onto the seventh, a good eight feet off the ground. "Thanks," I murmured, and continued climbing. Marc stayed at the base of the ladder, just in case.

The tenth step creaked beneath my foot, sending an adrenaline-spiked bolt of alarm through me, and the thirteenth was rotten under my hand. The seventeenth lodged a huge splinter in my left palm. But two steps after that, my head rose above the floor of the stand, and my cat's eyes focused easily on the small chest in one corner, thanks to the last rays of starlight now peeking from behind a cloud.

The first bit of daylight would shine shortly after 7:00 a.m., which gave us under two hours to get what we came for, get back to the car, and get the hell out of Dodge. *No pressure…*

I hauled myself up carefully, wincing when my cast scraped the floor, though it didn't hurt. I wondered if I would have smelled Brett's residual scent on the wood, if I were in cat form. Assuming he'd actually been where I now sat, a couple of days earlier.

Jace whined, and Marc asked the question for them both. "Do you see it?"

"Yeah. We are a go for an old wooden chest."

They both exhaled in relief from twenty feet below. Several patches of the floor looked suspiciously soft and dark, so I crawled around them on my knees and elbows, staying close to the right-hand railing. Crawling distributed my weight over a broader area, and my elbows kept pressure off my broken wrist.

The box was nothing more than a rough wooden cube, but I could see how a pair of small boys might call it a treasure chest. Might even have kept their own valuables in it.

The lid was a simple pine board, attached to the back of the box by a set of rusty hinges, which squealed when they were used. I lifted the lid slowly with my eyes closed, sending up a silent, fervent prayer that Brett had remembered this place. That he'd thought of it when he needed somewhere safe to store the evidence that could seal his father's fate, and save so many others.

I opened my eyes. And laughed out loud.

Relief bubbled up inside me like a fountain of joy, and it would not be stifled, even with dawn less than two hours away. Even though we were well inside enemy territory. Even though Kaci would die and my Pride would be slaughtered if we were caught.

"Is it there?" Marc demanded as Jace continued to whine softly, begging for information.

"Yeah. He even put them in plastic." I lifted the gallon-size bag and held it up. Inside were two huge feathers, striped with a distinctive pattern of colors I couldn't make out without more light, even with my cat vision. But I saw the dark smears of blood, and I could smell it, even nearly a week old and sealed inside plastic.

On the front of the bag was a white strip, and Brett

had printed on it, in clear black letters. "Thunderbird feathers. Lance Pierce's blood."

Brett, wherever you are, I hope you're being spoiled rotten in the afterlife. "Jace, your brother's a saint."

Jace huffed, as if he had a dissenting opinion to add, but I only laughed. And when I glanced into the box again, I laughed even harder. "They're still here!" I called. "Brett's pop guns and your knife. They're all still here! Do you want me to bring them down?"

For a moment, there was only silence. Then Jace huffed again, but I couldn't interpret that one without body language to add nuance, so Marc called up with a translation. "I think he wants you to leave them there. For Brett."

He must have gotten that right, because Jace didn't contradict him. So I closed the box and left the abandoned toys as a memorial to Brett, and to the childhood friendship he and Jace had once shared. Then I started back across the floor with the zipper of the plastic bag clutched in my left hand.

I was about a foot from the edge when my jeans caught on something, and my right leg refused to slide forward. I let go of the bag and propped myself on my good hand to twist for a better view. The hem of my jeans was stuck on a nail sticking up from the floor.

"Shit!"

"What's wrong?" Marc asked immediately as Jace whined louder in question.

"I'm caught on a nail. Hang on. I think I can get it." I pushed myself slowly backward and shook my foot to dislodge the nail. When that didn't work, I shifted my weight onto my left hand and reached back toward the nail with my right.

The deer stand creaked, and fear spiked my pulse. My hand broke through the floor. Jagged edges of wood raked the length of my forearm, pushing my sleeve up in the process. I screamed. My face slammed into the floor, and I bit my lip. Blood poured into my mouth.

"Faythe!" Marc shouted. Jace growled, a deep, fierce sound, and Marc's next words were directed at him. "Let go!" But Jace only growled harder.

"I'm okay," I said, but it came out as a whisper, with my left cheek still pressed into the wood. Still, the guys heard me.

"I'm coming up!" Marc called, and Jace's growl grew even fiercer.

"No!" I said, when his meaning finally became clear. "It won't hold you. I'm okay. Just let me pull myself out of this hole."

"Let go of me, or I'll cave your face in," Marc said, his voice soft and dangerous. Jace growled once more for good measure, then must have let Marc go, because he voiced no further complaint. "Can you get up?" Marc called to me.

"Yeah." *I hope.* "Just a minute." My left arm was useless, hanging beneath the floor from my shoulder on. The lower half of it was on fire, the pain so acute and encompassing that I couldn't tell exactly where it hurt.

"You're bleeding. A lot," Marc said, and twigs crunched beneath his boots as he paced.

"So I noticed. Just give me a minute, please." When

silence followed my request, I exhaled and braced myself for more pain. *Just do it quickly.* We needed to be out of the woods and out of sight before dawn, and we were running late already.

I closed my eyes and sucked in a deep breath, hoping against all logic that the rest of the floor would hold me. Then, since I couldn't support my weight on my right arm, I stretched over my head, flat on the floor, and rolled to my left.

Wood dug into my arm like daggers as it slid through the hole. I screamed again. I couldn't help it.

"Faythe!"

I lay on my back, breathing hard though I'd barely exerted myself, afraid to move lest the floor collapse beneath me. Marc's footsteps came closer, and wood snapped, dull and heavy. "Damn it!" he whispered fiercely, and my eyes popped open.

"Don't!" He'd broken the first rung of the ladder. The deer stand couldn't take much more damage without collapsing, and I desperately didn't want to be on it when that happened.

"Sorry." Marc's boots backed several steps away, and I made myself roll over carefully, avoiding even the briefest glimpse of my newly injured arm. It burned and felt cold at the same time, and I could barely stand the brush of my jacket sleeve against it. "Are you okay?"

"My arm feels pretty bad, but I'm not gonna look at it until I get down." Because I was pretty sure that if it looked as bad as it felt, my brain would tell me I *couldn't* climb down.

"Be careful."

"I will. Look, just…don't talk for a few minutes, so I can concentrate, okay? And catch this." Without waiting for his response, I shoved the gallon bag off the edge of the platform.

Marc's steps crunched forward. "Got it." Then he was blessedly silent.

I blinked and inhaled deeply, then pushed myself onto my knees and elbows, busying my eyes in the search for more weak spots in the wood, so I couldn't accidently look at my new wound.

But it was bad. I could tell from the strength of the scent of my own blood, and the pool of it I was now crawling through. I'd be light-headed soon, and I wanted to be safely on the ground before that happened.

I eased slowly toward the ladder, and after a few tense minutes found myself sitting on the edge of the deer stand. Marc stood in front of the ladder, with Jace at his side on all four paws. I could see them clearly thanks to my cat's eyes, and the slight lightening of the sky as dawn approached.

Damn it! We needed to be halfway back to the car already.

I pushed that thought away and took another deep breath through my mouth. Then I twisted to lie on my stomach and put one foot on the third rung from the top. The next step was a bitch, even once I was sure the rung would hold me, because I couldn't grip the ladder well enough with my casted right hand, and moving my fingers made my left arm explode in agony.

A whimper of pain escaped before I could lock it down, and Jace echoed the sound from below.

I stepped down again, and again gripped the bar, this time biting my still-bleeding lip to keep from crying out. So far, so good.

The next rung snapped beneath my foot.

Marc gasped. I screamed as my feet fell out from under me, and almost passed out from the agony in my left arm. I hung from it, my life dependent on a grip weakened by my shredded flesh.

"Let go," Marc said. "Let go and I'll catch you."

"No." I was too high. My body twisted, and my feet scrambled for the nearest rung, but it had been broken before we arrived, and the next hung a full foot below my feet.

"Faythe. Let go."

I glanced down at Marc, and if I'd seen fear in his eyes, I couldn't have done it. But I saw only confidence. If he said he could catch me, he could catch me. It was as simple as that.

So I closed my eyes and let go.

My hair blew back from my face as I fell. My cast broke through two more rungs, each impact reverberating in my broken wrist. My right foot slammed into the side of the ladder, and the blow radiated up my leg. Then I landed hard in Marc's arms.

He staggered beneath the impact, but didn't fall.

I clung to him and didn't even try to stop the tears. Screw being strong. I could be strong and hurt at the same time, right?

Because *daaamn*, I hurt.

Marc set me on the ground, and I caught his quick glance to the east. The sun would be up in an hour, and if anyone had gone for an early morning run, my screams had probably been heard.

He met Jace's gaze and tossed his head toward Malone's property. Jace nodded as his ears swiveled in that direction, on alert for any suspicious sounds.

"Let me see your arm." Marc knelt next to me, and I was glad all over again that he'd already mastered the partial Shift. Without it, he couldn't have gotten much of a look, because without our usual emergency trunk kit, we didn't have a flashlight.

I held my arm out straight, sniffing back more sobs as he carefully pulled my jacket off. I got my first look the same time he did.

"Oh, *fuck*," Marc whispered, and Jace turned to look. He whined in either sympathy or horror, but I was speechless. That couldn't be my arm. That piece of raw meat hanging from my elbow bore no resemblance to the forearm I'd had minutes earlier. Broken wood couldn't do that much damage. It wasn't possible.

A jagged section of the broken deer stand floor had ripped the side of my left forearm open from wrist to elbow, where my coat sleeve had bunched up, protecting the rest of my flesh. The muscle was exposed, and the whole thing was slick with blood.

If the wood had caught the underside instead, I'd probably already have bled to death.

Marc stood, and his jacket hit the ground. He ripped

a sleeve from his long-sleeved tee, then knelt again and stared into my eyes. "This is going to hurt, but I need you to keep quiet, okay?"

I nodded, and Jace nudged my shoulder with the top of his head for comfort, then went back on alert.

Marc wrapped my arm quickly and tightly, while I held back a scream with nothing but willpower. The pain was unlike anything I'd ever felt, and I couldn't stop silent tears. When he was done, Marc wiped my face with his remaining sleeve. Then he helped me get my jacket back on.

"Can you walk?"

"My legs are fine."

He pulled me up, and I let him, because I couldn't put weight on either of my arms. "If you start feeling light-headed at all, tell me. Don't let yourself pass out just because you're stubborn."

He got no argument from me.

I made it about half a mile on my own before the hill we were descending began to tilt on its own. "Marc…" My voice was barely a whisper, but he heard me. An instant later, the whole forest swam as he picked me up, cradling me in his arms like a baby.

He took two steps forward. Then everything went black.

Twenty-One

A familiar hum, the sounds of traffic, and the scent of leather told me I was in a car. The rental. We were in Kentucky, trespassing in Malone's territory. Sitting ducks, with both my arms messed up. I had no words strong enough to describe the pain. I'd literally been ripped open, and there must have been muscle damage, because my fingers didn't respond properly when I tried to curl them.

I opened my eyes, and the roof of the car came into focus. Next came Marc's face, peering down at me, lined in concern. Had my eyes Shifted back in my sleep? Marc repositioned himself, and I realized I was lying across the backseat with my head in his lap. "Hey. How does your arm feel?"

"Like I got it caught in the tractor." My left arm lay across my stomach, stinging, throbbing, burning endlessly, the pain spiking with each beat of my heart.

"Yeah, that's about what it looks like."

Great. At least he wasn't prone to sugarcoating. "My

fingers don't work right. I can't fight." My eyes watered at that realization, and his face blurred.

"We'll worry about that later."

The car turned right—with Jace presumably behind the wheel—and we passed a broad brick building, sunlight glaring in the windows. "How long was I out?"

"About forty minutes."

"You carried me the whole way?" I asked, and Marc only smiled. Of course he had. "Where are we going?"

"We're getting a room. You need to rest."

"No." I tried to sit up, but the world swam, so I lowered my head onto Marc's lap again. "We have to go get Kaci."

"We will," Jace said from the front seat, beyond my line of sight. "But we can't fly until we get you cleaned up, and we need somewhere private for that." He turned right again, and the car bumped over rough pavement. "It's nothing fancy, but they won't ask questions." He turned again and pressed the brake gently, then shifted into Park. "I'll get a key."

"They'll smell my blood," I said after Jace closed the car door. "They probably heard me scream. They'll be looking for us. I messed this up, Marc."

"No." He stroked my hair back from my face and let it trail over his leg. "They didn't hear you. We'd have heard them coming for us if they had. We were at least two miles from the main house. And they won't smell your blood unless they get close to the deer stand."

Or anywhere I'd dripped on the way back to the car. But neither of us said that. Just knowing it was scary enough.

Marc stroked my hair and I closed my eyes, trying to ignore the pain in my arm, which refused to settle into a quiet throb.

Jace came back minutes later with an old-fashioned metal doorknob key. He drove us to the back of the motel and parked in front of our first-floor room. I could have walked, but Marc insisted on carrying me, and I let him, because it made us both feel better. Jace hovered as Marc carefully unwrapped my arm while I sat on the edge of the first bed, then bundled his bloody, detached shirt sleeve in the plastic liner from the trash can in the bathroom.

I stared at the wall. I didn't want to see my arm in daylight. Or even in the murky glow from the bedside lamp.

Jace whistled, and still I didn't look.

"Well, at least it's mostly stopped bleeding," Marc said. And then I had to look.

I regretted it immediately. My forearm was one big scab. The gash was easily five inches long, and ragged, and now crusted with dried blood. It hurt to look at. It was unbearable to move.

"She can't travel like this," Jace said.

"She can if we wrap it well. But she needs antibiotics. And stitches—lots of stitches." Marc stood, and Jace shot to his feet, already pulling the car keys from his pocket.

"I'll go. Faythe, you want something to eat while I'm out? And you'll need some new clothes."

Marc growled and stepped between Jace and the door. "*I'll* go. I know her size."

I was beyond caring who went. I wanted nothing but an end to the pain. An end to this whole mess, so we could hand over the feathers and take Kaci home.

Marc grabbed the room key from the nightstand and knelt by the bed, looking up at me. "I'll be back as soon as I can, and we'll get you fixed up. Faythe?"

I made my eyes focus, and he squeezed the fingers sticking out of my cast. Then he stood and took the car keys Jace held out. "Call Greg and give him an update. And don't let her move her arm."

"I'm on it."

Surprised into awareness by Jace's easy compliance, I glanced up to see him watching Marc with an obedient, I'm-on-the-job expression. Marc hesitated, frowning, then reached for the doorknob.

"Hey, she's probably gonna need something stronger than Tylenol for the pain. Tequila?" Jace grinned suggestively at me with his back to Marc, and my pulse tripped at the memory of what happened the last time I drank with Jace.

I flushed. "No tequila!" Marc's brows shot up, and I stumbled over my own words. "Motrin's fine. I need to be thinking clearly."

Marc nodded, then slipped out the door, and Jace locked it behind him as the car engine hummed to life outside.

"You did that on purpose!" I eyed Jace, and he shot me an innocent grin, blue eyes flashing mischievously.

"I like what tequila does to you. And what it does for *me*..."

"Not that." I shook my head, and the pain-fog cleared

a little more. "You volunteered to go for supplies because you knew that'd push Marc into going." Into leaving me alone with Jace…

Jace shrugged, and his grin grew as he sauntered toward me. "You seem to be thinking clearer. Must be feeling better."

"Hardly…"

"Anyway, he is better qualified for a supply run. Since he knows your sizes, and everything."

"When did you get so…" *Smart?* "Manipulative?"

"Proper motivation works wonders." Jace kicked his shoes off and sank on to the opposite side of the bed, leaning against the pillows with his arms crossed behind his head.

I turned to face him—an awkward movement without full use of either of my hands. "I wanna fight."

He shrugged. "Okay, but the first time you pin me, I'm staying pinned."

"I'm serious." I frowned and held both arms out, flinching at the spike in pain from my left arm. "I can't fight like this. Hell, I can't even brush my own hair."

Jace sat up and scooted closer, all humor gone from his expression. "Marc's right—we can worry about that later. We'll get you all fixed up for now, and Doc can do a better job when we get home. With Kaci. The important thing to remember right now is that we got what we came for, and Kaci's gonna be fine."

"I know." Though, I'd feel a lot better about that once we got her away from the birds.

"And frankly, considering how pissed off they are,

we're just lucky thunderbirds' bloodlust isn't triggered by the scent of blood." He gestured toward my ravaged arm for emphasis.

Jace was still talking, but I couldn't hear him over the roar of alarm ringing in my ears.

"*Damn* it!" I started to slam my fists into the mattress, and stopped myself just in time, pissed off even more because I had no outlet for my anger.

"What?" Jace's brows lowered over cobalt eyes, and his gaze flew instinctively toward the door, no doubt listening for intruders. But there were none. *We* were the intruders.

"The feathers aren't enough. They never were." All that work—and my arm *completely* fucked up—for nothing. Well, for very little, anyway.

I scooted to the edge of the bed without the use of my hands and stood to pace. "Brett was the real evidence. His testimony." I passed the cheap, two-person table and turned in front of the plain white wall. "Thunderbirds can't distinguish between individual werecats by scent. The feathers will help our council nail Malone into his coffin, but they won't do a damn thing for the birds. We were depending on testimony against Malone from his own son, and we don't have that anymore."

Jace's expression crashed through confusion to absolute rage in a fraction of a second. "Mother*fucker!*"

I stopped pacing and closed my eyes. "We have to go back in."

"What? In where?"

"Back *in,* Jace." I opened my eyes to see him watching me in conflicting dread and anticipation. "We have to convince Lance Pierce to testify."

"Wait, you think Lance is just going to give himself up? You think he'll tell the thunderbirds the truth out of the goodness of his heart?"

I shrugged and resumed pacing. "He might—when he hears they're gonna kill Kaci. What kind of enforcer would let a thirteen-year-old tabby die for something he did?"

Jace pulled a chair out from the table and sank into it. "The kind who would let thunderbirds decimate an entire Pride for the same reason. A coward."

Okay, I couldn't argue with that. "So we'll make him testify. What other choice do we have?"

"Faythe." He blinked at me, as if I weren't making sense. "The birds'll kill him."

"I know." My pacing picked up speed. "I haven't figured that part out yet. Maybe we can renegotiate. His testimony, in exchange for immunity."

"Yeah." Jace rolled his eyes as I stalked past him. "They'll go for that. You know, since they're so cooperative and forgiving." I turned at the wall to cross the room again, but Jace caught the fingers of my right hand and tugged me gently toward him. "Faythe, you don't want to do this." He pulled me between his knees and held me with both hands at my waist as I cradled my gored arm. "This isn't self-defense, and you're not a killer."

"This is Kaci-defense. They're either going to kill Lance or Kaci. Are you really willing to let her die to save the tom who started this whole mess?"

"Of course not." He ran his hands slowly over my upper arms through my sleeves, careful of my many deep bruises. "But there has to be another way."

I shook my head and ground my teeth, my squeamish conscience at war with the cold, logical part of me, which understood exactly what had to be done. "There's no other way. If we don't come up with proof the thunderbirds can understand and get it back to the nest in the next thirty-four hours, they're going to kill Kaci. Then they're going to come after the rest of us."

I took a deep breath, then stared straight down into his eyes. "The rest of *you*. They'll hand *me* over to Malone, who'll whore me out to one of your brothers." His hands fell from my arms and he leaned back in his chair, anger curling his lips at the very thought. "And you know I won't let that happen. I'll have to kill every bastard who lays a hand on me, then they'll have to kill me. So…it's Lance or us. And keep in mind that he's guilty, and we haven't done anything wrong." To the thunderbirds, anyway.

Jace sighed and opened his mouth, but I went on before he could speak.

"Besides, we don't know for sure that they'll kill him. We have another day and a half to figure a way out of that. But regardless, we need Lance."

He crossed his arms over his chest. "And how do you expect us to get him?"

I shrugged. "We go in after him. Tonight. After dark."

"Faythe, that's suicide."

I know. "Only if we get caught."

He shook his head, unconvinced. "There are only

three of us, and even when we get you sewn up, you can't fight with one arm shredded and the other in a cast."

"I know." *Unless…* Excitement tingled in my fingers and toes—I was suddenly high on possibility. "I think I need a bath. A long, hot bath."

Jace's grin was back, and his gaze strayed south of my face. "Now you're talkin'…"

I hurried into the bathroom and started to unbutton my shirt—until the first movement of my left arm sent fresh pain lancing through it. "Hey, can you give me a hand with my clothes?" *Damn it,* that *didn't come out right!*

Too late… He was in the doorway before I could think of a way to take it back gracefully.

"Jace, I know this is weird, but…"

"It's not weird, Faythe." He sat on the side of the tub in front of me and his grin was gone, replaced by a heat in his eyes so intense I caught my breath, smoldering on the inside.

I swallowed and forced the right words out. "I mean…I'm not trying to get your pants off."

"You don't have to try.…" His hands rose slowly toward the buttons on my blouse, and his next inhalation was ragged. His gaze followed his fingers as they worked their way down the front of my shirt. His hand brushed my bare stomach, and I held my breath. He eased my shirt off my shoulders and over my cast, then ripped the left sleeve and let the material fall away from my latest injury.

Then he reached for the front clasp of my bra. In spite of my constant pain, my pulse spiked, and his answered.

This isn't going to work.

"Jace." I lifted his chin with my casted right hand until his gaze burned into mine and his hands fell away. "It hurts to move my arm and my fingers aren't working very well. I just need help. That's it. Okay?"

"Yeah. No problem." But he shifted uncomfortably, and I glanced down to find a prominent bulge in the front of his jeans.

Uh-oh. "You sure?"

"Okay, maybe a small problem." He grinned. "But not *that* small…"

I stifled a frustrated groan. This was neither the time nor the place, no matter how good his hands felt on me. *"Jace…"*

"I can't help it." He shrugged, not the least bit embarrassed, though I could easily have sunk through a hole in the floor. "You're half-naked."

"You've seen me naked a million times." My voice went hoarse. Damn it.

"It's not the same anymore."

And suddenly I was glad *he* wasn't the one getting undressed. Because he was right.

"Okay. Never mind. I can do this myself. I'm sorry." My cheeks flamed, and I turned, then winced as I reached for the button on my jeans.

"No, wait." He took a deep breath and pulled me gently toward him by my right elbow, just above my cast. "I'm fine."

"You sure?" I asked again, and this time he nodded confidently. I had my doubts, but I could pretend if he could. "Okay. Let's just get this over with."

"Not what I usually like to hear while I undress a woman…" But he was grinning again, and I exhaled in relief. I could handle a joking Jace.

He unbuttoned my pants with perfunctory speed, and I bit my lip to hold back a groan as he pushed them slowly over my hips, touching me as little as possible. His attempt at chaste assistance was more like a criminal tease.

My jeans pooled at my feet and I stepped out of them, and Jace leaned back with one hand on the faucet. "How hot do you want it?"

I rolled my eyes and indulged a smile, trying to break the tension. "Does nothing you say sound innocent?"

He returned my grin. "Not if I can help it."

"I need it pretty warm."

He turned on the water, tested it with one hand, then adjusted the temperature and plugged the drain. "So…what exactly are we doing? I know you're covered in blood, but I'm assuming this is about more than hygiene?"

"Yeah." I held up my cast. "We're soaking this bitch, so we can cut it off."

"Faythe…"

But I interrupted, wishing it wouldn't hurt to cross my arms beneath my bra. "I'll have to Shift to heal this one, anyway." I held up my throbbing, stinging left arm. "So it only makes sense to heal them both at once, right?" He started to talk again, and again I rushed to cut him off. "And don't tell me I shouldn't Shift at all. I'm *not* staying behind, and you guys need to know I can take care of myself when we go after Lance. Otherwise I'll be a distraction and a hindrance. I'm doing this, no matter what you say."

His grin was back. "I was just going to tell you you're brilliant."

"I—" I blinked. "You were?"

"Yeah. If I knew how to get the damned thing off, I'd have suggested it before you climbed up the deer stand and nearly got yourself killed."

"Oh." Well, *that* was a pleasant surprise.

"But, you know you're going to have to Shift several times, right? Like, a dozen or more. And it'll hurt like hell, assuming it even works on a broken bone."

He spoke from experience. But if he could handle the pain, so could I. "I know. Let's get this over with. And hey…you know Marc's gonna be mad, right?"

Jace shrugged. "He stays pissed at me."

I laughed. "Yeah, me, too. Help me out." I turned my back to him and released the front clasp of my bra with my right hand, then let him slide it carefully over both arms. Then I used that same hand to push down first one side, then the other of my black boy shorts until they fell to the floor.

The tub was only a few inches full, but I stepped in, anyway, because that was better than standing there naked while he tried—and failed—not to stare at me.

The hot water felt great on my legs, but I had to scooch down to submerge my cast as the water ran. I set my left arm carefully on the edge of the tub and glanced at Jace as he settled onto the closed toilet seat with one ankle crossed over the opposite knee, guy-style.

"How long has Marc been gone?" I swished my cast in the water and wiggled my toes in the flow from the faucet.

Jace glanced at his watch. "About twenty minutes. How long do you think it'll take him?"

"Normally I'd say about an hour, but he'll rush this time. We may have another half hour." I swished my arm faster and willed the tub to fill. "I think we'll all be a lot happier if I'm out of this cast—and the tub—before he gets back."

"No argument there." Jace frowned. "Not that I can't take him. This just isn't really…"

"I know. And I don't *want* you to take him. Or vice versa. Which is why I need this to work fast." I wiggled my fingers, trying to work water into the cast from that end, to speed up the process. "Your new phone has Internet, right?"

"Yeah, why?"

"Can you find out how long it'll take to drive back to New Mexico from here?" Because we couldn't just knock Lance out and drag him onto the plane.

Jace dug his phone from his pocket and spent the next five minutes typing with his thumbs. "Shit." He glanced up, and the bad news was obvious in his expression. "Twenty-three hours, if we drive straight through. Which we can do, if we drive in shifts, but…"

"But that means we can't wait until dark to go after Lance."

He shook his head. "Not if we want to get there while Kaci's still breathing."

I closed my eyes and leaned my head against the

edge of the tub as the water lapped at my navel. "Okay, so we go as soon as I'm healed." Or at least healed *enough.* "But we'll have to get Lance alone. We can't take them all on at once."

"Yeah. We'll think of something." He started to put his phone away, but I shook my head.

"We should call my dad. I'll talk to him, if you want. He's probably gonna be mad, too, but I can leave you out of this. I won't tell him you helped me."

Jace shook his head, and his gaze held mine with a substantial weight. A determination I almost didn't recognize in him. "I'm in this with you, Faythe. The whole way. This is the only option we have. He'll see that. And if he doesn't..." Jace shrugged and grinned again. "We'll both be in trouble."

My heart beat so hard it ached. He wasn't supposed to be like this. Jace wasn't supposed to be so...wonderful. Distancing myself from him wasn't supposed to be so *hard...*

I was starting to think that giving him up would be like giving up air—and I already felt like I couldn't breathe.

"Okay. Call him."

Twenty-Two

Jace autodialed, and I stirred the water with my cast. When my father answered, I turned the faucet off with my foot. The bath wasn't as deep as I like it, but it covered my arm, and I wanted to be able to hear both sides of the conversation.

"Hey, Greg, it's me."

"Jace? You have an update?"

"Yeah. We're in a motel, about twenty minutes from…Cal's place." Which was once Jace's home. "We found the feathers, so we're all good on that front, and there's no way the council will be able to argue with the evidence. But…we don't think it'll be enough to convince the thunderbirds. They can't distinguish werecats by scent."

My father sighed, obviously frustrated. "I've been having similar thoughts." Then, more distantly, "Michael, did you hear that?"

"Yeah. Let me think for a minute. I'll come up with something."

"We have an idea." Jace glanced at me and smiled reassuringly. "We want to go after Lance."

"Go after him?" My father's footsteps stopped, and I could easily picture his skeptical frown.

"Bring him in. Take him to the thunderbirds."

"I see." There was a moment of near silence, but for the water swishing around—and hopefully inside—my cast. "Put Marc on the phone."

Jace sat on the edge of the tub, and my left hand brushed his thigh. "He went out for first-aid supplies."

"Who's hurt?" My dad's voice rose, and the distant scraping of Michael's pen against paper paused.

"It's just a scratch, Daddy," I said, knowing he'd hear me. "My arm went through a rotten board in the deer stand where we found the feathers."

My father's long sigh was more of a plea for patience. "Jace, is it just a scratch?"

Jace shrugged and mouthed a silent apology to me, then answered. "It's really more of a gash. The length of her forearm."

I lifted my right arm from the water to flip him off, but I'd expected no less. If he'd lied to our Alpha, I would have lost respect for him.

"Put Faythe on the phone."

"Just a minute." Jace covered the mouthpiece and knelt beside the tub. "Can you hold it?"

Not comfortably. But if I made Jace hold the phone, my dad would be focused on how badly I was hurt, rather than what I could accomplish once I'd healed. "Put me on speakerphone."

Jace raised one eyebrow but complied, setting the phone on the tiny bathroom counter.

"I can hear you, Dad. Go ahead."

"Why am I on speakerphone?"

"Because I'm in the tub. I don't want to drop Jace's phone in the water." It was the truth. Just not the *whole* truth.

"And you're in the tub because…?"

"I've found they come in handy for keeping oneself clean." *Technically not a lie…*

Michael snorted, but my father was much less amused. "Faythe…"

"Fine. I have to Shift to heal the gash in my left arm, and I can't do that with a cast on. So I'm going to heal both arms with one Shift." Or maybe more like a dozen Shifts. "I'm soaking my cast so we can cut it off."

"Somehow I don't think Dr. Carver would approve of your timing or your methods." He sounded weary, but in good humor, which was probably due entirely to the fact that they were no longer being attacked by kamikaze thunderbirds.

"I know, and I wish the doc were here." So I wouldn't be bathing naked in front of Jace, while on the phone with my father and brother. Our conversation had completely redefined the word *awkward*, and we hadn't even gotten to the hard part. "But Carver's not here, and we're on a pretty tight timeline. And we need all three of us in good working order, so I'm doing what has to be done." I hesitated, and took a deep breath. "Is any of that a problem?"

My dad sighed again, and I could almost see him scowling as he debated the possible answers. "The whole thing is one big problem, Faythe. You're deep in enemy territory, injured, and too far away for me to help. You're nothing but a stroke of bad luck away from being caught, and if that happens, we'll have to go full-scale against Malone in the next day and a half, because when the thunderbirds figure out you're not coming back, they'll relaunch their offensive, and we won't have the manpower to get you out. Am I missing anything?"

"Um…we're pretty sure that if we're caught, they'll execute Marc and Jace on sight for trespassing. And the thunderbirds will kill Kaci."

"And there's that…" Michael said, no trace of humor left in his voice.

I took a deep breath and held it for a count of five. "I get it, Dad. We've re-created mission impossible, and if you have a better idea, I'm all ears. But from where I'm sitting—" *or lying, in a lukewarm bath* "—our options are pretty limited, and our time is running out."

Leather creaked as my father sat in his favorite chair. "Are you neglecting to mention an easier way any of this could be done? Either your cast, or finding better evidence?"

Whew, an easy one. "Not to my knowledge. Believe it or not, I don't *try* to do things the hard way." It just works out that way most of the time. "I don't know what else we can do for evidence, short of convincing

Malone to confess, or another one of his men to defect. And I don't see either of those happening this decade, much less in the next few hours."

"You still have nearly a day and a half." I could practically hear the frown in my dad's voice.

"Not if they're going to drive." Michael had obviously guessed the rest of my plan. "It's not like they can shove Lance in a suitcase and check him at the airport with their other baggage."

"Not that we aren't tempted…" Jace smiled at me from the edge of the tub.

"Okay, so you're going to need to move quickly. I assume you're not expecting Lance to simply volunteer his services."

I forced a laugh. "We're anticipating a bit more trouble than that."

"And you're prepared to use aggressive persuasion?"

I exhaled slowly and phrased my response carefully, hoping to hide my discomfort with handing a fellow werecat over for execution, even though it was my own proposed operation. "With your permission, we'll use the least amount of force necessary to get the job done."

My father's hesitation that time was brief. "Since I see no other option, you have permission. But, Faythe, have you thought this through? You're talking about taking a Pride cat from his own home, against his will. There's no way to pull that off without anyone noticing, and even if you get away clean, as soon as they figure out what happened, every tom in the Appalachian ter-

ritory will be after the three of you. And there's no way
I can get backup there in time."

"I know." I leaned my head against the back of the
tub and stared at the dingy foam ceiling tiles. "We don't
have it all figured out yet."

"And then there's the political fallout," Michael said.
Over the line, a door closed, cutting off background
noise I'd barely noticed before. The office was now off
limits to eavesdroppers, and my father and brother were
presumably the only ones in the room. "We're talking
about Parker's brother. Jerold Pierce's son. Since Blackwell's remaining neutral…" Thank goodness he was
there when Brett gave us the full scoop on his father.…
"Pierce is now the swing vote. If we turn his son over
to the Flight, we can pretty much forget about him
siding with Dad over Malone for council chair."

"But does that even matter?" My bathwater was
cooling, and I desperately wanted to warm it, but we all
needed to be able to hear one another clearly. On the
bright side, my chill bumps were helping distract me
from the agony that was my left arm. "We're talking
about civil war, Michael. The vote is moot at this point.
Whoever wins the fight will be council chair. If there's
even a council left to lead afterward." Assuming there
was anything recognizable left from our culture, once
the blood had soaked into the ground.

Michael groaned with impatience. "But who do you
think is going to win the war, if one side has more allies
than the other?"

Shit. My eyes closed as his point sank in. "Okay, so

if we turn Lance in, Pierce might throw his manpower behind Malone, which means he'll have a larger contingent than we will."

"There's no 'might' to it," Michael insisted.

"Of course there is." I rolled my eyes. Michael was ever the voice of doom, but he was only seeing half the facts. "Why would Pierce turn against us for turning Lance in, when Lance effectively sentenced our entire Pride—including both a defenseless tabby cat and his own *brother*—to death by letting Malone blame this whole thing on us? Why would he side with Lance and Malone over Parker and us? Especially considering how many fewer people will die if the thunderbirds know who really killed Finn?"

Michael started to answer, but Jace spoke up softly. "Do you really think Calvin's going to tell Pierce the truth about why we gave Lance to the Flight?"

Shit! My head was spinning with details—or maybe with blood loss—and it was getting hard to hold all the facts in my mind.

"Of course not. Malone will accuse us of trying to save ourselves by turning the thunderbirds against him. Which is exactly what *he* did to *us*." I let my head fall against the edge of the tub again, and my teeth ground together so hard my jaws ached. "But that doesn't change anything. If we turn Lance in, Pierce will fight with Malone against us. But if we don't, there won't be enough of us left to fight Malone at all. And we'll lose Kaci."

I sat up and opened my eyes, pleased to find Jace's gaze still steadily trained on mine.

"And, Daddy, I'm not willing to lose Kaci."

"That's what I was waiting to hear," my father said, and his statement carried the bold weight of finality. He sounded almost as relieved as worried. "This is a tough call, Faythe, but it's your call—yours and Marc's and Jace's—and I need you all to be sure. I think you're doing the right thing, but I'm not going to ask you to kidnap a Pride cat and deliver him to his death if you don't agree."

I hesitated, and Jace's hand wrapped around the fingers of my left hand. He squeezed gently and smiled. He had my back, no matter what. "All right. We're going to do it. Assuming Marc's with us."

"He will be," my father said. "He'll always stand with you, Faythe."

"I know." I dropped my gaze from Jace's. I couldn't help it, though his hand was still warm in mine.

"Okay, I'll cash out your plane tickets and see if there's anything I can do to help you get out of the territory once you have Lance."

"Thanks, Dad."

"Be careful and keep me updated."

"I will."

Jace ended the call, and I turned the faucet on to heat up the water.

Fifteen minutes later, my cast was soft enough to bend with my bare hand, so Jace dug up a pair of scissors from the desk in the main room. They were old, and neither sterile nor sharp, but it was either that, or gnaw the damn thing off with my own teeth.

Jace took off his shirt and tossed it onto the bedroom floor to keep it dry, then helped me turn to face the side of the tub. I propped my cast on the edge, fist to fist with my gored left arm. "I'll try not to move your arm, but your bone hasn't fully mended yet, so this might hurt," he said.

"I don't care." It couldn't hurt worse than the other one. And if it could, I didn't want to know that in advance. "Just do it."

His brows rose and one corner of his mouth quirked up. "Again, not my favorite words to hear from a naked woman."

I laughed, grateful for Jace's apparently effortless ability to break the tension. Not that he always employed that particular skill to my satisfaction… "Okay, here goes." He started at the elbow end of my cast. The lower steel blade was cold as it slid against my skin beneath the warm, soggy padding and firm-but-pliable plaster. Jace squeezed the blades together, and muscles shifted in his bare arm as he forced the dull scissors through the cast. I held my breath, waiting for pain, but he was very careful and I didn't feel a thing.

Several endless minutes later, the scissors split the last inch of plaster just below my knuckles. "Almost done." Jace slid the blade in next to my thumb for the last snip, and a second later it was all over. I wiggled my thumb while he carefully pulled my cast open through the new split down the middle. "Okay, lift your arm."

I did, again bracing myself for pain that never came, and he slid the cast gently off my hand, where the plaster was bisected but not truly splayed. "Wow. I look…wrinkly." From the water, of course. My hands and feet were wrinkly, too. Other than that, my newly exposed arm didn't look much different from the rest of me. I hadn't worn the cast long enough to get a tan line—we didn't do much sunbathing in February—and I couldn't tell from looking that it had ever been broken. Or that it might still be.

"Does it hurt?" Jace asked.

I grinned. "Not my favorite words to hear from a guy while I'm naked." I couldn't help it. We'd indulged in innocent flirtation since I was fourteen years old, and just because the "innocent" part no longer strictly applied didn't mean the habit was dead.

His blue eyes glittered as he set the wet cast on the floor. "I take it that means no?"

"Which you're obviously used to hearing from naked women…"

"Oh, now you're just playing dirty."

My grin widened, and my gaze tracked him as he leaned back to set the scissors on the counter. "I'm trying…"

Jace's fingers trailed a strand of hair down my back and into the warm water. "Watch out, or I might decide I need a bath, too."

"It would take a lot more than that to clean you up."

"Oh? What would you suggest?"

"A bar of soap for your mouth, and a sponge on a ten-foot pole for the rest of you."

"Ten feet?" Jace eyed me with a mischievous glint. "You flatter me—but not by much."

We were still laughing when the hotel door creaked open.

"Shit!" I whispered, and Jace stood so fast I thought he'd slip on the wet floor. My heart thumped so hard I swear the bathwater rippled with each beat. I hadn't heard the car pull up. Or maybe I had. Several had come and gone since Marc had left, and I'd stopped paying attention.

"Faythe?" Marc called as the door closed, and plastic crinkled when he set down whatever he'd brought from the store.

Jace stood firm in the middle of the floor, facing the main room, but his pulse raced almost as fast as mine. I twisted in the tub, and water sloshed around me. Pain shot through my evidently still-broken wrist as I grabbed a towel from the rack overhead and pulled it into the tub to cover myself. Though, I could not have rationally explained why.

Marc had seen me naked. Jace had seen me naked. Half the south-central Pride had seen me naked. And we weren't doing anything wrong. But I didn't want Marc to see me naked with Jace, because we *had* done something wrong once, and the guilt from that carried over to transform this one awkward moment into a drama the likes of which daytime television had never seen.

Because we didn't *look* like we'd done nothing wrong.

Marc's footsteps thumped slowly toward the bathroom, and I could practically smell his suspicion. Neither of us had answered him—I, for one, had no idea what to say—and he'd heard both my curse and the slosh of water. And probably our twin racing pulses.

He stepped into the doorway with my torn, discarded shirt in one fist, Jace's in the other, and rage took over his expression faster than I could form words to explain. He didn't notice that Jace still wore his pants. He didn't see the ruined cast on the floor, or the scissors on the counter.

Marc took one look at us—me naked and soaked in the tub, leaning around Jace to be seen, both of us probably looking guilty as hell—and the specks of gold in his brown eyes glittered with fury and bitter betrayal.

"What the *hell* do you think you're doing?"

Twenty-Three

"**M**arc…" I said, and his gaze flicked my way. He took in the soaked towel I clutched to my chest in spite of the pain in my left arm, and the darkness in his expression swelled until I could almost see the edges of it emanating from him like an inverse glow.

"Start talking, Faythe," he growled from the doorway.

Jace bristled. "Leave her alone. She didn't do anything wrong."

Marc dropped my shirt and his fist slammed into Jace's jaw before the material hit the floor. Jace stumbled backward into the counter, and his phone slid into the sink.

"Stop!" Water sloshed around me as I tried to push myself up with my left hand. But the pain was too much, and I dropped into the bath. More water splashed onto the floor.

Marc marched past Jace, anger roaring like flames in his eyes, and reached down for me.

"Don't touch her!" Jace rubbed his jaw, his brows drawn low, and took a deliberate step toward us. His snarl was a perfect bookend to Marc's. "You will *not* lay a hand on her until you calm down."

Marc froze. Then he straightened slowly and met Jace's gaze, looking both surprised and furious. "I would never hurt her. You know that." He reached down again to help me up, and Jace growled.

The warning was too authentic to have come from a human throat. Startled, I glanced at Jace and realized that his eyes and canines—and evidently some part of his throat—had Shifted.

Oh, shit. I could practically taste his bloodlust, likely triggered by both Marc's violence and Jace's own overwhelming need to protect me. Until we calmed him down, he would be *looking* for a reason to attack Marc.

"Stand down, Jace," Marc ordered. He kept his voice even and his hands within sight. With Jace so close to losing control—and with his teeth already Shifted—he held an obvious and dangerous advantage. If he attacked, Marc would defend himself, and there would be blood on both sides.

"Jace…" I said softly, and his cat-eyed gaze flicked my way. "Rein it in. He's just going to help me up. I need help."

"If his hand so much as twitches around your arm," Jace growled, "I'll kill him."

Fuck. The first lick of true panic made every hair on my body stand on end.

Marc's eyes went wide even as his brows dipped in

confusion. He turned slowly to look at me—because sudden movements were a *very* bad idea. "Faythe…?"

But I couldn't look away from Jace. Not until I'd talked him down. "No. Jace, you have to pull it back. I know you're trying to protect me, but that's not what I need right now. What I need is help getting out of the tub. Please. Pull it in. Shift now."

Jace glanced from me to Marc, and his focus stuck there, though he still spoke to me. "Not until he moves away."

Damn it! "Jace, *listen* to me. Marc's not going to hurt me. He's going to help me stand. I want you to reverse your Shift. Now."

Uncertainty flickered across Jace's expression. "Are you sure?"

"Yes." I nodded to punctuate my certainty. He took a deep breath, then closed his eyes—a huge show of trust on his part. Marc and I didn't move. A minute later, Jace opened his eyes, and they were human again, as were his teeth. "Thank you." I was proud of how calm I sounded.

The toms eyed each other warily. In the past three minutes, *everything* had changed between them. Jace had never stood against Marc before. Marc had never considered him a serious threat before. All that was different now, and I understood in some deep, dark part of me that there was no going back from this point. We were changed for good, the three of us.

"I'm going to help her up," Marc said, explaining himself to Jace as he would never have done before.

Jace made no reply, nor any move to stand down, but his gaze flicked to mine, his brows raised in question. I nodded and he scowled, but stepped back.

Marc exhaled slowly, obviously trying not to look too relieved. He bent to lift me, careful of the talon-shaped bruises on my arms. His eyes were full of questions, but I could only blink in reply. I had no idea what to say.

Humiliated by my own dependence and vulnerability, I flushed as I held my arms up so Marc could wrap a dry towel around me. Then I let him help me from the tub, where the water had grown cold again. He knelt to pull the plug, wariness still obvious in his every motion. "Okay. Everybody ready to discuss this rationally?"

Jace remained silent, his fists clenched at his sides, so I answered for us both. "Yes. But can we do it while you work on my arm? We don't have a lot of time."

Marc's eyes narrowed. "Why not?"

I sighed and looked over his shoulder at Jace. "Could you give us a few minutes? Maybe find a vending machine? I could really use some caffeine."

"I got Cokes," Marc said, ever helpful.

I ignored him. "Some ice, then? Please?"

Jace's normally cobalt eyes darkened almost to midnight. "You want me to leave you alone with him?"

"Why shouldn't you?" Marc bristled, and his voice took on a dangerous edge.

"Because you came in here throwing punches."

"At *you,* not at her."

I rolled my eyes. "I'm choking on testosterone here,

boys." I was also freezing. "Marc's fine now. Right?" I eyed him expectantly, and he nodded.

"But he might not be in a minute," Jace insisted, eyeing me intently. I got the message: this was as good a time as any to make our confession and get everything out in the open.

But I disagreed. Strongly. Neither of them would ever hurt me, but they would definitely hurt each other if they were both in the room when I told Marc what had happened.

"What the hell is that supposed to mean?" Marc demanded.

"Nothing." I shot Jace an angry, censoring look over Marc's shoulder. "He thinks you're on a hair trigger. Because you came in swinging." Marc started to argue— vehemently—but I cut him off. "Jace, *please* go get us some ice. And maybe I could use a little tequila, after all." To ease the pain in my arms, and smooth out the upcoming Shifts. And to settle my nerves, which felt like they were about to short-circuit, and take my brain with them.

"Fine. I'll be back in fifteen minutes." Jace snatched his shirt from the floor where Marc had dropped it, tugged it over his head in a series of angry, jerky motions, and stomped out the door. Without the car keys. Evidently there was a liquor store within walking distance of the motel—no real surprise, considering what little I'd seen of the neighborhood.

When Jace's footsteps had faded from the sidewalk, Marc crossed the room and chained the door.

I sank onto the end of the nearest bed, wishing I

could tighten the towel wrapped around my chest—or maybe dry my own hair—without exacerbating the pain in my arms. "That's only going to piss him off."

"You can see how much I care," Marc snapped. He obviously no longer felt the need to be particularly civil, now that we weren't in danger of triggering Jace's latent, lingering bloodlust.

I sighed. "Marc, please. We don't have time for this. You're truly overreacting." *This time*... My arms were killing me, but I was not going to use pain as an excuse to avoid the subject. That would be like flashing a little cleavage to get out of a traffic ticket.

"Good. What happened?"

"Nothing." I forced myself to hold his gaze. "I can't use my fucking hands, so he was helping me." *Shut up. You sound guilty when you cuss*...

"That didn't sound like helping, Faythe. Don't lie to me. What the hell happened in there?"

I took a deep breath and sent up a silent thank-you for his blessedly restrictive phrasing. "We were just flirting. Joking around, like we used to. It was nothing, Marc."

"Oh, yeah?" He snatched all three of the plastic bags from the table. "Then why is he acting like...like your fucking *mate?*" He gestured angrily toward the locked door with his free hand, since Jace wasn't there to point at. "That wasn't the reaction of a good friend. That wasn't even the reaction of some poor fool with a crush. He's acting...possessive."

"No." I shook my head. *No.* "He's not acting posses-sive, he's acting *protective.* Because you came in swinging. He's an enforcer. Part of his job is to protect me, and he thought you were going to hurt me."

"Only because he's not thinking rationally. Because he thinks you're *his*. If not up here…" Marc tapped his temple. "Then in *here*." He poked his own chest hard enough to bruise, and I flinched.

"He's always been protective of me. You all have. Hell, he stepped in front of a *bullet* for me, Marc. That's no different from this." That was true, but did nothing to assuage guilt so thick and heavy I could hardly breathe.

"The hell it isn't." He dropped the bags on the bed-spread next to me but didn't sit. "He's never tried to defend you from *me*."

"Maybe he never thought he needed to before."

Marc recoiled like I'd punched him, and shame flooded me. "I'm sorry. I didn't mean that."

Neither of us spoke for a moment, and Marc began pulling supplies from the bags. Two bottles of hydrogen peroxide, a suture kit, sterile gauze, medical tape, a new pair of jeans, a long-sleeved T-shirt, and underwear. And finally he sank onto the bed, folding the jeans while I sat with my useless hands in my lap.

"He's not right, Faythe. He hasn't been since Ethan died. He's acting possessive of the Pride tabby.…" I opened my mouth to object—he *knew* how badly I hated being referred to as such—but he spoke over me, intent on making his point. "He's resisting orders, challenging his superiors, bristling under authority.…"

Only your *orders,* you *as his superior, and your au-*

thority. Jace had exhibited none of those reactions to my father. But I couldn't say that until I was ready to say the rest of it.

"He's acting like…" Marc looked up then and laid one hand on my leg to make sure he had my full attention. "Faythe, he's acting like a challenger." He hesitated, and I knew what was coming. I shook my head vehemently, but he said it, anyway. "He can't stay. Once this is all over, Jace has to go."

"No. *No,* Marc. He has nowhere to go." *Just like you.*

"Faythe, it won't work anymore. It'll be like this—" he spread both arms to take in the whole horrible confrontation "—every day. You know it. And eventually he'll challenge."

I shook my head again, insistent. "Jace would never challenge my dad."

Marc shrugged. "Of course not. There's no reason to. When your dad feels like he's no longer what we need, he'll step down, because unlike Malone, he truly has the best interests of his Pride at heart.

"But Jace will challenge *me,* for top rank among the enforcers. In his heart, he sees himself as a contender, and he can't help it. He can't make himself submit to my authority anymore, and we can't work like that for long. He'll call me out. And I'll have to kill him."

My pulse spiked so hard the room went gray around me for a long moment. I couldn't breathe.

"That's ludicrous." I stood and walked away from him, disguising my distress as pacing, my arms swinging stiffly at my sides in spite of the pain. "This isn't the Amazon. We're a little more civilized here, in case you haven't noticed."

Marc's reflection shrugged in the grimy mirror over the cheap dresser. "All that means is that it won't be tomorrow. He'll resist as long as he can, but, Faythe, he's a serious contender now, and someday he'll challenge." He hesitated and glanced at the floor in confusion. Or maybe self-recrimination. "I can't believe I never saw this coming. Greg didn't, either—he would have told me. We never took him seriously."

"Well, it's serious now." My back to Marc, I started to lean with my hands flat against the top of the dresser, but the first bit of pressure stopped me with a shocking burst of fresh pain in both arms. "But even if you're right, you don't have to kill him."

"Faythe." Marc stood, and when I met his gaze in the mirror I saw that his eyes were swimming with sympathy. The irony of him feeling sorry for me and Jace almost made me cry. "You saw him in there." He gestured vaguely toward the bathroom. "He won't back down, and I *can't*. I can't marry you and share leadership of the Pride with you after another enforcer challenges me and wins. That would give every Alpha with a chip on his shoulder grounds to claim I'm not Alpha material."

Shit. I closed my eyes and let my head hang in alarm so profound it was almost horror. He was right. If he and Jace fought—ever, for *any* reason—only one of them would walk away. And I honestly had no idea which one would win.

I turned, desperately wishing for the use of my hands. "Can we do this now?" I held up my left arm.

Marc blinked, surprised by my sudden subject change. "He'll be back in a minute, and we're gonna have to tell him something."

"Not yet, Marc." I unlatched the door, then crossed in front of him and into the bathroom. "We have to talk to my dad first, and we don't have time to explain all this until Kaci's safe. Now, are you going to help me, or do I have to pour hydrogen peroxide on my gored arm with my broken wrist?"

Marc scowled and grabbed an armload of first-aid supplies, then followed me into the bathroom. "Fine. But we're not done talking about this."

"Talk while you sew." I sat on the closed toilet seat and leaned forward with my left arm over the sink, my broken right arm on my lap.

He transferred his supplies into one arm and laid a clean towel over the back of the toilet tank, then arranged everything on top of that. "Why the hell did you cut your cast off, anyway?"

"Because I can't Shift to heal with a cast on and you two can't fight properly while you're looking out for me. I need to be able to hold my own, and this way I can heal both arms at once." The reproach on his face expressed his disapproval more clearly than words ever could have. "Don't start. My dad already knows and he's cool with it." Mostly because there was no other option.

Marc frowned. "Do you have any idea how bad this is going to hurt?"

I rolled my eyes and stared up at him. "What am I, now, delicate? I can take it. Just do it." Marc shrugged and unsealed a squirt bottle I didn't recognize. "What's that?"

"Sterile solution, to flush the wound. Which, in your case, is half your arm." He flipped open the lid and leaned over for a better view as he squirted the first stream right into my open wound.

I hissed and gritted my teeth. "Talk to me. Please."

Marc scowled without looking up. "Honestly, you're not going to want to hear what I have to say right now, Faythe."

Ditto. I exhaled in frustration. "You know he doesn't know about any of this, right?" I swallowed a groan and looked away from my arm. "I swear Jace doesn't know. He doesn't consciously want to challenge you." For rank, anyway. Or for me, either, though I was seriously starting to doubt his claim that he was willing to share. "He doesn't understand what he's going through. He hasn't thought it out."

Neither had I.

Marc continued squirting while I tried not to squirm. "Well, that explains why none of us saw this coming. But it won't take him long to understand. I just wish I knew what flipped his switch. Ethan's death was a huge blow, but still…"

I shrugged, my heart thumping miserably. "They've been best friends since they were five. They did every-thing together. Until he died, Jace was happy to do whatever Ethan wanted. Kicking bad-guy ass, chasing skirts, and partying. But now all that's gone. Now this

Pride is his whole life, and I think he wants to give it everything he has. Even if he doesn't know that's what he's doing. And when you were missing he really stepped up and probably surprised himself. It's no surprise that he doesn't want to go back from there."

Marc made a noncommittal sound. "Do you think your dad's noticed the change in him?"

"Some of it, yeah. He sent him here, right? If Jace weren't the best for the job, my dad would have sent someone else, no matter how close he and Kaci are."

"I know." But he didn't look up from my arm until he'd worked his way to the end of the wound and capped the saline. "Okay, we're done with that part. Next comes the peroxide."

"Joy."

"This part's not optional. Unless you want to die of infection."

"I know. Just get it over with."

He unsealed a round brown bottle and unscrewed the lid, then wrapped one hand firmly around my left arm, just above the elbow, to hold it still.

I closed my eyes. He poured. Fire consumed my arm.

"Motherfucker!" I shouted. Then I ground my teeth so hard it hurt to unclench my jaw. I stared at the wallpaper, trying to count the flowers above the toilet. But I only made it to four before the flames made thought all but impossible. "Shouldn't I be unconscious for this?"

Marc laughed and poured more liquid fire into my open wound, and distantly I heard the front door open.

"Jace!" I called, when it clicked closed. "Tequila! And a sledgehammer, if you brought one."

A paper bag crinkled and Jace laughed. Thank goodness *he* was amused by my pain—and evidently in a better mood. Jace stepped into the doorway, holding up a bottle of Cuervo. His gaze flicked to Marc, who didn't look up, and anger flitted across his expression. Then he found me again and raised one brow in question.

Did you tell him?

I gave my head a short, sharp shake, then tossed my hair over one shoulder to disguise the motion. *Do you think you'd be standing there whole if I had?* It was truly not the time for our confession. Kaci couldn't afford for us to be less than focused on the job at hand.

Jace frowned. "One minute." He set the bottle down and ducked into the bedroom, then came back with a cellophane-wrapped plastic cup from the tray over the minifridge. He opened it and poured it half full, then started to hand me the cup—until we both realized I couldn't hold it. "Sorry. Here."

Jace held the cup up to my lips and I swallowed convulsively, until the flames in my throat matched those in my arm.

"Are we done yet?"

Marc shook his head and capped the first—now empty—bottle. "It's still bubbling. If we're lucky, this'll keep your arm from rotting off before we get you to the doc."

The next bottle was no better, even with two more doses of tequila and a can of Coke. But by the time he got out the suture kit, I was feeling pretty good—arm notwithstanding.

Marc threaded the wickedly curved needle, and Jace poured more alcohol. "That's enough, *zurramato!*" Marc snapped, with a glance at the plastic cup. "She can't Shift if she can't focus."

Jace ignored him and tilted the cup into my mouth. "She'll be fine by the time you're done with that," he said while I swallowed. Marc glowered, but kept his mouth shut.

We had to move into the bedroom for the stitches, and they each took one of my upper arms, because the room was tilting by then. As was the bed. I lay on top of the thin bedspread and my towel gaped open over my left hip and thigh. I started to close it, then remembered I couldn't use my arms yet. So I left it open.

No one seemed to mind.

Marc stretched my left arm out on another clean towel. I couldn't feel it by then, and was starting to wonder if he'd cut the whole damn thing off. "Faythe, I need you to hold still."

Was I moving? "And I need you not to kill him." My head rolled on the mattress and Jace slanted into view on my other side, oddly tilted, though he sat on the mattress next to me. "And *you* not to kill *him.*"

"*Damn it…*" Marc whispered. Then, "Faythe, you're drunk. Just shut up and hold still."

"Don't talk to her like that," Jace snapped, scooting closer to my head.

"How much did you give her?"

"Enough so that she won't feel much of this."

"I'm seriousss," I insisted, raising my head to look at Marc. "You guys should be friends. You have so much in *common*."

That time Jace cursed, and Marc glanced up sharply. "He's right, Faythe." Jace slid off the bed onto his knees on the floor, eyeing me from inches away. He was trying to tell me something, but his eyes didn't match his words. "Just go to sleep. When you wake up, you'll be all sewn up and ready to Shift."

I tried to go to sleep, but my arm wasn't as numb as I'd thought, and the needle hurt. "Will I be able to fight when you're done?" I asked, rolling my head to face Marc again.

"I think so. You'll just need time to rest and finish healing, even after you Shift."

Jace made an unhappy noise in the back of his throat. "She's only got three hours."

Marc frowned and looked up from the neat stitches he was sewing in a jagged line down my arm. "Why?"

"Oops." I laughed, and Marc pinned my upper arm with one hand to keep me still. "Forgot to tell him that part."

Twenty-Four

"What the hell is she talking about?" Marc demanded, glaring across me at Jace.

"Sew while you yell," I insisted, and when Marc made no move to comply, I tried to poke him with my free hand. But Jace gently forced that arm back onto the mattress, and I stopped struggling when pain shot through my still-broken wrist.

"You're going to hurt yourself, Faythe. Just hold still." He rubbed my shoulder, and Marc bristled.

"She'd be easier to reason with if you hadn't gotten her drunk," he snapped.

"She's *never* easy to reason with." Jace grinned at me. Then he met Marc's glare and his brows dipped so that their scowls matched. "I hate seeing her in pain."

"You think I like it?"

"I don't know *what* you like."

"Shut up!" I laughed and rolled my head to glance from one to the other. "I know what you *both* like."

"*Fuck!*" Jace threw his arms into the air, then eyed me desperately until Marc gripped my chin and turned my face toward him.

"What does that mean?"

I laughed again, but then suddenly I was crying, and I don't know how that happened.

"Let go of her," Jace growled. "She doesn't know what she's saying."

"Yes, I do." I jerked my chin from Marc's hand and stared up at him, wishing I could wipe the stupid tears trailing down the sides of my face. "You both like *me,* though I can't figure out why right now."

Marc relaxed, and Jace exhaled slowly in relief. What had he thought I was going to say? I was drunk, not *stupid!* "Okay, now that that's out in the open, please be quiet and let Marc finish sewing you up."

Another sharp point of pain pierced my arm with the next stitch, and I bit my lip.

"That was never exactly top secret," Marc said as the thread tugged at my flesh. "Everyone knows about Jace's little crush."

Jace went stiff on my right.

"Not *everybody...*" I was horrified to hear myself say. Had Jace given me tequila or fucking truth serum? He squeezed my elbow, desperate to shut me up, and I smiled at him in sympathy. "I know. It's the tequila." Marc glanced first at me, then at Jace in confusion. Like I wasn't making sense! "Don't you remember what happened last time I had too much tequila?"

Damn it! Okay, maybe I was drunk *and* stupid...

Marc laughed, and Jace froze, until Marc turned back to the needle. "Now, that was a hell of a night!"

Jace scowled at me, and suddenly I remembered that tequila had given them *both* a chance to get back into my…life. And with that realization, I silently vowed to keep my mouth shut until the alcohol had left my system.

Fortunately, without my own voice to keep me awake, I fell asleep in spite of the repeated, prickling pain in my left arm. Sometime later, I woke up on the hotel bed, still wrapped in the towel. My left arm was encased in sterile gauze, which gave off an unfamiliar chemical scent. My right arm was bare and stretched out across the mattress. I was grouchy, in pain, and distressingly sober.

And alone. Or so I thought until I heard the soft rumble of male voices from just outside the window, where two familiar silhouettes stood side by side. "Damn it, Jace, this is suicide. There's no way we'll make it out of the territory with Lance."

"If we don't try, we're dead. And so's Kaci. And Calvin will wind up with Faythe."

"He will, anyway, if this goes wrong," Marc growled.

Jace's shadow shrugged beyond the thin curtains. "She's willing to take that chance for Kaci. For all of us."

"Of course she is. She has no concept of her own mortality."

I rolled over and levered myself up on my right elbow, careful not to let my hand or wrist brush the bed. The towel slipped halfway down my chest.

"Yes, she does." Jace sounded mad, but he was

holding it in. "She's courageous, not careless. She just values everyone else's life more than her own. That's an Alpha trait."

"You think I don't know that?" Marc paused, and I could practically hear him counting to ten in his head. "*Maldito sea!* When this is over, we have to have a *serious* talk...."

"Hey!" I called, knowing they'd hear, and Marc would shut the hell up. Was I going to spend the rest of my life standing between them? The door opened and Jace brushed past Marc to be first through the door. I shot him an angry look. Marc wouldn't put up with much of that, whether or not Jace understood what he was going through.

"How long was I asleep?" The alarm clock read 9:34—in the morning, presumably—but I had no idea what time I'd passed out.

"Less than an hour," Marc said, and I breathed deeply in relief.

"Good. Jace filled you in on the plan?"

He frowned and sank onto the opposite side of my bed. "You mean that slow-motion suicide attempt? Yeah. I got the basics. We sneak onto Malone's property, break into the guesthouse, and somehow drag Lance out without alerting anyone else. Then we run for our lives."

I frowned. "You got a better idea?"

"Unfortunately, no."

"Then let's have a look at my arm. I need to start Shifting."

"She's gonna need food." Marc scooted closer as I

held my wrapped arm out to him. "And we should probably eat, too." He glanced up at Jace, who obviously knew what was expected of him. But Jace couldn't bring himself to volunteer.

I closed my eyes, counted to five, then met Jace's angry gaze. "Jace, will you *please* make a food run?"

He nodded stiffly. "What do you want?"

"Burgers are fine. Three for me, and some fries. And whatever you guys want."

"Bring her four." Marc shook his head at me when I started to protest. "You'll need it. And probably more. You're going to have to Shift at least half a dozen times in the next couple of hours—possibly twice that—and you'll have to eat and rest in between, or you'll pass out. Again. And even if you look healed, you probably won't be one hundred percent, which means you only fight as a last resort. Got it?"

I started to argue, then got a vivid mental image of my wrist re-cracking when I threw my first punch. Which could very well get all of us caught, and both of them killed. "I got it. Now, can we get this off? I feel like a mummy."

"I'll be right back," Jace said, and that time he grabbed the car keys before heading out the door.

Marc unwound the gauze from my arm gently, and I didn't brave a look until it was bare.

"Oh, shit!" I whispered. I looked more like Frankenstein's monster than the Mummy. *All I need now is a bolt through my neck...*

Marc rubbed my back, and I leaned into his touch.

"I'm sorry I couldn't make it…neater. Hopefully there won't be permanent muscle damage, but it's gonna scar."

Yes, it would. A long, jagged gash ran nearly the length of my left forearm, my swollen skin held together with suture thread and a prayer. When I held my arm parallel to the floor, the new wound resembled an erratic heartbeat on a hospital monitor. Or a small, blood-crusted range of mountains.

I shrugged and blinked back tears. Enforcers weren't supposed to have smooth skin, anyway, right? "Don't worry about it. I doubt Dr. Carver could have done any better. Besides, it looks bad-ass, right?" I forced a teary smile, and Marc returned it.

"Without a doubt."

"Figures, though. My most obvious scar is from falling through a fucking deer stand, instead of fighting some ferocious foe."

Marc laughed. "So we make up a story. You were defending a huddle of innocent orphans from some psycho with a broken steel pipe. He caught you across the arm, right before you kicked his ass back to his padded room." He smiled, gold specks sparkling in his eyes.

My heart melted. "I love you." I leaned forward and kissed him.

He smiled. "I know."

"I wanna Shift at least once before Jace gets back. Can you help?"

"Of course." Marc held my elbow to steady me while I sank to my knees on the rough carpet. Holding my breath, I pulled my stitched left arm to my chest and tugged the towel free. It fell to the carpet, and Marc pulled it out of the way. My arm hurt, but not like it had hurt before. Closing the wound had helped, at least a little.

Careful of my broken wrist, I brushed the fingers of my right hand gently across the new stitches. My left arm felt oddly numb, with only an echo of the pain I should have felt. And the chemical smell was stronger up close.

"What's on my arm?"

"Benzocaine," Marc said. "It's a topical anesthetic. Normally you shouldn't use it on such a large area, or on an open wound. But technically yours is closed now, and I thought Shifting might be easier this way. It dulls pain in your skin, but won't affect your muscles or movement at all."

"Thanks."

"Thank Jace. He got it from the convenience store next door."

Oh.

"Okay, I'm ready." Except that I couldn't support weight with my broken wrist. "Crap. Suggestions?"

"On your side." Marc shrugged. "It's awkward, but it'll work. I had to do that after I broke my arm a couple of years ago. Of course, I wore the cast for three weeks first…."

I stared at him in surprise. "You broke your arm?"

"Some asshole swung a two-by-four from around a corner while Vic and I were trying to corral him. You were at school."

I'd been at school for five years and had rarely called

home. And even when I had, I hadn't asked about Marc, because I hadn't wanted to encourage him. I'd thought I was done with the Pride—that I would graduate, then get a job in the human world and live a normal life.

Turns out there are several different definitions of *normal,* and now I couldn't imagine living in a world in which the daily grind included little pummeling and almost no face smashing.

"You hit him back?" I asked, and Marc grinned.

"With my other fist. Broke his jaw."

"Damn right." I smiled, and his hand found my elbow again, helping me lower myself to the ground. I lay on my right side and stared at the bathroom door as Marc backed away, giving me space.

I hadn't Shifted since the night Kevin Mitchell had broken my arm nearly two weeks earlier, so I felt more than a bit overdue. Fortunately, I hadn't yet hit the point at which not Shifting would damage my health.

I closed my eyes and let my head rest on the floor, then inhaled through my nose—and immediately regretted it. I hated Shifting indoors, and especially hated Shifting in motels. Instead of the scents of pine needles, ferns, and fresh creek water—which long-term habit had taught my body to use as signals to begin the process—I got chemical cleaning products, and all the disgusting odors they hadn't been able to kill. Cigarette smoke, stale takeout, and bodily fluids I didn't even want to imagine.

Springs creaked as Marc sank onto one of the beds, and I resisted the urge to look at him. For the first time since I could remember, I didn't want to Shift, because I knew it would hurt. And that I'd have to do it over and over again.

I'd never considered how necessary the actual desire to Shift is to the process itself, until I finally found myself faced with the lack of it. I sighed, frustrated.

"What's wrong?" Marc asked, and I answered without looking at him, trying to keep the distractions at a minimum.

"I'm truly dreading the pain. Does that make me sound like a total wimp?"

He laughed. "It makes you sound like an enforcer. No one else would even consider Shifting with a broken wrist and thirty-seven stitches in a massive gash on her other arm."

"I wish I weren't considering it, either."

"Okay, think about it like this..." Marc slid off the bed and sat beside me on the floor. He started rubbing my back, and I began to relax almost instantly. He always had that affect on me—when we weren't yelling at each other. "If you don't Shift, we can't get to Lance, and Kaci's going to die."

I stared at him in horror, waiting for the punch line that never came. He wasn't joking. "Yeah. No pressure."

Marc cringed. "Wrong approach?"

I shook my head, and my scalp scraped the carpet. "Nope, right on target."

"Good. I have another one." He was smiling now. "If you don't Shift, you don't get to kick any Appalachian Pride ass. How's that?"

"Better…" I smiled. "Say it again."

"Shift, and you get to kick the shit out of any of Malone's boys who get in your way."

My smile became a grimace of pain. The Shift had begun.

Marc backed away as the initial wave of agony rippled out from my spine and over my upper arms and legs. My limbs convulsed, and I lay on the floor in a paroxysm of pain, unable to speak. Barely able to think. I'd never Shifted on my side before, and was surprised by how much the process differed with no weight bearing down on my changing parts.

My legs retracted toward my stomach. My arms folded up to my chest, and an inarticulate, guttural sound of agony erupted from my throat.

That wasn't just Shifting pain. That was *rebuilding* pain.

My body was tearing itself apart, joint by joint, ligament by ligament, and in the process of putting itself back together—albeit in a new form—it would heal much faster than it would have without the transition. But in addition to the typical pain of the process, my broken radius was being stretched and pulled. The bones in my arms and wrists narrowed and elongated as they reformed. The pain was like nothing I'd ever felt before, including the gash in my other arm.

Evidently ten days in a cast isn't enough to heal a broken bone. *Let's hope half a dozen Shifts are….*

My teeth ground together until I forced my jaw to relax, afraid I might crack it. I tried to let the pain take over, to let the change choose its own course through me, as I'd learned to do more than a decade earlier. But the agony in my arms—particularly the right one—was unbearable, and I found myself resisting the transition in my broken wrist, while everything else went according to the usual plan.

My back arched. My ball joints cracked in and out of their sockets. I moaned as my pelvis contorted to accommodate a quadruped's stance and posture. My mouth fell open out of habit when the Shift flowed over my head, creating new bulges and hollows in my face. Repositioning my eyes for a predator's vision. I gasped as my jawbone undulated with the lengthening of my blunt human teeth into longer, deadly curved points. Hundred of tiny barbs sprouted in a wave across my tongue, arcing toward my throat, so that I could now lick a bone clean of all edible tissue.

For several minutes, my body pulled itself apart and reassembled the pieces in my new shape, but the familiar licks of pain from my joints and restructured musculature never eclipsed the acute agony in my right arm. Toward the end, the soles of my feet and the palm of my left hand thickened and bulged into paw pads. My nails lengthened and hardened into sharp claws.

But my stubborn right wrist remained mostly human. I was stalled there, and my fur would not come.

"Finish it, Faythe...." Marc murmured, careful to keep his distance. I wasn't much danger to him at the beginning of my Shift, but I now had canines and three sets of deadly claws. If I lost control and he got in the way, it wouldn't be much of a fight. "Let it come. You can't finish until you let your arm Shift."

I know! I growled, but if he understood, he showed no sign.

"Do you really want to have to throw all your punches with your southpaw? Wouldn't it be more satisfying to throw some resisting son of a bitch's head back with your right fist? You can't do that until it heals. Let it heal, Faythe."

"Rrrrrgggghhhh!" I closed my eyes, clenched my newly formed jaw, and mentally shoved the Shift into my arm.

Pain exploded in my wrist. Both halves of my bone wrenched themselves into place, and I screamed again, an inarticulate expression of sheer torture.

Distantly, I heard the door open, and a brief, thin line of sunlight slanted across my in-between form. "Shhh!" Jace whispered as he closed and locked the door. The scent of sausage washed over me, and my feline stomach growled. "Faythe, you have to hold it down, or someone's going to call the cops. You sound like you're giving birth!"

Insensitive bastard. He'd never hurt like this. He couldn't have. He hadn't Shifted until he'd had several weeks to recuperate from his broken bones.

Deep down, I knew Jace was right. Knew I was being irrational. But in that moment, I didn't give a shit. I just wanted the pain to stop.

"You're almost there," Marc said. "Just your paw. Come on…"

I sucked in a deep breath, and once again directed the Shift toward my right hand. My fingers shortened. My palm lengthened. The agony in my newly formed wrist radiated halfway up my arm.

The instant my paw formed, my skin started to itch and burn all over. Fur sprouted in a wave across my back, rippling to rapidly cover the rest of me. And finally, as a sort of Shifting coup de grâce, the uneven line of fur flowed over my front legs. The gash in my left arm burned like hell as new fur sprouted to cover my new stitches and developing scar.

Then, at last, it was over.

I lay there panting from my physiological miracle, and the guys both stared at me. Marc sat on the floor a foot away, and Jace squatted several feet from him. "Damn," he said finally, staring at me. "I can't believe she really did it."

"I can." Marc smirked. He'd never had a doubt.

"I just know how much it hurt me after six weeks." When Marc had beat the living shit out of Jace for leaving his keys for me to use to run away from the ranch. "She's had less than two." Jace crawled closer and stroked the fur and whiskers on my exposed left cheek. "You're amazing, Faythe. I don't know of anyone else who would have even tried that."

I huffed at him. Then I licked his hand.

"I agree." Marc stroked the entire length of my newly compact, powerful torso. "Now, Shift back so we can eat."

Twenty-Five

The Shift back hurt just as badly, but it went a little quicker. And when I stood—naked and fully human—I could tell little difference in my broken arm. It still hurt like hell to move, so I kept it as still as possible.

Fortunately, the gash in my left arm had closed. It was red, and swollen, and tender—still a wound; not yet a scar—but it was no longer oozing blood, and it didn't hurt quite as badly. After one more set of Shifts, Marc would remove the stitches.

As soon as I stood, I grabbed my towel and clutched it to my chest. I'd never had qualms about nudity before—Shifters have to be naked to Shift, unless they want to ruin a lot of clothes—but as we'd already established, everything had changed. Marc always had heat in his eyes when he looked at me, and I didn't want to run the risk of Jace having a repeat *reaction* in front of him. Or me.

Unfortunately, with my wrist still in serious pain—much more than when it was immobilized in the cast—

I had to let Marc rewrap me in my towel. I still couldn't eat right-handed, but that didn't stop me from devouring several sausage, egg, and cheese biscuits and two cartons of hash browns in under five minutes. It turns out hamburgers are hard to find before ten in the morning.

"What's that?" I asked around a mouthful, nodding my head toward a plastic grocery bag on the far bed.

Jace swallowed a drink from his cup. "Duct tape, for Lance. Picked it up on the way to Burger King. I also got a brace for your wrist, in case you don't have time to fully heal it." Which was a definite possibility.

"Good thinking on both." I couldn't help smiling.

"So, let's talk details." Marc took a long drink from his soda, then set it down and focused on me as I swallowed the last bite of my biscuit. "When you're whole again, we're just going to sneak in—under the cover of glaring daylight—and do a quick snatch-'n'-grab?"

Jace snorted. "You make it sound dirty. It's a covert operation, not a quickie in a public bathroom stall."

I desperately wished he hadn't said *quickie* and *bathroom* in the same sentence. Not when Marc was suspicious enough of my cast-soaking bath earlier.

"My point," Marc continued, holding a hash brown patty aloft, "is that we need to know more than the broad strokes before we go in."

As soon as he heard *broad strokes,* Jace laughed again and choked on a drink from his soda. Marc glared at him, and I shot him a frown. I wished we had time for a leisurely breakfast, peppered with stupid sex jokes, but somehow, I never seemed to find time for such simple pleasures.

"Okay, look." Jace set his biscuit down on its paper wrapper and met my gaze across the table. He was serious now, and the transition was truly something to behold. I was fascinated by the fact that he could be so like Ethan one moment—bighearted and easygoing; all carefree jokes and smart-ass-ery—then so like Marc. So dedicated, and determined, and…formidable. "I think I know how to get into Cal's guesthouse, and I think I can get Lance out without making anyone suspicious. Or not *too* suspicious, anyway."

I raised my brows, and Marc nodded for him to go on.

"Well, my mom was begging me to come home the other day. After Brett died. I said hell, no, for obvious reasons. But what if I changed my mind?" His blue eyes shone with possibility. "What if I came to town, hoping for a peaceful reunion with my mother, but I didn't want to just drop in without calling first?"

Something eased deep inside me. Some horrible tension. Some deeply rooted anxiety over our obvious and distressing lack of a plan. "Jace, that's brilliant!" I balled up my wrapper one-handed and tossed it into the trash can beside the dresser, ignoring the sting and creepy *tugging* sensation in my half-healed gash.

Marc sat in silence for a moment, obviously weighing the idea. "Do you think they'll fall for that?"

"Cal?" Jace scowled—his usual response to his stepfather's name. "Probably not. But my mother will, and if I'm here under her invitation, it's not trespassing. He has no excuse to kill me."

I stirred the ice in my cup with the straw. "At least until he can drum up some bogus charge."

"I don't plan to be around that long. I'm thinking, I'll go home, have a quick and painful reunion with my family, then find some excuse to get Lance alone long enough to knock him out and do Marc's snatch-'n'-grab." Jace grinned and Marc ignored the reference. "I might even be able to talk him into going somewhere with me willingly. In which case, we all get in on the snatch-'n'-grab. It's more fun with a group, right?"

That time his grin was all for me. And I couldn't resist shooting one back—if only because his plan was actually good. Much better than my "sneak through the woods, create a distraction, grab the guilty party, and run" idea. And Jace's was much less likely to get us caught. Or at least more likely to give us a head start. Hopefully we'd have an hour or more before anyone realized Jace and Lance were missing, rather than just late.

Finally, Marc nodded, and neither of us missed the appreciative lift of his left brow. "Okay, sounds like a plan."

We decided I should Shift into and out of cat form one more time before Jace called his mother, because there was no way to disguise the sounds of the process, and if she heard me, our ruse would be over before it had even started.

The second set of Shifts was a little easier, but only because my recent meal had given me more energy. My right arm still hurt like I was being tortured for information, but by the time I sat up again in human form, my left arm had healed to a thick but raw-looking pink scar. It would have taken several days for it to heal that far on its own.

I talked Marc into removing the stitches while Jace called his mother, to save time.

"Jace?" Patricia Malone's voice rose into the dog whistle range in surprise. Evidently her son didn't call very often.

"Yeah, Mom, it's me." Jace crossed into the bathroom and sat on the closed toilet seat but left the door open. He couldn't stop us from overhearing, but wanted at least the illusion of privacy. I could only imagine how uncomfortable that conversation must be for him.

"Are you...? What's wrong?"

Marc used a tiny pair of scissors to clip the first stitch, then tugged it from my skin with tweezers. It felt weird but didn't hurt. With any luck, I'd regained full use of my left arm.

"Nothing. Well, Brett's dead." Jace leaned forward with his elbows on his knees and stared at the bathroom wall. "Do you still want me to come home? For the funeral?"

"Of course. Will you, please? It would mean so much to...Melody."

Jace sighed, and I heard genuine reluctance in the sound. I couldn't imagine how nervous he must be. Nor could I imagine having a father figure who hated me, and openly lamented not killing me as a kitten.

"Is Cal okay with it? Did you ask him?"

"Don't be ridiculous, Jace," Patricia snapped. "I

don't need to ask him if my own son can come home. You're always welcome here. When can you come?"

Jace lifted his head and met my gaze as Marc pulled out the third stitch. I nodded, the best I could do to tell him he could back out if he wanted to. We could find another way. He shook his head; Jace was fully committed. "I'm already here."

Patricia Malone burst into relieved, overwhelmed sobs, and Jace slid one strong hand over his eyes to hide the tears he didn't want us to see. Marc busied himself with the fourth stitch, but I could tell by his determination not to look up—and by the fact that he pinched my skin along with the thread—that he was listening, too. And that he was not unaffected.

"Where?" Patricia asked, when she had herself under control. "Where are you?"

"I'm…around. I just…I wanted to make sure Cal's okay with this before I come over."

His mother clucked her tongue. "I told you he's fine with it."

"No." Jace wiped his eyes and frowned at nothing. "You didn't. I don't want to make things worse."

He was telling the truth. But he was also setting it up perfectly. Malone would be less suspicious if he knew Jace was reluctant to come in the first place. And it wouldn't hurt if he thought his stepson was afraid of him. Malone could not know what a serious threat Jace had become, or he would never let his guard down enough to let Jace leave his sight.

"You won't. Come home, Jace."

Jace hung his head, hiding most of his face behind his hand and the small phone. "I'll be there in an hour."

He sat in the bathroom for several minutes after the phone call, then he closed the door and I heard water running in the shower. And I might have heard him crying softly, though I couldn't be sure.

"He'll be fine," Marc whispered while the water ran. "He'll do his job. Better now than ever."

"I know."

Marc was working on the last zag of my massive new scar when the bathroom door finally opened. Jace stepped out in a clean change of clothes from his carry-on, wearing his business face—completely void of emotion. Which is how I knew he was both nervous and eager. And dreading every second of the most personal assignment he'd ever accepted.

"How long will it take you to get there?" I'd slept through most of the drive to the motel, so I had no clue how far we were from Malone's home base.

"About fifteen minutes."

Which meant he'd have to leave in about forty. "That's not enough time. I can't fit in enough Shifts to fully heal before then."

"I know, but I can't just pop in and ask Lance to get in the car. I have to be there a little while. Talk to my mom. Deal with Cal. Let everyone think I'm really there because of Brett."

I started to protest, but Marc was faster. "He's right. But we only have one car." He looked up from my arm, now focused on Jace. "You'll come up with another one—one without Faythe's blood in the backseat—and we'll meet you out there once she's good to go."

"We need to leave town by four-thirty to be sure we'll make it to the nest in time," I said. "That gives us an hour of padding for bathroom breaks, and that's cutting it pretty damn close."

Jace glanced at the clock. It was five minutes to noon. "We'll aim for four, for the takedown," he said, and his eyes narrowed in concern as his focus settled on me. "Can you be ready by then?"

"I sure hope so." I could think of very few things I wanted to do less than spend the next four hours Shifting with a broken arm. "Where should we meet you?"

"At the deer stand."

I frowned over what felt like too big a risk. "What if they've already found our scents there?"

"Then we're already screwed," Marc answered, and Jace nodded grimly.

I swallowed, and my throat felt thick. "Okay. So, all we need is a car."

"I saw a rental place about a quarter mile east of here," Marc said. "They had several vans and SUVs in the parking lot. You can probably get something with tinted windows and plenty of room in back."

Jace nodded. "Walking's a bit of a risk, but since everyone knows I'm coming to town now, they'll all probably stay home, waiting to see Cal's head explode. Or waiting to see him kill me."

I frowned, and Jace shook his head. "I'm kidding. He wouldn't kill me." I raised both brows, and he shrugged. "Okay, he'd *totally* kill me. But not in front of my mom. I'll stick close to her until I'm ready to head out with Lance."

"What if Lance won't go?"

Jace shrugged again. "He will. And if he tries to balk, I'll take him aside and tell him I have a private message from Parker. He'll want to hear that, either because he still gives a shit about his brother, or because he'll see Parker as a way to gather intel on the enemy."

Marc crossed both arms over his chest. "And if something goes wrong?"

Jace's jaw tightened. "Plan B. Fight hard and run like hell."

My stomach flipped and twisted. If something went wrong, we wouldn't make it out alive. I had no doubt of that. Marc and Jace would die. Kaci would die. And if I couldn't escape, I'd eventually have to make them kill me. If my choices were death or Calvin Malone, I'd choose death, hands down.

I Shifted into and out of cat form twice more before Jace left, and during my last Shift, Marc went into the bathroom and closed the door to call the car rental place while Jace was still there to watch me Shift, just in case.

After my fourth set of Shifts, the pain in my right arm had downgraded from mother*fucker*-it's-breaking-all-over-again to it-merely-hurts-like-hell. I lay naked and sweating and gasping on the floor, my eyes closed, counting my own racing heartbeats in an effort to slow them.

"You okay?" Jace knelt on the floor beside me and

ran one hand gently over my shoulder. It was a casual gesture, and one any of my fellow enforcers would have made in his position, with me lying there in obvious pain and exhaustion. But his touch raised goose bumps on my overheated skin, and my heart raced in spite of my best attempts to calm it.

"Physically? Yes. Probably. Except for the fact that I don't want to move. Ever again."

He chuckled, and his voice went deep and wistful. "You're amazing, Faythe."

I turned my head just enough so that I could peer up at him. "Says the man about to walk into the lion's den armed with nothing but hope."

"And faith." Something about the way he said it made me wonder if he'd spelled it with a *Y* in his head. "How could I be afraid to face Cal when you faced down a whole Flight of thunderbirds with nothing but a cell phone? And look what you're putting yourself through to save Kaci."

"No." I shook my head. "I got her into this. I *have* to get her back."

"You were trying to keep her away from Calvin."

"Yeah, *that* went well."

"It'll work out," he insisted, as Marc's voice echoed from the tiny bathroom while he haggled with the rental car clerk. "We'll make it."

I sat up, and he wrapped the towel around me. I was tired of wearing white cotton, but saw no use in putting on the only set of clean clothes I had, when I was just going to get sweaty all over again with the next few Shifts.

When Marc came out of the bathroom, I was seated at the table with a plastic cup of ice water. "I got you an '06 Explorer. Tinted windows. They threw in the cargo net for free."

Jace nodded. "That should work. It'll be faster than a van." He turned toward me. "I gotta go. Wish me luck."

My heart thumped in fear for him as I shoved my chair back. I crossed the room in several quick steps and went up on my toes for a hug, pinning the towel between us before it could fall off. "Please be careful," I whispered as his rough cheek brushed mine. "Ethan's death was all I can take."

"Me, too." He squeezed me so hard it hurt, but I didn't complain. Some part of me knew there was a good chance I'd never see Jace again.

I let him go and tightened my towel. Jace looked at Marc over my head, and I followed his gaze. Marc's jaw was tight, his stance tense. But his hands hung loose at his sides. He wasn't pleased by the hug, but wasn't going to deny either of us a goodbye. Not under the circumstances. Not that he could have stopped it.

"Play it smart, Hammond," Marc said at last.

Jace nodded and held his gaze. "Take care of her." Neither of them looked at me; they were too busy staring at each other, each sizing the other up. Or maybe warning him.

"You know I will. If she'll let me."

Jace gave a short laugh, then looked at me, one hand on the doorknob. "Let him."

I nodded. Then he was gone.

Tears stood in my eyes, and a huge lump had formed in my throat.

"Eat something," Marc said, and I realized I was still staring at the door.

I started to argue—I was more nauseated from exertion than hungry—then realized I'd just said I'd let him take care of me. So I sat at the table as he unwrapped another biscuit. There was no microwave, so I ate it cold, while Marc avoided my eyes from the other side of the table.

"Marc?" I asked when I was finished, wadding my wrapper awkwardly in one hand. His silence could not be good.

He finally looked up, watching me in equal parts fear, anger, and grief. "He loves you."

I closed my eyes and counted to five, then forced them open again. Made myself meet his gaze. "I know."

Marc shook his head, his brows drawn low. "I mean, he really loves you. It's not just some instinctive need to possess the tabby, now that he's coming into his potential. He's *in love* with you."

"I know." My throat wanted to close around my next breath. "Could you please stop saying it?"

"When were you going to tell me?"

My heart ached. My eyes stung with unshed tears. My throat burned from holding back words that needed to be said. "What was I supposed to say? You already knew. You beat the shit out of him for it."

"No." He stood and stomped away from me until he got to the wall, then turned abruptly, anger flashing behind the gold specks in his eyes now. "I beat the shit out of him for being careless. It's his fault Miguel got to you."

I could have argued that point all day, but we'd honestly already beat it to death, so I kept my mouth shut.

"I knew he had a crush. A stupid, little boy's crush on the unattainable. But this is different, Faythe. This is *dangerous*." He rubbed his forehead as if he was fending off a headache. "Does your dad know?" Then, before I could answer. "He knows."

I shook my head, but Marc ignored me. "That's why he sent him. Sent both of us. He knows we'd die to protect you."

"I don't want that." My tears finally overflowed, and I wiped my cheeks with my scarred left arm.

Marc watched me, and I saw the very moment when his expression went unreadable. He'd closed me out and the room was colder from his silence.

We couldn't go on like this. I had to tell him as soon as Kaci was safe—assuming we survived the next day....

Twenty-Six

The sun was warm, but the northern wind was cold and bitter, even on the short walk to the rental car. During my last Shift, Marc had scrubbed blood from my jacket so the scent wouldn't attract unwanted attention, but that left my sleeve damp and my arm cold.

As Marc drove, my thoughts raced, circling the risks we were taking like buzzards around a fresh kill. If anyone spotted us, we were dead. We were deep inside enemy territory, and both sides had long since dropped any pretense of polite politics or manners. Jace's mother seemed to be the only one still clinging to such fragile reassurances, and I think that was solely the product of her own denial. She could not believe that her husband would order one of their sons to kill the other. And if she couldn't face the truth about Brett's death, she couldn't possibly understand what Jace was risking by coming to visit.

Even if he wasn't really making a social call.

I held Marc's backpack on my lap, fingering Jace's duct tape through the thick material. I was already wearing the brace on my right wrist, and it smelled like him, just because he'd taken it out of the package for me. The rest of the car smelled like Marc, and like the unseen traces of my own blood, still lingering in the backseat.

Neither of us spoke. We'd both said so much already, and the confession I still held inside was so staggeringly awful that I could hardly grasp the consequences of voicing it. Yet keeping my secret was unbearable. It had turned to acid in my gut and was surely consuming me from the inside out.

Did Jace feel the same? He must. He'd wanted me to tell Marc all along—had been waiting on me to find the right time and place.

But there was no right time, and certainly no right place. As badly as it hurt to keep quiet, I was starting to believe that we could never tell Marc what had happened. Not because he might leave me. Not because he'd probably hate me. Not even because of what it would do to the Pride.

If I told Marc, he and Jace would fight, and one of them would die.

My mind refused to move beyond that certainty. I couldn't entertain the idea of an "after," and wasn't even sure there would be one. So the Confession remained a hulking, dark cloud on my mind's horizon, a distant goal I was afraid I might never actually meet.

When we turned onto the old country road we'd

traveled the night before, Marc turned on the radio rather than speak to me. I shrugged out of my jacket and took off my brace, then stared out the window while I concentrated on Shifting just my right arm.

In the motel, I'd Shifted into and out of human form four times, for a total of eight transformations. The first four were the most physically painful experiences I'd ever had in my life, but after that, the pain began to ebb until—with the last one—Shifting almost felt normal again.

The gash in my left arm was completely healed, and the long, jagged ridge of a scar could easily have been a month old. There was no more pain, and I had regained all muscle control, except for an annoying— and hopefully inconsequential—weakness in my pinkie finger. It stuck out just a bit now, when I formed a fist, but didn't seem to hinder normal activity. That had been my biggest fear—the possible loss of function or flex-ibility in my left hand—and that had seemed likely in the beginning, when I couldn't make my fingers obey orders from my brain. But in the end, I was both grate-ful and relieved to have avoided catastrophe. No pun intended.

My right arm was another story. After eight Shifts, it no longer hurt to move my hand and I had regained most of the flexibility in my wrist. But the injury still felt very tender, and I was afraid that overuse—or even short-term stringent use—could lead to further, and possibly permanent, damage.

"What are you doing?" Marc glanced at my arm,

and his question broke into my concentration. My palm shortened and my fingers lengthened. Fur never got the chance to sprout.

"Just trying to be ready." I couldn't shake the feeling that something would go wrong on Jace's end, and if that happened, we all needed to be able to fight.

Marc sighed, and I had the overwhelming urge to touch his jaw. He hadn't shaved in a couple of days, and the stubble on his face had bypassed the painful, scratchy phase and slid right into soft-and-sexy. "Let's just forget about it for now, okay?" he said, and I realized we were talking about Jace again. About our little problem, and the desperate need for some kind of a resolution. Of the sort that wouldn't get anybody killed. Or even dumped, preferably.

"Okay," I agreed, because there was really no other option.

Marc nodded decisively. "We'll shovel his emotional shit after this is all over. For now, let's just focus on getting the job done. That's the only way we're going to be able to concentrate. Right?"

"Right." I'd become a parrot. I almost asked Polly for a cracker.

"I know this can't be easy for you, either," Marc conceded, and his reasonable tone made me want to cry. "He's put you in a tough position. Put all of us there, really. Not that he meant to…"

"I thought we weren't going to talk about it."

"Yeah." Marc linked his fingers through mine on the center console. "Sorry."

At not quite three in the afternoon, Marc parked the rented SUV on an overgrown dirt trail that ended several hundred feet into the woods, about a quarter-mile from where we'd parked the night before.

"Maybe we should Shift." I stepped onto the forest floor and my hiking boots crunched into several small pinecones. "If this goes bad, we're going to need claws."

Marc shook his head, then drained the last of his coffee, watching me from the other side of the vehicle. "You need to conserve your energy, and you should try to keep your weight off that wrist until it's fully healed. Besides, if nothing goes wrong, Jace may need extra hands to help with Lance."

"Okay, you Shift and I'll stay like this. Best of both worlds."

He couldn't argue with that. Marc stripped and handed me his clothes, then dropped to his knees in the fallen pine needles. I dug in his pants pocket for the rental keys, then stuffed his clothes into the backpack he'd stocked with bottles of water and snack bars, and locked up the car.

When he'd Shifted, Marc rubbed the entire length of his body against my leg, and I let my hand trail through his fur, all the way to the tip of his tail. He purred noisily, then walked off into the woods, expecting me to follow.

"Wait. We're early. Let's take a peek at the compound before we head to the deer stand." Though, the term *compound* was a bit flattering for Malone's collection of buildings.

Marc shook his head firmly and kept walking.

"We won't get caught. I just want to get close enough to make sure he's not in any trouble. I need your eyes and ears. Come on."

Marc refused to turn back, so I headed west without him. Before I could count to five, he huffed, then jogged after me so silently I never would have known he was there, if I hadn't been listening for him. Pine needles don't crunch like dead leaves.

Marc whined when he came even with me, and I understood the gist, if not the specifics. "I'll be careful. And thank you. I feel horrible sending him in there alone, with no backup. That's not how we work."

After that, we hiked in silence, out of caution this time, rather than discomfort. I scratched his head and ran my fingers down his back whenever the opportunity presented itself, and he rubbed against me almost as often. It was a much more pleasant silence than the one in the car.

We'd gone less than a mile and a half when Marc went suddenly still but for his ears, which swiveled toward the north. I froze, following his lead, though I couldn't yet hear whatever had put him on alert.

He tossed his head in the direction his ears were pointing, and we headed that way, slowly, to be sure we didn't make any noise. We'd only gone a couple hundred feet when the afternoon quiet was shattered by the unmistakable thunk of a shovel into soil, followed immediately by the dull thud of dirt being tossed to the ground.

I knew those sounds. Hell, I'd *made* those sounds. Someone was digging a hole. Never a good sign.

I started to move forward again and Marc stepped in front of me, blocking my path—a clear order for me to stay back. "Like hell," I whispered, and pushed him firmly out of the way. But before I could take the next step, a voice carried through the woods, on the tail of another clod of earth hitting the ground.

"That's deep enough. It's not like the fucker's going to dig himself up."

"Cal said six feet," a second, much deeper voice replied, and I didn't recognize either tom. Malone had hired new enforcers.

"He'll never know," the first voice said, and Marc took a careful, silent step forward. "It's not like he's gonna come out and bury the body himself."

"If he does come out here, you'll be the next one in the ground, Jess," Deep Throat said.

I followed Marc, careful to step where he had and watch for twigs and pinecones, which would crunch and give us away. Who the hell were they burying? Not Brett. Surely his mother would demand a proper funeral for her second born.

"I don't get why he keeps killing his own boys," Jess said, and metal clanked, like he'd dropped his shovel on top of something.

Malone had killed another of his sons? *Not Alex.* He was too loyal to his father. Like some kind of wind-up soldier, marching without any thought for the orders he carried out.

Marc was a full body length ahead of me now, but I was still moving forward, my attention split between the overheard conversation and every element of nature with the potential to make noise beneath my foot. It was sooo much easier to be stealthy in cat form.

"Jace isn't his," Deep Throat said, and I froze with one foot still in the air.

Noooo. Pain shot through my chest, constricting it, as if my heart no longer had room to beat. I couldn't breathe. Couldn't see beyond consuming pain and denial.

"He's Patti's, from her first husband," Deep Throat continued as my eyes closed, denying tears an exit. Crying wouldn't help. Anger would. "Jason Hammond."

"What happened to him? Cal get him, too?"

Marc's tail twitched, recapturing my attention, and I realized I hadn't moved since I'd heard Jace's name.

They'd killed Jace.

A storm of rage rolled over me, drenching me with hatred. I'd kill every bastard involved. Including Calvin Malone.

"Nah," Deep Throat said as I inched forward, rage racing through my veins, hotter than blood, more potent than adrenaline. "He went out after a stray with his enforcers and got killed on the job. Cal was there. He had to tell Patti."

Malone had been one of Jace's dad's enforcers? If that was true, what were the chances that Jason Hammond's accident was really an accident?

Jess huffed. "Hammond must have been an idiot, just like his kid. Like anyone believes Jace is here for the funeral. Cal's right—he's a fucking spy."

Wait! Jace *is* here for the funeral? Did that mean Jace was still alive?

I took careful steps until I reached Marc, then reached out to squeeze his shoulder. He nodded. He'd caught it, too.

"What's Cal gonna tell Patti? She's upset, but she's not stupid. She's gonna notice another son dying, and coincidence ain't gonna cover it."

There was a flash of motion between the branches, then the crack of plastic as Deep Throat opened what sounded like a bottle of water. "Jace won't die. He'll disappear, and she'll assume he went back to his Pride." We inched forward more and were now close enough to hear him gulp from his bottle. "Let's go," Deep Throat said, and I caught another glimpse of movement between two thick pines. I ducked, hoping he hadn't seen us. Deep Throat was a short, thickly muscled tom in his early thirties. "If we hurry, we can still watch. They won't be able to do it until they get him away from Patti."

Something else thunked to the ground, and Marc glanced up at me. I nodded and held up three fingers, then dropped the third, beginning a silent countdown.

Jess and his partner came into full view between two trees. Jess was taller and well built, like most enforcers, but not as thick as Deep Throat, who drank from his water bottle as they walked.

Marc's tail twitched silently. I dropped the second finger.

My pulse tripped in anticipation. I dropped the last finger.

My heart beat once more. Then I leaped between the trees.

Marc landed first, two feet from the shorter, thicker tom. Both men spun around, and Deep Throat dropped his bottle in surprise. Marc was on him in an instant.

I swung my left fist the moment I landed. My blow landed on Jess's jaw. His head snapped back. I swung lower, and buried my fist in his gut.

Jess grunted, but his return punch flew fast and low. His fist slammed into the left side of my rib cage. My breath burst from my throat and my feet actually left the ground.

I landed on my ass in a pile of pine needles. Jess dropped on top of me. I threw another left into his ribs. His next blow hit the side of my head, and everything went hazy. Color faded. His face blurred over mine. I shoved against his chest with my good arm, but Jess only laughed. "Well, who the hell are you?"

My head swam, then rolled to the side. Marc was there, his tail swishing furiously several feet away. But he couldn't see me; he was backing the big guy into a tree. I was on my own.

"What's your name, pretty puss?" Jess leered down at me, pinning me with his full weight on my hips and restricting my chest.

Move! I commanded my arms, but they were slow, the message from my brain sluggish.

"You idiot, that's Faythe Sanders," Deep Throat said, and Marc's growl deepened. Pine needles whispered, stirred by the furious sweep of his tail. "Who else could it be?"

Ha! I had a reputation. *Which you'll lose pretty damn quickly if you don't get your* ass *off the* ground!

"Get off," I whispered, with what little breath I'd regained. When Jess laughed again, I sucked in more air. "Get the *fuck* off me!"

"Nasty words from such a pretty mouth." Jess ran one finger over my lower lip and I swung at him, left-handed. My fist slammed into his ribs, and he grunted again. His smile disappeared. He caught my fist in midair and yanked it over my head, while I pulled against him. My right fist followed, and the brace was little help. Pain shot through my arm when I tried to jerk it free. A second later, both my wrists were pinned to the ground in his left fist.

Marc's growl grew louder, but Jess ignored him and glanced over his shoulder at his partner. "I must have done something right in another life—now the universe is throwin' women at me." His free hand trailed up my waist and over my left breast.

"Touch me again and I'll break your fucking face," I spat, adrenaline singeing every nerve ending in my body.

Pine needles rustled to my right, and Deep Throat groaned. "Shit, Jess, Calvin has plans for her, and they do *not* include your bastard kittens. Knock her out and give me a hand here."

Jess frowned, and his thumb rubbed over my nipple.

"You fucking bastard," I spat. Fury roared through me, and with my next blink, my vision Shifted. The forest faded into muted tones of green and brown, but Jess didn't notice. He laughed again and leaned to the right, reaching for something. When he rose from my hips, I threw my right knee up as hard as I could. My kneecap slammed through soft tissue and into the bone beneath.

Jess howled and fell over sideways, clutching his ruined parts and shouting an inventive stream of profanity.

I rolled onto my knees, then leaped to my feet. I pulled my right leg back, then let it fly. My foot slammed into Jess's temple. His eyes fluttered shut, and his head rolled to the side. His hands fell from his crotch to lie limp and half-curled on the ground.

I spared a moment to make sure he was still breathing, then turned toward Marc and the thick tom he had backed into the boughs of a broad pine tree. I stalked toward him, feeling more feline than human with my cat's eyes. "What's your name?" I asked, and was surprised to hear my voice come out as a half growl. Evidently more than my eyes had Shifted.

I ran my tongue over my front teeth and discovered they had Shifted, too. *Convenient.* And I'd barely felt it that time.

Marc's prey remained silent.

I dropped into a nimble squat and picked up a large branch with my left hand. The ground was littered with them, probably casualties of the recent ice storm. When I rose, Deep Throat's gaze followed me. "Last chance. Who the hell are you?"

His focus shifted from me to Marc—who growled— then back to me. But his mouth remained closed.

I shrugged. "Your choice." I swung the branch at his shoulder with both hands, my left arm carrying most of the force. Deep Throat brought his arm up in self-defense. The thick end of the branch slammed into his forearm hard enough to smash the stick. And his ulna.

The tom screamed once, then cut the sound off with a display of willpower I couldn't help but admire. His arm swelled almost instantly. I swallowed my horror and observed the damage with a buffer of detachment. His arm looked…bent. And not at the joint.

"Your name," I said calmly, while he stared at me in growing fear and anger.

"Gary Rogers."

Good boy. He gave up both names at once.

"Gary, is Jace still alive?"

"I don't know," he said. I knelt to pick up another thick branch, and he rushed on. "Really. They're waiting until his mom's out of earshot. He may still be okay."

"Where is he?"

Gary shrugged. "He could be anywhere." I lifted the new branch. "But Cal won't let him sleep in the main house. He's probably in the back outbuilding."

"Thank you, Gary." I lifted the limb and swung before he could protest. The branch slammed into his head. Gary crumpled to the ground.

I glanced at Marc and dropped the branch. "Let me tape them up, then we'll go." We couldn't afford for them to wake up and alert the rest of their Pride, and I wasn't going to kill either of them now that they were no longer an immediate threat.

Marc's backpack lay on the ground where I'd dropped it during my leap into the clearing, and I dug through it for the duct tape. Marc kept watch over Jess while I taped Gary's mouth and bound his ankles, moving awkwardly to spare my right wrist. Then I rolled him over and taped his wrists behind his back, taking no particular care with his broken arm.

Jess got the same treatment, but when I stood to stuff the tape back into the bag, Marc nudged the unconscious tom with his nose and whined.

"He's out cold," I said, zipping the bag. "Let's go."

But Marc only sniffed Jess's hands, then looked up and pointed his muzzle at my chest.

I rolled my eyes, finally understanding the question. "Yeah, the bastard groped me. But I broke his balls. I'd say we're even."

Marc shook his head and continued to sniff the tom's hands, then whined at me some more.

I exhaled slowly, dread sinking through me at his insistence. He wouldn't leave until I'd said it. "Right thumb to left nipple. But he's paid for—"

Marc shook his head again, then bent with his mouth open. An instant later, something snapped, and the scent of fresh blood flooded the clearing. Jess's body shuddered and his eyes flew open, then he began to thrash and moan behind the duct tape gag.

Marc backed away and something small and crimson fell from his mouth onto a bed of pine needles, now stained with blood. He ran his barbed tongue over first one side of his muzzle then the other to clean it, looking perversely satisfied. I glanced at Jess's hands, and nausea rolled over me.

His right hand was pouring blood from the gory stump that had once been his thumb.

Twenty-Seven

Before we left the clearing, I bandaged Jess's thumb with a torn strip of his shirt and some duct tape and patted down both toms for anything useful. I took a folding knife from Gary, then pulled both toms' cell phones from their respective pockets and checked their text messages. Gary had none. If he'd ever sent a text, I found no sign of it. I dropped his phone on the ground and stomped it to pieces, so it couldn't be used against us when he woke up.

Jess, on the other hand, obviously had an unlimited texting plan. Kind of funny, considering he'd now be texting one-handed.

Marc whined in question as I typed, ignoring the residual pain in my right wrist. At least I still had both thumbs. "He has a bunch of texts from Lance. I'm asking if they've taken care of Jace yet."

The reply came an instant later. Not yet. Soon.

I read it to Marc, then typed some more. Still digging. Wait for us.

Lance's second response came just as quickly. No promises…

"He's still alive, but not for long. Come on." I slid Jess's phone into my left hip pocket and started off through the woods with Marc at my back. We moved as quietly as possible, but neither heard nor smelled any other Appalachian Pride members. A mile and a half from Jace's premature grave, the sound of a car engine warned us that we were getting close to the house.

We slowed and veered toward the growl of the engine as it first idled, then died. Minutes later, the evergreen foliage began to thin, and a simple, black-shingled roofline came into view.

"There it is," I whispered, dropping into a crouch as Marc came to a silent stop beside me. A few shuffled steps later, the compound came into view. And *compound* was really the only word to describe Malone's property.

I knew from what little Jace had said about his childhood that when his father was alive, his Pride's enforcers had lived in a converted barn behind the main house. But after Malone's ascension to Alpha status, the barn had fallen into shameless disrepair and had to be torn down eight years later. Since money was tight in the territory, to replace the barn Malone had brought in two used doublewide mobile homes and had them set permanently into the ground and bricked up to the bottom of the windows.

The result was definitely nontraditional, and I'd heard people openly question the longevity of the housing arrangement. But the advantage to us was obvious. The back outbuilding was almost completely shielded from the main house by the middle one. If Jace was in the last one, we might just be able to get to him without alerting the rest of the Pride.

From where we stood near the tree line, we could see all three buildings from the side. "We should approach from directly behind the back building," I whispered, then glanced up to find that Marc was already on the move. I rushed after him, careful to avoid anything that could crunch beneath my boots, and we hiked a quarter of the way around the property.

The middle building had almost disappeared behind the rear trailer when hinges squealed suddenly, then a door slammed shut. I froze, Marc at my side.

"...just thought you might want to make something special tonight. You know, since Jace is home."

"Well, I hadn't really thought about it, but he always did like homemade stew. And maybe I could make some potato bread to go with it."

My heart ached at the familiar voice. Patricia Malone. A moment later, she appeared between the last two buildings, heading toward the side yard of the main house. She was facing away from us, but even from behind I could see that she was thinner than I remembered, her brown hair now streaked with gray.

Alex Malone guided her gently but firmly by one arm, encouraging her and making suggestions for Jace's homecoming dinner.

"Shit. They got rid of Patti," I whispered, and Marc

whined. We watched as the Malones circled the middle building and disappeared from sight, veering toward the back door of the main house. "Let's go."

From the edge of the woods at the back of the property, we could see through the windows of the last building. Unfortunately, two of them were covered by threadbare but mostly opaque curtains, and a third was a total blind spot, thanks to a set of plain white mini-blinds. But two others were uncovered, and by some stroke of luck, one looked into the kitchen, the other into the living room.

I was starting to wish we'd brought binoculars when a blur of movement drew my focus to the larger of the two windows, and I saw Jace sink onto the couch in the living room. He looked exhausted, and tense, and nervous.

I pulled my own phone from my right hip pocket and started typing again. Marc glanced over my shoulder, reading along.

They think U R a spy. We're out back. Can C U thru window.

I sent the message, and an instant later, Jace sat straighter on the couch and leaned forward to pull his phone from his back pocket. He flipped it open and went stiff—which is exactly why I hadn't texted Jace earlier. I didn't want his reaction to give us away before we were close enough to help.

But then Jace's posture relaxed, and he flipped his phone closed without glancing toward the window. Playing it cool. He said something to someone across the room, and though I couldn't read his lips from that distance—probably couldn't have, anyway—whatever he said evidently raised no suspicions in whoever else was in the room.

Jace leaned forward and drank from a can on the table, then said something else to someone we couldn't see. And when no one attacked him in the next two minutes, my attention began to wander. "Look." I pointed, and Marc's gaze followed my finger toward the four cars lined up side by side next to the last building. Jace's was third, but I didn't recognize the others.

There were probably several more parked in front of the main building, but while there was nothing I could do about those without getting caught, I might be able to disable the other three with minimal risk.

Marc's nose nudged my arm as I dug through the backpack for Gary's folding knife. "I'll be right back," I whispered as my hand closed around the cold steel. I set the bag on the ground next to Marc and flipped open the blade as he began to growl softly, warning me not to do anything stupid.

"I'm just going to give us a head start," I whispered. "Stay here. I'll be right back."

Marc's growl rose as I started forward, then transitioned to an angry whine when I broke through the tree line and ran hunched over toward the first car. But he didn't follow. As worried as he was about me taking a risk, he knew that if I was caught, I wouldn't be hurt, but I'd need him to help get me and Jace out. And that if Marc got caught, too, we'd all be screwed.

My pulse raced along with my legs as I crossed the

thirty feet from the woods to the first car. Breathing heavily—more from nerves than from exertion—I slid to the ground with my back against the side of the first car and waited for several heartbeats to see if I'd been spotted. The gravel was sharp and frigid through my jeans, the breeze stinging cold on my cheeks. The engine clicked at my back as it cooled. This was the car that had led us to the property.

When no one shouted or came outside after twenty seconds, I rose onto my knees and shoved the blade of Gary's knife into the wall of the front right tire. Then I pulled it out and made a second cut over the first, to form an X. Air hissed out of the rubber, and I flinched. My bright idea sounded very loud in the near silence.

Adrenaline pumping, I scrambled to the rear of the car and slashed another tire, then moved quickly toward the woods again and cut the front left tire on my way to the next in line. I skipped over Jace's rental and went on to disable the other two cars as quickly and quietly as possible. When I finished, I sat less than two feet from the end of the last outbuilding. Twenty feet from the back steps.

I stared at the woods, heart thumping, my nose numb and dripping from the cold. Marc was nowhere in sight, but I knew he was watching me. Waiting. I glanced at the steps, then craned my neck to see the window overhead and five feet away. I could get inside if Jace needed me. Together we could take care of whoever else was with him and knock Lance out, then carry him right out the back door and into the forest.

But what if Lance wasn't in there? Maybe that's why Jace hadn't made his move yet. If I went in and Lance wasn't there, the whole thing would be ruined.

Marc would tell me to wait. To get back into the woods with him and watch and listen. My father would say the same thing.

So I would wait.

Half-frozen, I squatted in the gravel, then ran hunched over past the first two cars. I was about to break for the rental car when footsteps thumped rapidly behind me. Someone was running, coming around the first outbuilding from the direction of the main house.

I dropped onto my knees in the gravel and for one anxious moment was sure that the crunch of my landing had given me away. Then I realized rocks were *still* crunching. The footsteps were coming from the gravel drive now and had covered my own noise.

My pulse thudding in my ears, I rose carefully and peered around the front of the second car just in time to see Alex Malone pass behind the row of vehicles, headed for the front of the last outbuilding. His jaw was firmly set, his mouth a straight, grim line. He was a man on a mission.

He'd come to kill Jace.

Shit. Hinges squealed, then the front door of the trailer thumped closed. I whirled on the gravel to face Marc, my back against the front bumper of the rental car. Glad none of the windows faced the row of cars, I waved one hand frantically. I couldn't tell if Marc saw me, but I was sure he'd heard Alex approach; his cat ears were much better than my human ones.

Hoping he was still watching, I pointed toward the back door of the trailer in an exaggerated motion, then walked hunched over in front of the first two cars until I reached the corner of the building. Now out of sight from the rest of the compound, I stood against the wall, scanning for any sign of Marc in the woods as I listened to the muffled voices from the trailer at my back.

The windows were all closed against the winter chill, and while that had worked in my favor while I was crunching on gravel, closed windows were a definite inconvenience for eavesdropping. Desperate for information, I inched my way along the wall, the brick ledge catching on my jacket, and the indistinct voices inside grew clearer with each step. I stopped next to the first uncovered window, my heart beating a frantic, staccato rhythm against my breastbone.

"…how stupid do you think we are?" Alex demanded, and my racing pulse pumped blood through my body so quickly my cat vision started to go dark around the edges.

Jace's response was too low and calm for me to make out, and I was suddenly glad I'd texted him. Otherwise, he would've been caught off guard by his half brother's accusation.

"Mom may believe that, but I'm not quite so…gullible. You didn't really think you could come spying for Sanders, then walk out of here with your face intact? Or, alive."

"Alex…?" Jace sounded wary, then there was a solid thump behind my head as something crashed into the wall. Jace groaned.

"Pick him up," Alex ordered.

Adrenaline spiked in my veins. That was my cue.

I glanced toward the tree line just as Marc stepped out of the woods, and I held out one palm, begging him silently to wait. If I could get Jace out without revealing Marc's presence, I would. Besides, we stood a better chance with him as surprise backup—if they didn't know he was there, they couldn't defend themselves against him.

Marc shook his head, and though I couldn't hear it, I was sure he was growling softly. Insistent, I waved him off again, and finally he nodded. But I knew that at the first sign—or sound—of trouble, he'd be at my back.

I was counting on it.

Still clutching the folding knife, I raced up the steps and threw open the back door, then stepped into a small kitchen walled with cabinets.

In the adjoining living room, Alex gaped at me in surprise, a hammer held high, ready to deliver a blow. Jace was on his knees on the worn carpet, his wrists bound at his back, the right side of his head swollen and turning purple. His eyes were unfocused, and he didn't seem to know I was there. In the second Alex spent in shock, Jace began to tilt to the right like a felled tree. He would have fallen over if not for the grip Lance had on his arm from behind.

It took me half a second to absorb what I saw. Then I dropped the knife on the countertop and launched myself across the kitchen. I vaulted off the end of the short bar with both hands, but my left arm took the brunt of my weight, so I flew crooked. As I swung into the living room, my right foot slammed into the side of Lance's head instead of his arm. He splayed across the couch, out cold.

Startled, Alex leaped back, and the hammer-wielding arm fell to his side.

"Jace?" I knelt by him, one eye on Alex, suddenly wishing I'd kept the knife. Jace's head was swollen from his ear all the way into his hairline, and his skin was darkening by the second. I couldn't tell if he had any cracked bones, but he'd been knocked silly. Almost unconscious.

He started to fall over again, and I lowered him onto his rump against an armchair—not an easy task with his ankles taped—hoping he'd come back to himself quickly. If he'd been hit with the hammer, his skull would have been caved in rather than merely bruised. So he must have been punched. Or kicked. Either way, he'd be fine.

He had to be.

I stood slowly, facing Alex and his hammer with nothing but my fists. Make that one fist—pain was shooting through my right wrist again, thanks to my vault off the countertop. "He's not spying, Alex." I tried to sound calm and confident, but I was unarmed and in enemy territory.

"Yeah, and you're proof of that, right?" Alex sneered. "That he's not spying for your dad?"

"I'm here for moral support." I stepped to the side, drawing his focus from Jace as I edged my way closer to the knife I'd left on the countertop. "He didn't want to come here alone. In case *this* happened." I gestured to the entire room with my right arm, glad my jacket hid my wrist brace, concealing my weakness.

"And you were what? Hiding in his trunk?"

But before I could answer, Jace stirred on my right, gingerly rubbing his head. "Faythe? What the hell are you doing here?"

Great. There went my half-assed cover story.

"Rescuing you," I hissed, shivering in the draft from the open back door.

Alex laughed and gestured with the hammer. "And doing a fine job of it. Now, if you'll sit pretty while I call my dad, I promise we won't hurt you. My father's going to be almost as happy to see you as I am."

I raised one brow. "Why don't *you* sit down and shut up, and I'll promise not to kick your face in on my way out the door?"

Alex's gaze flicked to my left. I turned as a blur of motion raced toward me from an open doorway. I barely had time to gasp. Pain gripped my neck, squeezing. My body slammed into the wall. Fresh pain shot down my spine and whipped around my head. Air exploded from my lungs in one violent rush.

I couldn't breathe past the hand tightening around my throat, pinning me to the wall. My feet dangled above the floor. My head spun. The blurred face in front of me wouldn't come into focus. Without air, I couldn't identify my attacker's scent.

I clawed at the hand, raking it with my nails. My

mouth sucked uselessly at the air. I kicked aimlessly, my boots slamming into his legs over and over, to no avail. My blurry vision darkened. My throat felt thick and useless. My ears rang. The pressure in my head made it feel huge.

"Hey, Faythe, good to see you again." The voice was vaguely familiar, and the sour mental aftertaste called forth unfocused memories of pain and anger. I rolled my eyes upward and forced them to focus on the towhead whose huge hand squeezed my throat.

I knew him. *How* did I know him? Without more oxygen, I couldn't place his face or remember his name.

"Damn it, Dean, let her breathe," Alex swore. "That's my future wife you're choking."

The hand around my throat loosened, and I sucked in several short, sharp breaths. But I still dangled above the floor from his grip on my neck. I still clawed at his fingers, trying to pry them from my throat. "She's not yours yet...." Dean leered down at me, and his gaze landed south of my neck. He could see right down my shirt.

"Not. Ever," I gasped, struggling to open my mouth in spite of the pressure his grip put on my jaw.

"Anyway, I think this particular puss is more than you can handle," Dean continued, still looking me in the chest. "She throws a hell of a left hook."

And suddenly I remembered. Tall goon with white-blond hair and more muscles than brains. *Colin Dean.* The idiot Canadian import I'd knocked out in order to save Brett Malone in Montana during my trial.

"Put her down," Alex growled. Dean shrugged, then

lowered me to the floor, his hand still around my neck. Still pinning me to the wall, though my fingers pried at his.

I threw my right knee up, but he blocked it easily with his free hand. "You're going to make me get rough, aren't you?" The gleam in his eyes said that's exactly what he wanted.

"You. Work. For. Malone?" I gasped.

Dean grinned. "For about a month now."

Malone was recruiting from outside the country. The bastard was drawing neutral parties into our civil war. That could *not* end well.

"Let her go," Jace ordered from the floor where he'd fallen, on the lower edge of my vision. His eyes were clear; he was back with us, thank goodness. But where the hell was Marc?

Dean laughed without turning, and Jace growled until Alex kicked him in the ribs. Jace grunted and tried to curl around his new injury, but with his limbs bound, the best he could do was pull his knees up as far as they'd go.

I tried to yell for him to leave Jace alone, but my effort ended in strangled coughing. I wasn't pulling in enough air to shout.

"Let the poor girl breathe," Alex ordered, and Dean's grip loosened a little more. His blood was sticky beneath my nails, the scent fragrant, now that I could inhale properly.

But I only had eyes for Alex. "You touch him again, and I'll kill you," I swore, still trying to dislodge Dean's grip.

Alex's brows shot up. "You'd kill me over *Jace?*" He stepped closer to me, and Jace growled again. Alex glanced from me to him, then back to me, and when I flushed, his eyes narrowed in sudden understanding. He knelt and jerked his brother's head back with a handful of hair, then leaned down to stage-whisper in his ear. "Are you *fucking* my future wife?"

Jace's jaws bulged with fury, but he could only writhe uselessly without the use of his hands or feet. I struggled harder against Dean, kicking and clawing, but kept my mouth shut for fear of incriminating myself. Marc was probably right outside, waiting for the best time to lunge through the open door.

Alex glanced up at me. "I don't think this is what they mean by 'all in the family.'" He turned back to Jace. "You know I'd kill your bastard kitten while it's still bloody, right? Just like my dad should have killed you. Guess the honor's all mine now…" Alex pulled the hammer over his head with both hands.

"No!" I let go of Dean's hand and slammed my left fist into his ribs. He grunted and blinked, then pinned my arm to the wall over my head with his free hand. "Alex, no! Please," I begged, blinking desperate tears from my eyes so I could focus on him.

Alex glanced at me. Something moved at his feet. I looked down to see Jace's right hand whip out from behind his back. He grabbed his brother's ankle and pulled.

Alex hit the floor hard, stunned. Jace rolled onto his knees and leaned over Lance, who still lay on his left. He straightened an instant later with a folded pocketknife in his hand. Alex swung up with the hammer. Jace blocked his brother's forearm. The hammer thudded to the floor.

Metal clicked. Jace twisted around behind his brother, still squatting. He pressed the knife to Alex's throat, and Alex froze. "Get up slowly," he whispered, and they stood in tandem.

Jace's left hand was now a fur-covered paw. He'd cut through the duct tape with his dew claw, a technique I'd discovered just two weeks earlier.

Alex stood with his hands loose at his sides, eyes wide and angry. One flick of Jace's knife and he'd be dead. Jace pulled his brother to the side, and we could all see one another.

"Let her go or I'll kill him," Jace said, and my pulse thumped against the hand at my throat. He'd do it. I could see that in his eyes.

"Let *him* go," Dean countered. "Or I'll kill *her.*" He could break my neck with one squeeze of his huge fist.

"You kill her and Cal will hang your bones from the porch for a wind chime. If Alex doesn't do it first."

"Cut her," Alex ordered, and I wasn't sure I'd heard him right at first. But Dean didn't hesitate. Without losing his grip on my neck, he dropped my arm and snatched Gary's knife from the counter where I'd dropped it.

I threw another punch he barely noticed. An instant later the tip of the knife pressed against my left cheek, just in front of my ear. Panic flooded me, and I froze. "Let him go, or I swear I'll slice her up." Dean stared down at me, eyes gleaming in anticipation.

"You guys need her. You not going to cut her," Jace insisted, but I knew better. In Montana, I'd bested Dean physically, then proved him a coward and a liar. He'd been sent home in shame, and he was eager for payback.

"Do it," Alex said, and my heart tried to break free of my chest. "It's not her face I need."

Dean grinned down at me. My blood rushed so fast I felt light-headed. I couldn't breathe, though my airway was clear. "Remember that left hook?" He pressed down, and the blade sank through my skin.

Twenty-Eight

"Ask me to stop," Dean whispered, the point of the knife piercing my cheek. "*Beg* me, and I'll stop."

My hands fisted at my sides. I wanted to scream. I wanted to hit him. I wanted to claw his eyes out with my bare fingers. But I was afraid to move for fear of pushing the blade deeper.

And I would not beg. For my life? Maybe. For someone else's life? Definitely. But not to avoid a little discomfort and an ugly scar. Not to indulge some vengeful psychopath's thirst for power.

So Dean dragged the blade through my skin. I held my breath and fought not to close my eyes. Not to look weak. He cut slowly, tracing the line of my cheekbone, and I stood frozen, screaming on the inside. The pain was minor compared to the jagged gash in my arm, but my eyes watered immediately. Tears stung my new wound, thinning the blood running down my face, dripping from my chin. I could smell it. I could see it, a haze of dark red on the lower left edge of my vision.

"Stop." The fury in Jace's voice was as bleak as Dean's future, as dark as my own rage.

Dean paused but didn't lift the blade from my skin. "Let Alex go and get down on your knees. The longer you wait, the longer I cut."

"No," I whispered, moving nothing but my lips. If Jace let his brother go, Alex would kill him. No hesitation. No self-indulgent torture. No bad-guy monologue. Just a single, fatal blow to the head. I would lose him *and* Kaci. "No, Jace."

Marc, where the hell are *you?*

I rolled my eyes toward Jace, and saw his features twisted in agony, as if he literally shared my pain, as well as my fury. The tip of his blade had pressed a dimple into Alex's neck, but had yet to break the skin. He took a deep, shaky breath, but held his ground, under my order.

So Dean cut some more. Slowly.

A feline whine leaked from my throat. My fists curled tighter. I wasn't worried about the wound; they weren't really trying to hurt me.

I'll admit it: I was pissed about the scar.

We can heal wounds quickly, but we can't erase them, so whatever Dean did to my face would be permanent. The bastard was carving his mark into me, and it would be there every time I looked into the mirror or touched my cheek. For the rest of my life, every time I saw my own face I would think of Colin Dean, and of what Alex had told him to do to me. Every time Jace saw me, he would remember.

So would Marc.

When he heard me whine, Jace flinched. "Drop the knife *now*," he growled, and my eyes rolled to the right to bring him and Alex back into focus. "Or I swear I'll kill him."

Dean shrugged, and the blade bit deeper as he dragged it slowly toward the corner of my mouth. "You kill him, and I get the girl. After I've prettied up her other cheek."

Alex growled in protest, but no one acknowledged him.

"What do you think, puss?" Dean continued. "How about a cute little flower on that side? Ooh, or maybe my initials? That way, no matter who you spread your legs for, one look at your face and he'll know I've already been there."

"Never happen…" I whispered through clenched teeth, trying not to move my cheek. Fury raged in me, hot, heavy, and completely impotent. But there was nothing I could do without making it worse. I couldn't Shift my teeth or my hands without him noticing. I needed an opening. Something to distract him long enough for me to make a move.

"Never say never…"

Finally, the tip of the knife reached the corner of my mouth, and Dean pulled the blade away from my face. I set my jaw firmly, trying to stop the tears from flowing. But they came, anyway, and I allowed myself one heartbroken, pissed-off sob. It was done. No matter what happened next—even if I killed him with my next breath—Dean's mark would always be there.

"Ready to let him go?" Dean's words were for Jace, but his psychotic leer never left me, and his knife hovered near my neck. When there was no answer, he raised the blade again and slid the cold, blood-wet steel down the scooped neckline of my T-shirt, between my breasts.

"Don't," I whispered, acutely aware that the knife was now inches from my heart.

"Dean…" Alex warned. "Her *face*."

Just as Jace growled, "Cut her again and I'll kill you. If she doesn't do it first."

Dean grinned. One quick downward stroke split my shirt right down the middle. The blade snagged on the front of my bra, then that gave way, too, and I was exposed from neck to navel. "Maybe your face isn't all we should decorate. I'm thinking concentric circles.…" He dragged the tip of the blade lightly over the curve of my left breast without breaking the skin.

My pulse pounded, and rage scalded me like the heat from a bonfire. I was ready for help now. I glanced at Jace again and blinked, begging him silently to do something. *Anything* to keep Dean from carving up my chest. Anything short of letting Alex go.

"What's wrong, Jace?" Dean taunted, and my skin crawled when he pushed the left half of my shirt aside with his pinkie. "Not gonna want her after our little makeover?"

Jace swallowed and glanced at the blade, the point of which trailed lightly toward my left nipple. He was afraid of making it worse. Afraid that any movement on his part would make Dean cut me again. Leave his mark elsewhere.

I was scared of the same thing. Terrified to take a deep breath for fear of pushing the blade through my own skin. But I would *not* be this monster's fucking pincushion!

"You bastard," I whispered. I sucked in a shallow breath through my still half-constricted throat. "What the hell is wrong with you?"

"That's what I was going to ask you," Dean purred, dragging the back of the blade around the curve of my breast. "Why would you give it up for the token stray *and* Malone's disposable stepson, but I get a big fat 'never'? Sounds like I'm the only one you're not wrapping your legs around these days."

Jace's growl rumbled through the room in a rapid crescendo. He pulled his own knife back and shoved Alex forward with his knee. Alex grunted in surprise, and Dean turned toward the sound, pulling the blade about an inch from my skin in the process, giving me the best shot I was going to get.

I grabbed Dean's fist—still clutching the knife—and twisted with all the strength of my rage. I shoved his hand away from me. Hard. The blade slid into his chest, low on his left side. It slid between his last two ribs, meeting no resistance from bone.

Dean's eyes went wide. His mouth dropped open. His left hand fell from my neck to clutch at the knife. Blood soaked his shirt, dripping toward his belt.

I sucked in a deep breath, then pushed him with both

hands. Dean stumbled backward and tripped over Lance's leg. He landed on his rump, still holding the knife handle. He stared at me in shock, obviously afraid to pull the blade out.

"Do something with him." I flinched at the pain tugging at my cheek when I spoke, then nodded toward Alex as I pulled one half of my ruined shirt over the other, then tucked them both into my jeans to hold them closed. Mostly.

"Suggestions?" Jace gripped his half brother by the neck with his now human left hand and spun him so that they faced each other, the blade again pressed to Alex's throat. "I should kill him. He was going to finish me, then…" His glance strayed to the remains of my shirt, and fury flashed in his bright blue eyes.

"He was gonna *try.*" I grabbed a three-inch-thick phone book from the end of the bar, then stomped across the floor, my footsteps shaking the whole building. I swung with both hands in spite of the pain in my arm. The book slammed into Alex's head. Jace let him go, and Alex's legs folded beneath him. He was dazed but not unconscious, so I squatted beside him and grabbed his chin, forcing him to look at me while Jace stood over him with the knife, just in case.

"I will never marry you. I will *never* have sex with you voluntarily. And the day you touch me without permission will be the day you swallow your own testicles whole. Do you understand?"

Alex gritted his teeth and glared at me. But he made no reply.

"Stupid, stubborn son of a bitch. If you keep following your father's lead, you're going to die just like him. I should probably kill you now, to save me the trouble of kicking your ass later." But I couldn't kill someone who wasn't actively threatening someone else's life. I was the *good* guy, and it was hard enough to remember that sometimes without making gray-area kills. So I stood and kicked him in the head, softening the blow at the last second to make sure he'd survive it.

His eyes fell shut, his head rolled to the side, and his jaw went slack. But he was still breathing. *Good.*

Now that the moment was over and I'd survived—mostly intact—my aches and pains were starting to surface. My right wrist ached sharply, and my face burned like I'd been flayed alive, thanks to the knife I'd brought to the party and the salt from my own tears.

I snatched a half-used roll of duct tape from the top of a narrow entertainment center and tossed it to Jace. "Tape them up?"

In the kitchen, I pulled the last paper towel from the roll on the counter and bent to peer at my face in the dented, grease-splattered toaster. I bit back a groan and blinked away more tears. The cut was long and straight, and blood stained everything below it, including my neck and the collar of my useless shirt. I wet the paper towel at the sink and carefully wiped away most of the blood, glad to see that it had stopped flowing. Then I knelt to glance under the sink for another roll—they'd come in handy on the road. Instead, I found a small, lidless box holding several pre-filled tranquilizer syringes.

Score. I shoved all four into the pocket of my jacket.

In the living room, I found Jace standing over his newly bound brother, watching me carefully, his expression a mixture of sympathy and heart-wrenching guilt. I knew that look. He felt responsible for my cheek because he hadn't been able to stop Dean from cutting me. I felt the same way about my cousin Abby's rape, though I wasn't even there when it happened. And it was even worse when I'd left Kaci with the thunderbirds, though I'd had no other choice.

"I'm fine," I insisted before Jace could ask. He looked unconvinced but knew better than to argue.

I turned to survey the room. Alex and Lance were out cold and bound hand and foot with duct tape. Colin Dean was bleeding all over the carpet, propped against the front of the couch, his face pale from blood loss, his eyes glassy.

"Can you pull the rental around back while I find Marc?" I asked Jace. I couldn't risk anyone from the middle building seeing me, and I was worried about Marc. If he could have helped us, he would have, especially when Dean was carving up my face.

Unless he'd heard too much.

If he knew I'd slept with Jace, would he leave us? Would he have let them kill Jace and hand me over to Malone? Would he have let Dean cut me?

No. I shook my head, trying to shake off thoughts and questions I wasn't ready to confront. Jace dug the car keys from his pocket, but as I turned to follow him through the open kitchen door, a small glint of light drew my focus to Dean, where he still sat with one hand around the body of the folding knife protruding from his chest. The flash had come from his other hand. *What the hell?*

Squinting, I came closer, and Dean tried to slide his left hand beneath his thigh. But I'd already seen what he held: his cell phone, flipped open and ready to dial.

"Nice try." I stomped faster than he could react and smashed three of his fingers along with the phone.

Dean howled in pain, and I held my open palm out to Jace. He tossed me the roll of tape, then headed straight for the car. I peeled off a strip of tape and slapped it over Dean's mouth, then pushed him onto his side—ignoring his wordless moan of pain—and bound his hands at his back.

With Dean silenced and immobilized, I marched toward the kitchen—and nearly jumped out of my own skin when Marc appeared in the open doorway, wearing nothing but a pair of jeans from the backpack I'd left with him in the woods.

"Damn it, you scared the shit out of me!"

"Chingao!" Marc crossed the trailer in an instant, brows drawn low, gaze trained on my fresh cut. "What the hell happened to your face?" He took my chin and carefully tilted my cheek toward the light. "It's straight and clean. Shallow, but it's gonna scar."

"I'm fine. What happened to you?" He was bleeding from a four inch gash on the left side of his rib cage.

"Found another one of Malone's men in the woods. Fucker had a knife. Now *I* have his knife." He patted his right pocket, where the outline of the folded blade stood out against his hip. "Your turn." He glanced pointedly at my cheek.

I avoided his gaze. "It doesn't matter. It's just a stupid cut."

"Faythe, it's your fucking *face*. Did Alex do this? *Pinche carbon!* I'll kill him."

I grabbed his arm, and before he could shrug free, Dean began edging away from us on the floor, stupidly drawing Marc's attention. "Is that...? Colin Dean?" He tugged loose from my grip and dropped into a squat beside Dean. "Did you do that? That why she stabbed you?" He thumped the handle of the blade, and Dean groaned miserably. "This was Faythe, right?"

Dean sucked air in through his nose so fast I thought he'd hyperventilate.

"You fucking *cut* her?" Marc demanded. "Why? Just to do it?"

"He marked her," Jace said, and I glanced up to see him standing in the doorway, looking three different brands of miserable. "Left his fucking calling card on her face."

Marc was fury given form. His fist flew before I could stop him. His first punch smashed Dean's nose, and blood spurted everywhere. Dean sputtered and choked on it. "How the hell is he supposed to breathe now?" I demanded, trying to turn the gory Canadian on his side to keep him from choking on his own blood.

"He's not." The next blow broke at least two ribs.

"Marc!" I pulled him back. "You're killing him."

"Damn right."

"No." I shoved him back and flinched at the pain in my wrist. "He's not worth it. Not for revenge." Death, we avenged with death. But I'd already cut Dean worse than he'd cut me.

Jace knelt and picked up Lance, tossing the unconscious tom over one shoulder. "We need to go." His voice was calm. Too calm.

Marc rounded on him, eyes flashing in fury, pupils too pointed to be fully human. "Where the hell were you while he was carving her up?" He stomped across the floor, but Jace held his ground. He looked guilty as hell, but the twitch in his right arm said he was ready to defend himself, even one-handed.

Marc pulled his fist back, and I raced across the room. "What good are you, if you can't protect her?"

I threw myself between them and shoved Marc with my left hand. "Stop it! Jace is the only reason Dean didn't carve his initials into my chest. And we do *not* have time for this *shit!*" Marc blinked and forced his eyes to focus on me. When he dropped his arm, I exhaled slowly and Jace headed out the door with Lance. "Help me lock up. Kaci's waiting for us."

Marc blinked again. His nostrils flared as he tried to rein in his temper. Then he spun around and stomped to the front of the trailer where he locked the front door, then started covering windows.

I rolled Dean over again, giving him at least a fighting chance to breathe, but his nose was a lost cause. It was swollen and still pouring blood. He bubbled and gurgled with each breath.

"Don't make me regret this," I said, then pulled the tape from his mouth.

Dean sputtered, spitting out his own blood, and rolled his eyes up to glare at me in seething hatred. "Does Marc know?"

I froze, my heart thudding in my throat. Marc turned from the last window to raise one brow at me in question. I shook my head. I was a deer frozen in the headlights; I could see disaster coming, but couldn't avert it. I couldn't even get out of the way.

Jace clomped up the back steps but stopped in the kitchen, warned by the sudden, obvious tension. "What's wrong?"

Dean laughed, then hacked up more blood. "He wouldn't fight for you if he knew you were fucking Jace…."

Marc went so still he could have been made of stone. His gaze burned into me, begging me silently to deny it. To explain it. To say something to ease the pain and betrayal suddenly swimming in his eyes.

But I couldn't lie. I wouldn't.

My heart splintered into a thousand pieces and my next breath caught in my throat, refusing to budge. My eyes watered, mercifully blurring his pain. Yet I couldn't breathe.

Marc looked from me to Jace, then back to me. His hands curled into fists at his sides. Then he stomped past me. "Let's go."

"Marc…" I jogged after him, but he pushed me away

before I could touch him, and my whole world crashed on top of me, crushing me.

With his eyes focused on the door, I thought he'd stomp right through the kitchen. But at the last second, he whirled around and buried his fist in Jace's stomach. Air rushed from Jace's lungs. He flew backward three feet and crashed into the cabinets left of the sink. His elbow went through one faux wooden door and he hit the floor hard enough to echo throughout the trailer.

The look Marc tossed my way was so cold, my hands started to shake. "Kaci's waiting." Then he stomped out the door.

Jace hauled himself to his feet, scowling. "I deserved that. But I won't take another one from him."

And with that, I lost the battle against tears.

"It'll be okay." Jace tried to fold me into his arms, but I stepped out of reach.

"No. It won't."

He held my gaze; he wouldn't let me wallow. "It won't be the same, but it *will* be okay."

I could only nod and head for the car.

"I'm gonna lock up. I'll be right there," he called after me.

"Marc already…" I stopped on the top step when I heard a familiar metallic click.

No…

As Marc closed the back hatch, blocking Lance from sight, I ran back through the kitchen. Jace knelt beside Dean, who still wheezed through bubbles of his own blood. "You ever touch her again, and neither she nor Marc will have a chance to kill you."

I sucked in a breath to say his name, to stop whatever was about to happen, but I was too slow. Jace shoved the blade of the folding knife through Dean's exposed left cheek and pulled it forward, slicing all the way through to the corner of his mouth.

Dean screamed and gurgled violently, and this time the sound carried. *Everyone* could hear him.

Jace flinched when he saw me watching him in shock. Then he jogged across the room and grabbed my arm. "Let's go."

Marc was walking back from the woods with the backpack he'd retrieved, but when he saw us coming— and heard Dean screaming—he raced back to the car and opened the front door for me. But instead of rounding toward the driver's seat, he climbed into the back without a word. He wouldn't sit with me.

Jace slid into the front seat and started the engine, then slammed the gearshift into Drive. "Where'd you park?" He stomped on the gas and took the turn around the building too quickly.

"The road we were on yesterday." Marc slammed the buckle on his seat belt home, then grabbed the door grip as I struggled to untangle my own belt.

The car skidded onto gravel, then spun out as the back door of the middle building flew open. Another of Malone's enforcers jogged down the steps and stared at us for a moment. But that was all it took for him to recognize me and Marc. He shouted something I couldn't hear over the engine, then raced toward the row of cars I'd disabled.

Our tires caught purchase on the gravel and the rental shot forward. More enforcers poured from the middle building, and I didn't recognize most of them. How many had Malone hired?

We shot past the middle building, then past the main house and onto the concrete driveway. With my belt now buckled, I twisted to stare out the rear windshield as we raced toward the road. The front door of the main house flew open and Malone appeared on the quaint porch, followed by an openly sobbing Patricia Malone.

Jace never looked back.

"I disabled the cars by the back building but couldn't get to any of those," I said, waving toward the three additional vehicles parked in front of the main house.

Jace shrugged. "They won't catch us." He turned onto the road too fast and we fishtailed, but then the car straightened and shot away from the house. I glanced back to see that—so far, at least—we were not being followed. Malone would send his enforcers after us, but with any luck, theirs were the tires I'd slashed, and it would take a few minutes for them to regroup.

I stared out the window at the trees as they raced past, afternoon sunlight blinding me in the gaps. Thoughts tumbled over themselves in my mind, but because I couldn't focus on them, they were more like background static than true cacophony. I was beyond the capacity for rational thought. Too stunned to focus.

In a matter of minutes, everything had changed for the worse. My days of blending into crowds were over, and I'd be lucky if Marc ever spoke to me again. And it would take a miracle to keep him from trying to kill Jace the moment he had time to indulge his rage.

Two long, tense minutes later, we turned from Malone's street onto the narrow, badly maintained road that cut through the woods and up the side of the nearest hill. "About a mile and a quarter," Marc said. "On an overgrown trail on your right."

Jace nodded acknowledgement.

"What did you do to Dean?" Marc asked, and I twisted in my seat to face them both, horrified all over again by the purple swelling taking over the right side of Jace's head.

He hesitated, as if he were considering his answer. Finally, he exhaled heavily. "Let's just say Colin Dean and the Joker now bear more than a passing resemblance."

Marc nodded curtly, then stared out his window. I tried to catch his eye, but he wouldn't look up, though the tension in his posture said he knew I was watching him.

Several minutes later, we turned right and pulled to a stop behind the rented Pathfinder. We scrambled out of the car and I transferred all of our stuff while Marc put the rest of his clothes on and Jace tossed Lance into the cargo hold, still bound and unconscious, but breathing. We shot him up with one of the tranquilizers to keep him quiet. Then we backed out of the drive and onto the road, this time with Marc behind the wheel and me in the passenger seat.

As we pulled onto the highway, I tried to touch his arm, but he jerked away from me, and my heart broke all over again. And guilt was like salt rubbed in the wound.

"Are we going to talk about this?" I asked, and Jace went still in the backseat.

"No." But a second later, Marc's fist slammed into the dashboard, leaving a sizable dent and a smear of blood. "Fuck! You two have incredible timing."

I swallowed thickly, wincing over my bruised throat, and refrained from reminding him that it was actually Dean's timing.

Marc stared out the windshield for several minutes, his hands so tight around the wheel that his knuckles were white. His neck was tense and flushed. I stared at my lap, my stomach churning, my heart one big, hollow ache. I didn't know what to say. Didn't know if there was anything I could do to make it better. Or at least not make it worse.

Finally, Marc glanced in the rearview mirror, and I twisted to see Jace returning his gaze steadily. "You're getting out as soon as we cross the border," Marc growled through gritted teeth. "If you're lucky, I'll stop the car. I want you off the ranch by the time we get back with Kaci."

"No..." I began, but Jace spoke over me, his voice calm and firm.

"That's not your call."

Marc growled again and dug in his pocket. "Fine." He dropped his phone in my lap. "Call your dad. Let's get his opinion."

"Marc, please don't do this." I wiped tears from my eyes with my jacket sleeve, flinching at the sting in my cheek. "Don't drag everyone else into this. Not now. Think about the good of the Pride."

"Is that what you were thinking about?" He demanded, and the speedometer crept toward eighty-five. "Are you thinking about the good of the Pride when you're *fucking* him?"

I glanced at Jace, and the car lurched forward again—Marc's temper directly affected the weight of his right foot. "It's not like that," I said finally. "It was only once."

"I knew something was different." He punched the dash again, and a new dent appeared, with even more blood. "But I never thought you'd go that far…" Marc ground his teeth together so hard I could hear them over the road noise, and I cringed. "And you told Dean about it?"

Jace huffed, and the wheel groaned beneath Marc's hands. "Alex made a lucky guess."

"And now the whole world will know," Marc spat.

I felt my face flush. He was right. Malone would use my infidelity against my father, and against our entire Pride.

"Marc, I'm so sorry.…"

"Save it," he snapped. "We're going to concentrate on getting Kaci back for now. But after that, we will deal with this." He glared into the rearview mirror again, and Jace nodded firmly.

"Looking forward to it."

Twenty-Nine

We drove in miserable silence for nearly two hours, exhausted, angry, and tense beyond words. And to say that I got the least of the physical pain would be putting it mildly.

The gash on Marc's left side was nasty. Not as long or as deep as my arm had been, but much worse than my cheek.

Jace's head was still swollen and discolored, and he moved stiffly, trying to spare his ribs from any unnecessary movement. I turned to check the dilation of his pupils every fifteen minutes or so. I also kept the music cranked and my window cracked, hoping the cold and the noise would keep him awake until I was sure he didn't have a concussion.

In spite of our injuries—or maybe because of them—we didn't feel safe enough to stop for first-aid supplies until we were more than a hundred miles from Malone's property. And even then, we hesitated, both because we were still in the heart of enemy territory and because none of us was exactly presentable.

In the end, we decided Jace should do the shopping, because with the bill of his hat twisted to cover the side of his head, he was the one least likely to prompt a call to the authorities. Marc's wound had bled through his shirt, and I had a cut-up face, a sliced-open top, and finger-shaped bruises around my neck. If we were seen, some kind stranger's concern could end in a call to 911.

But that was only part of it. Marc and I needed time to talk. Alone.

He parked near the back of a Walmart parking lot as the sun began to go down, and I jotted a list on a scrap of paper I found in the glove compartment. As soon as Jace was gone, Marc turned to me. "You should have let me kill him."

At first, I thought he meant Jace. But then Marc's gaze strayed to my cheek, and I understood. He meant Dean.

I ran one finger carefully over the cut. The pain had dulled a bit, but my anger had not. "Maybe so. But I think he'll suffer more now."

"If I see him again, I'll kill him."

Too tired to argue, I let my hand fall into my lap. "Fair enough." With any luck, the next time we saw Dean would be during full-scale war. His death would be justified. "If I don't kill him first."

After another minute of silence, Marc glanced into the empty backseat. "You know it's all I can do to be in the same car with him. Every instinct I have is telling me to kill him."

Clearly, we'd moved on to Jace.

"I know." My heart felt as bruised as my throat. "What about me?"

"I'm trying really hard not to hate you right now, Faythe."

I blinked back fresh tears. "I hate myself right now."

"Then why did you do it?" His teeth ground together audibly. "Just…why?"

I tried to speak and choked on a sob instead. There was no simple answer. No logical reason. Jace and I had connected in a moment of heart-wrenching grief, and no one was more surprised than I was to discover that that connection went beyond the physical.

"Do you love him?" Marc asked, each word harsh, like he'd almost gagged on them.

I forced myself to look at him. To give him eye contact, at least. "Yes." And that realization made my head spin violently. "I don't want to, but I do."

Marc fell back against the door, like I'd punched him, and that ache in my chest settled a little deeper.

"I didn't mean for this to happen. Any of it." I didn't want to make excuses—he deserved much better than that—but he obviously wanted an explanation. "You were missing, and Ethan had just died. His blood was still wet on the couch. And we were all hurting *so much*. Jace, just as badly as the rest of us. Maybe worse, because he didn't have anyone to turn to, and at the time, neither did I. Everyone was handling it differently, and I didn't know what to do."

I paused for a deep breath, and to gather my thoughts.

The words weren't coming quickly or easily, but they were the truth, and that seemed to be more important to Marc than my apology. Even if it didn't make things any better.

"I went to check on him." I couldn't make myself say Jace's name. Not then. Not to Marc. "He'd gotten hurt in the fight, and he'd closed himself up in the guesthouse, all alone. He was already drinking, and I had some, too. I wanted to make the pain go away, just for a little while." Silent tears pooled in my eyes and I wiped them away, hoping Marc hadn't seen.

"So, he gets you drunk, and you just lie down for him?" Marc spat, and I flinched at the venom in his voice, though I knew I deserved it. "Better not let that little secret out, or every tom in the country will show up on the doorstep with a bottle and a condom."

I shook my head slowly, sniffling. "It wasn't like that, I swear. He said he loved me. He said he *needed* me, and I...I made a mistake. Sleeping with Jace was a mistake. I know that, and I can't tell you how sorry I am. I wish I could take it back. But I'd be lying if I said it didn't mean anything. It did. It *does*. It changed both of us and made me face the truth about...about how I feel about him."

"You love him." That time it wasn't a question. That time his voice sounded dead, like I'd killed the part of him that supplied emotional resonance for Marc's voice.

I could only nod miserably.

"Do you still love me?"

"Yes! Desperately," I said, hoping the truth of my

statement shined in my eyes. Hoping he could see it in the near dark. Or at least hear it in my voice. "I know I've messed this up, and I honestly don't know where to go from here. But I don't want to lose you."

His eyes glazed over in anger. "Then you have to choose. It's me or him, Faythe. Once this is over, he and I can't exist in the same Pride. Not with you. We'd kill each other."

"I know." I'd known that all along, but that didn't make the choice any easier.

"Don't make this a political decision," Marc said, and even in the dim light from the parking lot, I could see what it cost him to say that. "I'm the better choice to help you run the Pride, when that time comes, but I'd be lying if I said that mattered. The truth is that you've learned a lot this year. With the rest of the guys at your back and your father as an adviser, you can run things just fine on your own. So you owe it to yourself to listen to your heart on this one."

I gaped at Marc. "You're serious?" I'd expected him to try to beat the shit out of Jace, or at least lobby harder to have him expelled.

He glanced down, and when he looked up again, the gold in his eyes glittered coldly. "I'm not being selfless. I don't have that in me right now. I can't stand the thought of living the rest of my life without you, even after all this. But it would hurt worse to wake up with you every morning for the rest of my life, knowing you regretted your decision. Knowing you *settled* for me."

"I wouldn't…" I began, but Marc cut me off with a look so fierce I lost my breath. His eyes had Shifted.

"I'm not done," he growled; something in his throat had Shifted, too. "If I see him touch you again before you make your decision, I'll break every motherfucking bone in his body. Or die trying. I swear I will."

I believed him. And then we'd have two more toms out of commission, because I wasn't the only one who'd grown up. Jace was no longer the low-ranking enforcer Marc had kicked the shit out of the summer before.

Before I could figure out how to respond, Jace thumped on the windshield, then got in the car with three bags full of stuff. He'd only been gone fifteen minutes, but had apparently bought out the entire store. Including the deli, based on the scent wafting from one of the sacks.

He tossed an exaggerated glance at the back of Marc's head, then shot me a questioning look, silently asking me how it went. I could only shrug. We were all still breathing, and at the moment, that was all I could ask for.

Marc drove to the back of the building and parked behind the massive Dumpster, and we worked quickly, temporarily hidden from the rest of the world. Every tube of ointment and bottle of peroxide they shared came through me. I was afraid to let them have direct contact. Jace's hair trigger was only slightly less sensitive than Marc's, and every look he shot my way was intense. Searching.

He was afraid Marc had convinced me to get rid of him, and he was ready to fight that decision.

Jace scrubbed blood from beneath his fingernails while I cleaned the gash on Marc's side. It probably needed stitches, but since we were in a hurry and my needlework left much to be desired, he settled for three Steri-Strips and antibiotic cream, all covered with a square of sterile gauze taped into place.

I helped him into a plain black tee, then tried not to squirm while he cleaned the cut on my cheek. It was straight and clean and shallow, and the wound had already scabbed over, so there was no need for stitches, though it would no doubt leave a thin scar. I left my cheek uncovered, because a bandage would only have drawn more attention to it.

When we were dressed, bandaged, and as clean as we could get without a shower, Marc pulled us out of the parking lot, and Jace passed out fried chicken strips, potato wedges, and bottles of water while I called to give my dad an update. We'd agreed to leave out our personal business, to keep from overloading our Alpha when he already had his hands more than full.

"Hello? Faythe?"

"Yeah, it's me," I said around my first bite of chicken. I was starving, and chewing on the right side of my mouth was the only concession I was willing to make toward the pain in my cheek. "We have Lance, and we're about a hundred miles west of Malone's property."

The relief in my father's sigh revealed the truth: he hadn't expected good news. His footsteps echoed across the floor of the office. "Prospects?"

"Lookin' good so far, but we're not out of the woods yet."

"How's Lance?"

"Unconscious but breathing. I'm crossing my fingers against brain damage." We'd need him healthy and coherent to testify before his execution.

"Blood loss?"

"Nope." I swallowed my mouthful of chicken before elaborating. "Hiking boot to the side of the head. Plus tranquilizers. Malone really shouldn't leave loaded syringes just lying around."

"Mmm. Casualties?"

"None," Marc said from the driver's seat. And he looked decidedly unhappy with that particular detail.

Springs creaked as my father sank into the rolling chair behind his desk. "You snuck into the heart of Malone's territory and made it out with one of his enforcers without a single casualty?"

"Not for lack of trying," Marc mumbled, flicking on his left blinker.

I sipped from my water bottle. "We were lucky."

"Don't discount your own skill," my father insisted, and I nearly fainted from shock. He didn't hand out compliments lightly. "Injuries?"

"On their side? Five toms bound and gagged. One ruptured scrotum…"

My father nearly choked. "I assume that would be your handiwork?"

I shrugged, though he couldn't see me. "He got grope-y. Anyway, one ruptured scrotum, two broken noses, several concussions, one slashed cheek, a knife to the lower chest—don't worry, he'll live—and one amputated thumb."

Another moment of silence. Then, "Do I even want to know?"

"That one was me," Marc growled. "He got grope-y."

"Oh. What about the three of you? Everyone okay?"

I answered with another chicken strip halfway to my mouth. "Marc has a gash on his side, but nothing a few Steri-Strips won't fix. Jace nearly got his skull bashed in. I'm watching him for swelling and signs of a concussion."

"I'm fine, Greg," Jace insisted, around an entire potato wedge.

"Faythe, what about you?"

I hesitated, and might not have answered at all, if I wasn't sure either or both of the guys would do it for me in the event of my silence. "I got cut. On the face."

"How bad is it?" my father asked without missing a beat.

That time, Marc spoke for me. "Colin Dean marked her from her cheekbone to the corner of her mouth."

Silence. Horrible, heavy silence, while I waited for his reply. Then, "Are you okay?"

"I'm fine. It's a shallow cut. Once it heals, the scar will be thin."

"The bastard did it on purpose," Marc repeated, and my father made no comment about his use of profanity in front of an Alpha; there was no question it fit.

The chair creaked, and paper shuffled on my dad's desk. "What is Dean doing in Appalachian territory?"

"Enforcing for Malone." I seized the opportunity to change the subject. "And he's not the only one. Malone's been on a hiring binge, and I didn't recognize most of the faces." Which meant they either came from territories I'd had little contact with, or he was seriously recruiting from north of the border, in areas with little distinguishable accent. But, based on their scents, none were strays.

"Well, I wish I could say that was unexpected, but honestly, it's the most predictable move he's made so far."

Jace took a deep breath. "Dean's gonna be a problem, Greg."

I whirled on him, begging him with my eyes to keep his mouth shut. But he wouldn't meet my gaze. Nor would he keep something he considered important from his Alpha. At least, something that didn't involve him sleeping with the Alpha's daughter.

"How so?"

Jace sighed and forged ahead, staring at his hands in his lap. "He went home from Montana disgraced. His dad kicked him out and told the Canadian council he'd been exposed as a coward. That a tabby beat him up and caught him in a lie. Dean blames Faythe for the whole thing. He cut her where it would show to humiliate her." He sucked in another breath and continued, while I ground my teeth at the memory. "When he recovers, he'll be gunning for her. Even more than he already was."

"Why didn't you kill him?" My father was clearly talking to Marc and Jace.

Both of them looked to me for a response, and I rolled my eyes. "I wouldn't let them. After he got a taste of his own knife, he was no threat to anyone." Physically, anyway. His mouth had done plenty of damage....

"His very *existence* is a threat to yours," my father insisted. I closed my eyes and let my head fall against the headrest. Was I being scolded for *not* killing someone? "Faythe, being a leader means making tough decisions. Often. You may think you can take Dean again, if it comes to that, and you may be right. But if you're not…it would be devastating for the entire Pride. Not to mention you personally."

We are not *having this conversation….*

"Sometimes one person has to die to preserve the greater good."

I opened my eyes just to roll them again, having reached the end of my patience. "You think I don't know that? It was *my* decision to turn Lance Pierce over to be executed. I'm very familiar with the concept of 'greater good,' thanks."

"Good. If you're in a situation like that again, I expect you to eliminate the threat. Or at least let one of the guys do it."

"That won't be necessary." My teeth ground together so loudly I was sure he could hear it. "I can eliminate my own threats."

My father exhaled slowly. "Faythe…it *is* self-defense, because he *will* hurt you if he gets the chance."

"He already has. But I hurt him back."

"I know," he said, and I could practically hear the smile in his voice. My father was satisfied that I would do as I was told. And I would. But the matter sat on my conscience like a stone at the bottom of a river.

"Call me when you get close to the nest."

"Okay." I raised my hand to stifle a yawn.

My dad sighed. "Boys, make sure she gets some sleep."

"No problem," Marc said, though he was at least as tired as I was. Maybe more.

Half an hour later, Lance woke up, his consciousness heralded by a series of angry grunts and kicks against the side of the van. Jace raised a single brow in grim amusement, then leaned over the back of his seat to peer into the cargo hold. "Hey."

I twisted in my seat to watch, and Marc kept glancing in the rearview mirror until I smacked his shoulder and pointed out the windshield. He was dangerous enough with his eyes on the road.

Jace glanced at me and I shrugged, so he leaned over Lance, then came up a moment later with a strip of duct tape.

"Where am I?" Lance demanded. "What the *hell* do you think you're doing?"

"Balancing the scales of justice," Jace said, his usual grin conspicuously absent.

"What does that mean?"

I closed my eyes, steeling myself, then unbuckled and climbed onto the backseat, where I leaned over next to Jace, trying to keep the left side of my face angled away from our prisoner. "Hey, Lance."

"Faythe?" He clearly didn't remember my awesome countertop-assisted kick to his skull.

"Yeah. Listen, I'm just gonna get right to the point." Because I had to be sure. I was perfectly willing to hand him over to the thunderbirds to save Kaci's life, but I needed to know that he was actually guilty, for my own peace of mind. Though, peace hardly seemed possible, after the week we'd had. "Parker's worried about you. Brett told us you were the one who killed the thunderbird, and Parker's afraid that if the truth comes out, Malone will throw you under the wheels of the political machine to save himself. So we're here on behalf of my dad, to offer you sanctuary."

"Sanctuary? You're serious?" His brows furrowed in skepticism.

"Yeah. Sorry about the whole snatch-'n'-grab. We didn't think Malone would let you just walk out."

Lance shook his head, his hair catching against the carpet. "He wouldn't have."

"So, I just need to clarify a couple of points, then we can let you ride up front with the rest of the grown-ups." I smiled, hoping he could see my friendly, reassuring expression in the fading daylight, but not the new slice across my face, which hurt with each word I spoke.

"Okay…" He was hesitant to trust me, and I didn't blame him. But I stood a much better shot at convincing him than Jace did.

"Are you the one who killed the thunderbird? We heard it was totally justifiable. He was trying to butt in on your kill?"

"Yeah!" Lance's face brightened, and his relief was obvious even in the dying light. "It was my kill. Anyone else would have done the same thing."

I smiled again and nodded like a bobble-head doll. "So you killed him?"

"Yeah, but it was…"

"Great, thanks." I turned to Jace. "Tape him back up."

"What? No!" Lance shouted, and resumed his struggle. But as long as he couldn't partially Shift his hands—and I'd certainly never taught him how—there was no way he could tear through the tape binding his wrists.

"You got it." Jace dug in the bag at his feet and came up with a roll of duct tape.

"Where the hell are we going?" Lance demanded as I returned to my seat.

Jace leaned over to hold Lance still long enough to tape his mouth. "To New Mexico." Our prisoner fought harder, actually rocking the van a couple of times as he kicked. "Oh, don't worry," Jace said, smiling at him coldly. "I'm sure you'll have a chance to plead your case in front of the thunderbirds."

Jace faced forward again, and we all tried to ignore the desperate racket from the back. After ten minutes of Lance's nonstop, wordless begging, Marc turned the radio up, and Guns N' Roses cautioned our passenger to live and let die.

If he got the message, I heard no sign.

The guys insisted I take the first sleeping shift—the only thing they'd agreed on since we left Malone's—but I was hesitant to leave them both awake at once. Unfortunately, my exhausted body won that particular battle of wills, and I slept for four straight hours.

After the switch, Marc napped, Jace drove, and I Shifted my right arm over and over, gritting my teeth through the pain, until it no longer hurt in human form. An hour into that leg of the trip, when he was sure Marc was asleep, Jace shot me a sideways glance, as I concentrated on the wave of fur rippling over my arm from the elbow down.

"What happened with Marc?" he whispered.

I glanced into the backseat before answering. Marc was truly sleeping; I could tell. "He said I have to choose. And one of you will have to go."

Several full minutes of tense silence later, he whispered again. "So...what are you going to do?"

I could only shrug. "I don't know." And I had no one to talk it over with. Everyone I would normally have gone to for advice was either busy running the Pride, itching to kill the other man in my life, or dead. How could I possibly be so alone, when I never seemed to have any privacy?

After twenty-two hours, two more doses of tranquilizer for Lance, four bathroom breaks, and four different sleeping/driving switches, Marc shook me awake where I dozed in the front passenger seat. I sat up, rubbing my eyes, and noted that the sun was low in the sky. Again. "What time is it?"

"Four-fifteen. We're about half an hour away from where we picked you up."

Barring disaster, and accounting for the part we'd have to walk, that meant we'd arrive with less than a quarter-hour to spare.

Lance was sleeping off his latest injection and Jace was snoring lightly from the middle row. "Want me to call my dad?"

He nodded stiffly. I'd hoped he'd warm up a little, given time, but so far he showed no sign of a thaw.

I autodialed my father and gave him an update, promising to call him as soon as we had Kaci. He swore he'd be standing by with a phone to toss out to Beck when the Flight was satisfied with the proof we'd brought.

"Faythe, are you okay?" my dad asked, after the details were worked out.

"Fine." Technically that was true. There was nothing physically wrong with me. But he could tell there was something we weren't saying.

I dreaded telling my father almost as badly as I'd dreaded telling Marc.

Jace woke up while I was on the phone, and when I hung up he handed me two bottles of Coke and four protein bars—the makeshift dinner we'd bought at the last pit stop. We ate in silence, and my nerves consumed me as surely as I consumed my meal.

We were almost there. The thunderbirds would either accept our proof or they wouldn't, and there was nothing we could do about their decision, either way. Kaci would either live or she wouldn't, and there was nothing we could do about that, either. But I was willing to die trying.

Twenty-five minutes later, Marc turned right onto the narrow gravel road leading to the nest. Three miles along, we met the first obstacle—huge rocks spanning the entire width of the road in a random arrangement I was sure the thunderbirds had personally placed. We had to leave the car there and hoof it the rest of the way.

Lance blinked in the last rays of sunlight when we opened the back hatch, and he began struggling immediately.

"Shut the fuck up," Marc ordered, and hauled him out with a grip beneath both of the prisoner's arms.

Lance wobbled at first, and danced like he had to relieve himself, which was no surprise, considering he hadn't had a bathroom break in nearly twelve hours, since the guys had stood guard while he took aim on the side of a dark road.

"I think he has to pee," I said, and Lance nodded frantically. Jace glanced away and Marc cursed rapidly in Spanish. We weren't willing to free the prisoner's hands, but neither of the guys wanted to help him out of his pants. Apparently they were dribbled on last time.

I rolled my eyes. "Fine. I'll help him."

Marc growled. "I got it." He hauled Lance to the side of the road and Jace and I stared at the ground as Lance did his business. Then we started walking.

The awkward, silent two-mile hike took nearly half an hour, even with us shoving Lance along when he started to drag. He was obviously reluctant to arrive at the site of his pending execution.

The sun hung low on the horizon when the nest came into sight, and Jace stopped cold, staring overhead with his face shielded from the glare by one hand. "Wow. How the hell are we supposed to get up there?"

"We're not." I followed his gaze, impressed all over again by the thunderbirds' mountainside enclave. "That's the whole point."

When we stood near the base of the cliff, staring almost straight up, the door overhead opened and four mostly human thunderbirds filed out to stand at the edge of the porch looking down at us. At some unseen, unheard signal, they leaped from the edge one by one, unfolding huge wings from their sides like dark angels.

They landed in front of us with a massive gust of wind and the thunderous beat of huge feathers against the air. Two of the birds were unfamiliar, but I recognized Cade and Coyt, though I could not for my life tell one from the other.

Like last time, the birds stood mute, so I stepped forward, hauling Lance with me by one arm. He planted his feet on the ground, refusing to move so that I had to literally drag him through the dirt. Like his resistance would mean a damn thing in the long run.

"Here's your proof, right on time." I shoved him forward another step. The thunderbirds eyed him in malice so deep and cold that I got a chill just from looking into their eyes. "Now bring Kaci down."

Cade—or maybe Coyt—shook his head. "You must present your evidence."

I huffed in irritation but knew I really had no choice. "Fine. But you're gonna need more ferry-birds." I gestured behind me, to where Marc and Jace stood as my silent backup.

Coyt—or maybe Cade—shook his head. "Only you and your evidence. Your men will stay here."

Thirty

"No way in hell." Marc's words were more growl than voice. "Where she goes, I go."

The thunderbirds didn't even spare him a glance. "If you're ready...?" The bird nearest me gestured with one wing-claw toward the nest high above us.

"Yeah. Just a second." I turned to Marc and Jace, fully aware that with my back to them, the thunderbirds could rip me in two before I even knew the blow was coming. At my side, Lance watched everything with wide, terrified eyes, pulling so hard against the tape binding his wrists that the muscles stood out in his arms, even beneath his long-sleeved tee.

Duct tape was truly the most awesome substance known to man—or Shifter—but even it would wear out over time. If they planned to hold him very long before...dealing with him, the birds would need to rebind him soon.

"Faythe, you can't be serious," Marc hissed, pulling

me away from the birds and closer to him and Jace. "What's to stop them from killing you and Kaci once they have you up there?"

"We would not harm her or your kitten, if Faythe Sanders has done what we've asked," either Coyt or Cade said, addressing Marc for the first time. He glanced up, then his focus returned to me, his scowl evidently permanently fixed into place.

"*That's* what will stop them." I gestured toward the birds, to include the statement of their intentions. "I brought what they wanted, and they won't go back on their word. And, anyway, there's nothing either of you could do even if they hauled you up there. There are at least fifty grown thunderbirds in there, Marc. We're on their turf. The best way for all of us to make it out of here alive is to play by their rules."

"She's right," Jace said before Marc could object. "It'll be worse for everyone if they feel threatened in their own home."

Marc ignored him. He was busy eyeing me in an intense combination of frustration and fear. "You keep going places where I can't protect you."

I blinked at him in surprise. "Yeah. I do. But I keep coming back." I reached out to run my hand over the delicious, dark stubble on his chin. "This is my job, Marc, and I swear I will do everything I can to get myself and Kaci out of there quickly and unharmed." I glanced at Jace to include him in what I was about to say. "But listen, even if they don't send anyone down here with you, they'll be watching you, and their eyesight is incredible. If you guys start bickering or making trouble, they will come down here and end it, and there's nothing I can do to stop them. So I need you to promise you'll just stand here and wait quietly. Everything else that needs to be done or said can be addressed later. Okay?"

"Like we have a choice," Marc grumbled, while Jace nodded mutely, the fists clenched at his sides the only indication that he was just as unhappy about the situation as Marc was.

"Thank you." Turning, I held up a one-more-minute finger for the birds, then faced Lance, who looked like he was about to be thrown into a volcano. I had no doubt that if he thought he stood a chance, he'd have already taken off into the woods. "If I take the tape off your mouth, can you keep quiet and listen to me?"

He nodded hesitantly, and I decided it was worth the risk. I was about to hand him over to his death. Surely the least I could do was tell him how he'd gotten there and ask for his cooperation.

I peeled back one corner of the tape over his lips, then carefully pulled it the rest of the way off. Fortunately for Lance—and the stubble that had grown on his chin and cheeks over the past twenty-four hours—removing duct tape doesn't hurt nearly as badly as pulling off a Band-Aid; I could attest to that personally.

"Okay. First of all, I'm truly sorry about the way this had to go down, but I want you to know that we had no other choice. You pretty much sealed your own fate when you killed Finn. Did you know that was the thunderbird's name?"

Lance shook his head, and his gaze jumped from me, to the birds now surrounding him in case he tried to run, to Marc and Jace, to the woods, up to the nest, then finally back to me. He was clearly terrified.

"Well, it was. So far you've acted like a total, spineless punk throughout this entire ordeal. But now you have the chance to act like a man. To represent your species honorably and to do the right thing."

He started to open his mouth, probably to ask a question, but I shook my head and rushed on.

"The thunderbirds have Kaci Dillon up there in their nest, and if I don't hand you over to them, they're going to kill her. And you know damn well that she has nothing to do with this. You were obviously willing to let an entire Pride full of toms die for your mistake, and in my opinion, you've outed yourself as morally reprehensible with that one. But are you willing to let them kill an innocent tabby? A *child?* Or will you redeem yourself and help me save her life?"

If Lance had any enforcer pride left, any vestiges of morality and selflessness still clinging to the rotting corpse of his honor, hopefully such an appeal would move him. Most toms had an ingrained soft spot for children—the future of our species. And all enforcers had sworn oaths to protect their Pride's tabby.

The truth was that I would trade him for Kaci whether or not he played along. But I thought he had a right to try to redeem himself before he died.

Lance blinked, then glanced at the waiting thunderbirds before turning back to me. "What do I have to do?"

A huge sigh of relief built inside me, but I swallowed it, unwilling to let him see how little faith I truly had in him, how surprised I was by the possibility that he might cooperate. And how doubtful I was that he would actually stand tall when he realized that doing so would not miraculously save his life.

"All you have to do is tell the truth. And my personal suggestion would be to offer a sincere apology and try to explain the difference between our culture and theirs. Throw yourself on their mercy." I thought the chances of such a plea actually saving his life were slim to not-a-chance-in-hell, but that would give him something to focus on, other than his own impending demise. And distraction was really all I had to offer him.

"And if that doesn't work, you have two options. You can go out like the whiny little bitch Malone considers you—he obviously didn't think you were man enough to stand by the truth—or you can hold strong until the end. Die with dignity."

Lance swallowed thickly, then nodded hesitantly, holding my gaze as if he needed me to hear something. To truly believe something. "Faythe…it wasn't my idea. I didn't really have a choice. It was either go along with Calvin or wind up…well, like Brett did. If he'd do that to his own son, what would he have done to me, if I'd tried to fight him?"

"No one ever said enforcing was easy, Lance." Nor life, for that matter. "Sometimes you have to make a tough choice, knowing it might get you killed. This time, you made the wrong one." Though, oddly enough, the result was about the same. All he'd gained was an extra week of life under Malone's tyranny.

I'd have chosen death over that any day.

"I think we're ready," I said, turning to Cade. Or maybe Coyt.

The birds nodded in unison, and with powerful, nearly simultaneous flaps of their huge wings, they took to the air, nearly blowing me off my feet in the process. Lance stumbled back, and Jace shoved him forward. An instant later, one of the two unfamiliar thunderbirds snatched his arms, his wrists still taped at his back, and as soon as he dangled in the air, the second bird grabbed him by both ankles.

Lance screamed as he was lifted into the air face-down. His eyes were wide, watching the earth fly by beneath him until the wind became too much and he had to close them.

I glanced up just as Cade—or maybe Coyt—flapped his wings over me, whipping my hair into knots that might never brush out. Strands lashed my forehead and caught in my mouth, and my very breath was stolen by the rush of air over my face. But I stood still and raised my arms, ready as I'd ever be for a trip I hoped never to suffer through again, once we had Kaci.

The first bird took me just below my shoulders, his talons squeezing mercilessly. But this time, I found the painful pressure comforting; surely a lax grip would have increased my chances of falling to my death. When I hovered twenty feet in the air, the second bird swooped to grab my shins. Then, with practiced ease,

the two birds synchronized the beat of their wings—
amazing, considering their proximity to each other—
and we rose steadily toward the nest, bobbing for a
heartbeat between each powerful flap before soaring up
with the next.

I risked a single glance at the ground, and through
the strands of long black hair whipping around my face,
I saw Marc and Jace standing watching me side by side,
each with a hand shielding his eyes from the crimson
glare of the setting sun. From so high up, the differences
between them were almost impossible to find. They
were two anonymous bodies on the ground, watching
helplessly as I was flown away from them both.

Cade and Coyt dropped me on the overhanging porch
with a bone-jarring thud, and I remained crouched on
the floorboards—a little frightened by the cracks I saw
between them upon such close inspection—until they
landed on either side of me, silent but for the last beat
of their wings against the air.

"What the *hell?*" Lance shouted, and I stood to find
him standing with his back—and his bound hands—
pressed against the front wall of the nest. He glared at me,
arms shaking, face pale. "You could have warned me...."

"About the trip up? Yeah, it's a bitch the first time."
I regretted the words before the last one had even fallen
from my lips; Lance's first time would be his last.

Flustered, I started past him toward the open front
door, beyond which dozens of thunderbirds waited for
us in varying degrees of human form. When Lance
didn't follow, I turned to him. "You have two options—

inside…" I gestured toward the open doorway. "Or down, the hard way. Which is it gonna be?" He hesitated, and I sighed. "*Dignity,* Lance."

He spared one fleeting, terrified glance at the ground below, then squared his shoulders and walked past me into the huge main room of the nest—where he stopped, apparently frozen, three steps from the door.

I knew how he felt. Before this flight, Lance had only ever seen one thunderbird, and that poor cock had been alone and pounced upon before he had a chance to take to the sky. And now we were facing fifty or so of his closest friends and relatives, a much more representative—and intimidating—sample of the thunderbird population and their tendency to stick together.

And to avenge their own at all costs.

When Lance hadn't moved several seconds later, I gave him a little shove, and he stepped forward slowly, trying to take in everything at once, his eyes already glazing over with the effort. He may have been going into shock, and frankly, that was probably better for all involved.

Before I could make a better assessment, or address any of the dozens of birds now staring at us, a door squeaked open overhead and I looked up to see Kaci step out onto the exposed second-floor walkway. "Faythe!" she shouted, and was running before the single syllable of my name faded into silence.

She raced along the hall and around the corner, nimbly avoiding the two fully human thunderbirds she passed in the process, and thumped down the stairs like a bull about to charge. But she was all smiles when she flew across the huge room and into my open arms.

"You came!" Kaci buried her tear-streaked face in the shoulder of my leather jacket.

"You say that like there was some doubt." I pried her just far enough away that I could get a good look. Other than her sob-reddened face and an unusually pale countenance, she looked…fine. Which supported my theory that the birds would keep their word, so long as we kept ours. "Are you okay?"

"Yeah." Kaci wiped fresh tears from her face with the sleeve of her shirt—the one she'd been wearing since the day we were taken. "Just ready to go home." Then she blinked and frowned, staring at my cheek. "What happened to your face?"

"It's fine. Barely hurts. Just a keepsake from an old friend."

Her frown deepened, and her hand rose as if to touch the scab, before she thought better of it and clasped her hands together. "That's a joke, right?"

A really bad joke… "Okay, he wasn't a friend. More like a mortal enemy." Now, anyway.

"Did you kill him?" Kaci asked without missing a beat, and it was my turn to frown.

"Of course not!" Though, apparently I was alone in believing I was right to let him live. "But he's gonna be in a lot of pain for a very long time."

"Good." Kaci glanced around at the crowd of thunderbirds watching us closely. Listening. Waiting. "Can we go home now?" she whispered.

"Come this way," called a screechy voice, uneven with age, drawing our attention to the far end of the room, where I'd last addressed a smaller crowd of birds.

"In just a minute," I whispered to Kaci, and waved Lance forward. He came slowly, still standing tall, but staring at me as if I were his one shot at salvation. The irony truly stung. How could he look at me like I was supposed to save him when I was the one turning him in?

Maybe I should have just knocked him out.

"Who's that?" Kaci stared at him openly.

"This is Lance Pierce," I said, and he met and held Kaci's gaze, as if his curiosity could not be denied. Maybe he wanted to know who I was trading his life for. Or maybe, like most toms, he couldn't turn away from the sight of a young tabby, the very treasure enforcers—and indeed all toms—were taught from infancy to protect.

Kaci's eyes widened and she edged closer to me as the circle of birds grew tighter around us, herding us to the end of the room. "Parker's brother?"

"Yeah." The floor of the great room was packed with birds now, and hardly a glimpse of empty floor showed, but for the five-foot circle surrounding us, putting us at the center of their unnerving attention. "He killed Finn." A single glance up confirmed my suspicion: the perches and ledges had been abandoned. Everyone wanted to participate.

"What's going to happen to him?"

I swallowed, then stood straighter, trying to emotionally distance myself—and Kaci—from whatever would happen next. Hopefully *after* we left. "That's not up to us."

"Faythe Sanders?" a voice called from behind us this time, and I whirled, but was too late to pinpoint the speaker. *And so it begins...*

"Yeah?"

"Present your evidence to the satisfaction of the Flight, and you and your kitten may go." I saw the speaker that time, a mostly human man with only the suggestion of a beak in the protrusion of his nose.

"Sure. No problem." I swallowed thickly and pulled Kaci closer. It sounded too easy. How exactly did they define *satisfaction?*

"This is Lance Pierce." I gestured toward him with one hand, but he didn't even glance at me, having evidently decided that I was the enemy, after all. We all were. But he had nowhere to go. I inhaled deeply and stared straight forward, avoiding looking at any particular bird, since I was speaking to all of them at once. And because I was far from comfortable with my decision. With what I had to do to walk out of there alive, with Kaci in tow.

"Lance killed your bird. Finn."

Thirty-One

The reaction from the crowd was immediate and terrifying. Every bird in the room suddenly seemed to swell, as if together they could suck up all the air in the room, suffocating the rest of us. But air wasn't the cause of the change.

It was feathers.

Suddenly everyone but the three of us had feathers. And talons. And wing-claws. And most had sharp, curved beaks. All in the span of a single breath.

Lance sucked in a startled breath and jumped back. Feathers rustled behind him and he whirled around, then turned again. He'd never seen the avian, like-magic Shift, and I could only imagine how terrifying it must be to see the show for the first time, magnified by five dozen. One cock came close enough to use his talons to cut the tape from Lance's hands.

Finally, Lance exhaled and made a visible effort to regain calm himself.

"Will you speak for yourself?" asked an elderly female thunderbird, one of only half a dozen who still sported a human mouth. Her cold, shiny black bird eyes were trained on Lance.

"I will," he said, and I turned to look at him, surprised by the strength in his voice. I was even more surprised by his mostly steady stance, and the direct gaze he leveled at the last bird who'd spoken. He'd taken my advice seriously. Would wonders never cease?

"Hey, Lance, just FYI," I said, and when his head swiveled toward me, I saw that the fear had been buried deep behind his eyes, replaced with a hot, ripe anger ready to burst through him like rotten fruit through its own skin.

Oh, shit. That was a dangerous look. One that said he knew he was going to die, but didn't plan to go down easy.

Lance wasn't composed; he was *contained.* And only barely, at that. Any resemblance to his brother that I'd seen in him was gone. Parker wasn't capable of that much rage.

But then, Parker wasn't capable of letting an entire Pride full of innocent people—including his own brother—pay for his mistakes.

"Yes?" Lance raised a calculating brow my way.

"You should know they have no Alpha," I said warily, shifting to subtly move in front of Kaci. "Regardless of who speaks to you, you're actually talking to all of them, so don't be thrown off by their round-robin routine."

Lance nodded curtly, then turned back to the bird who'd addressed him, dismissing me with apparent ease, though I found it much more difficult to reciprocate.

"The only right you have within our nest is the right to speak in your own defense. Succinctly," said another bird, this one a younger man, whose talons clicked over and over on the floor, like a metronome counting down the last seconds of Lance's life. "What would you say?"

Lance inhaled, then began to speak, glancing from one to the other of the birds who still bore a few human characteristics. He never even glanced at those who had fully Shifted, as if by keeping them out of sight, he could actually put them out of mind.

"Last week, I killed a thunderbird in a dispute over a meal. According to werecat law, it should have been my decision whether or not to share my meal, and I never offered…Finn a portion of my kill. By our law, my actions are justified, but I understand that your customs are different. I've broken one of your rules, and all I can do is ask for your mercy and plead ignorance of your laws. I swear I had no idea our cultures differed so dramatically."

"Your culture is irrelevant here," another bird said, while the woman beside her snapped her beak together over and over. "Your laws are simply words fallen on deaf ears. You killed one of ours in his own territory, and ignorance of our practices is no excuse."

I knew from what little I'd spoken to Kai that the thunderbirds were aware of other species' territorial boundary lines, if only so that they could avoid unnecessary encounters.

"I wouldn't have killed him if he hadn't fought back!" Lance snapped, gesturing angrily with one fist, and an alarm went off in my head.

Shut up! The silent shout reverberated in my skull, but I could not give it voice. It wasn't my place to defend him—not simply because we shared a species. Lance was in the wrong, for both his crime and for letting Malone blame us. People had died because of him.

"Do you intend to imply that Finn's murder was his own fault?" a young female demanded, her pale brown eyes blazing in fury. "That if he'd only submitted to an intruder's strange practices in his own land, he would still be alive?"

"That may be," said an elderly male bird, whose head feathers had begun to gray. "But none among us would debase himself for a few more years on earth. What good is life if you live it in dishonor?"

Lance had no answer for that. He had done the very thing the thunderbirds could not abide: he'd sacrificed his honor for his life. Worse yet, he'd let others pay for his crimes.

A petite woman stepped forward on small, sharp talons, weaving birdlike with each movement. "Have you anything else to say for yourself?"

Lance hesitated, his hands folded together at his back. "Just that I'm truly sorry for what I've done to Finn and for what I've allowed to happen to the south-central Pride. They are completely innocent."

My exhalation was so ragged and heartfelt that it echoed in the near silence. Kaci squeezed my hand, and I knew without looking that she was smiling up at me. Most of the tension had drained from her bearing with Lance's admission.

The small female bird turned to me. "Faythe Sanders, you and your kitten may go. Cade and Coyt will take you down."

"Thank you." I glanced at Lance, then turned toward the door. But Kaci's grip on my hand pulled me to an abrupt stop.

"What about him?" She nodded toward Lance.

"That's out of our hands, Kaci," I said, pulling her forward. "Let's go."

She shook her head and stood her ground. "But we can't just *leave* him. What are they going to do to him?"

"You should listen to your mother," Brynn said, and I glanced up to see her standing on the edge of the crowd, holding her ever-morphing daughter on one hip. "Lance Pierce will be put to death for his crimes, and you don't want to see that."

She was trying to help; I could see that. She considered Kaci my daughter—even if not biologically—and she was trying to help, from one mother to another. Unfortunately, outside of the giant aviary, telling a child that someone is about to be executed is not a good way to calm that child down.

"What?" Kaci's screech was almost bird-worthy. "They're gonna kill him, Faythe. You have to help him."

I pulled her close and made her meet my stern gaze. "Kaci, there's nothing I can do for Lance. We all have to pay for our mistakes, and Lance made a big one."

"So did I!" She glanced at him, then back at me. "I messed up a lot. People died. But no one killed me, 'cause I didn't know what I was doing. That's what you said. You said I wasn't really guilty if I didn't know what I was doing. And he didn't know what he was doing, either. You heard him. He didn't know thunderbird law, so he's not guilty, right?"

I shook my head slowly and closed my eyes, trying to figure out how to explain. "It's not the same, Kaci. Lance… I'll explain it to you later, okay? When we get home. Let's go." I turned toward the door, and again she refused to move.

"No. You have to help him, Faythe. That's your job. We can't leave him here."

My heart ached for her, and over my own reluctance to hand over a fellow werecat to be executed. But I'd made my decision and it was far too late to change my mind. "Kaci, my job is to protect *you,* and I've done that. We have to go. Marc and Jace are waiting for us outside."

But she only shook her head and turned back to Brynn. "How?"

"How what?" Brynn asked, and the baby bird on her hip Shifted its nose and mouth into a tiny, sharp beak and began nipping at her mother's arm in a bid for freedom.

"How will he die?" Kaci stood straight and tall, as if steeling herself for unpleasant information. Information I didn't want her to have, even if I didn't know precisely what it was.

"He will be eaten, of course." Distracted, Brynn set the struggling child on the floor as she spoke, and clearly had no idea the effect her words would have on Kaci. "Consumed by the family of his victim."

Oh, hell…

Kaci's eyes widened, and her mouth opened and closed, as if her response had been stolen by sheer horror. "You're going to *eat* him?"

Such a sentence was unheard of among werecats. Man-eaters were among the most reviled of our criminals, and those most severely punished before they were executed. And the idea held special horror for Kaci, because a few months earlier—starving and half out of her mind—she'd partially consumed a hunter she'd killed while stuck in cat form.

Nothing Brynn could have said would have upset her more.

We were all watching Kaci, me in concern, as I tried to herd her toward the door, the birds in detached curiosity. They obviously could not understand her reaction. But so focused were we on the young, near-hysterical tabby that no one paid much attention to Brynn's little chicklet, scampering from bird to bird, as if she were playing tag in a great forest.

No one paid attention, that is, until she gave a sudden startled squawk.

Every head in the room turned, and Brynn gasped in horror. "Wren!"

Lance stood in the center of the circle, holding the child by her currently human waist, her thin legs and talons dangling, his broad hand loosely gripping her neck. "Promise you'll let me go, or I'll kill her. I swear I'll do it."

"Lance…" I warned, as all around us, the birds who'd retained a few human features Shifted completely into avian form, and the entire throng pressed subtly, aggressively toward him. "You don't want to do this. This is not the way to get on their good side."

"They don't have a good side!" he snapped, glancing at me briefly before returning his attention to the birds posing the most immediate threat. "I mean it. Stay back or I'll pull her arm right off." His hand slid from Wren's neck to her pudgy little elbow, and the child giggled like it tickled. Then, as if in response to the touch, her arms Shifted into small, beautifully feathered wings.

Lance jerked in surprise and dropped her arm, then grabbed her neck again before anyone had a chance to make a move toward the child. By sheer, bumbling luck, he'd managed to grab the toddler with her back to him, and all her most dangerous parts—beak, claws, and talons—were facing away. He could hold her like that for quite a while, if necessary.

Kaci made an odd noise and I glanced over to see her staring at Lance in horror and mounting fury. She looked disillusioned, and I felt almost as bad for her as for the child Lance held hostage.

Wren began to struggle, obviously tired of whatever game she thought they were playing. She flapped her wings but couldn't reach back far enough to bother Lance. When that didn't work, she squeezed her eyes shut in concentration, and one wing Shifted almost instantly into a chubby little arm, though the other remained stubbornly feathered.

Wren fussed—an inarticulate stream of nonsense words and squawks—and waved her mismatched arms in the air.

"Lance, what do you plan to accomplish with this?" I kept my voice calm, hoping to talk him down rationally.

"Survival," Lance spat, glancing at me briefly. Then his focus flitted from thunderbird to thunderbird, though he still spoke to me. "You said they'd honor their word, so I'll let her go if they promise to let *me* go."

I started to tell him it didn't work like that. That they'd feel no obligation to stand by a promise made to someone who'd already proved himself dishonorable. They'd broken their promise to Malone for that very reason. But then I realized that explaining that would only make things worse. Make Lance more desperate. Instead I turned to Brynn. Or, to the bird I thought was Brynn. It was hard to tell when no one had a human face.

"Brynn, promise him," I said, but the bird only snapped her sharp beak, frighteningly close to my arm. *I'm guessing that's a no.* "Just promise him you'll let him go, and he'll put your daughter down." *Then you can kill him at your leisure.* I didn't think even Kaci would object to that now, after watching him threaten to kill a toddler.

"No," a voice said from several feet to my right, and I whirled to find Brynn's face peeking out at me from an otherwise avian body, her stance aggressive and angry. *Damn. Wrong bird.* I shrugged in apology to the woman I'd mistakenly addressed, then turned to Brynn, trying to communicate the importance of what I was saying with intense eye contact. But if she got my message, I saw no sign. "We will not give our word to a man with so little honor. That would disgrace us all. What good are our lives if our word holds no value?"

Damn it! Was she serious? She would let her child die rather than besmirch her reputation?

Lance turned toward the door so that I saw him in profile, and his fingers twitched around the child's throat. Wren squawked and reached for her mother, but Lance's arm was locked around her middle. "Let me through, or I'll kill her," he said to the birds now blocking his path. "I have nothing to lose if I'm going to die, anyway, right?" His eyes blazed with panic, and if I didn't know better, I'd have sworn he had scratch-fever. He'd truly lost it.

The three birds directly in front of him glanced around at their Flight mates for a consensus, and though I couldn't read the subtle body language and silent looks, their decision was clear. The two male birds went left, and the female went right. The path to the front door was now clear, and about ten feet long.

"You should know that as a species, we're very fast." Lance shuffled forward slowly, his gaze tripping from one avian face to the next. When talons tapped on the floor behind him, he glanced over his shoulder without loosening his grip on the chicklet. "You can jump me, and probably kill me, but not before I break her neck."

Several of the thunderbirds glanced at me, presumably to substantiate or refute his claim, and I could only nod. Cat reflexes are phenomenal, and Lance's were likely a little better than most, considering that he'd killed an adult thunderbird on his own, with only a scratch to show for it.

The birds shuffled forward as one, bobbing their heads, clucking and snapping aggressively, but no one came too close to him.

"Lance?" I said, announcing my presence as I approached him cautiously, Kaci still clinging to my left hand. "What are you doing? You can't get down. You have nowhere to go."

He didn't answer, nor did he turn, and I was virtually certain he had no idea what his next move would be. He was flying by the seat of his proverbial pants, and since he couldn't literally fly, there was no good way for this standoff to end.

Lance was five feet from the porch now, and Wren struggled in earnest. Her face was scarlet, her cries punctuated with the occasional squawk and high-pitched avian cry.

"Lance, put her down. You wouldn't hurt a child. What happened with Finn was…like an accident." I chose my words carefully, afraid that if I took his side to talk him into letting the girl go, the fifty thunderbirds at my back would take me at my word. They didn't seem to understand the art of manipulation. "But you're not a baby-killer. You won't be able to live with yourself if you do this."

He stiffened, and the child squealed when his arm tightened around her waist. "I'm not going to live at all."

"She's just a baby!" Kaci cried, and I glanced at her in surprise. "How can you kill her? No matter what else you've done, you don't hurt babies. Only monsters kill kids."

I squeezed her hand, as horrified as she was. What had happened to Parker's little brother? Did Malone corrupt everyone he came into contact with? Or could Lance truly be scared out of his mind? Could mere fear turn an ordinary—if spineless—man into a monster?

Lance stepped through the open doorway and onto the ledge. Kaci and I followed, and she let go of my hand to press her back to the front wall, unwilling to go near the edge.

Four thunderbirds followed us out—including Brynn, Cade and Coyt—and dozens more peered through the doorway and the huge windows, their talons scratching against the floor.

I held my breath as Lance stepped toward the edge, and finally, a foot from the end of the porch, he turned and addressed the three male thunderbirds who'd come out with us. "Take me down. Take me down and swear to let me go, and I'll give back the baby. I swear."

That time the birds didn't have to confer. It was Brynn who answered, reaching toward her child with now-human arms. "You will not leave our territory alive, and if you kill my daughter, you will watch us eat parts of your body for days. Your death will be so slow and painful you will beg for the end long before it comes."

Lance gaped at her, eyes glazing over in shock, shoulders slumped beneath the weight of the inevitable. Then, before I could process the sudden, insane upturn of the corners of his mouth, he stepped backward and off the porch, still holding the child.

Thirty-Two

"No!" Brynn launched herself off the porch, sprouting wings in midair. An instant later, a violent gust blew my hair into my face and feathered flesh hit my arm so hard I was pushed forward two steps. Cade—or maybe Coyt—dove off the edge of the porch.

I grabbed the porch support post and looked down. Cade—in his mad nosedive—overtook the flapping Brynn quickly. He was bearing down on Lance and Wren before I'd blinked twice. Talons extended, he grabbed Lance by both shoulders and threw out his wings to slow their descent.

But he was too late, and Lance was too heavy.

Cade was thrown off balance by the sudden weight he carried and veered to the left, struggling to rise with his burden. Then he overcorrected and careened madly toward the tree line. Another sudden twist kept Cade and his cargo from smashing into the trees, but halted his awkward upward progress. Mere feet from the ground, he managed one last powerful beat of his wings, and he and his cargo bobbed upward. Then, when they started to fall, he rolled them all to the side, using one massive wing to shield Lance—thus Wren—from the ground as it rushed up to meet them.

The trio landed hard, and even from two hundred feet above, I heard the muted crash-thud of the impact, and Cade's awful screech of agony. He was hurt—badly—but thanks to his sacrifice, his unwitting passengers were fine.

Lance stood and shoved the bird's body over, earning another terrible squawk from Cade. Then, as Brynn thumped to a landing thirty feet away, Lance stepped over the huge, broken wing and took off for the woods, Wren still in hand and screaming her half-human head off.

Shit! The forest was our home turf, and my guess was that since thunderbirds couldn't fly in such confined quarters, they spent very little time in the woods, even in human form. Brynn would never catch Lance, and neither would any of the half-dozen other birds who rushed past me and off the edge of the porch.

Below, Marc and Jace alternately stared up at us and watched the procession of birds dropping from the overhead dwelling, but I couldn't see their expressions in the fading light from such a distance. However, neither seemed eager to take off into the woods with the first few birds who Shifted, then ran naked into the forest. Not that I could blame my guys. They had no idea what had happened.

"Hey!" I grabbed the wing of the nearest bird before

he could leap from the porch and almost got my hand bitten off when he whirled and snapped at me. Then he dove off the porch, soaring toward the tree line on huge, spread wings.

Frantic, I turned, still clinging to the post, and spied Kaci pressed against the front of the building, her eyes wide in terror as bird after bird rushed by her. At her side stood a familiar male bird, naked and almost fully human in form. "Coyt!" I had to shout to be heard over the thunderous beat of wings, but the bird looked up. I had no idea why he hadn't already joined the procession, and there was no time to ask. "Take me down. Please!"

He shook his head, and I realized he was guarding us. And suddenly it occurred to me that we might not be allowed to leave if Lance wasn't caught. Somehow I was sure that having my evidence abscond with a baby thunderbird would not fulfill my part of the bargain.

I shoved my way through the birds still waiting to take to the air and laid one hand on Kaci's shoulder to comfort her, while I stared up at Coyt. "Take me down. You guys will never find Lance in the woods, but I can. I can get Wren back."

Coyt hesitated, glancing around as if looking for a consensus before making a decision on his own. But there were fewer than a dozen adult birds left on the porch—and even fewer still inside—and none of them paid us any mind.

I rolled my eyes and grabbed his arm to seize his attention. "You want her back? Take me down."

And finally he nodded. Without a word, Coyt

grabbed me by my left arm and pulled me roughly toward the edge of the porch. "Wait!" I shouted as his hand became a claw and feathers sprouted from his arms. "Her, too! Have someone take her to…my men."

Coyt glanced back at Kaci, who now stared at us both in horror, frozen in shock and fear. No doubt she'd hoped for a calmer, more peaceful rescue, but I wasn't going to leave her in the nest waiting for a more considerate ferry.

Coyt grabbed the nearest bird, and his voice was screechy when he spoke, pointing at Kaci. "Take the kitten down."

The other bird nodded curtly and stomped to the far end of the long porch, where there was room to literally spread his wings. Then he took to the air, right there on the porch, rising almost to the ceiling in three powerful beats of his wings.

He dove and reached for Kaci, but she cowered away from his talons, edging toward the door.

"Kaci! He's going to take you to Marc and Jace. Come on!"

She took a deep breath, then nodded and stepped forward, her hedging confidence based on nothing other than the fact that I'd asked her to do something. On her belief that I would never let her get hurt.

The bird seized Kaci by her arms and launched them both from the porch. Kaci screamed the whole way down.

I didn't wait to see them land. Instead, I turned to Coyt. "There's one more thing. Cats hunt mostly with their ears, and I won't be able to find them with your entire Flight stomping through the woods. I need you to call them off so I can hear Lance and Wren."

He frowned. "We will not stop looking for Brynn's daughter."

I shrugged and stared up at him, trying to convey competence and confidence in my gaze. "Well, you won't find her, either. I'm your best bet at getting Wren back alive, so you either call your people off or get ready for another funeral. Which will it be?"

Coyt's frown spread into a hard scowl as he considered. It took him three long seconds—more wasted time—to make up his mind. "I will call them back."

"Good." I raised my arms, ready to be flown. "Can you carry me on your own?" I asked, remembering that it had taken two birds to safely balance my weight before.

Coyt shrugged and spread his wings. "Down is easier than up."

Not exactly confidence-inspiring…

But before I could protest, he lifted himself into the air and grabbed my arms in both talons. An instant later we were in the air, my hair whipping around my face and neck, my arms bruised by his fierce grip.

We fell more than we flew, and Coyt used his massive wings like a glider, slowing our descent and directing us toward the tree line. Several terrifying seconds later, he dropped me two feet from the ground, then thumped to the earth behind me, already half-human.

I glanced back to see Kaci clinging to Jace in the middle of the road, and Marc racing toward me in the last rays of the scarlet sun. He may have been pissed, but he wouldn't let me hunt alone.

I ducked into the trees and veered sharply to the left of the path the human-form birds were stomping, to keep from getting trampled. My clothes hit the ground, and I shivered—nudity in February is rarely fun—then dropped to the ground on all fours, glad I'd taken the time to fully heal my right arm. I was halfway through my Shift—groaning over the popping in my joints—when Marc dropped to the ground next to me, already nude.

I'm a faster Shifter than he is, and I already had a head start, so when I rose in my newly feline form, I rubbed my cheek against his flank in greeting, then bounded off into the woods, on alert for the sound of rushed footsteps, or Wren crying.

Unfortunately, the woods were *alive* with footsteps. Human-form birds crashed through the forest all around me, and I couldn't distinguish one loud, ungainly set of feet from another. And if Wren was crying or calling for her mother, I couldn't hear her over the stampede in progress.

Damn it, Coyt!

I sat back on my haunches and was about to give as loud a roar as I could manage, when an unearthly screech ripped through the night. My feline ears were much more sensitive than the human version, so Coyt's appeal to his fellow birds was like fingernails raked down the chalkboard of my sanity.

Whining, I lowered my head to the earth and covered it with my paws until the sound stopped. When I rose, the footsteps were still there, but now they were crashing in the opposite direction: toward the road where Jace waited with Kaci.

When most of the birds had gone, I ventured forward silently, on alert for any movement around me. The sun had finally sunk below the horizon while I was Shifting, but the residual light reflected in the sky was more than enough for me to see by in feline form.

As I walked, I classified each sound as my ears picked it up. The scurry of some small animal through the underbrush. A rabbit? They don't hibernate. Wind rattling the skeletal branches of the deciduous trees sprinkled among the pines. The distant chatter and screech of dozens of scared, angry thunderbirds.

Marc joined me several minutes into my search, his approach even closer to true silence than my own. Together we walked and listened.

I was just about to point him in another direction—we could cover more ground if we split up—when an avian screech speared my brain. I froze, and Marc went stiff at my side. The screech was too loud to have come from the birds presumably gathered in the road.

Wren. It had to be, unless one of the thunderbirds hadn't heeded Coyt's call.

I whined softly, then tossed my head in the direction the sound had come from. Marc nodded, and we took off together.

Two minutes later, a human child's cry came from that same direction, followed by the distinctive snap of a twig beneath someone's foot. Lance was too busy trying to keep Wren in hand to worry about moving silently. She was going to get him caught. If he had let her go, he might well have gotten away.

A quarter of a mile later, I glimpsed movement between two trees, and froze. Marc saw it, too. He tossed his head to the right, and I nodded. We would split up and approach them from two directions. He went left; I went right.

I picked my way silently around clumps of evergreen brush and tall, broad pine trees, avoiding the sparsely sprinkled deciduous trees both because the lack of foliage left me exposed and because the fallen twigs would snap beneath my paws.

Lance crashed through the undergrowth fifteen feet away, struggling to hold on to the squirming, crying toddler who twisted to peck at him with her beak one minute, then reached up in the next instant to tangle human fingers in his hair. Scared and angry, the toddler went stiff and let loose an eardrum-bursting screech without letting go of his hair. He jerked in surprise, and she came away with two great handfuls of dark waves.

Lance shouted in inarticulate pain and stopped to reposition the child. He crooned to her for almost a minute as he went, and when that didn't pacify her, he started yelling. "Shut up! Just for one minute, shut the *fuck* up!"

A growl built in my throat, and I struggled to swallow it to keep from exposing myself, though I had serious doubts he could hear me over Wren's cries and his own yelling.

I edged along with Lance, unseen, waiting for Marc to get into place; his had been the longer, more circuitous route. And finally I caught a glimpse of movement beyond Lance. Just a smear of shadow among heavily laden pine boughs, but that was enough. Marc was in position.

I was all ready to pounce when it occurred to me that in cat form, I'd have no way to hold the child, even if he handed her over voluntarily. *Damn it!*

Beyond frustrated and out of options, I retreated as quietly as I could and squirmed beneath the drooping boughs of a pine tree to force one of the fastest Shifts I'd ever done, counting on Marc to keep up with Lance in my absence. They couldn't have gone far in under two minutes. Not with a screaming, struggling toddler in tow.

Fully human, I cursed silently as I crawled out from under the tree on my hands and knees, scratching my undefended human skin on pinecones, twigs and thorns. My hair caught in the pine needles over my head, and my toes sank into brittle leaves.

When I stood, naked, I couldn't stop shaking from the cold, and I had to grind my teeth together to keep them from chattering. Wincing each time a thorn dug into my foot or a branch slapped my bare torso, I picked my way quickly toward Lance, whom I could still hear struggling with Wren.

Minutes later, I had Lance back in sight, and after several seconds of searching, I pinpointed Marc in the foliage behind him. Thank goodness I'd left my eyes in cat form. The silent, curious angle of Marc's head illustrated his confusion and frustration over my Shift, but there was nothing he could do about it now. Nothing except back me up.

Lance stopped again to hoist Wren higher on his hip, still facing away from his body. She clearly felt heavier after a half-mile trek through the woods than when he'd first picked her up. She struggled and managed to catch his index finger in her beak while he adjusted his grip.

"Damn it!" Lance shouted. Blood welled from his finger, fragrant among the more bland scents of the winter-dead forest. "Hold still!" he shouted, trying to transfer her from one arm to the next.

Time to move. Very soon he'd either drop her, and she'd escape into the woods, or he'd lose his temper.

I took a deep breath and stepped out from behind the tree shielding me from sight. "Give me the baby, Lance."

He gasped and squinted at me in the dark, without the benefit of Shifted eyes. Movement behind Lance told me that Marc was there but would stay out of sight in case we needed the element of surprise. "Faythe?" Lance asked, still squinting.

"Who else?" I stepped closer, and his eyes only widened briefly when he realized I was naked. "Give her to me, so I can take her back to her mother. You don't need her anymore. Why didn't you let her go?"

"You don't understand. They'll hunt me, no matter where I go. This little shit machine is the only thing that will stop them from killing me when they find me."

"Okay." I nodded. "But they're not even looking for you. I told them I'd bring her back, and they're all waiting for us in the road. Give her to me, and you can run a lot faster."

His brows rose, and he repositioned the still squirming child on his hip again. "You'd let me go?"

I shrugged. "I don't care whether or not they catch you, since they're no longer blaming us for killing Finn."

"Won't they be mad if you let me go?"

"Probably. But how am I supposed to chase you down *and* bring Wren back to her family?"

He started to relax, the tension draining from his features as the truth of my words sank in. "So, I give her to you, and you just…let me go?"

I nodded. "I won't even try to catch you."

Lance thought about it. He knew he wouldn't get far with a kid on one hip. And if the birds caught him, they'd never give him the chance I was offering. Finally he nodded. "Here." He held the struggling toddler out with both hands, and I stepped forward to take her, my heart thumping in a sudden bout of nerves. She didn't know me any better than she knew him. Would she try to peck my eyes out all the way back to the nest?

"Wren?" I extended one hand slowly. "You want to go back to your mama?"

"Maaama?" she said brightly, and her moist eyes widened. She stopped struggling for the first time since Lance had picked her up.

"Yeah. Let's go find your mama." I took the child, and she let me pull her close, even as her arms Shifted into tiny, thin, feather-covered wings. "Let's get you home." I backed up a step, still watching Lance, just in case. "Thank you."

He nodded. Then he turned and ran.

Lance only made it few steps before a dark blur flew from the shadows. Marc landed on him midleap and they crashed to the ground together, with Marc on top.

Wren screeched in terror, and I held her close to comfort her, trying to ignore the cold, sharp talons now digging into my bare flesh.

Mental note: baby birds? Not cuddly.

"You promised!" Lance howled as Marc's jaws gripped the back of the tom's skull.

"I said *I* wouldn't try to catch you. I never said anything about Marc." I stared down at him, surprised by how little sympathy I felt.

Marc whined at me in question, and I held the child closer, running one hand over the hair currently flowing from Wren's head. "Turn him over."

Marc backed off of Lance but kept his muzzle close enough to rip out the other tom's throat at any moment. Lance rolled onto his back slowly and stared up at me as I came closer. Wren began to struggle when she saw Lance, so I stopped several feet away, unwilling to further traumatize her.

"Lance Pierce, you've killed three people," I said, surprised by how strong my voice sounded.

"What?" He started to protest, but changed his mind when Marc growled inches from his throat.

"Finn was just the first," I continued. "By letting Malone blame his death on us, you've also killed Charlie Eames and Jake Taylor. And seriously injured both my brother Owen and my cousin Lucas. You got me and Kaci kidnapped by thunderbirds, and almost got her killed. And you kidnapped a toddler and threatened to kill her in a despicable, cowardly attempt to preserve your own life."

Lance was silent now. He couldn't argue with the truth.

"The thunderbirds are demanding your life. They want to eat you alive as revenge for killing Finn. But if I give you to them, Jake and Charlie won't see justice. So you can consider this a mercy killing." With that, I nodded firmly at Marc.

Marc cocked his head at me. *You sure?*

I thought about my father telling me leaders have to make tough choices. I thought about Kaci, and the person I'd have to become to truly have the power to protect her. If I made this choice, I could never go back. I could never again be just a tabby, or even just an enforcer, expected to do as I was told. Alphas order executions, and giving such an order was as good as declaring my intent to someday challenge—however peacefully—for leadership of the Pride.

Marc's acceptance of that order would be a promise of support for my bid.

I took a deep breath. "Do it."

Lance's eyes went so wide I thought they'd pop from their sockets.

Marc lunged for his throat.

It was all over in an instant. Lance's death was quick, which was more than the thunderbirds would have done for him.

Wren made an odd, content clucking sound near

my ear, where her head rested on my shoulder. She was watching. And she was completely unbothered by the bloodshed.

Twenty minutes later we emerged from the tree line onto a road crowded with thunderbirds milling in various stages of mid-Shift. I was freezing—literally shaking from the cold—but they'd huddled together for warmth. The current of tension and anger was so palpable I could almost taste it. Until the first beady bird eye spotted us.

"Wren!" Brynn screeched and raced across the road. The moment the toddler heard her mother's voice, she began struggling in earnest, and I set her down carefully. Wren toddled toward her mother on one talon and one chunky human foot, flapping half-formed wings as if she might take off at any moment.

Brynn scooped her daughter up and rocked her, crooning in familiar, tuneless notes. Apparently comfort transcends species.

Behind me, Marc carried Lance's body over one shoulder. He followed me into the center of the circle the birds formed. Brynn stood opposite us, still rocking her exhausted daughter.

Marc bent and dropped Lance face up on the ground. His bare back was stained with the dead tom's blood. Lance stared sightlessly at the starlit sky, while nearly fifty thunderbirds stared down at him. As they stared we quickly dressed in the clothes we'd picked up in the woods on our way back, eager to be warm again.

"He is dead," said one young cock as I zipped my jeans, obviously speaking for the entire group.

I nodded. "Yes, but your child is not. We couldn't take him alive, but his body is yours to dispose of as you will." As badly as I hated to hand the corpse over—as sick as the thought of them consuming it made me—that was the only compromise I could think of that might actually satisfy the thunderbirds and get us out of there intact. "I assume he is proof enough that we didn't kill Finn."

"Of course." Brynn spoke that time.

So relieved I could barely breathe, I turned to peer over the heads of the birds surrounding us. Fifty feet away, Kaci stood pressed into Jace's side, his arm around her shoulders. She shook with the cold, and likely with fear, but the moment she saw us she stood straighter, determined to show her strength.

"I've done my part." I dug my phone from my pocket as I turned back to Brynn. "Call off the rest of your birds."

She nodded, and I flipped open my phone and auto-dialed my father.

He answered on the first ring. "Faythe?" he said, tension thick in his voice.

"Yeah. We have Kaci, and we're coming home."

"Thank goodness." In the background, I heard masculine cheers and my mother's massive sigh of relief.

"Can you give your phone to Beck?"

"Just a minute." My father sounded exhausted, and I wondered if he'd slept at all since we'd left.

I tossed my phone to Brynn, and when Beck's voice came over the line, she told him to execute a full retreat.

When my father came back on, he promised to release Kai to his Flight mates immediately.

By the time I slid my phone back into my pocket, two of the largest thunderbirds were already ferrying Lance's body up to their nest. I nodded once at Brynn, an all-purpose thanks-and-goodbye, and turned to leave. Then her hand landed on my bare arm.

I turned to find her watching me in the closest thing to friendliness I'd seen yet from one of her species. "We are in your debt, for the return of my daughter," she said. "And we would like to repay you as soon as possible."

The sentiment was more of a "We'd rather not be in your debt" than a "Thanks, how can we ever repay you." Still, it was better than a swift kick out the door and a plummet from two hundred feet.

"Um...okay." Saying thank-you seemed simultaneously trite and inappropriate. "I'll let you know if I...come up with something." But an idea was already beginning to form. As cold and ruthless as they were—or perhaps because of those very qualities—the thunderbirds would make a formidable opponent in war. My Pride had already seen that firsthand, and I had little doubt that my father would be just as eager as I was to turn the proverbial tables on Malone.

I was still basking in that possibility when I folded Kaci into my arms a minute later.

She squeezed me tightly, and only let me go long enough for me to put on my jacket. Exhausted, I forced a smile for Kaci's benefit, trying to ignore the way Marc and

Jace went out of their way to avoid each other, yet stay close to me. Then I slid one arm around Kaci's shoulders.

"Can we go home now?" she asked, staring up at me in exhaustion and uneasy relief. Neither of us would truly feel safe until we were far away from the thunderbirds and their prison in the sky.

"Absolutely." We would go home, if only long enough to rest and plan our full strike. Because if the blood-soaked feathers of a murdered thunderbird weren't enough to convince the other Alphas that Calvin Malone should be removed from power, we'd be prepared to do it the hard way.

And sometimes, the hard way is the only way to go.

* * * * *

There's one more battle to face!
Don't miss
ALPHA
Coming in Oct 2010.

Acknowledgements

Thanks first of all to my critique partner, Rinda Elliott, whose suggestion changed the last third of this book—for the better. Thanks for showing me the forest, in spite of the trees.

Thanks to Elizabeth Mazer and everyone at MIRA for all the behind-the-scenes work it takes to turn a manuscript into a book.

Thanks to my editor, Mary-Theresa Hussey, for her patience and dedication.

Thanks to my agent, Miriam Kriss, who makes things happen.

And thank you so much to the readers who have hung in there with Faythe and her Pride. Your words of praise and encouragement—and even the occasional distraught letter of disbelief—keep me writing, determined to make each book better than the last.

NEW YORK TIMES AND USA TODAY
BESTSELLING AUTHOR

HEATHER GRAHAM

At a Vegas casino, Jessy Sparhawk is just collecting her much needed winnings when a man with a knife protruding from his back crashes into her, pinning her to the craps table.

Private detective Dillon Wolf is fascinated by the redhead beneath the victim—and soon the two begin an investigation that takes them from the glitz of the Vegas strip to Indigo, a ghost town in the desert. Years ago, blood was shed on that very ground, and now history is about to repeat itself, with Dillon and Jessy fighting not only to stay alive but for the chance to build a future.

NIGHTWALKER

Available wherever books are sold.

REQUEST YOUR
FREE BOOKS!

2 FREE NOVELS
FROM THE SUSPENSE COLLECTION
PLUS 2 FREE GIFTS!

YES! Please send me 2 FREE novels from the Suspense Collection and my 2 FREE gifts (gifts are worth about $10). After receiving them, if I don't wish to receive any more books, I can return the shipping statement marked "cancel." If I don't cancel, I will receive 3 brand-new novels every month and be billed just $5.74 per book in the U.S. or $6.24 per book in Canada. That's a saving of at least 28% off the cover price. It's quite a bargain! Shipping and handling is just 50¢ per book in the U.S. and 75¢ per book in Canada.* I understand that accepting the 2 free books and gifts places me under no obligation to buy anything. I can always return a shipment and cancel at any time. Even if I never buy another book, the two free books and gifts are mine to keep forever.

192 MDN E4MN   392 MDN E4MY

Name	(PLEASE PRINT)	
Address		Apt. #
City	State/Prov.	Zip/Postal Code

Signature (if under 18, a parent or guardian must sign)

Mail to **The Reader Service:**
IN U.S.A.: P.O. Box 1867, Buffalo, NY 14240-1867
IN CANADA: P.O. Box 609, Fort Erie, Ontario L2A 5X3

Not valid for current subscribers to the Suspense Collection
or the Romance/Suspense Collection.

Want to try two free books from another line?
Call 1-800-873-8635 or visit www.morefreebooks.com.

* Terms and prices subject to change without notice. Prices do not include applicable taxes. N.Y. residents add applicable sales tax. Canadian residents will be charged applicable provincial taxes and GST. Offer not valid in Quebec. This offer is limited to one order per household. All orders subject to approval. Credit or debit balances in a customer's account(s) may be offset by any other outstanding balance owed by or to the customer. Please allow 4 to 6 weeks for delivery. Offer available while quantities last.

Your Privacy: Harlequin Books is committed to protecting your privacy. Our Privacy Policy is available online at www.eHarlequin.com or upon request from the Reader Service. From time to time we make our lists of customers available to reputable third parties who may have a product or service of interest to you. If you would prefer we not share your name and address, please check here. ☐

Help us get it right—We strive for accurate, respectful and relevant communications. To clarify or modify your communication preferences, visit us at www.ReaderService.com/consumerschoice.

MSUS10

RACHEL VINCENT